To Richard, with my love

KT-145-856

Her embroidered bag was full of books and heavy. She stopped for a few seconds on the landing to put it down. As she looked up the four steps that led to her rooms, a shadow passed behind the frosted glass in her door.

'Mr Jamshed,' she called. 'Is that you?'

He'd mentioned that morning he might come up later to look at her broken tap. She heard the sound of running water from down below. A slash of sizzling oil and then the smell of spices.

'Mr Jamshed? It's Viva,' she called softly.

She picked up her bag and opened the door.

She saw the soft outlines of a body lying down on her bed in the shadows of the corner of the room.

The shadow stood up. It was Guy Glover. He was wearing his black coat. He was waiting for her.

Julia Gregson worked as a model for Hardy Amies before moving to Australia, where she became a journalist. She was sent to New York and Los Angeles, India and Vietnam as a foreign correspondent for Sungravure magazines, and has worked for *Rolling Stone*, *The Times* and *Good Housekeeping* magazines. Married with one daughter and four step-children, she lives in Wales with her husband, Richard, two Welsh cobs, a Shetland and two dogs.

By Julia Gregson

East of the Sun
The Water Horse

East of the Sun

JULIA GREGSON

An Orion paperback

First published in Great Britain in 2008
by Orion
This paperback edition published in 2008
by Orion Books Ltd,
Orion House, 5 Upper St Martin's Lane,
London WC2H 9EA

An Hachette Livre UK company

Typeset at The Spartan Press Ltd,
Lymington, Hants

Printed and bound in Great Britain by
Clays Ltd, St Ives plc

The Orion Publishing Group's policy is to use papers that
are natural, renewable and recyclable products and
made from wood grown in sustainable forests. The logging
and manufacturing processes are expected to conform to
the environmental regulations of the country of origin.

www.orionbooks.co.uk

Chapter 1

LONDON, SEPTEMBER 1928

Responsible young woman, twenty-eight years old, fond of
children, with knowledge of India, will act as chaperone on
Tilbury to Bombay run in return for half fare.

It seemed like a form of magic to Viva Holloway when, having paid
three and six for her advertisement to appear in the latest issue of
The Lady, she found herself five days later in the restaurant at Derry
& Toms in London, waiting for her first client, a Mrs Jonti Sowerby
from Middle Wallop in Hampshire.

For the purposes of this interview, Viva wore not her usual mix
of borrowed silks and jumble sale finds, but the grey tweed suit she
loathed but had worn for temporary work as a typist. Her hair – thick
and dark and inclined towards wildness – had been dampened and
clenched back in a small bun.

She stepped into the genteel murmurings of the tea room, where
a pianist was playing a desultory tune. A small, bird-thin woman
wearing an extraordinary blue hat (a kind of caged thing with a blue
feather poking out of the back) stood up to greet her. By her side was
a plump and silent girl who, to Viva's considerable amazement, Mrs
Sowerby introduced as her daughter Victoria.

Both of them were surrounded by a sea of packages. A cup of
coffee was suggested, but disappointingly, no cake. Viva hadn't eaten
since breakfast and there was a delicious-looking walnut cake, along
with some scones, under the glass dome on the counter.

'She looks awfully young,' Mrs Sowerby immediately complained
to her daughter, as if Viva wasn't there.

'Mummy,' protested Victoria in a strangled voice and, when the
girl turned to look at her, Viva noticed she had wonderful eyes: huge

and an unusual dark blue colour almost like cornflowers. *I'm sorry, I can't help this*, they were signalling.

'Well, I'm sorry, darling, but she does.' Mrs Sowerby had pursed her lips under her startling hat. 'Oh dear, this is such a muddle.'

In a tight voice she, at last, addressed Viva, explaining that Victoria was shortly to go to India to be a bridesmaid for her best friend Rose, who was, and here a certain show-off drawl entered Mrs Sowerby's voice, 'about to be married to a Captain Jack Chandler of the Third Cavalry at St Thomas's Cathedral in Bombay'.

The chaperone they had engaged, a Mrs Moylett, had done a last-minute bunk – something about a sudden engagement to an older man.

Viva had set down her cup and composed her features in what she felt to be a responsible look; she'd sensed a certain desperation in this woman's eyes, a desire to have the matter speedily resolved.

'I know Bombay quite well,' she'd said, which was true up to a point: she'd passed through that city in her mother's arms at the age of eighteen months, and then again aged five where she'd eaten an ice cream on the beach, and for the last time at the age of ten, never to return again. 'Victoria will be in good hands.'

The girl turned to Viva with a hopeful look. 'You can call me Tor if you like,' she said. 'All my friends do.'

When the waiter appeared again, Mrs Sowerby began to make a fuss about having a tisane rather than a 'normal English tea'.

'I'm half French, you see,' she explained to Viva in a pouty way as if this excused everything.

While she was looking for something in her little crocodile bag, the silent daughter turned to Viva and rolled her eyes. This time she mouthed, 'Sorry,' then she smiled and crossed her fingers.

'Do you know anything about cabin trunks?' Mrs Sowerby bared her teeth into a small compact. 'That was something else Mrs Moylett promised to help us with.'

And by a miracle Viva did: the week before she'd been scouring the front pages of the *Pioneer* for possible jobs, and one Tailor Ram had placed a huge advertisement for them.

She looked steadily at Mrs Sowerby. 'The Viceroy is excellent,' she said. 'It has a steel underpinning under its canvas drawers. You can get them at the Army and Navy Store. I can't remember the exact price but I think it's around twenty-five shillings.'

There was a small commotion in the restaurant, the clink of cutlery momentarily suspended. An attractive older woman wearing faded tweeds and a serviceable hat had arrived; she was smiling as she walked towards them.

'It's Mrs Wetherby.' Tor stood up beaming and hugged the older woman.

'Do sit down.' She patted the chair beside her. 'Mummy and I are having thrilling talks about jods and sola topis.'

'That's right, Victoria,' Mrs Sowerby said, 'make quite sure the whole restaurant hears our business.' She turned to Viva. 'Mrs Wetherby is the mother of Rose. The one who is going to be married in India to Captain Chandler. She's a quite exceptionally beautiful girl.'

'I can't wait for you to meet her.' Tor was suddenly radiant with happiness. 'She is so much fun, and so perfect, everybody falls in love with her – I've known her since she was a baby, we went to school together, we rode ponies . . .'

Viva felt a familiar pang – what a wonderful thing to have a friend who'd known you since you were a baby.

'Victoria,' her mother reproved. The blue feather poised above her eyebrow made her look like a slightly miffed bird. 'I'm not sure we need to tell Miss Holloway all this yet. We haven't quite decided. Where is darling Rose by the way?'

'At the doctor's.' Mrs Wetherby looked embarrassed. 'You know . . .' She sipped her coffee and gave Mrs Sowerby a significant look. 'But we had the most exciting morning before I dropped her off,' Mrs Wetherby continued smoothly. 'We bought dresses and tennis rackets, and I'm meeting Rose again in an hour at Beauchamp Place – she's being fitted for her trousseau. The poor girl will be absolutely dead tonight; I don't think I've ever bought so many clothes in one day. Now, who is this charming young person?'

Viva was introduced to Mrs Wetherby as 'a professional chaperone'. Mrs Wetherby, who had a sweet smile, put her hand in hers and said it was lovely to meet her.

'I've done the interview,' Mrs Sowerby said to Mrs Wetherby. 'She knows India like the back of her hand, and she's cleared up the trunk business – she says the Viceroy is the only one.'

'The girls are very sensible,' said Mrs Wetherby anxiously. 'It's just quite comforting to have someone to keep an eye on things.'

'But I'm afraid we can only offer you fifty pounds for both girls,' said Mrs Sowerby, 'and not a penny more.'

Viva literally heard Tor stop breathing; she saw her mouth twist in childish apprehension, big eyes trained on her while she waited.

She did some quick sums in her head. The single fare from London to Bombay was around eighty pounds. She had one hundred and twenty pounds saved and would need some spending money when she arrived.

'That sounds very reasonable,' she said smoothly as if this was something she did every day.

Tor exhaled noisily. 'Thank God!' she said. 'Oh, what bliss!'

Viva shook hands all round and left the restaurant with a new spring in her step; this was going to be a piece of cake: the gawky one with the blue eyes and the mad-looking mother was so clearly desperate to go; her friend, Rose, was about to be married and had no choice.

Next stop the Army and Navy Hotel to talk to a woman called Mrs Bannister about another prospective client: a schoolboy whose parents lived in Assam. She scrabbled in her handbag to check the piece of paper. The boy's name was Guy Glover.

And now she was sitting with Mrs Bannister, who turned out to be an irritable, nervy-looking person with buck teeth. Around forty, Viva estimated, although she wasn't good at guessing the age of old people. Mrs Bannister ordered them both a lukewarm cup of tea with no biscuits or cake.

Mrs Bannister said she would come to the point quickly because she had a three-thirty train to catch back to Shrewsbury. Her brother, a tea planter in Assam, and his wife, Gwen, were 'slightly on the horns of a dilemma'. Their son Guy, an only child, had been asked to leave his school rather suddenly. He was sixteen years old.

'He's been quite a difficult boy, but I'm told he's very, very kind underneath it all,' his aunt assured Viva. 'He's been at St Christopher's for ten years now without going back to India. For various reasons I don't have time to explain to you we haven't been able to see him as much as we'd like to but his parents feel he'll thrive better in India after all. If you can take him, they're quite prepared to pay your full fare.'

Viva felt her face flush with jubilation. If her whole fare was paid, and she had the fifty pounds coming from Mrs Sowerby, she could buy herself a little breathing space in India, thank God for that. It didn't even cross her mind at that moment to enquire why a boy of that age couldn't travel by himself, or indeed, why his parents, the Glovers, didn't come home to collect him themselves.

'Is there anything else you'd like to know about me, references and so forth?' she asked instead.

'No,' said Mrs Bannister. 'Oh well, maybe yes, you should give us a reference, I suppose. Do you have people in London?'

'My present employer is a writer, a Mrs Driver.' Viva scribbled down the address quickly for Mrs Bannister, who, fiddling with her handbag and trying to catch the waitress's eye, seemed half in flight. 'She lives opposite the Natural History Museum.'

'I'll also send you a map of Guy's school and your first payment,' said Mrs Bannister. 'And thank you so much for doing this.' She produced all her rather overwhelming teeth at once.

But what had most struck Viva, watching the back of Mrs Bannister's raincoat flapping in her haste to enter her taxi, was how shockingly easy it was to tell people lies – particularly when it was what they wanted to hear. For she was not twenty-eight, she was only twenty-five, and as for knowing India, she'd only played there innocently as a child, before what had happened. She knew it about as well as she knew the far side of the moon.

Chapter 2

'She seems all right, doesn't she?' Mrs Sowerby said to Mrs Wetherby after Viva had gone. 'She's very good-looking,' she added, as if this decided everything, 'if you discount that appalling suit. Honestly, Englishwomen and their clothes.' She made a strange hood of her upper lip when she said the word 'clothes', but for once Tor couldn't be bothered to react.

How balloon – they had a chaperone, phase two of the plan had fallen neatly into place. Her mother's pantomime of careful consideration might have fooled the others, but it hadn't fooled her. They'd fought so bitterly that summer that a hairy ape could have applied for the job and her mother would have said, 'He's perfect,' so desperate was she to see Tor gone.

And now, the excitement was almost more than she could bear. The tickets had come that morning, and they were leaving in two weeks. *Two weeks!* They had a whole day ahead of them in London in which to buy clothes and other necessities from a thrilling list that their Bombay hostess had provided.

Her mother, who normally had all kinds of rules about things – for instance, only lemon and water on Tuesdays, and no cake on Wednesday and saying 'bing' before you went into a room because it made your mouth a pretty shape – had relaxed them, even to the extent of allowing her walnut cake at Derry & Toms. And now she knew she was definitely going, all the other things that normally drove her completely mad about Mother: the way she went all French and pouty as soon as she got to a city; the embarrassing hats; her overpowering scent (Guerlain's Shalimar); not to mention the other rules about men, and conversation, seemed almost bearable – because soon she'd be gone, gone, gone, hopefully never to return, and the worst year of her life would be over.

*

After coffee, Mrs Wetherby flew off to pick Rose up at the doctor's.

Tor's mother was sipping a hot water and lemon – no tisane had been found – she had her silver pencil and notebook out with the clothes list inside.

'Now jods. Jodhpurs. You'll probably go hunting in India.'

It seemed to Tor that her mother was speaking louder than usual as if hoping that the people at the next table would know that, for once, they were the exciting people.

'Ci Ci says it's too stupid to buy them in London; she knows a man in Bombay who'll run them up for pennies.'

Ci Ci Mallinson was a distant cousin of her mother's and would soon be Tor's hostess when she arrived in Bombay. She had also heroically agreed to organise Rose's wedding without ever having met her. Her letters, written on thrilling brittle writing paper in a slashing hand, spoke of constant parties, gymkhanas, days at the races, with the occasional grand ball at the governor's.

'Such a good idea,' she'd written in her last about a recent ball at a place called the Bombay Yacht Club. 'All the decent young Englishmen are rounded up, and the girls spend ten minutes with each of them and then get moved on – great fun and usually quite long enough to know if one can get on.' Before she'd signed off she'd warned, 'People out here really do try to keep up, so be sure to send out a couple of issues of *Vogue* with the girls, and if it's not too much of a bore, one of those divine silk tea roses – mine was munched upcountry by a horde of hungry bog ants!'

'Quinine,' her mother was ticking away furiously, 'face cream, darling, don't forget, please. I know I nag about unimportant things, but there really is *nothing* more ageing and you are already quite brown.' This was true; Tor had her ancestors' smooth olive-brown skin. 'Eyebrow tweezers, darling, I *am* going to take off your own caterpillars before you go.' Eyebrows were an obsession of her mother's. 'Evening dresses, a camp stool – oh, for goodness' sake! I think that's too Dr Livingstone – I'm going to strike that – and . . .' she lowered her voice, 'she says you'll need packets and packets of you-know-whats. They're wildly expensive there and I—'

'Mummy!' Tor frowned at her and moved away; any moment now she felt her mother would blight her beautiful morning by talking about 'Dolly's hammocks', her code for sanitary towels. 'Mummy,' Tor leant across the table, 'please don't cross out the camp stool. It sounds so exciting.'

'Oh, how pretty you look when you smile.' Her mother's face suddenly collapsed. 'If only you'd smiled more.'

In the silence that followed, Tor sensed a series of complicated and painful thoughts taking place under her mother's hat; some of them she was all too familiar with: had Tor smiled more, for instance, or looked more like Rose, all the expense of sending her to India might have been saved; if she'd eaten less cake; drunk more water and lemon on Tuesdays; acted more French. Her mother seemed always to be adding her up like this and coming to the conclusion she was a huge disappointment.

But now, how strange, an actual tear was cutting a channel through the loose powder on her mother's face and had lodged in her lipstick.

'Hold my hand, darling,' she said. When she took a deep sobbing breath, Tor couldn't help it, she moved her chair away. Her mother in this mood seemed horribly raw and human, and there was nothing she could do about it. It was too late, and the harm had already been done.

It was impossible to find a taxi that day, and even though they weren't normally bus people, an hour or so later Tor was on top of an omnibus, looking down on drops of rain drying on the tops of dusty trees in St James's Park. The bus swept down Piccadilly towards Swan & Edgar, and Tor, feeling the perfumed bones of her mother sitting so unusually close to her, was surprised to feel another stab of sorrow.

This felt so exactly like the kind of outing a happy mother and daughter might have had, if she hadn't been so difficult: a father left at home with a plate of sandwiches, the 'girls' up in town for the day.

From the top of the bus she could see the vast bowl of London spreading out to the horizon: splendid shops with mannequins in the window, interesting people and already a much bigger world.

Bars of sunlight fell across her mother's face she leant to look out of the window. The blue feather in her hat wiggled like a live thing.

'Darling, do look!' she said. 'There's the Ritz – oh God, I've missed London,' she breathed. And all the way down Piccadilly she pointed out what she called 'some smart waterholes' (when Mother got excited her English let her down), places she and Daddy had eaten in when they had money, before Tor was born: Capriati's, the In and Out – 'dreadful chef' – the Café Royal.

8

Tor heard a couple of shopgirls behind them titter and repeat, 'dreadful chef'.

But for once, she told herself she didn't give a damn – she was going to India in two weeks' time. *When you're smiling, When you're smiling, The whole world smiles with you.*

'Darling,' her mother pinched her, 'don't hum in public, it's dreadfully common.'

They'd arrived at the riding department at Swan & Edgar. Her mother, who prided herself on knowing the key assistants, asked for the services of a Madame Duval, a widow, she explained to Tor, who'd fallen on hard times and who she remembered from the old days.

'We're looking for some decent summer jods,' her mother had drawled unnecessarily to the doorman on the ground floor, 'for the tailors in Bombay to copy.'

Upstairs, Tor mentally rolled her eyes as Madame Duval, removing pins from her mouth, complimented Mrs Sowerby on how girlish and slim she still looked. She watched her mother dimple and pass on her famous much-repeated advice about lemon juice and tiny portions. Tor had been forced to follow this starvation diet herself, all through the season, when her mother had only agreed to buy her dresses in a size too small to blackmail her into thinness. Sometimes she thought her mother wanted to slim her out of existence altogether: their fiercest row – they'd almost come to blows – was when her mother had found her one night, after another disastrous party where nobody had asked her to dance, wolfing half a loaf of white bread and jam in the summer house.

That was the night when her mother, who could be mean in several languages, had introduced her to the German word *Kummerspeck* for the kind of fat that settles on people who use food to buck themselves up. 'It means sad fat,' she'd said, 'and it describes you now.'

'Right now, I've got the larger size.' Jolly Madame Duval had returned with a flapping pair of jods. 'These might fit. Are we off to some gymkhanas this summer?'

'No,' Tor's mother as usual answered for her. 'She's off to India, aren't you, Victoria?'

'Yes.' She was gazing over their heads at her reflection in the mirror. *I'm huge*, she was thinking, *and fat.*

'How lovely, India!' Madame Duval beamed at her mother. 'Quite an adventure. Lucky girl!'

Her mother had decided to be fun. 'Yes, it's *très amusant*,' she told her. 'When these girls go out they call them the Fishing Club because there are so many handsome young men out there.'

'No. Mother,' corrected Tor, 'they call us the Fishing Fleet.'

Her mother ignored her. 'And the ones who can't find men there,' her mother gave Tor a naughty look with a hint of challenge in it, 'are called returned empties.'

'Oh, that's not very nice,' said Madame Duval, and then not too convincingly, 'but that won't happen to your Victoria.'

'Um . . .' Tor's mother made the little pout she always made when she checked her face in the mirror. She adjusted her hat. 'Let's hope not.'

I hate you, Mother. For one brief and terrible moment Tor imagined herself sticking a pin so hard into her mother that she made her scream out loud. *I absolutely loathe you*, she thought. *And I'm never coming home again.*

Chapter 3

There was one last arrangement for Viva to make and the thought of it made her feel almost light-headed with nervous tension. An appointment at seven o'clock at the Oxford and Cambridge University Club in Pall Mall with William, her guardian and executor of her parents' will.

It was William who had, two months ago, inadvertently set off the whole chain of events that now led her to India by forwarding a letter – written in a quavery hand on cheap writing paper – telling her about a trunk her parents had left in India. The writer, a Mrs Mabel Waghorn from Simla, said the trunk, which contained some clothes and personal effects, was being kept in a shed near her house. The rains had been heavy that year and she was afraid the trunk would disintegrate should she leave it there much longer. She said that after the funeral the keys of her trunk had been left with a Mr William Philpott, at the Inner Temple Inn in London – if they weren't in her possession already, she could collect them.

William had attached his own letter to this. The sight of that careful cramped handwriting had brought a slap of pain.

'Forgive me for being brutally frank,' he wrote, 'but I don't think you need do anything about this. I would send the old lady some money and get the trunks disposed of. I have the keys should you want them.'

Though she hated to agree with him, Viva had at first been convinced he was right. Going back to India would be like throwing a bomb into the centre of her life.

And what would she find there? A Rider Haggardish child's dream of buried treasure, a glorious reunion with her lost family?

No, it was ridiculous, only pain could come of it. When she thought about it, she literally saw it in her mind as a step back into darkness.

For, finally, after six months and two dreary typist's jobs in

London – one for a drunken MP, the other for a firm that made iron locks – she'd fallen into a job she adored as assistant to Nancy Driver, a kind, eccentric woman who churned out romantic novels at an impressive rate and who was generous with advice. Her new job paid thirty shillings a week, enough for her to move from the YWCA into her own bedsit in Earl's Court. Best of all she had started to write herself, and had experienced for the first time a feeling of such relief, such pleasure it felt almost cellular. She'd found – or was it stumbled into? – what she knew she wanted to do with her life.

She dreaded seeing William again – their relationship had become so soiled and complicated. She wrote to him asking if he could post the keys, but he'd refused.

So why, given all these new and wonderful opportunities in life, had another vagrant part of her leapt hungrily into life again at the thought of seeing her parents' things?

In certain moods she could barely remember what her family even looked like. Time had blurred those agonising memories, time and the relative anonymity of boarding school and, later, London – where, at first, she had known nobody. Indeed, one of the things she most liked about the city – apart from all its obvious attractions, the theatre, the galleries, the exhilarating walks by the river – was that so few people ever asked you personal questions. Only two ever had: first, the form-filler at the YWCA, querying the blank she'd left after 'Family's place of residence', and then Fran, the plump friendly typist in the next bed in her dorm. She'd told them both they had died in a car accident years ago in India; it always seemed easier to dispose of them both at once. She didn't tell them about Josie at all. *You don't have to say* was something she'd learnt the hard way with William.

He was waiting for her outside the grand Graeco-Roman façade of the Oxford and Cambridge Club when she ran up the steps around a quarter to seven. As usual he had arranged his backdrop carefully – placing himself on this occasion between two imposing Corinthian columns, his thin hair lit by the golden glow of lamps from the luxurious rooms behind.

A fastidious man, he was wearing the pin-stripe suit she had last seen folded over the arm of his chair in his flat in Westminster. She remembered how he'd lined up his sock suspenders on top of his underpants, a starched collar, his silk tie.

'You're looking well, Viva.' He had a sharp, slightly barking voice, used to great effect in the Inner Temple where he now worked as a barrister. 'Well done.'

'Thank you, William.' She was determined to stay calm. She'd dressed herself carefully for this occasion: a coral silk dress – one of Miss Driver's cast-offs – the silk delicate as tissue. A purple rose covered the scorch marks on the bodice, the reason for it having been given away.

She'd got up early to wash her hair under a cold tap because the geyser was on the blink again. It had taken ages and a shilling's worth of coins in the meter to dry. She'd dampened down its glossy exuberance and tied it back with a velvet bow.

'I've booked us a table.' He was steering her towards the dining room, which smelt of roast meat.

'There was no need to do that,' she said, moving away from him. 'I could take the keys and leave.'

'You could,' he said.

A waiter led them towards a table set for two in the corner of the grand dining room. Above them, hung in a straight line, portraits of distinguished academics looked down on her gravely, as if they too were considering her plans.

William had been here earlier. A bulky envelope – she presumed it held the keys – lay propped against a silver pepper pot.

He settled his pin-striped knees carefully under the table, smiled at her blandly and told her he had taken the liberty of ordering a bottle of Château Smith Haut-Lafitte, a vintage, he told her in that prissy, self-satisfied way she now recoiled from, of which he was particularly fond.

The waiter took their orders, brown soup and lamb cutlets for him; grilled sole for her, the simplest and quickest thing on the menu. She was ashamed of herself, in spite of everything, for feeling hungry.

She glanced at him. Still a commanding presence with his impeccable clothes, his air of slightly impatient authority. Still handsome in a bloodless sort of way – although a bad go of malaria during his tour of India had left his skin a permanently waxy yellowish colour.

A few stiff pleasantries, then William glanced around the room and lowered his voice.

'Are you sure you really want these?' He closed his hand over the envelope.

'Yes,' she said. 'Thank you.' She had made up her mind before this interview not even to try to explain herself.

He waited for her to say more, manicured nails beating like drums on the tablecloth. How clean their half-moons were, the cuticles neatly trimmed. She remembered him scrubbing them in the bathroom.

'Are you going back?'

'Yes.'

'On your own?'

'On my own.' She bit the inside of her lip.

She heard him make a whistling sigh. 'Can I remind you, you have no money – or very little.'

She forced herself to say nothing. *You don't have to say.*

He squeezed his bread roll, scattering its crumbs over the side-plate. He looked at her with his cold, grey eyes – eyes that had once shone with sincerity. The waiter brought his soup.

'Well, for what it's worth,' he took a careful sip, 'I think it's an absolutely dreadful idea. Completely irresponsible.'

'Soup all right, sir?' Their chirpy waiter had approached them. 'A little more butter for madam?'

She waved him away.

'Stay where you are,' William said coldly for she had moved her chair back.

He waited until the waiter was out of earshot.

'Look, Viva,' he said, 'whatever may or may not have happened between us, I still feel responsible for you. I can't allow this to happen without getting a few more details.'

She looked him straight in the eyes. 'Are you in any doubt about what happened to us?'

'No.' For the first time his eyes met hers. 'But there'll be nothing in India for you,' he said, 'and I'm worried it will upset you.'

She gave him a quizzical look. 'It's a bit late for that, William,' she said. 'Don't you think?'

She'd pined for him once like an animal, haunting streets near his flat, hoping for a glimpse of him; she'd learnt to cry without sound under the pillows after lights out.

'Viva, I . . .'

'William, please.'

As she picked up the envelope, a few grains of rust seeped through the cracks and left a trail near the salt pot. He frowned as she put the keys into her handbag. 'I've made up my mind,' she said. 'One of the advantages of being an orphan, I would have thought, is that I'm free to do what I like.'

'How will you support yourself?'

'I have already found two people willing to pay my fare – I am to be a chaperone and then I have some addresses in India.'

'A chaperone! Do you have any idea how irresponsible you are?'

'And I'm also going to be a writer.'

'How can you possibly know that?' She could see bright spots of colour on his cheeks. He simply couldn't bear not being in control, she could see that now. He preferred the wounded bird.

'I've made a start,' she said. She wasn't going to tell him how much it terrified her.

He shook his head and briefly pouched his fingers over his eyes as if to block out her many stupidities.

'Do you know, by the way, there's a small rip at the back of your dress?' he said. 'The colour suits you, but I wouldn't wear it in India – they don't like women who go jungli out there.'

She ignored this. Now that the keys were inside her bag and she had said what she meant to say, she felt a surge of power, like oxygen in the bloodstream. She suddenly felt really hungry.

She raised her glass of Château Smith Haut-Lafitte towards him.

'Wish me luck, William,' she said. 'I booked my passage on the *Kaisar* today. I'm going.'

Chapter 4

MIDDLE WALLOP, HAMPSHIRE, OCTOBER 1928

On the night before she left England, Rose Wetherby had such an attack of cold feet that she seriously thought about going to her parents and saying, 'Look, scrap the whole thing; I don't want to go,' but of course it was too late.

Mrs Pludd, the family cook for fifteen of her nineteen years, had made her favourite supper: shepherd's pie and gooseberry fool. When it came Rose wished she hadn't asked for it, because the nursery food made her feel even more desperate and clinging, and everyone was making a huge effort to pretend nothing special was happening. Her father, who looked even paler than usual, tried to tell them a joke he'd obviously saved up for the occasion: a terrible joke, about a man who really thought that cuckoos lived in clocks, and when she and her mother fluffed their parts and laughed too quickly and in the wrong place, he'd given her such an unhappy smile that the shepherd's pie had turned to stone in her stomach and she could have wept.

I shall miss you so much, Daddy; Jack will never replace you. The violence of this emotion surprised her.

After dinner she'd gone into the garden. The last puffs of smoke from a bonfire of leaves rose and drifted above the tall branches of the cedar tree. It had been a cold but perfect day, with the sky clear as polished glass and frost on the trees in the early morning. The garden stripped of its summer finery, but still with the skeletons of summer roses amongst the Virginia creepers and bright, fresh haw hips, had never looked more beautiful.

She walked past the orchard where her ponies, Smiler and Bertie, had been buried under the apple tree and where she and Tor, dressed in solemn robes and holding candles, had buried all the rabbits and dogs. Her feet flattened the rougher grass as she took the shortcut from the orchard to the stables.

She was going, and now that the light had changed, what was usually taken for granted felt almost unbearably painful and precious: the crunch of gravel, the smell of the bonfire as it rose into darkening sky, the silky slither of the stream disappearing underneath the drive.

She looked back at the house and thought of all the life that had gone on there: the laughter and the rows, and shouts of 'Bedtime, darlings', the blissful sound of the supper gong when she and Tor and her big brother Simon, whom they'd idolised, had been racing around in the garden building dens, or playing cricket or pretending to be Germans, or playing pirates in the stream. Big brother Simon baring his teeth and threatening the plank to all dissenters.

Her last pony, Copper, had his head over the stable gate. She gave him his bedtime apple, and then, looking furtively to the left and to the right, let herself into his stable and collapsed over him weeping. Nothing in her life had ever made her feel this bad before, and at a time when she was supposed to feel so happy.

Copper pushed her gently with his head, and let her tears fall into his mane. She knew she wouldn't see him again, or the dogs, Rollo and Mops, who were getting on. Maybe not even her parents. Her father's wretched bout of pneumonia only last winter had left him with what he called a dicky motor and the doctor called a serious heart condition. He had not recovered. They talked about her wedding as if he was bound to make it, although both of them knew he probably wouldn't.

She was aware, too, of all the painful thoughts tonight would bring to all of them about Simon. Darling Simon, so tall and gangling and blond and half grown, had had all her father's goodness and gallantry as well as his steelier qualities. He was killed in France in the last month of the war. It was ten days before his twenty-first birthday. Her parents rarely spoke of it; but it was always lurking there, like an iceberg under the sunny surface of things.

Now she was sitting in the garden shed, on a stack of piled-up chairs surrounded by the neat boxes of apples twisted into tissue that her mother had put away for winter, and a dusty collection of wicker chairs and croquet mallets and old cricket bats. Across the lawn, a light went on in her father's study, casting a dark square shape on to the lawn. She pictured him bending over his books with that look of desperate calm he wore when he was trying not to think of upsetting things, knocking ash from his pipe into the brass ashtray he'd bought in Egypt, or winding up his gramophone to hear his beloved Mozart.

Her fixed point, her magnetic north; but now everything was being moved. She wished she smoked, like Tor did. Tor said it really did help when one was in a state.

She stayed for a while, desperately trying to calm herself. *Soldiers' daughters don't cry.*

Going up the backstairs to her room, her mother called out from her own bedroom, 'Are you all right, darling?'

'Yes, Mummy,' she said. 'Absolutely fine, I'll be in in a minute to say goodnight.'

Inside her room, all her new clothes had been hung outside her wardrobe like ghosts waiting for their new life to begin. They'd had such a lovely day up in London with Tor and her mother, Jonti. They'd bought such pretty things – a floaty dress with pink tea roses on it from Harrods; new pink suede shoes to go with it; a tennis dress that Mother had frowned at but was too sweet with a sort of kick pleat in the back and satin bindings.

Her mother had taken her to a powder-puffy little salon in Beauchamp Place that Tor's mother had recommended, all ribbons and chandeliers and flattering peach lights. They'd bought her trousseau there: thirteen pairs of cotton drawers; a corset that laced at the back; nainsook bloomers; two silk petticoats, and then the long peach silk negligee with a lace trim which made her feel like a glamorous stranger. After Madame had taken her measurements and complimented her on her 'perfect proportion', Rose had looked at her reflection in the mirror.

Her shoulders, her waist, even the small buds of her nipples seemed on display and scandalous. The next time she wore this, she'd be in Jack Chandler's bed. Mummy, whose face had suddenly swum into view behind her in the glass, must have been thinking along these lines too. She'd given a funny little grimace and shut her eyes. This was all so new for both of them.

That might have been the best time to have asked her about the bedroom side of things, but she'd been too shy. All that had happened in that department was a hot-making visit to Dr Llewellyn, an old family friend who hunted with her father, but who had offices in Harley Street. Blushing furiously and avoiding her eyes, he'd fished around inside her, hurting her horribly, and then handed her a small sponge. He'd said she was to use it when she was no longer a virgin. 'You put it in like this.' The back of his tweed suit had strained as he'd creaked into a squatted position and poked it between his legs.

He'd given her a little cloth bag, into which it must return washed and powdered when it wasn't in use.

She longed to ask her mother for more information about the terrifying event that would bring this thing out of its cloth bag, but her mother, who'd left her at the gate of the doctor's surgery almost scarlet with embarrassment herself, had said nothing. She wanted to ask Tor, in fact had asked her one night, when they were joking about kissing boys, but Tor had been irritatingly vague in the way she was when she knew nothing.

And now, her enormous new Viceroy trunk stood in the corner of the room. Earlier in the day she'd half packed it, clothes carefully wrapped in sheets of tissue paper with heavy things at the bottom; she was trying now to learn to be sensible and womanly like Mummy. She got into bed with the pile of women's magazines that had been her constant companions since Mrs Sowerby had handed them over. Mummy, who subscribed only to *Horse and Hound* and *Blackwood's Magazine*, thought they were a frightful waste of money, but she found them her only source of information on 'it'. On the problem pages of *Woman's World* a writer called Mary said her readers could ask her anything.

'Dear Mary,' one girl wrote. 'I am getting married shortly and have asked my mother to tell me the facts of life. She says I am thoroughly nasty and morbid and shall find out soon enough.' It was signed Ignorant Betty.

Mary had written back: 'Send a stamped addressed envelope and I will tell you all you need to know.'

Rose had thought, several times, of sending her own letter to Mary and enough stamps to get any reply to Bombay; but the thought of Ci Ci Mallinson, or her husband Geoffrey, opening it by mistake was too mortifying. She also hoped there would be time to find out on the voyage, not in a practical way of course, but because there were bound to be lots of parties and older people.

She turned to an article about how men simply love women who are a little bit secretive. 'Keep him guessing just a little bit,' said the writer. 'Besides, you will be much more appealing if, instead of telling him all your hopes and fears, you ask *him* about himself.'

She'd met Jack at her friend Flavia's twenty-first, at the Savile Club in London; he'd told her he'd been asked along as a spare man and he had seemed so much older and more experienced than the other silly boys. He was handsome too, with his fine tall physique and blond hair. He wasn't at all a good dancer, and at first they'd both been hopelessly flustered and tongue-tied bouncing around the floor together to the New Orleans Rhythm Kings.

He'd asked her to come downstairs so they didn't have to shout, and then she had asked him about India. And been initially impressed rather than bedazzled. He seemed to her a proper grown-up man, and to have done so much: pig-sticking and chasing tigers and helping Indian people learn so much about themselves. He was very modest about this, saying he was simply doing his bit, but she could tell he'd been brave.

Now she wanted so much to love him in what *Woman's World* called 'not a dull rub-along sort of way', but to try, as they suggested, 'to intrigue him and keep a sense of mystery alive'. So far, the mystery part had been easy – he'd proposed four weeks after that first meeting and gone back to India a week later. But the real test, the only one that counted, would be when they were alone in India together.

A soft knock on the door: her father. She hoped he couldn't see how red her eyes were from the big blub in the summer house. He looked slowly around the room at the packed trunk, the rose dress, Jack's photograph on her bedside table.

'Do you think you'll be all right, Froggie?' he asked.

'Yes, Daddy, I will.'

He sat down on the bed beside her. The fervent way she said 'I will' must have made him think of the wedding. 'I'm jolly well going to try and make it,' he said. 'I'm quite jealous of him, Frog.'

'Daddy, no!'

'I am.' His fingers, papery and old-looking in the lamplight, were plucking at the bedspread. 'My darling girl.'

When he turned, she was shocked to hear him swallowing, the breathless rasp of his lungs. The first time she ever saw him cry. Outside her window she saw the dark branches of the cedar tree moving in the wind. That tree had shaded her pram, held her tree house, been part of the den she built with Tor.

'So, who are these blasted poodle-fakers?' he said in quite a different voice, picking up *Vogue* magazine and glaring at the manne-quin on the front. This was their game when she was young: he was a ferocious character called Colonel Bluff who roared at her in a way he never had in real life. 'Extraordinary kit! Waste of good British money.'

She put her arms around him, burying her head in the softness of his moleskin waistcoat. How thin he was now! She inhaled him, pipes and soap and dogs, and fixed him somewhere deep inside of her.

'Goodnight, Daddy. Sleep well.'

Goodnight, sleep tight, hope the fleas don't bite.

'Goodnight, my darling, darling girl.' She felt his shuddering breath under her fingers.

'Would you mind turning off my light?'

'Will do.' The door clicked and the room went dark. She knew, and he did too: it was their last night together under the same roof.

Chapter 5

The *Kaisar-i-Hind* would sail the next day and now Viva's taxi was passing through an avenue of dripping rhododendron bushes towards St Christopher's School in the village of Colerne, near Bath.

It had rained steadily since she'd woken up early that morning. From her basement in Nevern Square she'd watched the usual procession of mud-splattered ankles, galoshes and buttoned shoes tramping through puddles on their way to work. In the train, the mist had drawn in so tightly she felt as if she was moving through a grey fur tunnel.

The taxi was splashing through puddles towards a large and gloomy Victorian house. To her right, a group of boys ran like small grey ghosts around the edges of a field, watched by a herd of cows hock deep in mud.

A maid showed her into the visitors' room, cold and sparsely furnished. A small fire in the hearth had two upright wooden chairs on either side of it.

'I've come to pick up Guy Glover,' she told the maid. 'I'm his chaperone. I'm taking him back to India.'

'Mr Glover's in the parlour,' the maid said, 'but Mr Partington, his housemaster, would like a quick word with you first.'

Mr Partington, an exhausted-looking man with nicotine-stained white hair, entered the room softly. She thought he looked old for a schoolmaster. 'Miss Viva Holloway, if I'm not mistaken.' He shook her hand limply. 'Well, well, well, off to India then.' He rubbed some chalk off his trousers and cleared his throat.

'Yes,' she said, 'tomorrow morning from Tilbury. We're going down tonight.'

She waited for him to say the usual things masters say when boys are leaving, 'Good chap' or 'We'll miss him' or some such, but nothing came.

'Do you know Guy?' he said after an awkward pause. 'I mean, are you a friend of the family?'

'No, his parents contacted me via an advertisement in *The Lady*.'

'How strange,' he said softly.

'What do you mean?'

'The way people lead their lives. Hah!' He seemed to have some constriction in his throat. 'So, hrggghh! – you don't know them at all?'

'No.'

He looked at her for a while, pressing his lips together and tapping his pen against the desk. She heard the squeaking of shoes in the corridor, above them someone was playing the piano badly.

'I've got something for you to take with him.' Mr Partington slid a letter from under the blotter and across the desk towards her. 'It seems, hah! that nobody has told you.'

Their eyes locked.

'Told me what?'

'Guy's been expelled. Two boys in his dorm reported money missing; another boy lost a travelling clock. He owned up right away. It wasn't a great deal of money, and there are some mitigating circumstances, hah!' When Mr Partington drew out his handkerchief to blow his nose, a shower of elastic bands flew to the floor. 'His parents keep him very short of funds. In fact he had to borrow from us last term. But the point is, it's led to certain problems with the other boys,' his pale eyes blinked at her, 'an understandable lack of trust. We sent a letter saying all this to his parents a few months ago, but they didn't reply except to send a telegram last week to say you were coming.'

Partington plucked another letter from underneath the blotter. 'Would you mind awfully giving this to them too? His report and his exam results. A disaster, I'm afraid – all this blew up before them. Shame. Hah! On the right day and given a fair wind, he's perfectly capable of passing them – depending on his mood, of course.'

'On his mood?' Viva took the letters and put them in her bag, trying to sound calmer than she felt.

'He's not a strong boy mentally at the best of times. But his parents reassured me you were responsible and experienced and I—' He was about to say something else when a bell rang, and there was a scattershot of feet in the hall outside. The piano above them stopped; she could hear the squeak of its lid as it closed.

The maid appeared. 'Mr Bell wants to speak to you in the lab,' she

23

said to Mr Partington. 'You may have to take his class there. He's forgotten to tell you he has to go to the dentist.'

'Oh God,' sighed Partington.

'Well, I won't keep you.'

Mr Partington took her hand in his. 'The boy's waiting for you just across the hall. Take him when you feel like it. We've said our goodbyes.' He pointed towards the door opposite and then scurried off in the opposite direction down the corridor. He seemed in a hurry to get away.

She walked into another chilly reception room across the hall. It had a highly polished sideboard on which was a green vase with peacock feathers in it. A tall pale-faced boy stood up without smiling. He was wearing a long black overcoat; pimples stood out on his chin through the beginnings of a beard.

'Hello, my name is Viva Holloway. Are you Guy Glover?' she said.

'That's the name,' he said.

'Well, I'm very pleased to meet you.' When she held out her hand, he shook it reluctantly.

'Charmed,' he said. 'I'm sure.'

When at last he smiled, she noticed he had the same buck teeth as his aunt. Also that his eyes couldn't quite meet hers. She could feel herself starting to dislike him already, but felt that this was very unfair of her. If anyone should understand how awkward a person could feel being picked up at a school by a perfect stranger, it should be her.

'Well, shall we collect your things?' she said. 'The taxi's waiting outside; we're going straight to Tilbury.'

'Who's paying for it?' he asked her sharply.

'Paying for what?'

'The taxi, of course. I haven't got a bean.'

'Your aunt,' she said, determined not to resent his tone. Their arrangement was five pounds in travel expenses.

As she followed his long thin legs upstairs, she tried to neutralise the sense of panic she'd felt at Mr Partington's words. Her own trunk was packed, the entire trip organised, she couldn't afford to exaggerate his crimes and after all, she rationalised, lots of children did a bit of amateur thieving. She and her friends had pinched the occasional pear drop or something harmless like a pencil from the sweetshop near school. They'd done it for dares; it was almost part of growing up.

'So, how long have you been here?' They'd reached the first landing and she stood beside him.

'Ten years.'

'Gosh, long time.'

'Um.'

'It must feel rather strange leaving.'

'Not really.' His voice was so completely without expression. She felt she must stop asking him questions. For all his assumed nonchalance, he might be upset – even mortified – at the thought of leaving this place under a cloud.

The door at the top of the stairs had a large wodge of felt underneath it to keep draughts out. When he'd pushed the door open with his foot, she saw a row of white beds, probably ten in all, with green counterpanes folded neatly at the base of them. At the end of the room, a large window looked out on to a sky ready to dump more rain on to sodden fields.

He led her to a bed halfway down the room with two suitcases beside it.

'My trunk's gone on ahead,' he told her.

She was struck by the silence, the cold in the dormitory, and then relieved to see a note pinned to his pillow with his name written on it in an untidy schoolboyish scrawl, assuming it was someone wishing to say goodbye. Without reading the letter, he tore it up and dropped the pieces of paper into a wastepaper basket underneath the bed.

'There,' he said. 'All done now.'

The note had brought a flush of colour to his otherwise chalk-pale cheeks. His young man's Adam's apple bulged in his neck. She pretended not to notice. *He is more upset than I realise*, she told herself, remembering how she'd both hated and felt safe at her own freezing-cold convent boarding school in North Wales.

'Shall I put these in your case?' she asked. There was a razor strap and a soiled vest underneath his bed. The vest had worn thin and had yellow sweat marks under the armpits.

'No, I'm leaving them behind.'

'So,' she said with an attempt at brightness, 'shall we be off? I've already spoken to Mr Partington.'

'Yes.' He was moving around his bed like a large stunned animal, looking about the room for the last time.

'Do you want this?' She picked up a photograph face down on the washstand.

When she turned it over she saw a tall, square-shouldered man in khakis making a self-consciously jokey face at the photographer with what looked like mile after mile of bleached sand dunes behind him.

'My father,' he said. He unclipped his suitcase and crammed the picture on top of some badly packed clothes.

'Are you sure it won't break there?' She was conscious already of sounding like an irritating grown-up.

'I'll risk it,' he said. He closed the suitcase.

She carried one of his cases downstairs; he took the other. They crossed the polished hall together. She closed the door behind him and it was only when she was sitting in the taxi and they were halfway to the station that she realised that nobody: no boy; no maid; no servant; no master, had come to the door to say goodbye to him.

When their taxi drove through the iron gates at the end of the drive, he turned in his seat and looked back towards the school. He whispered, 'Bastards,' and then he said with a bright insincere smile, 'I'm sorry, did you think I said something?'

And her thought was: *The sensible thing now would be to ask the taxi driver to turn round and drive him straight back to school.* She would say, 'I'm very sorry, but I don't think this will work.' But that would mean no ticket and no India, so she ignored her feelings and told the driver to take them to the railway station in Bath.

Chapter 6

The *Kaisar-i-Hind* was a swarming hive of activity by the time Tor and Rose arrived. Red turbaned lascars flew around with luggage; crates of fruit and boxes of food were being hauled up the gangplank; bells were ringing, and on the quay, a pensioner band was wheezing its way through 'Will Ye No' Come Back Again?'. And all Tor could do was smile and try not to stare too openly at all the men walking up the gangplanks: sunburned men in naval uniforms, old colonels bundled up against the cold, clever, pale men, young civil servants and one heavenly-looking man, who looked half-Indian, in the most beautiful cashmere coat who turned and gave her what she was sure was a meaningful look.

Oh, it was almost unbearable to feel this excited.

Close to the gangplank, Rose's parents stood conversing quietly with Miss Viva Holloway, who had been joined by a tall pale boy in a long dark coat, her other charge. Tor saw him glance at her mother, who was making a noisy hand-waving fuss about boarding passes and trunks, but today she hardly gave a damn.

All of them had flown around for most of the morning exploring the ship, which was astoundingly spacious and opulent. 'Quite like a first-class hotel,' her mother kept saying. 'I mean, very like the *Meurice*.' Its gleaming wooden floors smelt of fresh polish; it had deep armchairs in smoking rooms, lushly painted murals in the dining room, Persian carpets, fresh flowers, and when they walked in to look at the dining salon, a buffet was already being laid out with huge turkeys and hams and a sweet trolley, quivering with blanc-manges, and neiges au crème, fruit salads and – Tor's favourite – lemon meringue pie.

Her mother had gasped with admiration and then spoilt it by stage-whispering, '*Somebody* will be in their element.' And then,

'Darling, please do try not to overdo it, there is *no more money* for any frocks.'

And for once, Tor's silent father had taken her side. 'Leave her alone, Jonti,' he'd said, his voice throbbing with emotion. 'Don't go on at her today.'

At the clang of a loud bell, the pulse of the ship had quickened; feet scampered above their heads, orders were shouted, the music on the quayside swelled to a sobbing pitch, and her parents had been sent ashore.

Tor's last view of her mother had been of her standing on the quay, a few feet away from her father, tiny and determined, a coloured streamer caught in her fur tippet. When Tor looked down, her mother looked up, lifted her bosom and gave her a significant look. '*Posture*,' her mother mouthed and Tor had immediately straightened up. *Her performing seal*, she'd thought bitterly, *right up until the end*.

Then the band had played a rousing farewell and suddenly she'd felt this lurch like a giant heartbeat and they were off. And while other passengers had wept and waved and strained their eyes towards the shore until their people were dots, Tor's heart had floated upwards and outwards in an ecstasy of flight. She was free.

An hour later, Rose and Tor stood in a thumping wind on A deck clinging to each other. The seagulls that had followed them from Tilbury were, one by one, turning to go home.

Rose's new coat suddenly ballooned above her head, making them both laugh a little too wildly.

'Are you all right?' Tor said. Rose looked as if she'd been crying.

'Yes, Tor, I'm fine – excited – *really*. But I do think I'll go down to the cabin now and unpack. What about you?'

'I'll be down in five minutes,' said Tor. 'I'm about to throw my corset into the drink.'

Rose scrunched up her eyes and tried to laugh. 'Your mother will kill you.'

'She can't swim,' said Tor, flashing her great headlamp eyes. '*Shame*.'

The corset. Her mother had brought a new one up to Tor's room while she was packing and laid it on the bed like a shrivelled pink baby.

'I brought it back from Paris,' her mother whispered, 'as a surprise.

It's called a waspy and makes your waist *comme ça*.' She'd given a silly conspiratorial smile and held her hands in a tiny circle. 'If you don't wear it under your peach crêpe de Chine it really will look like a rag, and I warn you, Ci Ci Mallinson is very, very smart,' she'd said, bringing up their dragon hostess in Bombay yet again.

And in spite of all her good intentions not to row before she left, Tor had raised her voice and said, 'Mummy, *nobody* wears them now,' which of course was not true, and then she'd added illogically, 'Besides, if my brains are melting in the heat I shan't be able to.'

For a second, Tor had expected to be struck across the face, her mother could be free with her fists when riled, but all she'd said was, '*Oh, pouf.*' She'd waved her away with her hand like some sort of nasty fly, and Tor had seen pure contempt in her eyes, which in a way was worse than anger. *Be fat and ugly then*, her mother might as well have added, *I give up.*

'Darling.' A wan-looking Rose joined her on the deck again. 'This is so stupid but I can't find Miss Holloway, or our cabin – they all look the same to me.'

She was trying hard to smile and keep the wobble out of her voice, but poor Rose was in quite a state, Tor could see that. At school, Rose had always been the calmly efficient one, packing Tor's pencils and finding forgotten homework; now Tor was the one holding Rose's hand as they wove their way down the deck, both feeling slightly nauseous. As the wind drew them in a sucking motion towards the steps, she saw the strange boy who'd been with Miss Holloway earlier, sitting on his own on a deckchair. He was staring out to sea and, at the same time, tapping his foot rhythmically as though he was listening to a piece of music.

'Oh, hello,' said Rose, 'we're looking for Miss Holloway. Have you any idea where she is?'

'Not the foggiest,' he said. 'Sorry.' He turned away from them and looked intently at the sea again.

'Gosh, how *rude*,' Rose said as they walked down the stairs towards the purser's office. 'I jolly well hope we don't have to eat every meal with him.'

'We don't,' Tor said firmly. 'Because I won't. I'll talk to Miss Viva Holloway about it. I'll make some excuse.'

At the bottom of the steps, a brick-faced colonel was giving orders to a tiny Lascar seaman who was struggling with his trunk: 'Left hand down, hard at it, jolly good, well done!' A smart woman was checking her lipstick in a mirror and saying to a small boy, 'Yes, it is rough but there's nothing I can do about it.'

It would take them all a while to settle in.

'I'm afraid we've been very silly and lost our keys,' Rose told the purser, who was instantly charmed by her. Rose had that effect on men: a dewy softness, a tentative confiding air that made them melt. He said he was going off duty but would take them down to their cabins. He led them past the bar where a band was playing 'Ain't She Sweet?', and then past the dining salon where waiters in snowy-white uniforms buzzed about setting tables.

'First journey east?' he asked Tor impersonally.

'Yes,' Tor said. 'My friend is about to be married, and I'm chief bridesmaid.'

'That sounds very nice,' he said. 'Bombay or Delhi?'

'Bombay.' She felt she had taken on somebody else's life.

They went up a flight of carpeted stairs and then up a narrow corridor smelling faintly of petrol.

'There you go, ladies,' he said. 'B 34, your cabin. Your chaperone is in B 36. Mr Glover is next door to you in B 35. Bon voyage.'

Alone in their cabin, Rose and Tor sat on opposite bunks and grinned at each other. The tiny room was already chaotic, they'd been down earlier and left heaps of clothes on the floor, too excited to unpack properly. Now they examined in detail the twin brass beds, the rich-looking monogrammed blankets, the Lilliputian chest of drawers. Rose hung her wedding dress, a swinging corpse in its cloth bag, on the outside of the cupboard. 'I'll give it to the purser later,' she assured Tor. 'It takes up too much space here.'

They lay on their beds in silence for a moment, exhausted by the day. Tor had taken the bed next to the porthole through which she could see the tumbling sea. Rose said she'd rather be closer to the bathroom.

They were chattering again when there was a knock on the door, and their tiny steward walked in ('I mean *literally* monkey-sized,' Rose wrote in a subsequent letter home, 'in this wonderful blue and white uniform'). He smiled at them radiantly. 'My name is Suday Ram,' he said. 'Babies want bat?'

'Sorry?' Rose said politely. 'I didn't quite catch that.'

Tor knew she mustn't look at Rose; they were both in a mood to giggle.

'Do babies want *bat*?' he repeated more firmly.

He took them into the miniature bathroom, which had thick white towels and new soaps. He showed them how to get the rust-coloured seawater out of the taps and how to flush the water closet, which was most embarrassing. When he left, they exploded with laughter and said, 'Baby want bat,' several times until they'd perfected their Indian accents and Tor was so happy to see Rose laughing. She'd been crying again, she could see that, even though Rose would rather die than admit it.

'Rose,' she said in her Indian voice when the man was gone. 'Go back into the bathroom, rub your tummy and make a vish. I have big surprise.'

When she heard the bolt slide, Tor took the most magical thing she possessed out of her trunk and held it reverently in her arms. Its red leather box, with the little dog Nipper and a horn inscribed on its lid, still made her tremble with happiness.

'Don't come out yet,' she said. She removed the pair of silk stockings she'd put into the horn chamber to stop it getting dented. 'Eyes tight shut!' She took a tin out of the silk pocket in the lining and took the red (loud) needle from a square of cotton wool. A few seconds later, the cabin exploded with the pratfall squeaks and bangs of J. B. White's 'Shoo Fox'.

'Oh, Tor.' Rose Charlestoned out of the bathroom in her stock-inged feet. 'Thank God, *thank God* you're here.'

They danced together for a while and then collapsed on the bed.

'Oh bother!' Rose's wedding dress was falling in a silken avalanche on to the floor. 'I must put it away.'

'Yes, yes, yes.' Tor poured them both a crème de menthe and they lay on the bunk together, with their eyes shut, feeling the ship speeding them onwards.

Then Tor read the letter from their captain that had been left on their beds.

'We're invited to a cocktail party tonight, in the Taj Room. Voyage out will take three weeks. We'll stop at Gibraltar, Marseilles, Malta, Port Said and Bombay. Dancing each night in the Persian Room to the Savoy Havana Band.

'No second-class passengers to even think of showing their com-mon little mugs in first class,' Tor continued, 'and there will be

31

fancy-dress parties, deck quoits and bridge evenings, a talk on snake bites and sunstroke in the Simla Bar given by Lieutenant Colonel Gorman when we get to Port Said. Dinner jackets and long dresses to be worn each night. Oh! And fornication.'

'Oh, Tor, stop it.' Rose took a sip from her glass and then put it down. 'What's that?' she said. There was a great creaking noise coming from the direction of the porthole, followed by the thud of an engine, the running of feet above their heads.

'Only the wind, my lovely.' Tor glanced towards the porthole, towards the waves, grey and tumbling. 'Following us into the fathomless depths.'

'I shan't have any more crème de menthe,' said Rose, who was looking a bit green.

'Well, I will,' said Tor, 'otherwise I might just die of excitement.'

Chapter 7

BAY OF BISCAY

The sea: long glistening hollows laced with creamy foam;
broken ice creams, clamour, bang, smack of waves. Reptilian
hiss of ship as it glides through sea. Colour of potato peelings
at Tilbury, now a deep dense green.

'NO CLICHÉS,' Viva Holloway wrote in capital letters in her new
leather-bound journal. 'GET ON WITH SOME PROPER WORK.'

This habit of writing bossy notes to herself often resurfaced at
times of strain. When she was a child, and at her convent boarding
school in Wales, she'd imagined them being dictated by her father,
Alexander Holloway, railway engineer, late of Simla, who was in
heaven but looking down on her, monitoring her progress. Later, in
London, where she'd arrived at the age of eighteen, this moving
finger moved too, full of advice on how she should survive this big
bad city where she knew nobody and was frighteningly poor; it was
always ready to tick her off about dithering or regrets or extravagance
or self-pity.

She turned the page.

'<u>THINGS TO DO IN INDIA</u>,' she wrote.

1. WRITE FOR A MINIMUM OF ONE AND A HALF
   HOURS A DAY.
2. LOOK FOR WORK IMMEDIATELY, BUT <u>NOT</u> AS
   LADY'S COMPANION OR NANNY.
3. WRITE TO MABEL WAGHORN ABOUT
   COLLECTING TRUNK.

'You must NOT go to Simla,' she bossed herself in the margin, 'until you have earned enough money to do so. <u>VERY BAD IDEA!</u>'

Money was something she worried about constantly. Guy Glover's aunt had promised to send her one hundred and sixty pounds in a banking order before the ship left, but the posts had come and gone, and the fare plus the money for their train tickets had come from her own dwindling savings.

At the last moment her old employer, Nancy Driver, had slipped a ten-guinea bonus into the leather journal that had been her farewell present. She'd been given twenty-five pounds by Rose's mother and twenty-five pounds from Tor's, but now survival depended on her being able to supplement her income by writing articles.

She turned another page and took a deep breath. She was sitting in the far corner of the ship's writing room where, at other lamp-lit desks set at discreet distances from her own, a handful of other passengers were dutifully scratching away. From where she sat, she could see grey waves and grey skies and a horizon that moved up and down like pantomime scenery. They were in the Bay of Biscay, and the steward who had ushered her in here had cheerfully assured her that the waves would get rougher as the morning went on, a piece of intelligence she was determined to ignore.

'THE FISHING FLEET by Viva Holloway', she wrote in bold letters at the top of the page; she added a fancy squiggle to both Fs while she put the top of her pen in her mouth.

'There are, roughly speaking, three kinds of women on board the *Kaisar-i-Hind*,' she began.

She stared out to sea for a while, trying to decide whether she would post this, or try to send it by telegram, which would be shockingly expensive. Its final destination would be a shabby bedsit in Bloomsbury, where *The Voice*, a feminist magazine begun by two suffragette sisters, Violet and Fiona Thyme, had its headquarters. Mrs Driver had introduced her.

If they liked the story, the sisters had promised to pay her ten pounds for one thousand words. 'Forget elephant hunts and spicy smells, dear,' said Violet, who had once been to jail with Emily Pankhurst, and who smoked small cheroots. 'Lift the lid on what really happens to all those women going to India, and what they think they'll do when the whole thing collapses.'

'First,' wrote Viva, 'there are the memsahibs – the name in Hindi means "the master's women", all of whom are travelling on this ship

34

by first class.' ('Check there is a second class', she wrote in the margin for she hadn't had much time yet to explore.)

I have seen them in this ship's elegant dining room, and their plumage is quite varied – some favouring the more dowdy feathers of the shires: dun-coloured tweeds, silk dresses in various shades of potato, sensible shoes and thick stockings. Some look as if their hearts have already been half-broken by India.

Others are extremely elegant, maybe they already know there will be little else to do when they get there but go to the club, the tennis court or the shoot, where the same small crowd will watch each other with hawk-like fascination and be quietly determined not to let themselves fall behind in the fashion stakes.

Next, we have the skittishly nervous young girls who are collectively and unkindly called the Fishing Fleet. They are going to India to look for husbands, and they've been going there with their hooks baited ever since the early nineteeth century.

('WHEN EXACTLY? YOU MUST TALK TO THEM' she scrawled in the margin.)

Most come after the London season is over and where, presumably, they have fallen at the first fence of that glorified marriage market. India, where men of their class outnumber women by three to one, will be their last chance to find a husband.

She put down her pen for a while and thought of Rose, who smelt of Devonshire violets, and who was – Tor was right – ravishingly pretty. She seemed to epitomise a peculiarly British kind of innocence: fine-skinned, appealingly shy, unsure of men.

On their first night at sea, she'd gone down to the girls' cabin to see if they were all right. The door was unlocked, and when she'd put her head round the door, she'd found Rose lying face down on the bed quietly weeping. The girl had leapt up immediately and mumbled something about her brother, or maybe it was her father – that poor man had looked so devastated as she'd left – and apologised for being such a wet. And Viva had experienced what she imagined it felt like to have a maternal impulse; she had longed to put her arms around her, but knew it would embarrass them both.

She's petrified, she thought. *And why not?*

For some, this could turn out to be a voyage into nightmare: it was vessels like these that took those who were hacked to death in Cawnpore out to India. Others will discover what it is like to want to die of heat; or they may be shot at, or have their children die of tropical diseases or taken away from them at an early age and educated half a world away.

Viva put her pen down. This, of course, would be the natural moment to tell them about her own father's death. Or not. Experience had taught her that telling meant enduring other people's moistly sympathetic looks, their embarrassment, the long accounts of other people they knew who'd lost people abroad, or, worst of all, attempts to think of some uplifting moral that would make sense of it all. And besides, the car-crash story now tripped off her tongue so easily it felt almost real.

And next, there are women like myself: single women with no sahib and no wish for one, who love India and like to work. You see, nobody ever really writes about them – the governesses, the schoolteachers, the chaperones – but we have our tales to tell.

'True, <u>all</u> like to work?????' she scribbled to herself. Well, it would do for now. She was about to describe their plumage, which in her case was quite atypical. Now she'd returned the woolly tweeds to Mrs Driver, she was back in her own clothes that morning, a scarlet silk dress, a dark ballet top left over from school and a barbaric-looking silver necklace inherited from her mother.

All of a sudden, her mouth filled with liquid and she put her pen down as the floor rose and fell along with her stomach. She glanced at the leaping room, its lamps and green leather desks – when did leather ever smell so sickening? – to see how the other passengers were doing. The walls creaked as she stood up. How hot-making! Not thirty-six hours out from Tilbury and she was going to be sick.

'Excuse me, madam.' A waiter appeared with a grey and pink box and a glass of water.

Oh no! Was it that obvious? She sat back with her eyes closed, trying not to feel the suck and swell of the waves. *Breathe! Breathe!* She tried not to listen to the faint tinkle of the glasses or the stupid laughter of people who thought rough weather was funny or the woman in the booth next to her who was asking for 'a plate of egg sandwiches and some Earl Grey'. Egg sandwiches, uuggggh, how disgusting.

'Missy.' The waiter stood at the door. He smiled kindly at her as she stumbled out on to the deck and into the deafening boom of the waves.

'Thank you. I'm fine, thank you.'

She rested her forehead on the railings and stayed there until she felt slightly better. The phrase she had been about to write swam mockingly in her head, the words dancingly disconnected. 'You see I was not made for marriage, I was born with a knapsack on my back.'

The steward brought her a deckchair and a rug. When she was sitting down, she thought, briefly, about Ottaline Renouf, one of her heroines, who'd gone halfway round the world in an eccentric variety of crafts: Danish fishing boats, banana boats, trawlers, Turkish caiques, never once mentioning seasickness. What if she wasn't strong enough for this? What would that mean?

By the time she stood up the sky was one huge grey and yellow bruise over the still rearing waves. Night was falling and the lights had gone on. From the ship she could hear laughter and faint arpeggios of piano music rising and falling. How tinny it sounded against the animal roars of the waves.

When she looked up again, she saw Guy Glover sitting on a deckchair behind a glass screen that sheltered him from the worst of the wind. He was wearing his black overcoat and smoking a cigarette. When he saw her looking at him, he held her gaze for a moment and raised his cigarette to his mouth. The look in his eye said, *Try and stop me.* He inhaled deeply and exhaled, making a fishy shape with his lips as the wind blew his smoke ring away. He ground the cigarette under his heel and sauntered over to her. Pathetic, she thought, in his too large coat, trying hard to be what? Perhaps Valentino in *The Sheik*, complete with cape and dagger in boot, or maybe a rake on his first night at sea trying to decide which virgin to take to bed.

He's just a child, she tried to reassure herself, for the sight of him

37

had made her anxious again, *a foolish self-conscious child. Nothing to be frightened of.*

She'd shared a similar background, and her current thinking about him went as follows: like many boys of his class and background, he'd been turfed from the nest too young. Without parents on hand, or, in his case, siblings to chivvy him along, he'd become a permanent defensive guest, unsure of his welcome, uneasy in his skin. Underneath the studied indifference, the coldness, there was, she was almost certain of it, a boy hungry for love, angry about having to ask for it. She should at least try to understand him even if she couldn't like him.

'I meant to tell you,' he shouted over the waves, 'there's some people on board my parents want me to say hello to. The Ramsbottoms from Lucknow. They've asked us for a drink in the music room tomorrow night. I'd like you to come too.'

Well, well, well, he'd made one unsolicited remark to her.

'Of course,' she said. 'Perhaps you and I and the girls can have dinner together at the early sitting first. We can all get to know each other.'

As she said this, she wondered again whether she should have warned the girls to lock their cabin, just in case Guy was still a little on the light-fingered side.

He looked startled. 'I'd rather not do that,' he said. 'I don't want to eat with other people.'

'Why not?'

He mumbled something that the waves drowned out.

'I can't hear you,' she shouted.

'My parents said we'd be eating alone,' he shouted so hectically that she took a step back.

'Shall we talk about this later?' She felt too sick to lock horns with him now, or to think about food for that matter, and the girls were hardly going to mind.

'Of course.' He beamed his blank and insulting smile and shouted something else about parents that was swept away by the wind. He was going to be a handful; there was no doubt about it.

After this exchange, Viva went down to the cabin she was sharing with a Miss Snow, a whispery and apologetic schoolteacher who was going back to teach in a school near Cochin. The two had come to this arrangement in order to save money, but hadn't yet exchanged more than a handful of words.

Miss Snow was asleep under a mound of bedclothes with a green pail underneath her bed. Viva put a damp flannel on her own head and lay down on her bunk and thought about Guy again and all the sympathetic things she'd thought about him earlier flew out of her mind. The scaring thing was, she thought, that Guy Glover was her creature now, her responsibility and no doubt her punishment for the lies she'd told.

A wave of anxiety swept over her. Why in God's name had she taken all this on, particularly at a time when she had, at last, achieved a kind of independence?

It couldn't surely just be for the chance to open that wretched trunk – Mrs Waghorn couldn't have been more frank about the chances of her finding anything in it – but she had flung her life on to this slender thread. Why?

She thought back almost longingly to her basement flat in Nevern Square, not an abode of bliss, to be sure, with its gas ring and narrow bed, but a home nevertheless.

Her bathroom – shared with an elderly librarian and a woman who had an unusual number of gentleman callers – was behind a curtain in the hallway. It had a rough green bath, and was full of damp and dripping stockings and odd ends of slimy soap and a rusting green boiler called the Winterbourne which, when you touched its innards with a match, exploded like a volcano for three scorching minutes and then went achingly cold.

In winter she'd slept in her liberty bodice and a variety of jumpers; her blood, it seemed, had been thin ever since India. She'd sallied forth each morning for a variety of temporary jobs, going to work in the same foggy darkness that she came home in.

An older person might have seen nothing but drudgery in this existence, but for her, young and determined to survive her tragedies, independence had been a kind of drug. No more school dorms, no more spare rooms where relatives had to move things around to fit her in. This room was hers. In a state of childish excitement, she painted its walls a pale pink – she had in her mind the kind of dusty pinks you find in Rajasthan – but the effect was more of calamine lotion.

On a lumpy single bed near the boarded-up fire, she'd put her only real heirloom, an exquisite patchwork quilt, made up of sari fabrics in jewel-like colours: bright greens and yellows, pinks and blues, with a border embroidered with fishes and birds. It had once been on her parents' bed in Simla, and in their other houses in Nepal and Kashmir, and the houseboat in Srinagar. She had a brass lamp, a few kitchen utensils hidden under the bed ('*No kitchen privileges*', said the sign in the hall), boxes and boxes of books and typing paper and a Remington typewriter perched on a packing case. The secretarial course was only a means to an end. What she wanted more than anything in the world was to be a writer. After work each night, she changed into some warm clothes, lit up one of the three Abdullah cigarettes she allowed herself each day, touched her little green glass statue of Ganesh – Indian god of writers amongst other things – and set to work.

She found happiness in that room hearing the clack of her typewriter and the occasional whoomph of the Winterbourne, the last lavatory chain being pulled. Around midnight, stiff and yawning, she undressed for bed and as soon as her head hit the pillow, fell dead asleep.

And then, via the agency she did temporary typing for, she was sent to work for Mrs Nancy Driver, who was the real thing: a prolific writer of romances, two of them set in India, where her husband, now dead, had been a major in the Indian Cavalry. Mrs Driver, who spent much of her day furiously typing in a camel-haired dressing gown, might have seemed at first, with her Eton crop and fierce pouncing style of conversation, like an unlikely fairy godmother, but that was what she'd been.

She and Viva had settled into a routine together. At eleven-thirty, when Mrs Driver had bathed and eaten her breakfast, she wrote furiously in longhand for an hour or so while Viva dealt inexpertly with her correspondence. After lunch, while her employer relaxed with another glass of sherry and a cheroot, Viva would type up the morning's work and, if a large red cross was in the margin, she was allowed to add what were called 'the spoony bits'. Mrs Driver was convinced, quite wrongly, that Viva, being young and good-looking, was having lots of exciting romances.

It was Mrs Driver who subscribed to the magazine *Criterion*, and who first introduced her to the poetry of T. S. Eliot. 'Listen to this! Listen to this!' She'd struck a dramatic pose with her cheroot still smouldering between her fingers and her eyes closed, declaiming:

> *April is the cruellest month, breeding*
> *Lilacs out of the dead land, mixing*
> *Memory and desire, stirring*
> *Dull roots with spring rain.*

And it was in this flat, typing and proofreading and drinking coffee, that it gradually dawned on Viva that as far as being a writer was concerned, she was in kindergarten. Before, she'd bashed out her stories and when she came to the last full stop sent them out. Now, she watched how hard Mrs Driver struggled to find 'the right way in', how she paid close attention to the smallest and oddest things, often writing about them in her many notebooks; how she talked her stories out loud when she got stuck, how she'd leave them in drawers for several months to mature.

'There is no magic recipe,' her employer said. 'Each one cooks in its own way.'

When Viva, shaking with nerves, told Mrs Driver over sherry one morning that she had dreams herself of writing some stories, Mrs Driver had been kind but pragmatic. She told her if she was serious and needed to earn money immediately (for Viva had been unusually frank about her dire financial straits) she should try and sell to women's magazines like *Woman's Realm* and *The Lady*, the kind of gentle romances they published on a regular basis.

'Awful tripe,' Mrs Driver had warned. 'And you will write from your own heart eventually, but it will get you started and give you some confidence.'

She'd showed her how to prune her stories ruthlessly ('Sharpen, lighten, tighten,' she'd written all over her margins) and in the last six months, Viva had penned thirteen stories in which a variety of granite-jawed heroes seized women of the blonde, helpless and dim variety. Back had come ten rejection slips but three had been published.

And oh, the impossible elation of that first moment of hearing that her first story had been accepted. She'd got the letter after work on a wet November evening, and run around Nevern Square on her own in the dark. She'd been so sure then – ridiculously sure in retrospect – that this was a turning point and from now on she would be able to survive by her pen. No more dreary jobs, or school dorms, no more spare rooms. She was young, she was healthy, she could just about afford the three guineas a week for her flat, and whoopee, she was now going to be a writer.

So why, with everything at last moving in the right direction, had she decided to change all her plans? Surely not because some old girl had written to her out of the blue to tell her she had a trunk in her shed with her parents' things in them? Or was all that just an excuse to get back to India, which, bizarrely, when you thought about everything that had happened to her there, she still missed – a permanent ache as if some vital organ had been removed.

Miss Snow was still asleep, snoring with a puttering sound and occasionally moaning as though she was wrestling with her own demons. When she sat up suddenly, Viva's typewriter fell with a clunk on to the floor, followed by a ream of loose paper.

Kneeling to pick up her scattered pages, Viva saw navy blue water rushing past her porthole in coils like a snake. She went to the basin and washed her face. There was an hour and a half before the first sitting for dinner; she was determined to bash out a first draft of her article before she ate. She was still mulling over the title, 'The Fishing Fleet' or perhaps 'The Price of a Husband in India'. One day, even the memory of it would make her burn with shame.

Chapter 8

POONA

'Master,' Jack Chandler's bearer called softly through the bathroom door. 'Wake up, please, time is marching. *Jaldi!*'

'I'm not asleep, Dinesh,' Jack Chandler called back, 'I'm thinking.'

He'd been lying in the bath for almost an hour. It was dark now; the new electric lights were still more off than on. His eyes were closed as he brooded about marriage and why men told lies, and Sunita, to whom he must soon say goodbye.

Normally, this was a favourite time of the day, when he peeled off clothes that smelt satisfactorily of horse sweat and stepped into warm water, with a whisky mixed just the way he liked it, and allowed himself the luxury of floating like an almost inanimate sea creature before Dinesh dressed him and he went to the club. But tonight, he was a bundle of nerves. That afternoon, he'd been to the dusty cantonment church to talk to the vicar, a faded uninspiring man, about arrangements for his marriage in four weeks' time. He'd written down all the details on a piece of paper – Miss Rose Wetherby, spinster, of Park House, Middle Wallop, Hampshire – but the vicar had informed him that you didn't need banns to get married in India, so many people, he had implied without actually saying it, did it on the spur of the moment here. And this exchange had further rattled Jack who was, generally speaking, a man with a logical brain who thought things through.

'Time spent in reconnaissance is seldom wasted,' was one of the rules he'd lived his life by. A sergeant major had bellowed it out to his class of gawky recruits at Sandhurst in the first week of their terrifying induction there and it had saved his life more than once since then. So why, well, it was too late to bother about this now, but why had he recklessly ignored this, jumped in eyes closed, in the matter of finding a new wife?

43

He'd set himself the task of writing to Rose earlier that night and posting it to her in Port Said, where her ship would arrive in twelve days' time by his calculations.

'My dearest Rose,' he'd written. 'Today, I went to the church where we are to be married and—' He had crumpled up the letter, irritated with the banality of his thoughts and for not having the right words at a time when, surely, they should be tumbling out.

But more and more, he found communications with her stilted, like a grown-up and more fateful version of the letters they had been forced to write during Sunday morning sessions at his English boarding school. The excitement of their earlier letters had petered out into a dull exchange of plans beefed up with endearments – *my own little fiancée, my soon-to-be darling wife* – which now seemed to him artificial, if not downright over-familiar.

He owed Rose's mother a letter too. They'd met twice, the first time at an Easter party at her house, where a dozen random relatives covertly inspected him and congratulated him on his sudden engagement, and talked a lot of rot about India. Now Mrs Wetherby had written him several letters, full of baffling bits of advice about the wedding, and, last week, to tell him that Rose's father had come down with a bad case of bronchitis after her ship had sailed. 'But probably better to keep this to ourselves,' she'd written. 'They are very close and she has so much on her plate.' For some reason, the words 'on her plate' had annoyed him too, making him feel as though she regarded him as some sort of unpleasant green vegetable that would soon have to be faced and gobbled down. And if he was such an unknown quantity, why had these two sensible, fond people let the marriage go ahead? In certain moods he almost blamed them for it.

He stood up in the bath: a tall man with a fine, sensitive face, wary eyes, strong sloping shoulders and the long muscular legs of a horseman. He was far better looking now at twenty-eight than he had been when he first came out to India six years ago. Then, he was a tall boy just one year out of Sandhurst, skinny in spite of all the punishing exercise, the yard drills, the riding, the expeditions in mock deserts with thirty-pound weights on his back, all things designed to take the softness out of young men.

'Sir, please.' Dinesh stood smiling at the door, a towel in his hand. He'd come to Poona three years ago, a refugee from a flooded farm in Bengal. Jack had first met him quite by chance in the house of a friend in Delhi, and had been struck as everybody was by the open radiance of his smile. Dinesh counted this job as his one blinding stroke of good fortune in a life full of tragedies. A sign that his karma, his wheel of fortune, had taken a turn for the better.

Dinesh and Jack were a team now. The fact that Jack was a young officer with an Indian, rather than a British Cavalry regiment and could – after quite a slog, for he was not a natural linguist – converse with Dinesh in almost fluent Hindustani was a point of pride with Dinesh who, like many good servants, was a snob who looked down on the other servants in British regiments who had to speak English to their sahibs. They had been through so much together, some of the finest moments of their lives – the parades, the equitation school in Secunderabad, the yearly camps in the mountains where Dinesh, as thrilled as Jack had been by the adventure, had cooked for him over one of dozens of little fires that sprang up as soon as night had settled. He'd served with a reverence and a passion that both humbled and worried Jack, for the wheel was turning again. All of Jack's servants – Dinesh and his wash man, his cook and her young daughter – were acutely aware of their various positions in the house; they watched each other like hawks for any changes in the pecking order. The arrival of Rose, no question about it, would ruffle their feathers, and Jack hadn't found the words to explain that to her yet.

He walked into his bedroom. In the plain, low-ceilinged room an ancient fan ground away over his single bed with a mosquito net above it. There was a rush mat on the floor and on the bare walls only one faded landscape of the Lake District, left by the last tenant. He'd asked the regiment's stores for a double bed six weeks ago, but things moved very slowly here; he'd have to remind them again.

On the bamboo chair in the corner of the room Dinesh had laid out a pair of linen trousers and a white shirt, all beautifully pressed. Against the wall – it had taken Dinesh hours to do when they'd first arrived – he'd draped a red cloth like an upright altar, against which he had hung whistles and spurs, his Sam Browne belt and sword.

Beside his bed his servant had placed a silver bowl full of Eno's fruit salts, in case he should need them after a heavy night at the mess and, touchingly, as if to say, 'I am going to try and like her,' he'd surrounded the photograph of Rose with a garland of marigolds, as if she was a goddess.

Now Dinesh came out of the shadows thrown by the hurricane

lamp, dried Jack carefully with his towel, helped him put on his underpants, then held open the waistband of his trousers so he could put first one leg in and then the other.

There was a time when Jack had loathed being dressed like this. The first time it happened he had offended Dinesh by laughing nervously and snatching his clothes away. It was embarrassing, demeaning, like two grown men dressing dolly. Now he rather liked it. The way he explained this to himself was that he now understood so much better what each job meant to each person in this house. But if he was honest, Dinesh's tender ministrations made him feel less lonely here, and, also, his deepest instincts told him that such cosseting would not last for much longer.

Everything was changing, everybody knew it. Nobody talked about it much, but it was always there, like the scuffling of rodents under the floorboards. On top of the house, the masters were still having their bridge nights, their endless cocktail parties; the servants in the basement were burning the furniture.

Arun, one of the high-class Indians he played polo with, had recently returned from a year reading law at Cambridge University. 'And do you know what I most loved about Trinity?' he'd teased Jack in his lazy Home Counties drawl. 'Having one of your lot clean my shoes and leave them at my door.'

Only the week before that, Jack – he'd been in tennis flannels at the time strolling home from the club – had been spat at in the street. He'd stood there in absolute astonishment with another man's phlegm on his shoulder, completely unsure as to whether to ignore him or strike back.

He ate supper on his own in the dining room. A nondescript room with mismatched chairs and an annoying light that was belching out paraffin fumes. That would have to be fixed now, too.

Dinesh brought him a simple kedgeree for supper. Normally, it was one of his favourite meals; tonight he pushed it around his plate – too nervous to eat much.

He drained a glass of beer, thinking about how contrary a man's mind could be. Six months ago, when he'd first met Rose, he'd felt an emptiness at the centre of this life, which in many ways he loved so much, a hunger for someone to talk to about something other than politics or polo or parties, the staple diet at the officers' mess and the club. But now, a goblin in his head was whispering to him about the bliss of bachelorhood: not having to tell anybody when you're coming home from the club, being able to work until midnight when the heat was on, as it had been recently with the Awali Riots in the Punjab. The thought that his colonel, who was against his men marrying young, might exclude him from active service was unbearable.

All of a sudden he stopped thinking, buried his head in his hands and heaved a shuddering sigh. Why not be honest, at least to himself? It was Sunita who filled his thoughts tonight. Sunita, darling Sunita, who knew nothing about the changes ahead and had done nothing to deserve them.

'Master, tonga man will come in ten minutes. Do you wish pudding? There is junket, jelly even.'

'No, Dinesh, but thank you. The kedgeree was very good.' Dinesh took his plate. 'I'm just not particularly hungry.'

Jack went out on to the verandah to smoke a cigarette. The night was hot and humid, unusually hot for this time of the year in Poona – eighty degrees by the glass thermometer tied to the verandah railings.

The fly screen closed with its usual squeak, the old pie dog that hung around their kitchen door waiting unsuccessfully for food slunk away into the violet shadows, and across the dirt to the servants' quarters he could hear the sounds of laughter, and a tabla being played.

Could she take the heat? Would the dog with its revolting hairless tail scare her? Would the dreary cocktail party he'd been forced to attend by his colonel last night have bored her as much as it had bored him? This was the area in which he had started to lose his nerve. He simply didn't know enough about her.

'Tonga is here, master.'

A skinny old horse and tonga waited by the kitchen door. Inside its creaking interior, he sat tensely, feeling like a criminal and wondering why even the prospect of marriage had made certain areas of his life – Sunita, his bar bills, Dinesh's ministrations, even his habit of liking to lie in the bath for hours when he had a problem to solve – seem like guilty secrets.

Sunita's house was in the old part of town – twenty minutes and a world away from his. No distance at all, really. Lots of men carried on with their women after they were married, but he didn't want to. His own father – a hearty, distant man's man – had been a cavalry man himself with the Eighth, his hero for years – an explorer, an adventurer, a county-standard cricket player. He, as he often reminded Jack, had known some proper fighting, in his case mostly in

47

Mesopotamia. But he'd also been a philanderer, and the pain his lies had caused had seeped into all their lives like a slow poisoning.

'All men lie,' Jack's mother had once told him and his three sisters. 'They can't help themselves.'

Only three years ago, during one particularly wretched home leave spent at his parents' house in Oxford, the atmosphere had become so intolerable that his father had eaten his meals at a different time from the rest of the family, in his study, although it may as well have been in the dog house.

Three days before Christmas, his mother, red-faced, wild-eyed after too many gins, had explained what the fuss was. His father, it seemed, had a new woman, a young girl he'd set up in digs in Oxford. The girl was about to have his child.

'Do you know,' his mother had said, her face contorted with rage, 'all my life, I've never really understood men and never really liked them. Now I do understand them and I hate them.'

And he'd been horrified and repelled by the pain on her face, hung his head, and felt as guilty as if he had committed the act himself. He didn't want that for Rose. In old-fashioned language that strangely appealed to him, he had plighted his troth. He knew he had his father's wildness: loved shooting and riding horses too fast, getting drunk in the mess, making love, but he still prided himself on having a more logical streak. If he was to be married, this wildness must now be curbed. He wanted to make her happy, to earn her trust and keep it.

So much of his life he already saw through her eyes now. Would she take to India in the way he had? He'd tried to be honest with her about the bone-shrivelling heat of summers here, the poverty of the people, the constant moves, the hard life of the army wife.

But he'd been desperate to woo her at the same time. Desperate in the way a man is who has fallen for a girl like a ton of bricks but who knows he only has a week's home leave left. A certain hard-headed practicality had crept into his warnings.

He'd met her first at a deb's party in London, roped in as a spare man by a friend of his mother. 'Decorative,' she'd called him, to his considerable irritation. He'd walked up Park Lane on his own to get there, more nervous and shy than he liked to admit. The London he'd visited during the grim, desperate last days of the war had been covered in wreaths, full of funeral processions, its parks frowsy and unloved. This new London had shining little cars buzzing up and down Park Lane, frightening the horses. The girls had horrible new hairstyles and blew smoke in your face.

Partly to spare him from the miserable atmosphere at home, his mother had kept on getting her friends to ask him to parties, but the parties had thrown him. At one, he'd seen a couple openly copulating on top of a pile of overcoats in the spare room and had backed out scarlet with embarrassment and wanting to punch both of them for making a spectacle of themselves. At another, bewildered by a group of excited people sniffing up a pile of powder, he'd caused laughter by asking what they were doing, and been told rudely, 'It's naughty salt, you ignoramus. Cocaine.'

But Rose. She wasn't like that. At the Savile Club, where he'd stood in his dinner jacket underneath the ceiling painted with fat cherubs, she'd appeared beside him, endearingly gawky in an evening dress that was too old and slightly too big for her, but unmistakably a beauty with her silky blonde hair and sweet smile. The band had started to play a foxtrot and she'd raised her eyebrows slightly and smiled at him.

'Dance with me,' he'd said, and she'd stepped into his arms. They'd bellowed at each other over the music for a hopeless few minutes during which he'd stepped on her toes.

'Do you have a chaperone here?' he'd asked her after several dances.

'I do,' she said with her delicious smile, 'but unfortunately she's downstairs playing bridge.'

'Have you seen the pictures downstairs?' he said. 'They have some wonderful portraits in the reading room.'

The oldest and corniest line in the world, but she'd said, with sweet gravity, 'No I haven't, but I'd love to see them.'

And it was there, in the soft glow of the reading room, underneath a picture of a man wrestling with wild-eyed foaming horses, that he'd simply taken her in his arms and kissed her soft lips, feeling at first a shy resistance, a stiffening in her arms and then her yielding.

'Um,' she'd licked her lips thoughtfully, like a child tasting the last remnants of a sweet, 'I don't think I've been kissed before – not like that.'

And it was at that moment, with this divine, slim, fresh young creature in his arms, smelling of Devonshire violets, the same scent that his mother used, that he thought of Sunita, his mistress, and how much he owed her. She'd taught him everything. After three lonely

49

years of bachelorhood in the mofussil, he'd gone to her like a bull in rut, and she'd bathed him and oiled him, slowed him down. Teasing and laughter had also gone into it, a sense that lovemaking could be practised and refined as well as sublime abandonment. He'd been like a man trying to play a symphony on a penny flute; she'd given him the whole orchestra.

They'd reached her street: a row of battered terraced houses with wrought-iron balconies that had seen better days. The same groups of rickshaw men were gossiping on the corner, waiting for their fares, and, as usual, she'd left a candle burning for him outside her door. Inside her room, she had a glass-fronted cabinet where all the little presents he'd given her – a silver box from a London antique market, a bottle of scent, a scarf – were proudly displayed. But tonight, in his pocket, he had a cheque to give her after his speech, a donation he could ill afford, towards her future. His heart sank as he walked up the stairs. For the first time in her life she might feel like a prostitute. He felt like a brute; but he had to do it. Jack Chandler was about to be married.

Chapter 9

GIBRALTAR

Mr and Mrs Percival Wetherby
Park House
Nr. Middle Wallop
Hampshire

21 October 1928

Darling Daddy and Mummy,
We arrive in Gibraltar in about an hour's time, so will try and post this then.

I've been lying in my bunk – Tor is still asleep – reading my Spanish phrase book, and have just read this: *Gracias a la vida que me ha dado tanto.* (Thanks be to life which has given me so much.) Isn't that lovely? It made me think about all the splendid things you have given me: not just Park House as a place to grow up, but the ponies, the dogs, the camping trips, you and all the wonderful times we have had together.

I hope you are not too sad at not having your Froggie at home, but rest assured she is excited about all that lies ahead and Tor and I are having the most balloon times.

There are so many nice people in first class, and also, don't worry about Miss Holloway being so young. She is very kind and keeps a good eye on us and knows India like the back of her hand because she grew up there. We are also very spoilt by our cabin steward, Suday. I don't know why people talk down to natives. I have nothing against them at all, and he is perfectly sweet.

Every night there are parties or entertainments planned and supervised, and we have found it easy to join in. One of our new best friends is Nigel, who has a junior post in the civil service somewhere in the west of India; he is fairly quiet, but very clever and has a good sense of humour. Unlike most people on the *Kaisar* he is sick at heart at having to go back to India because he's done four years there in a remote province and wants to stay home. Last year he said a local man came to him with his wife's ear wrapped up in a piece of newspaper. He had cut it off in a jealous rage, but now he had forgiven her and was wondering if Nigel could think of any way of putting it back!! The other bods on board are tea planters, army officers and so on, also quite a few children and their ayahs.

We've also met Jane Burrell (rather horsey and noisy) and her three friends. Frank, the ship's junior doctor, is a very good egg. He's working his passage to India so he can do some research out there on some sort of malaria, can't remember what, but a kind I hadn't heard of. He's also keeping an eye on us and now tells us lots of gruesome things about suicides at sea and doing operations during force-nine gales. He is great fun and very good-looking. I think Tor has her eye on him!

<u>Later.</u>
Sorry, didn't finish! Will post in Malta.

A party of eight of us went ashore, so there were lots of people to keep an eye on us. Frank (the doctor) knew a respectable restaurant overlooking the harbour with sawdust on the floor and a fat senorita who waddled around in her sandals.

For lunch we had some sort of fish, caught that morning and prawns, then she laid out three puddings of such deliciousness I thought I was dreaming. (Much more of this and I shall simply waddle down the aisle. Food is an obsession on board. There are about fifty dishes on the menu each night.) Frank made us laugh by telling us a story about one Fishing Fleet girl who got so fat on board that when she arrived in India her new husband didn't recognise her.

It was almost dark by the time we got out and Tor and I and assorted bods from the ship walked down towards the harbour and the sight of it all lit up and with music wafting out and so much for me to look forward to made me feel how wonderful it was to be alive.

Mummy, darling, help, please. I've been reading my wedding etiquette book and getting into a fizz. For example, they say that speeches are out of fashion but if someone must prepare a toast it should be some old family friend. Who should I ask? I hardly know Ci Ci Mallinson so it seems rather forward. Could you write to Jack and ask? Also is it de rigueur in India to have a wedding breakfast? Do you think I should wear the pink silk georgette to that, or is it a bit much?

When you write, send your letter to Cook's Office, 15 Rue Sultan Hussein, Port Said. You can also send a telegram.

The breakfast gong has gone and there is a lot of scuttling above my head.

Write soon. Give Copper a big kiss for me and a handful of carrots.

With bestest love,
Rose

But she'd suddenly lain down on her bunk again and thought about her father and their last camping trip together in late summer.

They'd gone fishing on a small trout stream in Wales that he particularly loved near the village of Crickhowell. All the familiar paraphernalia had been loaded into the back of his ancient Daimler: the rickety Primus, the two dogs, with their beds, the big tartan thermos, rods, camp beds and the stout old army tent that had seen active service in Africa. She'd loved these camping excursions as a child – Tor often came too and her father would instruct them in all kinds of boy things: épée fencing with pieces of stripped alder; trout casting; how to fold a tent, and make a tree house – he'd even brought one of his guns up once and they'd had a competition shooting tin cans out of a tree, which Rose to her amazement had won hands down and been called Dead-Eye Dick for the rest of the trip. She and Tor had swung on a rope over the river; they'd burned sausages over fires at night.

She'd only been dimly aware then of trying to be as brave as Simon – the boy her father had lost and wanted back so badly – but on that last trip, when they were alone together, the view had changed. One night, after they'd fried up the salmon they had caught and he had lit a fragrant pipe, he'd said to her clearly and urgently that he hoped he and Mummy hadn't let her rush into this Jack thing. He'd said that he wanted more than anything else in the world for her to find a man who was worthy of her. He'd looked at her anxiously and his voice had trembled with emotion as he'd told her that finding the right person was the greatest gift of your life. And he'd suddenly looked so old and anxious, sitting hunched on his stool in the fading light, that she'd known that even if things weren't a hundred per cent perfect when she got to India, it was her turn to protect him now.

Chapter 10

Tor woke up in darkness hearing the noise again. It was coming from the boy's cabin next door. A series of escalating moans, like something being held down and tortured, then broken words, then the sound of the bunk creaking, then silence.

She lay back in the dark, frightened. If the boy had been a friendlier type, she might have gone straight away to see if he was all right, but she found him odd and disturbing. They often saw him on deck smoking and glaring out to sea, and only a few nights ago, at a ball in the Siena Room, he'd made quite a spectacle of himself. The orchestra had been playing, the kind of waltzes that appealed to the colonels and the older people, and he'd suddenly stood up and danced wildly and inappropriately by himself. Because they were, so to speak, neighbours, and because the older people had been tutting, she'd tried to smile at him, but he'd turned hurriedly away.

He'd also made that fuss about only eating with Viva, which was a great relief to them because he wasn't exactly laughing gas, but they were sorry not to have more time with Viva, who was, Tor had decided, mysterious and exotic.

'I bet I'm no more than three years older than him,' she'd complained to Rose, 'but he makes one feel such a maiden aunt.'

'Don't forget,' said Rose, always kinder about these matters than Tor, 'how absolutely vile we could be at that age.'

'You were never vile, Rose,' Tor said. 'I was vile for both of us.'

The noises stopped as suddenly as they had started and because Tor wasn't sure what to do, she put her head on the pillow to think about it and fell asleep and forgot all about him.

The sun woke her five hours later. She basked in it like a cat on a windowsill and thought, as she had almost every morning since she'd been at sea, *How wonderful. I'm free.*

Only three months ago, she hadn't even been allowed to wear face powder without her parents' permission or stay up after one-thirty a.m. or walk alone in London without a chaperone, and every other week, she'd had to go to deportment classes with Mrs Craddock in Salisbury.

But today would start with tea in bed and a good gossip with Rose about the night before, then a wonderful breakfast, maybe kippers, or eggs and bacon, and delicious coffee, which she had only just started to drink and which made her feel so sophisticated. All kinds of games in the morning, and perhaps a turn around the deck with Frank, the ship's junior doctor, who was so good-looking and who, yesterday, had appeared on deck just as she and Rose were looking out to sea. And then, at six o'clock Viva, who had been wonderful about leaving them alone during the day, would appear in the cabin, for what they now called a bishi, the Marathi word, Viva had told them, for a female party.

Last night, during their bishi, the conversation had turned to the topic of what qualities they should look for in a man, and Tor, without meaning to, had told Viva, who was a very good listener, about Paul, the man who had broken her heart last summer.

'Perfect at first,' she said sadly. 'We met on the lawn of his parents' house at Tangley, which is not far from where we live. He was very dark and sophisticated, sort of tortured-looking. He'd been away working in Rome as an art historian for three years; my mother was nudging me like mad as he was talking to me. She thought he was the perfect catch because his parents have money and we've become quite poor since the war.'

She was trying to make them laugh at her stupidity, but it hurt even now to remember how fated that first meeting had seemed: the scent of old-fashioned roses, the clink of champagne glasses (it was his parents' thirtieth wedding anniversary) and this dream of a young man in a summer suit and panama hat, who had really talked to her and made her laugh and, at one point, playfully kissed her hand.

'He was three years older than me,' she said, still trying for a light-hearted tone, 'and more interesting by a mile than the other men I'd met. He took me to concerts where he read the scores, lent me this book called *Middlemarch*. Have you read it, Viva? It's rather good – he was horrified I hadn't. He even told me what colours I should wear. I didn't even know I had olive skin until he told me.'

'Do you remember that lovely letter he sent you?' Rose was going along with the joke even though she'd seen her sobbing in the summer house afterwards.

'Oh yes, oh yes, hang on,' said Tor, 'let me see if I can remember it,' even though it was branded on her mind. ' "The world is so rich," ' she recited in a stagy voice, ' "so throbbing with rich treasures and interesting people. Forget yourself." '

'But he does sound interesting,' Viva had laughed – she seemed to love listening to their stories even though she never told them a thing about herself. 'What happened next?'

'He disappeared.' Tor suddenly hadn't felt like finishing the story. It wasn't that funny and she'd run out of steam. And the truth, still too painful to admit, was that by the time summer was over, she'd been so sure it would work out, she'd all but named their children and dreamt of the houses they would have.

And then, for reasons she still didn't understand, it had all gone so wrong.

This had happened one morning, it was in early autumn, he had asked her mother – who adored him even more now that he spoke to her in fluent French – whether he might take Tor on a picnic to Magdalen, his old college in Oxford. Her mother, sensing a proposal in the air, was ecstatic; she saw no reason why they needed a chaperone.

He'd gone to the Bodleian in the morning to look up some ancient manuscripts and after lunch, under a willow tree near some historic bridge, he'd rolled up a towel and tucked it under her head. And suddenly – it had happened almost without her thinking – she'd felt so bowled over by the river and the ducks and the smell of new grass and the blue sky and the fact that she was here with her own beau that she'd turned to him, taken his face in her hands and kissed him.

And then, horrible, he'd leapt to his feet almost shouting at her. 'Please never do that again.' He'd brushed the grass from his trousers.

'Why not, silly?' She'd tried for a flippant tone that would not come.

He'd stood glaring and looking down at her with the sky all around him.

'I can't do this,' he had said. 'It's ridiculous.'

She'd felt her sandwich go like a stone inside her. 'I don't understand,' she said, and even now it made her wince to think of it. 'I thought we . . . I thought you said you loved me.'

'You do have an awful lot of growing up to do,' he'd said as if somehow it was all her fault, and walking back, to make it even worse, she'd caught her heel in the hem of her dress, which had come down and added to the crushing, humiliating sense that she had let herself down and him.

She'd cried all the way home, hating her tears and at one point begging him to reconsider. But he hadn't. The next week he'd appeared, charming and kind again, to tell her a job had come up in Rome and he simply had to go. If he had, at any point, given her the impression of an engagement, he was terribly sorry. She was really the most terrific girl. Some other fellow would be very lucky.

Her mother had stopped speaking to her for two whole days. It was Rose who had held her in her arms, who had told her he was an absolute cad and swine, that he would regret the loss of Tor for the rest of his life. They had stayed up all of one night in the summer house talking about it, and she'd cried until there were no more tears to shed, and she'd smoked so many cigarettes that her tonsils were raw the next day. Rose's kind words had helped, and being on the *Kaisar* was a tonic, but part of her was still bruised and bewildered, which was why she probably shouldn't have embarked on the story in the first place.

'What fun it must be to be young on a ship like this,' Major Smythe, one of the passengers, had said to her wistfully only the night before. And so it was: the dancing, the games, the flirting, but what Paul had left with her was hunger. Hunger for the world he'd shown her a glimpse of, *throbbing with rich treasures and interesting people*, hungry to be loved for herself with her hair down and her corset off. Was that completely and utterly impossible?

The sun was rising in the sky, the sea a sapphire blue. Suday was walking into their cabin with a tray in his hands.

'Chai, my ladies.' Without a word of reproach, he walked around the dress and the feather boa that Tor had stepped out of the night before and left on the floor. 'Chai and fruitycakebiscuit, hot roll, *irrawaddy*.'

Neither of them had the slightest clue what *irrawaddy* meant, but every morning their laughter made him laugh delightedly, like a child.

He poured tea for them with a flourish from a silver pot, and then took hot rolls from a napkin and put them on their plates. He smiled when they told him what an absolute brick he was and shut the door behind himself still beaming.

'I love Suday,' said Tor sentimentally when he had gone. 'Now, get into bed with me, Rose I need a gup.'

A gup, their new word for a gossip, was gleaned from the series of lectures they'd been going to called 'Kitchen Hindi for Memsahibs', given by Lieutenant Colonel Gorman twice a week in the Wellington Room. Rose had listened avidly; Tor had gone along to keep her company.

Rose climbed in at the opposite end to Tor. 'Now don't kick me,' she said, 'else I'll scald you with my tea.'

'First item on the agenda,' said Tor. 'Marlene and Suzanne?'

Both of them were fascinated by Marlene and Suzanne – easily the two most glamorous girls on the ship. They had one of the best cabins – really a kind of suite – on A deck. 'They're only secretaries, really,' Mrs Gorman, the colonel's wife, had said meanly – it was rumoured that Marlene's last job had been with an Indian who imported carpets and was terribly rich – but Tor and Rose and half the crew were mesmerised by their highly varnished shingles and succession of brilliantly beaded frocks, their smouldering eyes, their matching jet and pearl cigarette holders.

'I saw Marlene was dancing with Jitu last night,' Tor reported. 'He had his hand on her back like this.' Tor demonstrated with her own hand placed near the elastic on her pyjamas. 'And while Mrs Gorman and I were watching agog, she said she'd known another girl like that who went out to India last year. She'd worked in the scarf department at Lillywhites, was very pretty and smart and she'd ended up in a maharajah's palace, and guess what he'd asked her to do? He'd made her take six baths a day – that was all.'

Rose looked nonplussed. 'Why?'

'No idea. I suppose he liked looking at her.'

'Golly.' Rose had gone a faint pink. 'How very embarrassing.'

'Next item,' Tor continued quickly, hoping she hadn't put her foot in it – although it was hard to imagine Captain Jack Chandler wanting to stare at Rose in a bath. 'What were those terrible sounds last night?'

'What sounds?'

'From the boy next door. Didn't you hear him?' Tor said. ' "Oh my God! Oh God! Oh! OH! OH!" '

'How awful.' Rose's eyes were round and blue. 'He must have been having a nightmare.'

'I don't know.'

'But didn't you go and ask him if he was all right?'

'Well, I meant to, but I fell asleep.'

'Oh, well done you. Brilliant. Just the kind of chap one wants to go into the jungle with.'

'I know. I was bad. But I had one of those Singapore Sling things and I was sleepy.'

'Well, we'd better ask him later,' said Rose. 'And tell Viva. She's usually in the writing room about now.'

'I tell you what, let's forget it.' Tor was munching now on her second hot roll. 'If anything bad happened, I'm going to feel a beast.'

'Oh, don't be so dramatic,' Rose pinched Tor's toe, 'and stop dropping crumbs on my foot. He probably ate too much like us and has the trotagees.' Trotagees was their made-up Hindi word for diarrhoea.

Don't get married, Rose, thought Tor, listening to Rose laughing, and feeling her warmth beside her. *I'm going to miss you so much.*

'I'm going to have a bath,' said Tor a few minutes later. They'd finished breakfast and were lying in the same patch of sun on the pillow.

'In a sec. I haven't finished my gup.' Rose stretched out luxuriously. 'Who were all those people you were dancing with last night? I got buttonholed by Mrs Llewellyn-Pearse, who told me all about the forty-seven varieties of rhododendron she saw in Simla last year. I told her to be sure and show you the photographs.'

'Oh goodness, absolutely everyone. Philip, he is such a show-off. Colonel Green, who breathed garlic down my neck. Rose, if I gave you a chocolate would you put my bath on? I'm absolutely exhausted already.'

'And Frank?' Rose widened her eyes. 'Were we dancing with Frank, Frank, Frank, Frankeee?'

'Oh, Frank.' Tor kept her voice carefully neutral. For the first time since the Paul fiasco, her heart had leapt when she'd seen him walk across the dance floor to ask her to dance. He was so endearing in his white dinner jacket and untidy hair. And a doctor was exciting, even though Mummy would think that was beneath them. But danger! her heart had said. Red alert! Don't talk about him to anyone!

'He's a sweet boy,' she said offhandedly. 'Oh, and I meant to say, he asked if you and I had any plans when we get to Port Said. He knows a splendid restaurant there – everyone's going.'

'Oh, darling, you know we can't,' said Rose. 'We promised your mother we wouldn't go ashore after Gibraltar, you know that.'

'She's obsessed with the white slave trade,' said Tor. 'It's ridiculous, and Frank is a grown-up: he's been on board lots of ships, well, at least two, and he's medically trained if anything happens to us.'

'Well, let's think about it,' said Rose in her sensible voice.

'Well, you can think about it, Rose. I'm going.' Tor got out of the bunk and walked through the heap of fallen clothes. 'And if you're going to get married soon, I suggest you learn to think for yourself.'

A shadow crossed Rose's face and Tor wished she hadn't said it.

'I'm not saying it to be bossy,' Rose said. 'It's just that you don't know him and—'

Tor knew exactly what she was thinking: *I don't want to see you hurt like that again.* But, a few moments later, when Tor was sitting in the bath, she firmed her jaw under her floral bath cap and thought, *I don't care. I'm ready again. For everything this time.*

Chapter 11

'What Price a Husband?' Draft Six. By Viva Holloway.

Viva was sitting on her bunk, her typewriter balanced on a pillow; she was trying not to cry with frustration. Miss Snow had just walked in full of apologies – Sorry, sorry, sorry! – and was now organising what she called in a jocular voice 'her kit': her underthings, her dusty-coloured dresses and her books.

'You look awfully uncomfortable there,' Miss Snow said rather pointedly. 'Don't you find the writing room a more suitable place for work?'

She had tried. It was impossible. Four of the senior memsahibs on board – intimidating with their braying laughs and confident county voices – had taken it over for a regular bridge four and the silence was punctuated by cries of 'Four in spades' or 'I say, what a wily bird you are' or 'Well done you!'

Yesterday, when the writing room had been deserted (there had been some kind of sporting competition on deck) and she'd been taking another run at draft four, a young steward had come in, cheekily handsome in his P&O uniform, leant over her shoulder and made her cheeks turn scarlet. 'Are you writing lots of secrets, madam?' he'd breathed confidentially.

Later, hearing him josh in the same over-familiar way with Marlene and Suzanne on deck – they'd shrieked with laughter at him and made him laugh back – she thought if she was a proper writer she might have tried to get to know him better too. Maybe flirted with him a bit, gained his confidence, and got him to tell her about any bad behaviour on the ship. But she was hopeless, far too shy. The same thing applied to Frank, the ship's junior doctor, who she could tell was a bit of a ladies' man. It was clear Tor and most of the other women on the ship were already in love with him. She'd watched him yesterday walking down the deck, a slightly bandy, cocky-young-male-in-his-prime walk. And observed female heads stiffening as he passed by.

He didn't flirt openly – it was, Tor had already explained to them, forbidden for him to do so. 'He's not allowed to start conversations with us, but can reply if we talk to him,' she'd reported. But he didn't have to flirt, for even Viva, who mistrusted him, had to admit he had a wonderful smile.

She put another piece of paper into her typewriter and moaned softly with frustration. Having got off to such a flying start with 'The Fishing Fleet', now definitely renamed 'What Price a Husband?', she was finding the damned thing almost impossible to finish. Each time she read it it seemed a little more stupid and brittle, even mean-spirited considering she hadn't actually had the gumption to talk to the women she was writing about. Not yet anyway. She'd imagined herself sauntering casually up to one or two of the young women she'd seen dancing and playing deck quoits – women like Marlene and Suzanne with their flashing smiles, or one or two of the nannies or even Miss Snow. She might have walked around the deck with them and engaged them in interesting conversations, but now it seemed an absolute cheek buttonholing complete strangers and asking them intimate questions about their lives.

So far, apart from the evening bishis with Rose and Tor, she'd spoken to no one, apart from Miss Snow. The other young female passengers were perfectly polite to her, said their good evenings when they passed in the dining room and so forth, but she was a chaperone after all, so they, for most part, excluded her from further intimacies. Sitting in the writing room, or on deck, she'd heard snatches of their conversations.

I told Mummy to turn him out to grass; I'll hunt him next winter . . . Oh, of course she's a pukka Able Smith . . . Such a good little man . . . Christopher's suit, literally half the price . . . Of course we know them: we shot there last winter . . . We went as circus people to their party.

Their confident voices and endless changes of clothes made her angry with herself at times. Why mind being rejected by people she didn't want to be friends with anyway? It was absurd, illogical.

But there they were, the old insecurities that reared up, particularly when her work was not going well, and which made her feel not the confident free-spirited bohemian who had stepped on to the boat, but more of an outsider, one of life's gooseberries. It was possible that she'd been one all her life, what with her isolated childhood, her parents constantly on the move; and possible too that she'd talked herself into this idea of herself as a person who craved solitude, her lamp in the darkness, her books, her writing. You didn't always choose.

She shook herself out of these gloomy thoughts. She liked Rose and Tor more and more. They were very silly and young, of course, but their evening bishis were fun. Last night Tor had wound up the gramophone and handed out the crème de menthe and taught her the Charleston.

It was impossible not to like Rose, so blonde and wholesomely charming, so ready to laugh and be kind, so entirely unaware of how good-looking she was. She was someone who expected to be happy, who probably usually was. Viva had listened to her yesterday confiding to a group of enchanted older people about her upcoming wedding. *Yes, I'm very excited. It will be such fun. We're having the reception at the Bombay Yacht Club . . . Oh good! I've heard it's lovely . . . not absolutely sure about the dress, but I've brought Mummy's veil.*

At Tilbury, she'd observed her from a distance saying goodbye to a collection of relatives and well-wishers who clearly adored her. Viva had felt a familiar pang watching them: a whole family in action, an interconnected organism like a colony of ants helping to move her from one life to another. They'd straightened her hat, squeezed her hand; her father, a gaunt, beautifully dressed older man, had watched her with an expression of quiet anguish on his face.

There was a knock on the door.

'Viva,' Miss Snow looked down at her, 'I forgot to tell you, but I just bumped into your young man in the corridor looking very pale and loitering. He wants to know if you are going up for the first or second sitting for lunch today.'

Dammit! Dammit! Dammit! thought Viva. She'd imagined when she'd taken on the job that once on the ship, the Great Sulky, as she now unkindly thought of him, would pal up with people of his own age, leaving her time to write. But not a bit of it: all he seemed to want to do was to gloom around the decks on his own, smoke cigarettes and sit and eat with her. If he'd made even the most minimal effort with her, she might have forgiven him, but he was almost impossible to talk to. It wasn't, as she'd argued with herself a number of times, as if she was bursting to play gin rummy, or flap paper frogs with a rolled-up newspaper along the deck, or sit in the games room with a piece of paper with Mary Queen of Scots stuck on her forehead, but these japes were part and parcel of shipboard life and his total lack of enthusiasm for any of them was really starting to affect her. It was almost as if both of them had become walled up in his shyness, if that is what it was.

'What did you tell him?'

'That you'd have a confab with him after you'd finished whatever it is you're doing.'

It was clear that Miss Snow found their relationship odd. She had asked Viva, more than once, why his parents hadn't chosen an older man for his chaperone, or an older woman at least, and seemed certain that Viva would have been having 'an awfully jolly time on this ship' without him. 'But never mind, my dear,' she'd annoyed her by saying a few days ago, 'we'll be there in just under two weeks, and India is teeming with men looking for young women like you.' As if her writing was just a brave front for far deeper ambitions.

But Miss Snow, to be fair, had her own problems – a new school in a new district, fear of loneliness there, not enough money, and guilt about an elderly mother left in a Dorset boarding house for gentlefolk.

The first-class dining room was humming with conversation when she entered it later that night. Such an elegant room with its richly painted murals, sumptuous chandeliers and mirrored walls. For a girl who'd been living on tinned sardines and baked beans heated up on a Primus hidden under the bed, it was like a dream to sit here and see the uniformed waiters buzzing around with silver platters, the sideboards heaped with exotic fruits and fine wines, the occasional glimpses of the scurrying, steaming world of the kitchen behind the swing doors.

So what a bore to look up and see in the corner of the room that Guy Glover was waiting for her, looking pale and put upon. He looked up as she approached and gave her a wan wave.

Now that the weather was so much warmer – 102 degrees, according to one of the passengers, a Colonel Price, who had buttonholed Viva that morning with the latest reports from his pocket thermometer – the other passengers had changed into summer clothes: lighter dresses for the women, dinner jackets for the men. But Guy, still wearing his long black coat, stuck out like a pallbearer at a wedding party.

Three waiters leapt into life as she sat down at their table. Guy didn't stand up.

He hadn't shaved very well, she noticed. He'd left a piece of gosling fluff on his chin and a cut, which he'd covered with a bit of cotton wool.

The waiter handed her a menu. She heard a burst of laughter coming from a nearby table. 'The Young', as the older people on board called anybody under thirty, had begun to eat at each other's tables. Rose and Tor were sitting with two other women, whose names she didn't know, and a young civil servant called Nigel. She saw Rose's blonde hair fall forward as she laughed. A young naval officer was pouring wine into Tor's glass. Tor, who had confessed to her that she was longing to be 'seized', was batting her eyelashes at him.

'I'm sorry I'm late,' Viva said.

'I hadn't noticed.' He met her eye briefly and unwillingly and then looked away.

'Have you ordered?'

'Not yet.'

She picked up her menu with a heavy sense of duty.

'So, what would you like?'

Oh my God, if only I knew.

'Sole Véronique is the dish of the day. I think it's very good.' She hadn't a clue really, it was something to say. 'There's a steak Rossini. Lobster thermidor.' The food was famously good on the *Kaisar*, something to do with the wood-fired ovens, she'd been told. 'Oh good,' she said, 'pommes dauphinoise is on too.'

'I can actually read by myself.' Sarcasm had been added to his own limited menu lately.

'Sorry,' she said.

At first she really had tried with him: admittedly aunty-ish stuff about whether he was looking forward to going home. 'Not really.' And what kind of sports he'd played at school. 'None.' But you had to start somewhere. She'd admired the murals on the dining-room walls, the beautiful chandeliers, wondered at the songs the pianist played, but now she had just about reached the end of her patience.

'Water?'

'Yes, please, and,' he gave her a look of barely concealed truculence, 'a bottle of Pouilly-Fuissé. Waiter!'

She'd offended him on the first night by asking him whether his parents allowed him to drink and he had not forgiven her. 'You do realise, don't you, that I am eighteen years old?' he'd said. Mrs Bannister had said he was sixteen and he certainly didn't look any older, but she let this pass. 'Not eight. I can't imagine why my parents thought I needed a chaperone.'

'So what about food?' she said. 'Are you ready to order?'

'Not yet.' He disappeared behind his menu.

She buttered a roll; passed the bread; listened to the distant laughter of other diners and the strains of the pianist playing 'Clair de Lune'.

This, she thought, *is how I imagine it must feel to be really unhappily married. An endless landscape of slowed-down meals you don't want to have together, a place where talk is an exhausting chore, a form of mental housework.*

'Well, I'm going to have a tournedos Rossini,' she said. 'Medium rare.'

When it came, she listened to their knives and forks on the plates; watched the waiter take their plates away; looked at the old married couple on the table beside them who had also eaten in silence.

'It's Saturday night,' she told him. 'They've got a band up in the ballroom. They're supposed to be rather good. Do you feel like going?'

'No, I don't think so.' He sighed heavily and pursed his lips in a self-conscious way.

'So, is there anything else you'd like to do then?' Oh, she honestly felt like striking him sometimes.

'Just say the word.'

'You Great Sulky,' she said under her breath.

The pudding trolley arrived bearing lemon meringue pies and fruit jellies, an apple soufflé, ice creams and the Indian julebis, which she found a little sickly.

'More wine, sir?' The wine waiter's smile was a beam. 'We have some very nice Beaumes de Venise to go with the crème anglaise. Madam?'

'Just the lemon meringue for me, thank you.' She drained her wine glass. 'I think we've had enough.'

'I'll have a bottle of Beaumes de Venise,' the Great Sulky told the waiter. When he lowered his head and looked at her like that, he reminded her of a young bull about to charge.

'Who is going to pay for this?' she asked him in an angry whisper after the wine waiter had scuttled off.

'My parents,' he said prissily. 'Do stop fussing.'

As she watched the Young, chattering and laughing and starting to

67

move upstairs, she felt what a luxury it would be to box him soundly around the ears. The room was half empty now and he was scowling at her again with that look of barely concealed contempt.

'Will both your parents be in Bombay when we get there?' She asked the question quite deliberately, knowing where it might lead.

'I don't know.' He squinted at somebody beyond her head, in a way which suggested they were far more interesting than she was. And she felt a sudden desire to make him feel something, anything – hurt, embarrassment, a sense that she existed too.

'My parents won't be there,' she said.

'Why not?' It was the first question he'd ever asked her.

'My parents and my sister died in India when I was ten. That's why I came back to England. One of the reasons I'm going back now is to pick up their things. They left some trunks there.'

He gazed at her, so blankly at first that she thought he hadn't heard. When he stood up his chair fell on the floor.

'Were they assassinated?' The expression on his face was one of genuine, even exaggerated horror. 'Did Indians kill them?' His face was contorted with disgust.

She felt a spurt of shame move from her stomach to her chest. She simply couldn't believe she'd blurted it out to him of all people, but now it was too late – he seemed gripped, horribly so, by her story.

'No.' She held her hands up as if to tamp him down.

'Were they shot?'

The elderly couple at the next table were staring at them.

'No,' she said.

'So why?'

'They just died,' she whispered. She felt a wave of heat go over her. 'I don't really want to talk about it. It was a car crash. I don't know where.' She hated it when people asked for details.

'I don't know what to say. Tell me what I should say.' His voice had risen and she wished she'd kept her mouth shut – she seemed to have unhinged him and wanted the silent boy back. He rushed off.

When she went on deck to look for him, the air felt thick and warm and the moon lay in a basket of cloud.

'Guy,' she called out, but the rush of bow-water and faint echoes of music from the ballroom muffled her voice. Other passengers appeared through lit windows like a series of still lifes: some women playing cards, a white-haired old man extracting a cigar cutter from a waistcoat pocket, a group toasting each other and laughing. In a dark corner near the funnel, a couple were embracing, dark and oblivious like shadows.

'Guy?' She was near the lifeboats now, a warm wind rushing through her hair. 'Guy, where are you?'

Half of her was inclined to let him stew in his own juices, but she was starting to feel more and more worried about him. His almost hysterical reaction to her story, the wearing of that dreadful overcoat, even now with the glass regularly hitting 100 degrees, the bright insincerity of his smile at times as though he were centre stage at the Old Vic – what if he was barking mad rather than simply churlish and self-engrossed?

After a fruitless search down empty corridors and on the landing of A deck, she found him at last, hiding in a lifeboat, stretched out in his long dark coat. He was smoking a cigarette.

'Look,' she said. 'Lots of people have parents who died in India, so don't worry about it too much. I also don't really give a damn whether you're interested in me or not.'

The moon had gone behind a cloud but she could still see the wet of his cheeks and the desperate intensity of his eyes. He was drunk, she was sure of it, and in pain.

'Why is life so awful?' he said.

'It's not all awful,' she said. 'Things change, improve. I really shouldn't have said it. I don't know why I did.'

'They're gone now, gone for good.'

'Yes.'

'Your whole family.' Moonlight washed his face in a greenish glow. 'Gone for good,' he repeated. 'For ever.'

She was almost certain he was thinking about himself again.

'No,' she said. 'No, I don't believe that. Not really. Do you?'

He sat up and stared at her.

'Look, forget about me for a moment,' she said, realising that this might be her only chance. 'I want to ask you about yourself. You probably think I'm a hundred years old, but I'm not, and I do remember what it's like to be torn out of one place and put in another, that it's—' Her voice was stumbling but it was the best she could do.

'No, that's not it,' he interrupted. 'Not at all. Look, sorry . . . I'm going to bed.'

As he hauled himself out of the lifeboat, the cotton wool fell off his shaving cut. It was bleeding again. She watched him walk away with his stiff, high-shouldered gait. He disappeared through a lit doorway.

'I've betrayed you,' she said out loud.

'I'm so sorry,' a voice said from behind a pile of deckchairs. 'I feel I'm eavesdropping but I'm not.' A shadow stood up: it was Rose in a gauzy white dress, her blonde hair burnished by the moonlight.

'I came out here to think,' she said. 'The others were so noisy.'

'Did you hear all that?' said Viva.

Rose looked embarrassed.

'Not all of it. I used to argue with my brother all the time – isn't it absolutely *de rigueur*?'

'I don't know if I can stand him.' Viva was shaking. 'He's so contemptuous.'

A waiter had followed Rose in case she wanted anything, just as men would probably always do.

'Coffee, madam? A nice liqueur? A cocktail? Emmeline Pitout will be singing her songs in the music room soon.'

'I tell you what.' Rose was smiling at her. 'Let's go mad and have a brandy. I think the worst thing about him not being your brother is you can't give him a fourpenny one. It would be so satisfying.'

Rose had a wonderful laugh, warm and throaty. Its hint of wildness was what stopped her seeming too good to be true. She scrunched her eyes up like a child and abandoned herself to it.

When Viva looked up, the moon was chasing their boat, spinning a faint golden mist over the haze of stars.

'It must be so strange for him going back to India.' Rose sipped her brandy. 'After all those years on his own.'

'Ten years,' said Viva, trying to calm down. 'And it is hell leaving India as a child – one moment, sun and freedom and blue skies, and lots of people running around after you who adore you. The next, well, he hasn't spoken much to me about it, but you're breaking the ice on a washbasin in some freezing school.'

'Like being kicked out of paradise,' Rose said.

'Yes, but India isn't paradise. It has other ways of being awful.'

'Examples, please, but nothing too horrid.'

'Well, the heat for one thing. You have never, ever felt anything like it in England, it's like being clubbed over the head sometimes, the flies, appalling poverty, but if you love it, as I do, it gets to you, it bores its way into your soul. You'll see.'

70

This was the longest proper conversation they'd had together since coming on board. Although her part of it had brought Viva close to tears, she was glad to be having it.

'It's so odd to think I'm going to be married there soon,' said Rose. The tip of her perfectly straight nose was showing above her stole, which she'd pulled up like a blanket. 'There is quite a lot to think about.'

Frightened, thought Viva. *All of us.*

Rose had confessed to her the day before, as if it was a splendid joke, that she'd only met her fiancé a grand total of four times, five if you counted a point to point they'd been to near Salisbury.

And Viva had wondered, *How could you give yourself away so carelessly?* Why had her parents allowed it? It wasn't even like an arranged marriage in India where the families would have known each other for generations.

'Yes, I can imagine,' said Viva. She wanted to touch her childish soft hand, or to put an arm round her, but she couldn't. Instead, she thought of her own mother in her wedding dress, her laughing brown eyes, the gaiety of her expression. It made you feel dizzy to think about it. *I've been frozen, frozen since that moment.*

'It's been such fun on the dear old *Kaisar*.' Rose was twisting the sapphire ring on her wedding finger, her voice dreamy and far away. 'All our new best friends, the sense that you're always on the way to somewhere else. In fact . . .' she looked at her watch '. . . we should be able to see Port Said soon, or so our waiter told us.'

She jumped up and walked towards the ship's railings, her dress like butterfly wings in the moonlight.

'Look. Oh, do look!' She pointed towards the horizon. 'You can see the lights already.'

Viva didn't want to move. She shouldn't have said all that to Guy.

'Do come! Do look! It is so thrilling. Is it Port Said? It must be.'

Together they looked out at a faint necklace of lights across a dark and crinkling sea. A foreign town where foreign people were cleaning their teeth and washing up their supper dishes and thinking about going to bed.

'Is it true we're allowed to sleep on deck now? That sounds such fun.'

When Rose beamed like that, you could see how sweet she must have been as a child.

71

I hope he's a nice man, thought Viva. *I hope he deserves her. What a hideous gamble.*

'Do you know it?' Rose's voice broke through her reverie.

'Not really – I've been there twice before.' She had been six or seven the last time she was here. She remembered it in snapshots: her first taste of fresh orange juice in a café in the square; her father playing horsey with her up on his shoulders.

'Tor's desperate to go ashore,' Rose said, sounding anxious. 'Frank's going with a group and he's asked us all. What do you think of him, by the way?'

'Not sure,' said Viva. 'Except that he seems rather sure of himself and of his effect on women. I hope he doesn't hurt her.'

'I do too,' said Rose. 'She had such a rotten time during the season. I don't know why men aren't nicer to her.'

She tries too hard, Viva thought. *She doesn't mean to but she does, because she thinks she's not pretty enough.*

'Colonel Patterson told me yesterday that Frank had an older brother who was killed at Ypres,' she heard Rose say in the middle of these thoughts. 'That's why he became a doctor. Colonel Patterson thinks Frank puts on a jolly front because he's still getting over it. He said it only came up because the colonel's son was killed there too.'

'Are you sure?' It took Viva a few seconds to absorb this information and feel the jolt of shame that came with it. *I do this all the time with people. I write them off before I know them, or I think that friendliness, a certain kind of openness, is a form of weakness.*

'That's what the colonel said.' Rose's beautiful blue eyes suddenly gleamed with tears. 'My older brother died in France – the one I used to row with, because I was so much younger than him and wanted to do all the things he did. Oh, let's not talk about it now. It's too awful. I can't bear it sometimes. I think it's part of the reason my parents sent me away, because they can't bear it either and it's awfully quiet at home now. The thing is,' she said in a firmer voice, 'Frank knows the most wonderful restaurant there, and a trip we can do to the Pyramids. Tor's simply longing to go, but I did promise my pees I wouldn't go without a proper chaperone, so would you?'

'I'd love to come.' Viva tried not to sound too eager. 'I mean, I don't know it that well but—'

'There'll be other people coming,' said Rose, 'but they're boys, and I don't want it to look wrong. People do gossip so. I shouldn't mind, but I do.'

'I understand,' said Viva, 'of course I do.'

'But what about the boy?' Rose's expression was warily polite. 'I mean, he can come if he likes, but we probably seem like a crowd of ancients to him.'

'He wasn't keen when we talked about it earlier,' said Viva. What he'd said was, 'So, camel stools, perfume factories. How *splendid*,' his voice breaking on the splendid.

'He might actually like a day on his own.' Rose sounded hopeful. 'But do bring him if you have to.'

No, no, no, thought Viva. *I don't have to. He has made it perfectly clear he wants a day on his own.*

She had made up her mind already, and one day she would pay for it.

Chapter 12

PORT SAID, 1,300 MILES TO BOMBAY

Tor got up early, woken by the shouts of the boatmen in Port Said Harbour and a sense of queasy excitement about the day ahead. Picking up a bundle of clothes she crept around Rose and headed for the bathroom. She locked the door and put on a white toile dress first, the one her mother had insisted she buy in Swan & Edgar. She stood on the stool and lined up her reflection in the mirror. She took the dress off again. Too sugared-almondy and twee.

Her linen suit with its short jacket seemed boxy and ordinary. Ten minutes later, sweating and agitated, she stood in the middle of a clothes mountain in a pale green cotton frock and a pair of jade earrings, trying to imagine what Frank would think of her in this.

She lifted a hand mirror up to see what she looked like in profile, moved her lips in conversation to see how she appeared to others when she was talking, and finally gave a silent and experimental laugh.

'Oh God,' she said to herself, coming back to earth with a bump, 'why is it that every time I like a man I turn into my mother?' If she wasn't careful, soon she'd be checking her reflection in restaurant spoons, or wearing frownies in bed at nights. Frownies were the sticky bits of canvas her mother wore between her eyebrows at night to prevent worry lines.

While her bath was running, she thought back to that awful afternoon at home before she'd left for India, a turning point in a way. For months the argument about whether she should be allowed to go or not had been batted backwards and forwards between her parents. Her father, who spent most of his days in a book-lined bothy (he called it his bunker) researching ladybirds, listening to music and trying to resist his wife's furious attempts to change him and the house, had been against it.

74

'I like Tor here,' he said. 'And I think we're in for a bumpy ride in India.'

One night, over a stormy dinner, he'd begged her mother to just for one second stop talking about parties and polo matches, and consider the impossibility of two thousand Englishmen trying to control one-fifth of the world's population. Her mother had said, '*Pouf*,' and told him to stop trying to frighten Tor, it was very mean of him. She'd slammed the door and left the room.

Tor had tried one morning after a sleepless night to confide in her mother about the Paul fiasco.

They were in the flower-arranging room. Her mother, who seemed now in a more or less permanent huff with her, was cutting rose stems and thrusting them into wire baskets with unnecessary force.

'Have you quite finished?' her mother had said when Tor's tearful outburst was over. 'Because I've made up my mind to be very frank with you, my darling.' She'd put down her flower scissors. 'You see, when you are young, you think the time for being chosen and married will go on for ever and it doesn't, and if a mother doesn't tell you these things, who will?' And then, worse than the rage really, she'd taken Tor's hand and given a regretful smile. 'Darling,' she said after a sufficient pause. 'How shall I put this? You are a reasonably attractive girl; you'll do for most known purposes. When you put your mind to it you can be a very nice girl, but you're no oil painting and in general, you,' and here her mother had spaced the words out, 'Are. Going. To. Have. To. Work. Much, *much* harder, because it is work.'

Any moment now, Tor could feel it coming, her mother would be producing one of her lectures about love being like a ballet performance, a beautiful lie, a twirling, smiling lie that masked the pain. Mother even had a special mask-like smile she produced during this talk.

'Mother! Please!' She had covered her ears with her hands. 'I was trying to tell you about Paul and what went wrong. I mean, he didn't even want to kiss me.'

Then her mother, scarlet with indignation, had let her have it with both guns.

'You went and had your hair cut like a ridiculous boy. What did you expect? You wear shoes like baby shoes. You make the most ludicrous fuss about wearing nice clothes. If Daddy and I are spending all this money on your coming out, the least you could try and do is to look nice. That's all. Now, is that so unreasonable?'

Her mother had stormed off again, this time to play bridge; her father had bolted the front door; Tor had sat in the summer house – where she and Rose had played dolls, and vets, and schools – and downed half a bottle of kitchen brandy.

Later, she'd gone up to her parents' bedroom half drunk; she'd stripped down to her knickers and brassiere and decided to face the truth at last. Was she ugly, perhaps hideously so?

She'd sat at her mother's kidney-shaped dressing table – a shiny pink confection underneath which her mother always kept her pink satin slippers with their frou of ostrich feather on the toes. When her foot had wedged in them she'd kicked them halfway across the room.

She'd stood up and looked at herself in the long cheval mirror near the window. She was taller, it was true, than was strictly speaking necessary, and browner than was fashionable. Her body was broad-shouldered, athletic. But she was not fat. *She was not fat.* Her hair was an undistinguished mid-brown with no curl in it whatsoever. She had her father's huge, blue, tragicomic eyes; they were what people always commented on. A perfect mongrel, she decided, watching them fill with tears.

She'd lain on the carpet and looked at herself in the mirror again. The early afternoon light was remorselessly bright.

'I love you,' she said, wondering how she'd looked to Paul that day. *Ugly, ugly, ugly,* a goblin voice said back.

'Kiss me, Paul,' she'd said to her reflection, watching her face contort with tears, for she was very drunk by now.

She'd unlocked the large walnut wardrobe that dominated the room. She'd taken out her mother's pride and joy: a peach silk Balmain dress – hand-pleated, each sequin sewn on by hand, as her mother never tired of telling her – bought in Paris years ago for a glamorous life that had never quite taken place. It felt blasphemous even to unzip its cloth bag and remove its complicated straps from the hanger.

It had surged over her head – a flood of apricot silk. She'd shivered.

'You could make yourself beautiful if you tried harder,' that's what Mother said.

She put the dress on and sat at the dressing table. Three versions of her face looked back at her. She'd opened the drawer underneath her and found, next to the hair pins and the swansdown powder puff, a packet of cigarettes. Narrowing her eyes, she smoked a cigarette from a long ebony holder. She drained her glass, and helped herself to a blast of Shalimar from a cut-glass bottle with a tassel on its lid.

She'd put on some lipstick and looked at herself in the mirror and said at last, 'I don't want to be you, Mummy, I *really* don't.'

Her father, who'd come up to look for his slippers, had walked in and found her crying. For the first time since she was little he had taken her in his arms, had really hugged her.

'I think you'd better go to India,' he'd said. 'I'll talk to her tonight.'

But now she was feeling all wobbly and chameleonish again, which was annoying, only this time it was Frank, and to nutshell the problem, she had the most hideous crush on him. When he'd asked her, in the most casual way possible, if Rose and she had any plans for Port Said, she'd been sitting in the bar chatting to Jitu Singh. Jitu was the urbane young maharajah, down from Oxford and rumoured to have at least twelve servants in the hold, organising his immaculate suits and writing paper and special food. Beside him, Frank, who had just worked a five-hour shift, looked adorably rumpled and creased. Frank had said he'd be off duty at twelve the next day and maybe they could all meet for a drink and lunch. When he'd smiled, she'd felt her hand go clammy around her glass and her heart skip. She'd started to look forward to him arriving every day, rehearsing in advance amusing things she could say to him. Only yesterday, he'd walked around the deck with her and, in between saying polite good mornings to the Groans (anybody over thirty), muttered scandalous accounts of their lives under his breath. *Murdered wife's best friend in a moment of sordid passion*, he'd said as they passed Major Skinner, quietly settling down to a few desk quoits with his family. *Senior member of opium gang*, towards Miss Warner, who had been sitting on her deck-chair at the time reading her Bible.

'Well, it's certainly a thought,' she'd said to him, when he'd told her about the quick trip to Cairo they could do from Port Said. 'It sounds rather fun.'

She was proud of herself for sounding as if they had a million other possibilities there.

'I'll be up near the purser's office at ten tomorrow morning collecting my post,' he said. 'No need to let me know before then.'

How spontaneous.

'Honey pie,' Rose's voice came through the keyhole, 'any chance of using the bathroom before we get to Bombay?'

'Oh Lord!' Tor yelped. 'What time is it?'

'Don't panic, it's only nine, but do come and look, you can see Port Said – all kinds of funny little men in boats are selling things. I can't wait for today.'

Fifty minutes later, Tor saw him standing near the purser's office.

'Oh, hello, Frank.' She was annoyed by her silly grin. 'Did you sleep well?'

Oh, how wonderfully original.

'Hardly at all,' he said. 'I was on call and we were quite busy.'

'Any good scandals?'

'Lots,' he said. That devastating little pulse was going in his jaw again. 'But I'm not allowed to tell you, or at least not until I've had at least three grenadines in the Windsor Bar.'

'Beast,' she said. 'Well, you may get one because we're coming.'

'I can't come until lunchtime,' he said, 'but I've got you a safe driver, he'll take you to the station at twelve fifteen when the train leaves and we'll get to Cairo about four hours later. We can have lunch on the train. You'll have time to shop this morning if you want to.'

She felt a warm glow as she watched his tanned hand scribbling. He was so much manlier than the pale and artistic Paul Tattershall. She hoped it wouldn't be too long before he seized her.

When she went upstairs, Viva and Rose were already on A deck ready to leave the ship. It was a dazzlingly bright day, a blue sky stretching to a shimmering horizon, and below, the harbour buzzed with small crafts all filled with excitable men trying to sell them things. A gully-gully man was shrieking and bringing birds out of his armpits; small boys dived for coins.

The wind was frisky. Holding the hem of her green dress down, Tor, thrilled by all this, leant over the side of the ship. And then the most embarrassing thing happened.

'Mummy, Mrs Queen, look here!' A small man, his arms covered in bracelets, shouted up at Tor from a boat down below. 'Mummy will buy!' He put his head endearingly on one side and gave her a white-toothed grin.

He was the most naked man she'd ever seen – nothing but half a handkerchief held round his waist with a thread.

'Yes, please, Mummy. Mrs Queen. Very nice.'

She and Rose started giggling but stopped suddenly. A gust of wind had blown the scrap of cloth aside; Rose, Viva, Miss Snow and Brigadier Chorley Haughtington all saw his 'thing' – a length of conker-coloured piping surrounded by luxuriant reddish-coloured hair. It was enormous. Miss Snow shrieked. Tor's mouth went dry. *So this was it*, she thought, *that mysterious bit of male plumbing for which continents were crossed and lives ruined.* Rose, holding a letter from Jack in her hand, turned away aghast.

And Tor, who knew exactly what she was thinking, clutched her hand. Marriage was such a huge step in the dark; terrifying actually, when you thought about it.

Seven hours later, Tor, Viva, Rose and a group of friends from the ship were in the Windsor Bar, in Shepheard's Hotel in Cairo. They were sunk deep into chairs made of old barrels, with piles of shopping bags full of what Frank called 'ill-considered trifles' all around them. For Tor a piece of embroidery and a sola topi made with ostrich feathers around its brim. For Rose a copper tray for her new house and a badly cured high-smelling belt for her husband-to-be, which she was already worried about. Viva had bought a dusty notebook with a camel on its cover and a twist of paper with some frankincense in it, which she said made a lovely smell when burned.

'Isn't it heaven being on terracotta again?' said Tor, looking luxuriously around the hotel's bar.

'Darling, I think the phrase is *terra firma*,' said Nigel.

Nigel, the young civil servant, was one of their new best friends. He had lank sandy hair and a languid body. His pale fine-featured face quivered with intelligence.

'I would adore a lime and soda,' Rose told Frank, who was ordering.

Tor thought Frank looked wonderful out of uniform. He was wearing a crumpled linen suit. She liked men who didn't try too hard with their clothes.

'A pink lady for me,' said Tor. 'Do try one,' she said to Rose. 'They've got grenadine at the bottom and brandy on top and they taste like pear drops – you'll love them. I say, it's not every day you have breakfast in Port Said and supper in Cairo.'

Tor's hair felt gritty from the train, her legs ached from the camel ride that had made them all shriek earlier – one had spat at Nigel straight in the eye – but she felt happy in a keyed-up sort of way. There was Frank, smiling his sleepy smile and looking relieved to be off duty; her friends, Tor and Rose and Nigel, all drinking grenadines now. Through the window, she could see red sky; sun setting through palm trees with actual dates on them.

'See all this.' Nigel waved his glass towards the Windsor's antique carpets and polished floor, the stuffed animal heads on the wall. 'It was once a very smart English officers' club; it'll soon be a piece of history.'

'Nigel is frightfully clever,' Rose explained to Viva. 'He—'

'Nigel, don't start all that hell in a handcart stuff,' Tor pleaded. 'We're having a jolly day out.'

'But it's true, though, isn't it?' Nigel turned to Viva.

When Viva looked at him and smiled sadly without saying anything, Tor thought how beautiful she was today, her scarlet dress, the barbaric necklace, her loose hair looking artistic and dishevelled and vaguely gypsy-like. She was an original, Tor decided, and admired the way she never looked as if she tried too hard. Frank was looking at her too, both men waiting eagerly for her to talk.

'Another grenadine, please,' Tor told Frank. 'Too delicious for words.'

The waiter arrived, plump and smiling with a napkin over his arm. They ordered far more than they needed: dishes of fat olives and plump little tomatoes, chickpeas, hummus and mouth-watering mounds of chicken and tabbouleh, all washed down with some local wine.

Frank insisted that they tasted the *roz b laban*, Egyptian rice pudding with raisins and cinnamon. 'Like Mother never made.'

'Teach us a good Egyptian toast, Mustafa,' Frank had said to the waiter.

'May a camel arise from your arse,' came the bawdy reply.

Tor loved the sound of Frank laughing next to her. His tanned hand around his glass. When he turned to talk to Viva, she watched them from the corner of her eye. There was a stillness about Viva that she envied. She kept herself apart. But hang on, he must have made a joke for she suddenly seemed to glow, and then she leant forward, saying something emphatic and mischievous to him that, irritatingly, Tor couldn't catch but which made him laugh.

Why do I never understand this? thought Tor, feeling her happiness *drain away. That charming people charm everyone – they're not just people that clever old you has discovered. Even the dreaded Paul had absolutely fascinated Mummy.*

'Have one of these.' Viva offered Tor a dish of olives, deliberately involving her again. 'And tell me if Frank is lying to me. He tells me some archaeologists have just dug up this new pharaoh's tomb at Moukel al Tes and found inside it mountains of old hairnets, tweezers and pots of face oil.'

'He's probably lying.' Tor didn't mean to sound so sour.

'I'm not.' When Frank turned round to look at Tor, she was happy again.

'Why wouldn't good looks be as important to them as to us? We didn't invent vanity.'

'I feel a quote coming on,' said Viva. 'Hang on.' She thought for a moment. ' "I am convinced that nothing in a man's life has as much importance as the conviction that he is attractive or unattractive." Tolstoy.'

'Perfect,' said Frank. 'My case rests.'

Tor, who had never read Tolstoy, gave a knowing smile.

Frank turned away from Tor again. 'Where are you going to live when you get to India?' he asked Viva.

She hesitated. 'I'm not sure yet. I have a few introductions. I'll be living on my wits for a while.'

She picked up a dish of Turkish delight and handed them around.

'Will you live there on your own?'

'Probably.'

Everybody waited for her to say more, but she didn't.

'Do you think you'll go north – isn't that where you grew up?' Nigel was intrigued too.

'Maybe,' she said. 'I haven't decided.'

That was the secret, *be more mysterious*. She blabbed to everyone.

'So,' Nigel turned to Tor in the silence that followed, 'what are *your* plans post Bombay?'

'Well—' Tor was about to be elusive too when Rose interrupted.

'She's my chief bridesmaid,' she said loyally, 'and bestest friend in the whole world.'

'And is this a full-time job?' Frank teased.

'Yes,' Rose said, 'I'm hideously demanding.'

Tor had never heard her role in India sound so mundane, so childish.

81

'As soon as Rose is hitched,' she blew out some cigarette smoke, 'I'll be off like a shot, travelling, having adventures and so forth.'

'Oh!' Rose stood up. She looked as if she'd been slapped. 'Do excuse me,' she said. She pushed back her chair and walked off in the direction of the ladies' room.

'Is she all right?' Viva mouthed to Tor.

'I'm sure she is.' Tor was puzzled. Rose had never in her life walked off in a huff. 'I'll go and see her. Maybe she's not feeling very well.'

Rose was standing by an ornately tiled washbasin crying when Tor walked into the ladies' room.

'What on earth's the matter, Rose?' she said.

'You.'

'*Me?* Why?' Tor had never seen her so angry.

'I'm sorry, Tor,' Rose said. 'But I thought you were a little bit excited about being a bridesmaid and that when we got to India we would spend some time together enjoying things. Certainly that's what your mother and mine thought. But now, you seem completely bored by the whole thing. And, well, I'm starting to think . . . to think . . .'

'What, Rose?'

'That you couldn't give a damn about it.'

And suddenly Tor was shouting at Rose, because the whole day was turning out to be such a disappointment and she was absolutely fed up with being on the edge of everybody's dreams.

'Oh, so is my sole function in life to be your wet nurse?'

'No! No! No! But all you talk about now is going away and having adventures.' Rose gave a great whoop of despair and tears ran down her face. 'Can't you see, can't you see at all how strange this will be for me?'

For a few seconds, they both glared at each other, breathing heavily. Outside the iron bars on the bathroom windows, they could hear a donkey braying and the sound of men shouting in foreign languages.

'Oh, Rose.' Tor put her arms round her. 'I'm so sorry.' She stroked her hair. 'I really and truly am. I was showing off to Frank, and it's just that sometimes other people seem to have such interesting lives and I want one too.'

'You'll have one, Tor, I know you will.'

'Yes.' Tor straightened Rose's hair. 'I'll have one.' Her voice seemed to bounce in a hollow way off the tiled walls.

'Friends again?'

'Yes.' Tor hugged her. 'Friends. In fact, if you're not careful, I'll be on that honeymoon with you. Shall we go back and join the others?'

'Yes,' said Rose. 'Sorry if I was a bit of an idiot, but it is so strange.'

They walked back to their table. Nigel was sitting on his own reading a book of Arabic poetry. Frank and Viva had disappeared.

'Where is everyone?' asked Tor.

'Gone,' he said. 'While you were out, a chap came from the *Kaisar* and told Viva to get back to the ship as soon as possible. Something about an incident on board.'

'Where's Frank?'

'He went with her.'

'What about us?' said Tor.

'He's ordered a car to take us to the ship.'

'How thoughtful.' Tor felt her heart turn to stone again. 'He's thought of everything.'

Chapter 13

POONA

'Sunita,' Jack Chandler called through the door. He was standing on her little verandah with its clay pots filled with bougainvillea and geraniums. Around each pot was a circle of damp where she had watered them earlier. He put his forehead against the door. *Sunita, Sunita, I'm so sorry.*

Behind the door, he could hear the gentle percussion of her bangles as she walked towards him.

'Jack.' She was smiling at him so wholeheartedly. She held nothing back. That was one of the things he most admired about her. She was wearing one of his favourite saris: pale green with a faint mauve underneath, reminding him of the sweet peas in his mother's garden in Dorset.

She put the palms of her hands together and made a namaste.

'My sweet pea,' he said.

'Sweet pea?' She looked confused.

'A beautiful flower.'

He followed her trail of attar of roses into the undistinguished room where his life had been changed for ever. Their bed, a low divan with a white sheet on it and a mosquito net, was there and the small brass table with its ornate lamp. Beside the bed, she'd already laid out the bottle of brandy he bought at the mess, his favourite cheroots and a carafe of water.

Her hair fell in a flood of silk as she leant forward to fill his glass.

'You look tired,' she said. 'Shall I get you something to eat? I went to the market earlier and bought two beautiful mangoes: alfonsos.'

Sunita was a mango connoisseur.

'Just a drink,' he said. He was too nervous to eat. 'Thank you, Sunita.'

Watching her fingers prise the skin away from the fruit, he was horribly aware of what he must soon lose: her gentle presence, her tender mouth, the proudness of her bearing. She was a *Rajput*, one of the warrior class, with all the gentleness of the truly strong.

'Sunita. I . . .' He held her hand and turned it over, tracing the shape of the pink pads underneath her fingers. She closed her eyes and smoothed the sides of his hair.

'Plenty of time to talk when you've had a drink.'

While he drank the brandy, night fell outside her window, as suddenly as it always did in India, like a fire curtain coming down on a play. Light then dark.

They'd been together now for three years. She'd been introduced to him by a fellow officer who'd been going home to England, and who said she was a very superior type, not a street girl, but a direct descendent of the *Nautch* girls who had so captivated Englishmen with their wonderful dancing and singing, their refined ways of enthralling men, before India had, as he put it, 'become almost as doily and prissy as the British and clamped down on them'.

Before her there'd been a few flings at Sandhurst with sporty girls, mostly army daughters, who'd been almost as shy as he was; then a brief fling with a junior officer's wife in Jaipur. She was a short, plump, lonely woman with all her children in English boarding schools and her husband away for months at a time. She'd had the most wonderful arse – unfashionably plump, and round and high – and that was all he remembered about her now. And there had been fumbles with other women, but nothing like this.

'Here.' Sunita took off his shoes and bathed his feet.

'Sunita—' He had meant not to be a cad: to say what he had to say, make his salaams and leave.

'Here.' As she unbuttoned his shirt, he smelt his own sweat. The proper thing was to tell her immediately and not sleep with her.

But he was hard now, and helpless. The smell of her, the swish of her hair against his chest; the sense of having been cut adrift from himself, from all the stuffy apparatus of cantonment life with its games and uniforms and sense of being on show, made this room part of what it took for him to feel alive.

Her skin felt soft and slightly damp beneath his hands. He could feel her ribs under the silk of her sari, as he lowered her down on the bed, and then her long narrow waist and then his lips on hers. And now he was floating with her again, floating in the dark: happy and helpless.

'Wait! Wait.' She put her hand over his mouth. 'I have some music for you. Shall I put?'

The wireless gramophone had been one of his most successful presents to her. He'd bought it on his first home leave, in a shop off the Camden Passage in London. She'd opened the box it came in so reverently, with such tenderness, that it brought tears to his eyes. He gave it to her, but she gave it back to him many times over by introducing him to Ustad Hafiz Ali Khan who'd just begun to make his recordings at the Tiger Studio in Bombay. She'd introduced him to the richness of the Indian ragas – the sacred music used to greet dawn and sunset, summer, spirits and fire. He remembered the night he'd put on *Madame Butterfly* for her and how they'd laughed after a few bars when she'd put her hands over her ears and said, 'Stop! It's horrible – like cats going oooohhhhh,' and she'd howled in real pain.

But now she said, 'Listen!' She put on the music and then lifted her arms above her head and briefly made a snake of her body. Generously, gracefully she had shared that body with him.

Now she had slipped under the sheet and was gently massaging his neck, singing, '*Chhupo na chhupo hamari sajjano*,' – do not hide from me, my beloved – softly into his ear. It was their song.

Patient as a mother, she'd nursed him through the days when for all his easy manners, his correctness in the outside world, he'd been a peasant in the ways of lovemaking, with a peasant's tongue. Like a farm boy in rut, speaking the language of the squaddie because he hadn't known the words then. *I want to fuck you. Fancy a root? Are you ready for it?*

She'd watch him in the dark with her beautiful seaweed-coloured eyes, playing him like a virtuoso. Sometimes she massaged him and watched him rise, making him feel that she was the source of every exquisite sensation he'd ever felt, stretched out and prolonged with appalling sweetness until she released him.

She was refined, beautiful, well educated, well connected, even: her father, a liberal cultivated man, was a lawyer in Bombay, but she was not wife material. Never a wife. It wasn't as easily explained as snobbery, although, and he had faced this squarely, snobbery did come into it. The problem was this: he loved his regiment and his fellow officers with a passion that bordered on the obsessional. No woman, Indian or English, would ever really understand what they meant to him, and as a group they strongly disapproved of fellows who took on native women and went what they called 'jungli'.

All of the men he knew were, to some extent, split in their natures: privately bawdy and schoolboyish, publicly courtly and reserved with women. Sunita had healed the split. But even if they had approved of her, some part of him knew he would never have married her. In the end they were just too different.

With my body I thee worship. No problem with that. *With my soul I thee wed.*

That was the rub. If he had a soul (which he sometimes seriously doubted) it had been, in a hundred thousand ways, forged so differently to hers. In the end and notwithstanding the painful night ahead, it would be so much easier to marry a girl like Rose.

'You're very quiet tonight,' she said when they'd made love. 'What are you thinking?'

With one fluid gesture, she got up and wrapped herself in her sari.

He put on the silk dressing gown she kept for him there and put his arms round her.

'Sunita, I'm getting married soon,' he said. 'I'm so sorry.'

He could feel her breath changing under his hands.

In the silence that followed, he heard the fan churn, the sound of an insect buzzing outside, wheels turning in the street outside.

'I knew you would,' she said at last.

She went over to the table where a candle was dropping wax on the postcard he had sent her from England, three weeks after he'd met Rose. It was an absurd card – he was ashamed of it now – a duck trying to ride a bicycle. She'd kept it like a holy relic just as she'd kept everything else he'd ever given her: a handbag, a toy car, a phial of Evening in Paris scent, still in its cardboard box. All the presents placed on a shelf where candles were lit in front of Shiva.

'When is the wedding?'

Her back was graceful, erect.

'Next month.'

'Do you know her? Or was it the old matchmaker?' She turned and tried to smile.

'I know her. Not very well. We met on my last home leave in England.'

'Is she pretty?'

'Yes, but—'

'Is she a good woman?'

'Yes, I do believe she is.'

'Tell her I shall set the *goondas* on her if she isn't.'

She gave up trying to move the candle and blew it out. She was a warrior's daughter. He'd never seen her cry and she didn't now.

'She is lucky, Jack.'

'I hope we'll be all right,' he said. 'The jury is out.'

'What jury? What do you mean?'

'Nothing.'

'My father wants me to get married too,' she said. She was sitting on the divan in the half-light. Her voice sounded so sad. 'He's fifteen years older than me, but very kind, handsome, suitable.'

None of us is free to choose, he thought. Rose had been chosen for more or less the same reasons: the right class, right voice, right look, nothing to frighten the horses, his colonel, his men.

'Do you think I should marry him?'

'Oh, Sunita, I don't know. I can't—' He stopped himself. If she was brave he must be too.

I hardly know the woman I'm marrying either. That was how he felt driving home sobbing in the rickshaw alone, and all through the cold sweat of the sleepless night that followed. He hoped he would not feel this way tomorrow.

Chapter 14

PORT SAID, ELEVEN DAYS FROM BOMBAY

When Viva got back to the ship, Mr Ramsbottom, an acquaintance of Guy's parents stood at the bottom of the gangplank. Beads of sweat stood out on his forehead, and he was so angry he could not look at her.

Viva felt her mouth go dry. 'What's happened? Where's Guy?'

'You'd better come down and talk to him,' he said. 'I'll tell you what I think of your behaviour later.'

She followed his squared shoulders and squeaking brogues up the gangplank and then down three flights of narrowing stairs, down into the bowels of the ship where oil-covered sailors looked surprised to see them.

'You had no right to fob him off on to us,' he flung over his shoulder. 'We know his parents a little, but we don't know *him* at all. Incredibly embarrassing.' His brogues carried on squeaking, down and down. 'I mean, where were you all day? It's not my job to look after him, and my wife's got a heart condition.'

'Look,' she said. 'Tell me quickly, is he all right?'

'Well, you'll see him in a minute – he's being held in the ship's lock-up, brig or whatever damn thing they call it.' He was still spitting mad.

A uniformed officer took them into a small, airless suite of rooms that smelt faintly of urine and Dettol.

'Ah! Miss Holloway, the chaperone, good of you to drop in.' The duty officer, who was red-headed and high-coloured, was sitting behind his desk waiting for them. 'My name is Benson.' The two men exchanged looks full of male understanding about the unreliability of women. 'Mr Glover's been rather a busy boy during your absence.'

'Can I see him on his own for a while?' she said.

Ramsbottom closed his eyes and put the palms of his hands up as if to say, 'Nothing to do with me.' The officer unlocked the door.

When she walked in, Guy was lying on a narrow bunk with his face to the wall. It was hot in the room, 105 degrees or so, but he was huddled in a grey blanket. His overcoat was hanging up on a hook on the wall. She could smell him from the door: alcohol and sweat.

'Guy,' she said, 'what happened?'

When he turned over, his face looked as if someone had stamped on it: both eyes purple and swollen, his lips twice their normal size. A cut at the corner of his mouth was leaking a watery blood.

'Why aren't you in the hospital?' she said.

He raised his voice and looked beyond her, to the officer who was keeping a protective eye on both of them.

'I want her away from me,' he said in a slurred voice. 'It's not her fault. Silly old sod Ramsbottom keeps blaming her.'

'Guy, Guy, shush, please.' As she sat down at the end of the bunk, she was conscious of the door closing softly.

'Look, he's gone,' she whispered, 'so tell me quickly what happened.'

'Nothing,' he mumbled. 'That's all you need to know.' He crumpled up his face like a child about to cry, then closed his eyes and seemed to sleep.

'Miss Holloway,' Benson appeared at the door, 'he's been given a sedative injection, so I don't think you'll get much more out of him tonight. If you wouldn't mind,' he added softly, 'we'd like to ask you one or two questions.'

'Of course.' She touched Guy on the foot. 'Are you sure there's nothing I can do for you?'

'You can bring me a bottle of bleach,' he said, 'and I can drink the lot.' He turned to look at the wall again. 'A joke,' he mumbled.

Even *in extremis*, he didn't want her.

'He has to see a doctor,' she told the duty officer.

They were sitting in his cubbyhole of an office. Sweat was dripping from Benson's face on to the blotting paper, and his thin red hair was plastered to his temples. He switched the fan on.

'Much hotter, isn't it?' he said pleasantly. 'I think they recorded 110 degrees at Bab-el-Mandeb yesterday.'

'What happened to him?' she said. 'Why isn't he in the san?'

'Madam.' A steward walked in with a cup of tea for her, and she was dimly aware of the ship moving forward again. 'You left your shopping on the deck, Miss Holloway.' When the steward handed her the parcel with her new notebook and twist of frankincense inside, she felt a fresh wave of shame. This was all her fault; she should never have left him alone.

'What happened?' she said for the third time to the officer when they were alone again. He still didn't answer.

'His eyes are so swollen,' she said. 'He must see a doctor.'

'Absolutely.' He scratched his damp forehead. 'I'll organise one right away, but what we'd most like to do is move him back to his cabin.'

'Wouldn't it be better if he was in the sanatorium?'

Benson started to shuffle some papers. As he uncapped his pen and found the form he was looking for, she found herself wondering whether she could ever love a man with ginger hair on his knees.

'Well, it's a bit complicated.' He swivelled his chair round to face her. 'While you were out shopping, or sightseeing, or whatever you were doing, Mr Glover attacked and then insulted one of our passengers.' His pale eyes watched her take this in. 'An Indian passenger, name of Azim. They're a prominent Muslim family from the north. Mr Azim apprehended Glover in his cabin with a pair of cufflinks and a small silver ornamental sword in his coat pocket. A scuffle ensued, nothing too serious at first, but then, according to Azim, one moment they were chatting conversationally and the next Mr Glover hauled off and punched Mr Azim hard in the face and then in the ear. Azim was in the san for five hours; they've discharged him now. At the moment, he says he does not want to press charges. That may change.'

Sweat broke out on her own forehead; she could feel some dripping down her dress. 'Who beat Guy up?' she said.

'Well, that's the point, we don't think anybody did. Your boy was seen approximately half an hour later by two members of staff, banging his own head against the stern railings.'

'Oh good Lord!' She stared at Benson in disbelief. 'Why?'

'We don't know, but now we have to sort out the best way of dealing with him. You appreciate that with roughly two hundred and fifty other first-class passengers on board we'll have to put our thinking caps on. But as a matter of absolute fact,' Benson put the cap back on his pen and looked at her again, 'he said he did it for you.

Something about being in love with you and voices telling him to do it.'

A large pipe gurgled above her head like a giant stomach, and the Dettol and urine smell seemed to move towards her.

Benson's face looked carefully blank.

'This is madness,' she said.

'Well, it may be,' said Benson, 'but, assuming that Azim doesn't press charges, and to be frank, your young man will be extremely lucky if he doesn't, here are our options: do we get the police involved, which could mean you disembarking and hanging around in Suez for an indefinite period; do we keep him locked up here and cause a scandal; or do we take the chance that it won't happen again? What do you think? You know him best. And technically, I suppose, he is yours, although, may I be frank, I'm surprised that his parents gave so much responsibility to someone of your age.'

She looked at him for a moment, trying to think. Her head had started to ache and her mouth was still dry from the grenadines she'd drunk what seemed like days and days ago.

'Do you know Frank Steadman?' she said at last. 'He's one of the medical officers on board. I don't know him well, but I'd like to talk to him before I make up my mind; he could check Mr Glover over at the same time.'

'That sounds like a very good idea.' The duty officer looked so relieved he actually smiled. 'Worse things happen at sea and all that. What if we arrange for Mr Glover to be taken back to his cabin tonight? I could arrange for Dr Steadman to meet you there.'

'Thank you,' she said. Her headache was starting to make her feel sick, and she was worried that soon she might get a migraine.

'Just one more thing,' he said as she was picking up her bags. 'I wouldn't tell anybody about this incident if I were you. Ships are funny places: rumours, fears spread like wildfire. I've said the same thing to Mr Ramsbottom and he agrees.'

'I won't say anything,' she said.

'It wouldn't look very good for you either,' he added slyly. 'It wasn't perhaps the wisest thing to leave him alone like that. It could have been very much more serious.'

'Yes,' she said. The right side of her face was starting to tingle; his outline was breaking up into wavy lines.

They looked at each other warily. She walked towards the door and closed it behind her.

It took two sailors to bundle Guy, still groggy from the sedatives, back to bed in his own cabin. When they left, Viva bolted the door behind them and collapsed in a chair. Guy fell asleep almost instantly, purple eyelids twitching, the blood on his lips congealing.

As she watched him sleep she felt a cold contempt for herself. She didn't like him, that was true, but it was dreadful of her to have left him behind.

Before they'd parted, Benson had warned her again that she could be held responsible if any legal charges were pressed. When she asked him what that meant, he had told her 'it was not his part of ship' to explain the full legal implications to her, but he'd implied that they could be serious.

She slept lightly, and then a soft knock on the door made her spring to her feet.

'Can I come in? It's Dr Steadman. Frank.'

Relief flooded through her like new blood.

'Come in and lock the door behind you,' she whispered.

He was back in his white uniform and seemed like an entirely different person in this setting: professional, impersonal. She was grateful for that: in her current state of mind, jokiness or familiarity would have been unbearable. He sat down on the chair beside Guy's bunk, a small leather bag at his feet.

'Don't wake him for a second,' he said. 'Tell me what happened.'

When she opened her mouth to speak, the boy's swollen eye flickered.

'Ah, Doctor,' he said through his cut lip. 'Good of you to drop in.' When he tried to sit up, she caught the smell of his stale air, his sweat and vomit.

'Stay where you are for a second.' Frank moved closer to him and gently touched the corner of the boy's eye. 'I want to have a look at this.'

Viva noticed the boy's face softening, the faint beginnings of a smirk from his cut lip. He seemed to be enjoying the attention.

Frank rolled back his sleeve on an expanse of brown arm. He scrutinised the boy's face.

'You were lucky that whatever hit you missed your eye,' said Frank. 'What was it, by the way?'

'A thunderbolt.'

'What kind of a thunderbolt?'

'The usual kind.'

'I can't help you if you're going to play silly buggers with me,' Frank said softly. 'It looks like someone gave you an almighty punch. Was that it?'

'My business, not yours.' The boy turned his face to the wall.

'Look,' Frank said evenly as if the boy hadn't spoken at all, 'before you go to sleep, I'd like to clean up your lip and put something on your eye to take the swelling down and then, maybe,' he looked at Viva for permission, 'I could talk to Guy on his own. Man to man.'

'Of course,' said Viva. She picked up the boy's bloody shirt and said, 'I'll give these to Guy's steward. And tell him,' she gave Frank a significant look, 'not to bother us for a while. Benson said I should lock the door behind me when I leave.'

'Come back in about half an hour,' said Frank, 'and then perhaps you could come to the surgery with me and get something to help Guy sleep.'

Numb and still woozy from her headache, Viva walked quickly down the corridor hoping when she passed Rose and Tor's cabin that she wouldn't see them.

A heavily made-up man wearing a frock suddenly appeared from one of the cabin doors. He tittered when he bumped into her and said, 'Pardon!' in a silly voice. More people appeared from behind him, giggling and self-conscious, dressed in feather boas and clown suits.

'Rotters,' shouted a middle-aged woman dressed as a crossword puzzle. 'Wait for me.'

'Oh, diddums,' the clown shouted back and then he smiled at Viva, yellow fangs, red lipstick. For a few confused seconds they seemed part of her developing migraine, and then she remembered it was the Eccentrics party that night. She had said she might go with Tor and Rose. For the next few hours at least, a lot of people from their corridor would conveniently have deserted it for the ballroom on A deck.

She'd reached the purser's office. The clock outside said eight thirty-five; the lights were on inside. To fill in time and to hide from the partygoers, now shrieking with laughter in the corridors, she went in to ask whether there was a letter for her.

The clerk handed her a buff-coloured envelope with a telegram in it.

It was from the *Pioneer Mail and Indian Weekly*. 'Sorry,' it read. 'Insufficient funds to take on another correspondent in our Bombay office this month, but do come and see us if you are passing by.' It was signed Harold Warner. He was an old friend of Mrs Driver who'd been sure he'd be able to find 'some little job' for her.

'How was your day, Miss Holloway?' the purser, a thickset Scotsman with a relentless smile, was locking up his glass cage. 'Did ye enjoy your quick trip to Cairo?'

'Great fun,' she said. She couldn't even begin to explain how bad it felt.

And now another lifeline had been cut.

'D'you want to put that in here?'

'Thank you.' She threw the crumpled telegram into the wastepaper basket.

'So, will you be after the silly party tonight?'

'No,' she said. 'Not tonight. I've had enough excitement for one day.'

She glanced at her watch. She could hardly see the time. She'd been gone for ten minutes and would go back in ten.

The worst thing about being on a ship was there was nowhere to hide when things went wrong. If she went to her cabin, Miss Snow would be there, no doubt brimming with good advice and I-told-you-sos. If she went into supper, she'd have to face the Ramsbottoms. The only person she felt temporarily safe with was Frank.

Walking slowly back to the cabin, she thought about him. He seemed so light-hearted, even faintly flirtatious, something to do with his sleepy green eyes, the smile.

But if Rose was right and a brother had been killed at Ypres, he'd suffered and now perhaps concealed his pain too well. She wondered if the brother had been killed outright, or had to take his chances in one of the ad hoc medical centres on the battlefield steeped in mud and blood, and whether, as a consequence, the luxury of this ship angered Frank – he'd joked once or twice about the rows of passengers that waited for him outside his surgery in the mornings to have ears syringed and smelling salts renewed.

Mad-making, when you thought about it. She wondered if he ever talked about it, and somehow doubted it.

*

He was still sitting in a chair by Guy's bed when she walked in. He'd placed a shirt over the cabin's wall light so that the room was darker and full of shadows.

'How is he?' she said.

'Agitated for a while,' he whispered. 'But fast asleep now; he will be till morning.'

'Can we talk here?'

'Well, it's not ideal,' he said, 'but at the moment, I can't think of a better place.'

There was a silence for a while.

'How old are you?' he asked suddenly.

'I'm twenty-eight,' she said.

'You don't look it.'

'Don't I?' She didn't like lying to him but it seemed important to keep her story straight.

'Do you know anything about his parents?'

'I met an aunt once at my interview. She said something about his father being in the tea business near Assam. Originally they'd hired an older chaperone, but she let them down.'

'They should never have put you in this situation.' He ran his hand through his hair and shook his head.

'What situation?'

'Would you mind if we went into the bathroom?' he said. 'I don't want him to overhear.'

They crept into the bathroom together where they sat awkwardly at either end of the bath.

Guy's paisley silk bathrobe was hung behind the door. A grubby-looking shaving brush lay in the sink, hairs stuck in the congealed soap. The steward hadn't been in to clean up.

'Look,' said Frank, 'before we start you must understand that this is in confidence, and I don't have all the answers.'

'I understand.'

'Can I speak openly?'

'Of course.'

Frank didn't seem to know where to begin, or look. 'To start with, how do you get on with Guy?'

'Honestly?'

'Yes,' he glanced at her quickly and smiled, 'always.'

'I can't bear him.'

'Well, that's pretty unequivocal,' he said.

'Look, I know boys of his age struggle with conversation,' she said, 'but he's barely uttered a word for the last two weeks, and when he does, I get the feeling he hates me.'

Frank thought about this for a while. 'He doesn't hate you,' he said at last. 'He hates himself.'

'But why?'

'That, I'm not sure of. Have you seen him in his own setting, at school for instance?'

'Well, I drove down there to pick him up, but when he left all the other boys seemed to be out playing sport. His dormitory was deserted.'

'That's pretty unusual, wouldn't you say? He told me he was leaving school for good.'

'He was.'

'Do you know why?'

'Yes, I do. Look, this is all my fault. I should have said something earlier. He'd taken things from the other boys. I didn't take it seriously enough.'

'What did he take?'

'Not very much, the normal pilfering.'

'Don't blame yourself too much,' said Frank. 'The thieving might be part of a bigger problem.'

'Such as?'

'I'm not sure yet. When you were out of the room he told me he hears voices sometimes. He said they come through his wireless.'

'But that sounds absolutely—'

'I know. He also said something about you being his chosen mother. He said he hates his real one now.'

Viva felt her skin prickle.

'What should I do?' She didn't wait for an answer. 'I shouldn't have left him. Do you think he's dangerous? Will it happen again?'

Frank put his hand on her shoulder.

'Here's the tricky bit, I don't really know. His reaction did seem quite extreme. Obviously I'll have to talk to my senior, Dr Mackenzie, about it, but my instinct is to keep an eye on him for a couple of days. I'll attempt to persuade him to come into the san; we'll try and keep the lid on things. It's only ten days to Bombay and the weather will be too hot for anyone to do much in the Indian Ocean.'

'What's the alternative?'

'To put him off the ship at Suez, but then he'd have to wait for his parents to come and that won't do anything for his state of mind.'

'What if he won't go to the san?'

'Well, the other alternative is to keep him under some form of house arrest in his cabin. They'd fit his door with an extra lock, but how would you feel about that?'

She shuddered and shook her head. 'I honestly don't know. Did you know that his cabin is right next door to Tor and Rose's?'

'No,' he said. 'I didn't.'

'Shall I tell them?'

'Not for the time being. No point in frightening them.'

'What would you do if you were me?' she asked.

'I'd review the situation first thing tomorrow. I'll talk to Dr Mackenzie; you won't be left alone with this. And then,' he stood up, looked at his watch, 'it's ten-thirty, so I'd go upstairs and find someone to have a drink with. You could do with a break.' He looked at her again. 'Are you all right?'

'Yes. Why do you ask?'

'You look very pale.'

'I'm fine, thank you.' She didn't want to tell him about the migraine.

'It must have been a shocking day for you.'

'No. No. It's all right.' She took a step back from him. It was so instinctive not to ask for help, a habit she couldn't break. She shook his hand formally. 'But thank you,' she said. 'You've been most helpful.'

He smiled at her, the smile that made the other girls go weak at the knees.

'Part of the P&O service, madam.' He was back to his bantering self again.

He turned off one of the lights in the cabin and straightened the blankets over Guy. She collected her wrap and her bag.

'Don't worry too much,' he said. 'I'm sure he'll be all right.' He brushed against her arm as he locked the cabin door behind them. She stepped backwards into a figure in the corridor. It was Tor. She was dressed in a black hooded cloak, with a rope tied round her neck like a noose. Attached to the noose was a bottle with the label 'The last drop' written on it. When she saw them both she stopped smiling.

Chapter 15

THE STRAIT OF BAB-EL-MANDEB

28 October 1928

Dearest Mummy,

I picked up your letter in Cairo and was thrilled to hear from you. Mummy, thank you for all the useful information about placecards and flowers and article about corsages. It was kind of you to send it too to Jack – I'm sure he can send it on to Ci Ci Mallinson if he finds it all too confusing! I don't think he'll think he's marrying into a monstrous regiment of women, he should be grateful to have a mother-in-law who is so thoughtful.

It is hot, hot, hot here. Tor and I have put our winter clothes away in the trunk and have brought out our summer clothes. The crew are wearing their white uniforms, and instead of serving us broth in the morning, we get ice and melons.

Mr Bingley, who is a jute planter and one of dozens of new best friends on the ship, does forty turns around the deck (in flapping shorts) each morning. He announced today that it is now over 100 degrees in the shade. At nights after supper our stewards haul our mattresses on deck – men on one side of the deck, women on the other!!!! The sunsets are out of this world, and though the wider parts of the Suez Canal got rather dull, we've now passed the Gulf of Suez, which is only about ten miles wide, and so we can watch the most fascinating sights from the steamer – camels, men in long flowing nighties, women with pots on their heads and all kinds of biblical scenes.

I am still taking my kitchen Hindi lessons from Colonel Gorman. *Bearer, khana kamre ko makhan aur roti lana, ek gilass pani bhi* – bearer, fetch me a glass of water, and butter and jam into the dining room. I've probably spelt it all wrong. Tor and I speak it in our cabin and have fits of laughter. Our ladies' meetings are called bishis.

Mr Bingley's wife, who is v. sweet, has also lent me her 'indispensable bible', viz *The Complete Indian Housekeeper and Cook*, written by a Mrs Steel who's lived there for ages – full of good info incl. recipes, lists of servants, best places to buy things, etc., so you see I am hard in training for the life of a *pukkamem*.

(By the way, Mrs Steel's advice on how to deal with awkward servants is to give them a ticking-off, followed by a large dose of castor oil.) *Memsahib tum ko zuroor kaster ile pila dena hoga* – the memsahib will have to give you castor oil.

Do try that on Mrs Pludd and tell me how it goes!

Darling Mummy, too hot to write any more and the bell has just gone for deck games. I have a million more questions to ask you but will think of them later.

Your affectionate and devoted daughter,
Rose

P.S. Tor not v. well, nothing to worry about, says it's the heat and she's feeling much better now. Don't bother telling Mrs Sowerby.

P.P.S. Another fancy-dress party on Saturday night, mind complete blank as to what to go as.

Chapter 16

Tor had looked forward to the Arabian Nights party ever since she'd arrived on board. Held on full-moon nights, on the day before the ship slipped into the Red Sea, experienced travellers on board said it was one of the highlights of the voyage and she'd worked herself up into a fine froth even thinking about it. Exotic costumes were expected and the dress she'd planned to wear – long, slinky and made of fine gold silk – begged for a cigarette holder, red lips and a weary expression. It was a vamp's dress and any other mother but hers would have flatly forbidden it.

A few days ago when she'd hung it in the steamy bathroom to get the creases out, she'd literally shivered with anticipation at the sight of it. She'd decided to wear it with a short gold mask, a long rope of pearls and lipstick. She was to be an Egyptian goddess in it, which one she wasn't sure of, her knowledge of such things being hazy, but certainly one who was autocratic, who was splendid and who was above the law. Every time she'd thought of the party, she ran a little film in her head in which Frank took off her mask of gold, and looked deeply into her eyes. Sometimes he told her she had wonderful eyes, sometimes he simply led her terrified but thrilled down to his cabin where he made a woman of her. And, once again – what was wrong with her? – her mind had raced ahead to babies and houses and photograph albums.

On the morning before the ball she woke early, furious with herself all over again. The gold dress swung limply on a hanger outside her wardrobe door, taunting her now with its idiotic promises. How long, she wondered, would it take her to get it into her fat head that men didn't like her? The only part of her plan that now appealed was the mask, because she felt so wretched.

She thumped her pillow and turned over. Jealousy was such a horrible emotion, she decided. From the moment she had seen Viva and Frank leaving the boy's room it had stolen into her sunny picture like a pantomime villain, with pitchfork and gleaming eyes and smoke coming out of his ears.

The sight of them – so conspiratorial, so somehow changed-looking – had made her accept that Frank, in spite of their jolly turns around the deck, was not, and never had been, the slightest bit interested in her. Why, with the memory of her humiliating attachment to Paul Tattershall so recent in her mind, she'd ever imagined he was, was a complete mystery to her now. But this time, she told herself, squaring her jaw on her pillow, this time she would behave like a grown-up. *Stop caring so much* had been her stern message to herself over the past few days, *simply cut them out of your mind*.

Last night, when their group had met up in the bar for a few pegs, she'd flirted and danced with everyone to show just how fine she was. When Frank had arrived suddenly, had a quick drink and then left just as suddenly with Viva, she, conscious of Rose shooting her a protective look, had turned away. And laughed nonsensically at something somebody else had said. She'd danced with Nigel, who was a sweetheart but too gentle and poetic for her, and then with Jitu Singh, who, she and Rose agreed, was the most exotic man they'd ever seen. Now because she'd drunk too much she had a thumping headache and a horrible taste in her mouth.

As she looked for some Eno's salts in the bedside table, she thought for no particular reason of a girl who she'd had a crush on at school who had seemed even then to have some elusive quality that she entirely lacked. The girl's name was Athena, and she was dark and beautiful and used to spend her school holidays in South America, where her father did important and secret things for the government.

After the school holidays, most of the girls would get on the train and talk without drawing breath until the train arrived in Cheltenham where their school was. All except Athena who, while they babbled about shrimping in Salcombe, or having wizard fun in the Isle of Wight, would sit enticingly silent.

'Please, Athena,' they'd beg, 'tell us where you've been.'

'Buenos Aires,' she might say, in her not quite English accent, and then she'd wait, smiling.

'And? Come on, Athena, you beast! Tell!'

'Oh, you know, the usual things: parties, boys.'

As Tor had waited hungrily with the rest for more scraps which never came, she saw how powerful silence could be and even tried it once herself.

On a school trip to London she'd forced herself to keep a secret (so important but for the life of her she couldn't remember what it was now) until Reading at least. But by Didcote, she'd blabbed to Athena, who, to add to the humiliation, had politely raised her eyebrows, and said 'Golly' with the same dying fall that her own mother said 'Anyway' when she wanted people to get off the phone.

Another memory surfaced about Athena: when they were out on school trips, and given sandwiches and bars of chocolate to eat at lunch, she kept hers until lunch.

Tor had usually demolished hers by about a quarter to ten. No self-control, Mother was right about that.

Viva was like Athena. When Frank had asked her about her plans, she hadn't babbled helplessly as Tor would have done, or seemed to ask for his approval or advice. She'd merely said, 'I'm not sure yet,' and Tor could tell he was completely hooked.

It had been left to Rose and herself to fill in the tantalising gaps, by telling him that Viva was going to be a writer; that she may or may not go to Simla, where her parents had been killed – nobody knew exactly how – and where there was this mysterious trunk waiting for her, probably filled with jewels and things, and that in the meantime, she would probably try and live on her wits in Bombay.

Tor's biggest problem, she decided, was that she had no idea of how to wait: for food, for love or for people to find her interesting, which she wasn't.

Tor, creeping across the cabin in the half-light of dawn, took down the invitation that had been stuck behind a mirror and studied it again.

CAPTAIN AND CREW HAVE GREAT PLEASURE, ETCETERA, ETCETERA, ETCETERA, CHAMPAGNE AND ORIENTAL DISHES TO BE SERVED WHEN THE MOON RISES AT 7 P.M.

What a horror the whole thing sounded now. She briefly considered the possibility of crying off – Rose could tell people she was in the cabin with a raging fever or Delhi belly, but then Frank might appear, avuncular and kind, with Viva at his side. Also – she glanced at Rose, calmly asleep in her bunk – this time she really didn't feel like involving Rose. She was just so tired of being her ugly sister, the eternal gooseberry, the child with its nose pressed wistfully against the window of love when all Rose had to do was look at a man and he fell fainting at her feet.

But, darling, Rose might reasonably have said, *you hardly know him,* or she might speak to her more generally about shipboard romances, which would make her feel slightly common.

I melt, I rage, I burn.

Hard to imagine Rose melting, raging or burning. Life just seemed to happen to her, maybe because she was so pretty. *I try too hard.*

Her groan woke Rose up. She sat up in her lace nightdress and stretched her perfect arms towards the ceiling.

'Um, divine,' she said sleepily, 'I had the strangest dream that I had this little baby and it was riding an elephant in the tiniest topi you've ever seen and everyone was saying it was too early but I was so happy with it.'

'Gosh.'

In the silence that followed Rose said, 'Oh golly, it's that Arabian Nights thing tonight. Can we have a clothes chat?'

'Sorry, but no,' Tor said. 'I'm asleep. Goodnight.'

'All right, but do you think my floaty pink thing will do if I use the shawl part as a veil?'

'Couldn't be less interested. Sorry.'

'You actually owe me this, Tor, because you were very noisy last night – you were thrashing around like some mad fish in a net.'

'I'm asleep, Rose, sorry. No further bulletins.'

It isn't as if Frank is even madly good-looking, she thought as soon as she heard Rose breathing regularly again. A lovely smile, a quick wit, but not quite tall enough for leading-man material and slightly bandy-legged if one was being absolutely brutal. And Mummy wouldn't have been thrilled about him being a doctor, although he wasn't really a ship's doctor; he was, when he got to India, going up north to research into something horrible.

And if he preferred Viva, fine. She wasn't going to make a meal of it or even give them the satisfaction of a scene. If living well was the best revenge, that's what she'd do tonight. Dance and flirt and not care, not care at all. There were plenty of men who would dance with her.

She switched on the fan above her bed, finished the glass of water beside her bed, still half listening for sounds that might or might not be coming from the cabin next door. Why they'd been in that cabin was still a complete mystery to her. Where was Guy Glover, come to think of it? She hadn't seen him for days. When she'd asked Viva about why she'd rushed back to him, she'd laughed it off as a false alarm.

Rose had noticed nothing but with only six days to go before they got to Bombay, her mind was understandably caught up with meeting Jack Chandler, another reason why she shouldn't be burdened with the trivial business of why Frank didn't want her. It was a shipboard romance. She'd done it again: woven a ridiculous fantasy out of nothing.

The Arabian Nights party was in full swing when Tor went up on deck later that night. The sky flamed with the colours of coral and claret and all the faces of the partygoers were bathed in its light. The crew had scurried around all day, wrapping tables in pink cloths and piling fruits – figs, mangoes, paw paw and sweetmeats – and Turkish delights on the tables. There were coloured lights hung around the deck rails, and what was usually the sports deck had been magically transformed into a sultan's tent.

There was a fire eater inside the tent and a throng of shouting people in masks and Turkish sandals, saris and flowing robes. Colonel Kettering, in a long caftan, swayed to the music of the Egyptian band.

Tor took a deep breath. *Shoulders back. Head up. Smile. Walk.* Her destination was the other side of the crimson deck where she could see her group drinking and laughing.

'Heavens,' said Nigel, bowing elaborately. He was wearing a sharkskin dinner jacket and a fez. 'It's Nefertiti, and how, um, how ravishing she looks.'

'Thank you, Nigel.' Tor kissed him on the cheek.

'Who are you?' she asked Jane Ormsby Booth, the strapping young woman by Nigel's side, who was not a natural candidate for the sari.

'Unsure,' came the good-natured reply. 'Someone foreign.'

'Thank you, darling.' Tor took a glass of champagne from Nigel and arranged herself casually against the deck railings. Her golden mask was in her evening bag in case it all got too much. 'Isn't this divine?'

'It's our last proper sea before India,' said Jane. 'How are we ever going to adjust to real life again? I—'

She was interrupted by a group of people saying, 'Ooooohh!' Rose had appeared in brilliant pink silk, and as the band struck up 'Ain't She Sweet?' she did a little jig in the direction of the colonels and the mems who were sitting at their own table. 'I'm Scheherazade,' she told them gaily, 'and I've got lots of stories that I'm not going to tell any of you.' They laughed indulgently.

The band flared, trumpets sounded and there was another general intake of breath. Marlene and Suzanne had appeared masked and in daring and sumptuous evening dresses, followed by Jitu Singh, swaggering across the deck and flashing his eyes and teeth. He was wearing a blue silk jacket, baggy trousers and soft leather boots into which, Valentino-like, he had casually stuck a dagger. Around his waist there was a leather belt with some cartridges in it and on his head a silk turban with a large diamond.

'Jitu,' they called, 'come over here and tell us who you are.'

He smacked first Marlene and next Suzanne gently on their bottoms and then walked over and salaamed deeply, touching eyes, mouth and chest.

'My name,' he announced, 'is Nazim Ali Khan. I am a Mughal emperor. I bring gold and perfume and diamonds.'

As he nuzzled Tor's hand with his lips, she hoped Frank was watching.

After the sun set in a final blaze of glory, the stars came out and the partygoers danced and then ate sitting on silken cushions arranged inside the tent. Afterwards, they played a parlour game called Who Am I?, in which you had a strip of paper stuck on your forehead with the name of somebody famous on it. You had to ask the others questions to guess who you were. It caused great mirth and when it was ended most of the elderly passengers went to bed.

The Egyptian musicians were ferried back to their villages – their boats causing a brilliant bubbling mass of phosphorescence. The resident band appeared and played breathless foggy late-night music; couples danced cheek to cheek; shadows were seen kissing in the far corners of the deck.

Tor watched it all from a table littered with snapped streamers and lipsticked cigarettes. Her dress was damp with perspiration and she had the beginnings of a corn on her heel. Nigel had just left and she was summoning up the energy to go to bed when Frank suddenly arrived at her side. He looked pale and out of sorts.

'Have you had a good evening, Tor?' he said with unusual formality.

'Marvellous,' she said. 'How was yours?'

'I'm tired. I need a drink.' He poured some wine. 'You?'

'No, thank you.'

They listened to the waves swish and the sleepy croaky sound of the trumpet player.

'Tor,' he said.

'Yes?'

'Hang on a moment.'

He looked at her very intently and for one heart-stopping moment she thought she'd got it wrong and that he might kiss her after all, but instead, he removed a piece of paper from her forehead and gave it to her.

' "Virginia Woolf," ' he read. 'No, I don't think that's you at all.'

'Who do you think I am?' she asked. She'd hoped the question would sound light-hearted, but waited, absurdly tense, in the moonlight. 'Theda Bara? Mary Queen of Scots?'

He shook his head, refusing to play her game.

'I don't know,' he said at last. 'I don't think you do either.'

She felt her face grow hot with dismay. And then she stood up and called, 'Jitu, don't sit on your own, come and have a drink with us.' Not because she wanted him to but for something to do.

'None of us know.' Frank was staring glumly into his glass. 'We—'

But Jitu had arrived. 'I've been summoned by a goddess,' he said, sitting next to her. 'Might a mortal even dance with her?'

She opened her bag and put her mask on, just in case, for Frank's reply had really hurt her, and the whole evening put her in a strange, unhappy, slightly unhinged mood. When a tear rolled down underneath the cardboard she was glad it was too dark for anyone to notice.

She smiled at Jitu, stretching out her arms to him. 'She *will* dance with you. Thank you for asking her.'

He led her out to the dance floor where he held her in an expert impersonal grip. A few couples were dancing cheek to cheek. The band was playing 'Can't Get Enough of You'. She was shocked to see Marlene kissing a cavalry officer she'd seen her with earlier, in full view of the kitchen staff.

'I love this song,' she told Jitu, whose hand had moved an inch or two up her back. 'It's so balloon.'

Why was she always saying things she didn't mean? This song was making her feel miserable, she was longing for bed.

She felt him move closer towards her, his fingers splayed and casually probing her spine. His long-lashed eyes were fixed on hers, as if to say, 'Can I go this far? How about this?'

'So, Jitu,' she was trying to keep him at arm's length, 'did you have a good time tonight?'

He gave that most Indian of gestures: neither yes nor no but a wiggle of the head from side to side.

'It was fine. A necessary party.'

'What a funny word to use.'

'Well, you know.'

'No, I don't.'

'One more sea to cross, then I'm home.'

'But isn't that good?'

'Not for me. I've been away for a long time.' He sighed and moved closer, bringing a whiff of spicy perfume with him. 'I've been so free in Oxford and in London,' he said. 'You know, parties, cosmopolitan things. I shall miss naughty girls like you.'

She wanted him to release her now. He was too male, too highly scented, but she was the one who had summoned him out of the shadows, showing off and commanding him to dance. And now, with such skill that she hadn't noticed, he had danced her off the small moonlit floor and into a dark cosy corner near the ship's funnel.

'You have wonderful eyes,' he said when her back was wedged against the wall. 'So big, so blue.'

'Thank you, Jitu,' she said primly.

He put one hand swiftly between her legs and tried to kiss her.

'Jitu!' She pushed him away, horrified.

'You've been drinking,' he admonished, pushing her back. 'You wicked thing,' he breathed.

She felt the tip of his tongue in her mouth. He guided her hand towards the big rubbery thing that had sprung out of him.

'For God's sake, Jitu. Stop it!' she said.

It took every ounce of her strength to push him off, but before she ran downstairs she turned and saw him smack his head with the side of his hand; he was as confused as she was.

Chapter 17

The day after the party, Viva, pale-faced from lack of sleep and air, sat on a deckchair in the shade trying not to think about Guy for a few moments. They'd just passed Steamer Point and the *Kaisar* was surrounded by a tribe of young Arab boys in little canoes, all of them naked except for white loincloths. They were waiting for coins to be flung into the shark-infested waters around them. When the anna coins were flung, the boys hurled themselves into the bright green depths, vanished from sight and then, after a long interval, burst out again, appearing one after the other, their woolly heads dyed red with lime and henna leaves and usually with a coin between shining teeth.

The contrast between these exuberantly alive boys and the white and slug-like Guy, who had not stirred from his cabin for days now, could not have been starker. Viva, looking longingly down towards the water, checked her watch and with a deep sigh went down to his cabin again.

When she walked in, he was lying in bed playing with a crystal wireless set, unshaven and miserable-looking. He had a sheet and a blanket wrapped around him even though the temperature was around ninety-seven degrees.

The cabin was now littered with papers and old sweet wrappers and some nuts and bolts that he'd removed from his wireless. He'd forbidden the cabin steward to enter his room for the last two days and became irritable when Viva tried to tidy up.

She switched on the fan. The smell of old socks and stale air moved around the room and a few sweet wrappers flew away.

'Are you feeling any better this morning, Guy?' she asked.

'No,' he replied. 'I'd like you to get off my airwaves for a start.'

Her heart sank. She hated this wireless talk.

'I'm not quite sure what you mean when you say that,' she said.

'You do know,' he said. He gave her a bright I-wasn't-born-yesterday sort of look. 'You know you know.'

'Guy,' she tried again, 'Dr Mackenzie is coming to see you today. He needs to decide the best thing to do with you. We'll be in Bombay in five days' time. Your parents will be there.' He closed his eyes when she said that but she ploughed on. 'The thing is that Dr Mackenzie says there are quite a few people in the ship's sanatorium with upset stomachs but he can easily make room, if that's the best place for you.'

'I'm not ill.' He pulled his lips back over his teeth and looked over her head. 'Why do you keep telling people I am?'

She ignored this.

'What do you want me to do today?' she said. 'I think Frank will be looking in on you too in half an hour.'

'Stay until he comes and then go.' He sounded half asleep again, and was thumping his pillows.

'Before you nod off, Guy, I do think you should wash yourself and get the steward in here to clean your cabin,' she pleaded. 'Do it before Dr Mackenzie comes.'

'Can't,' he mumbled. 'Too tired.'

While he slept, she watched him warily. Doctor Mackenzie, who'd talked to him once but only for five minutes, seemed keen to avoid having him in the san.

Frank wasn't sure. Every night now since Port Said, he'd come down to sit with her in Guy's cabin. When Guy had fallen asleep, she and Frank had sat together in the half-light, talking to each other about a range of things – books they liked, music they liked, travel – nothing too personal except for one night when he'd told her about his brother, Charles.

'He didn't die at Ypres,' he said in a low and scarcely audible voice. 'It's just easier to say that to most people. He was invalided home. He had injuries to his throat and trachea, and he wrote down on a piece of paper that he would like me to stay with him until the end. He asked me to talk, so we held hands, and I wittered on.'

'About what?' Viva felt herself stiffen – too much emotion in the room.

'Oh, I don't know,' his voice was far away, 'daft things: family cricket matches at Salcombe where we went for summer holidays, camping trips in the New Forest, eating Eccles cakes in Lyon's Corner House, a trip to the National Gallery where we saw the Turners for the first time, family meals, the usual sort of stuff. It was difficult for him though – he would whisper something to me and then I'd tell him what I remembered.'

Frank said it had been the strangest five nights of his life and the saddest, and that afterwards he had felt so relieved it was over that he'd gone out and stolen a chocolate cake from the pantry and eaten it all by himself and then felt dreadfully ashamed, but it was the sheer relief of knowing that his brother wouldn't have to live with his dreadful injuries.

Viva fell silent after this outburst – what was she supposed to say? What if he cried in front of her?

'Do you think that's why you became a doctor?' she said at last.

'Possibly,' he'd said, standing up. 'It's a fairly impressionable age, eighteen – Charles was ten years older than me.'

He'd turned towards Guy and adjusted his blanket. 'I'm worried about this chap,' he said in a brisk new voice, 'and the amount of time you have to spend with him. It's not healthy, and it's not much fun for you.'

She'd gazed at him mutely, conscious of having failed as a confidante.

'No, it's not,' she said. 'But what can one do?'

'It's tricky, but I think it's time to explain the situation to Rose and Tor, for their safety if nothing else. They must be wondering where you are.'

'I sort of explained my absence by saying he was ill with an upset stomach.'

She didn't tell him the rest – that when she'd told Tor she'd reacted very strangely.

'Oh, don't bother to make up a story,' she'd said with an icy look. 'I knew it from the start.' And then she'd walked off in the other direction.

Dr Mackenzie was due in half an hour. She sat down to wait for him.

Reading was impossible in Guy's cabin, because he liked to sleep with the curtains closed, and writing seemed temporarily beyond her; all she felt capable of at the moment was a kind of dull worrying about him and about her. Everything was starting to feel precarious.

But then came a small break in the clouds. She'd just crept to the sink in his bathroom to wash her face when she heard him singing softly behind the thin partition wall. It was a song she remembered her own ayah singing '*humpti-tumpti gir giya phat.*'

She put her head round the door. But the mound of bedclothes was silent again.

'*Talli, talli, badja baba,*' she sang to him and his pleased snort felt like the first bit of good news she'd heard all morning.

'Did they all sing the same songs?' He opened one bloodshot eye.

'Probably,' she said. 'Mine told me lots of stories that began "*Ecco burra bili da* – there was a large cat,"' she said sing-song, like an Indian.

'You can tell me a story if you like.' His voice sounded softer, more childish.

Her mind raced furiously and then went blank.

'Tell me about your school.'

'Um, well, *ecco burra bili da,*' she said to play for time. 'I'll tell you about the first time I went back from India and saw my prep school if you like.'

The mound under the bedclothes moved again; she heard another soft grunt.

'Well, it was a convent boarding school in North Wales. I was seven years old. My mother, my sister and I came back on the ship together, we stayed at a small hotel close to Waterloo Station in London, and there Josie and I changed into our grey uniforms and blue shirt and tie. Is this boring you, Guy?'

'No, no, keep going.' He shifted impatiently.

'My mother had seen our school, but we hadn't. I remember that we walked up a pebbly beach together and I looked up and saw this gaunt, grey, forbidding place on the edge of the cliff. To stop my mother crying I said, "Don't worry, Mummy, at least it isn't that place." She had to tell me it was.'

'Did they beat you?' His face had appeared above the blankets. His mouth had dropped open into a perfect round. 'Were they horrible too?'

'They were very strict, we were hit on the hands with rulers and made to do penances, but that wasn't the worst thing. Homesickness was, missing India.

'In India we'd step over beaches as soft as silk, we swam in water as warm as milk. At school we had to crunch over huge, sharp pebbles into grey waves that smacked you bracingly round the face. The nuns had all sorts of strange punishments – one of them, Sister

Philomena, she wore a leg brace, used to make us stand in a bath if we were naughty, then she'd turn the hose on us.'

He gave a short bark.

'Go on, go on,' he said eagerly, 'you're good at this.'

She hesitated. This was the part she wasn't sure about telling him.

'I was so unhappy that I decided to make myself really ill. I used to pour the contents of my water jug over my blouse at night and sit by an open window and hope to get some tragic kind of illness that would make everyone feel sorry for me and make Mummy come and take me back to India.'

'What happened then?' His breath smelt when he left his mouth open like that. She reminded herself to try at the very least to get him to clean his teeth before he saw Dr Mackenzie.

'Nothing much. I got a very bad cough and spent a week in the san, and then things got better. I made friends.'

Damn. Not very tactful, when he'd seemed so friendless.

'Looking back,' she resumed quickly, 'I just wish somebody had told me that schooldays are often a pretty dreadful time of your life, but that they go so fast, they really do, and other things like being independent, making your own money, your own decisions, are so much more fun later.'

'I don't think I'm going to have fun later,' he said. He sat up and lit a cigarette and when the smoke had cleared, looked her in the eye. 'You see, I've more or less decided to kill myself.'

'Guy, please. Don't even say that as a joke.'

'It's not a joke,' he said. 'I wish it was.'

She knew that she should reach out to him, touch his hand, put her arm around him, but the smell of his socks, the heat, the pointless gloom of it all, made it impossible.

'Guy, please! Get up, get dressed, clean your teeth, do something. There's so much to look at outside, the canal is so narrow in places you can stand on the ship and see children and flamingos, pelicans, geese. It's extraordinary. Do get up. I'll take you up, I'll stay with you.'

'I might, but I'm still going to kill myself, you know.' He gave her a sneaky infant grin. 'You'd better tell Dr Mackenzie that when you see him. He should know that too.'

'Well, you can tell him yourself, he's coming to see you this morning.'

'I don't want him in now. I've changed my mind,' he said. 'He's on my airwaves too.'

She looked down at him. The skin around his eyes was still yellowish and marbled, but she could see it healing day by day. It was his eyes and their strange scattered expression that troubled her. This was the moment she decided to get help.

The ship's surgery was on B deck and ran from nine-thirty until noon, when it closed for lunch. When Viva arrived at five past twelve, she stubbed her toe on the door.

She ran downstairs again and in desperation knocked on Tor and Rose's door, not expecting to find anybody in.

Tor opened it. She was barefoot and had a dab of face cream on both cheeks.

'Look, I wonder if you could help me?' said Viva. 'I'm in a bit of a pickle.'

'Oh?' Tor's frozen expression hardly changed.

'Can I come in?'

Tor's shrug wasn't enthusiastic but she stepped back from the door.

'Look, I'm sorry I raced off the other day,' Viva started and, because Tor was looking grand and blank, added, 'You know, at Shepheard's, when we were having such a good day.'

'Good for you, maybe,' was Tor's strange reply.

Viva spent the next ten minutes trying to explain about Guy and his increasingly odd behaviour and how impossible it had been trying to decide where to put him.

'I didn't tell you before because I didn't want to worry you,' she said. 'Frank's been wonderful, he's given him sedatives and me moral support, but neither of us feel it's right to keep you in the dark any more. Guy was expelled from his school. He stole things from the other boys. There may be a good reason for this – his parents keep him very short of money – I haven't been able to discuss it with him, but it's only fair to warn you.'

It was a surprise to feel Tor's hand on her shoulder and then to feel her quick hug.

'I'm sorry,' she said. 'Poor you – you look absolutely done in,' and then she shook her head and hugged her again. 'I've been so cheesed off with you, but don't let's talk about that now, this is important.'

*

Tor opened up a miniature of Drambuie, split the contents between two glasses, and said, 'Are you sure he's as bad as you say? I mean, I was fairly doolally myself at his age. I was always threatening to kill myself.'

'No, Tor, I'd like to think that, but this is different: much worse.'

'And my own father is quite odd at times too,' continued Tor, 'but that was mustard gas during the war. The thing is to give him plenty of treats, something to look forward to each day. I could take my gramophone in and play him some tunes.'

'Oh, Tor, you are kind.'

'I'm not very kind actually,' said Tor, 'but we'll be in Bombay in a blink of an eye, so surely between us all we can keep him amused, then it's his parents' hard cheese.'

Rose appeared, pink from a game of deck quoits.

'What's going on here?' she said. 'A drinking den? Can anyone join?'

Tor sat her down and put her in the picture, ending up with 'So I'm sure the poor child doesn't need flinging in the brig or whatever they call it.'

'Don't feel you have to say yes,' said Viva, noting Rose's slight hesitation. 'I would understand.'

'Well, I would like to talk to Frank first,' Rose said.

'Oh, of course.' Tor smiled. 'We've all got to talk to Dr Frank.'

'And aren't you forgetting something, darling?' Rose looked at Tor.

'What?'

'Those noises you heard him making.'

'What noises?' said Viva.

'Do them,' said Rose to Tor.

Tor started to groan theatrically. ' "Oh my God! Ow! Oh God!" I thought someone was killing him. I should have gone to help him.'

'It was probably best to leave him alone.'

'Why?' both of them said in unison.

'Well.' Viva looked at the carpet. 'Those are the sounds boys make when they're masturbating.'

'What?' Rose looked bewildered.

'Well, you know, they touch their thing and it makes them feel excited, happy.'

All three of them went pink.

'What?' Rose still looked confused. 'What are you talking about?'

'Well, to put it another way, it's how a man's body goes when he is about to make love or a baby.'

'Oh my gosh.' Rose swallowed. 'But he's so young. Are you sure?'

'No, of course I'm not sure, but that might be what it was. I'm pretty sure he didn't need your help.'

They looked at her, shocked and impressed.

'And is that all you're going to say about it?' said Tor. 'Come on, Viva, for once in your life *spill the beans*. You know so much more than we do.'

'Later maybe, not now.'

'Will you *promise* to come back later and tell us the rest? We haven't had a bishi for days.' Tor's face was on fire. 'And I do think there comes a time when one has to know everything.'

Poor Rose still looked so bewildered that Viva made a reluctant decision.

'I'm not an expert,' she said. 'I've only had one lover, I'll tell you about him later.'

'The love bits as well as the story,' said Tor.

'Maybe,' Viva said distantly, although she never wanted to think of him again.

Chapter 18

THE INDIAN OCEAN, 500 MILES FROM BOMBAY

Although Rose had decided to avoid the boy next door as much as possible, she had started to feel a strange and unhappy kinship with him. Viva had told her that he hadn't seen his parents for ten years, that his terror was growing as they drew closer to India. She said he now slept with his head muffled under thick blankets.

She understood. Yesterday when she'd used the term 'fiancé' to describe Jack to one of the mems, the word had stuck in her mouth like a pair of badly fitting false teeth. And this morning when she'd woken up, she'd actually been sucking her thumb, something she hadn't done for years. She'd picked up the photo of a uniformed Jack dressed up to the nines in his brass buttons and swords and wearing a strange proud smirk, almost willing her heart to swell with *something* at the sight of it, but what she'd really felt was an almost giddying sense of loss. In two days' time they'd be there, her goose would be cooked and one door would close for her on her childhood and a sort of freedom, and another would open on a world as foreign to her as the moon.

This thought brought a gnats' swarm of other fears into her brain. Would Jack even recognise her after their six months apart? And assuming he did recognise her, would he be disappointed? The setting for that first kiss at the Savile Club – the moonlight, the staircase, the gambolling cherubs above – could not have been much more perfect, but now was now, and so much depended on where you met a person and how you were feeling that day. When she stepped off the ship, every flaw highlighted by a merciless sun, would he look at her and think, *Huge mistake*? Or would she look at him and know in an instant *I got it wrong – he's not the one*?

In the bathroom, she filled the basin with water and splashed her face angrily. It was odd, she thought, tying back her hair and putting two spots of cold cream on her cheeks, not to have told Tor how nervous she was feeling. It felt like an act of disloyalty, but whether to Jack or to her oldest friend she could not tell, that was how scrambled up her thoughts had already become. She dared not think about her parents – she'd cried herself to sleep several times on the voyage even thinking about how unhappy they would feel now that she'd really gone. She couldn't bear to think of the most trivial things connected with Park House, like who would play chess with Daddy, and take him a cup of tea and a piece of lemon cake in the afternoon, or how would Copper feel now that she was no longer around to mince up apples and carrots for him. They'd feed him, but no one would know that special place underneath his chin where he liked to be scratched and she'd been too shy of seeming babyish to tell them.

She brushed her hair. Should she wash it today? Now that they were out in the middle of the Indian Ocean, everyone went on about how much fresher and more vital the air seemed; all of them dripped with sweat by lunchtime.

Even Tor, her thoughts resumed, had never been rash enough to give her life away to a man she hardly knew, and anyway, she seemed to be palling up with Viva and helping the boy next door.

That morning for instance, Tor had taken off with her portable gramophone and a stack of 78s, and right now Rose could hear the muffled sounds of 'Blue Skies' and three voices singing, 'Nothin' but blue skies from now on . . .'

The boy's mood, according to Tor and Viva, was still very up and down, but Tor had discovered he had a passion for jazz and for cinema and during his good moments she nattered away to him like an old friend.

Last night, Tor had told her, she'd had a real heart to heart with him. Guy had even talked with remorse about stealing from the boys at school. He said he'd done it because they all came back with cakes and buns, which they shared around. He wanted treats to share around. He said when he went to stay with relatives during the holidays, they were cross with him for arriving empty-handed.

Rose had failed to be moved by the twisted logic of this story. In fact, thinking about the boy released the gnats again. Call her selfish, but she actually didn't want to step off the boat with this slightly odd child as part of her set. He'd probably start smoking and scowling and swinging his hips, or wear that ghoul-like overcoat. What would Jack think of that?

She personally thought that they should have handed him over to

Dr Mackenzie right away, and had said so quite firmly when the matter had been discussed over drinks with Frank. But Tor, who had previously been so mean about him, had annoyed Rose by turning out to be the sympathetic one. She'd said they could all form a safety circle round him until he was handed over to his parents in a few days' time.

They'd missed their chance anyway now: a consignment of bad Indian Ocean oysters had laid three passengers low. There were no more beds available in the san.

Rose closed her eyes and put her head against the cabin wall. Another kind of music was coming from next door: Indian raga music, hesitant and foggy and infinitely sad. When it stopped, she heard Tor's voice, blunt and jolly, followed by a burst of laughter.

Dear Tor, she thought suddenly, with her beloved gramophone and her music and her hunger for life. It was so clear that she still had the most appalling crush on Frank. Those huge eyes hid nothing.

The thought that Tor was now keeping secrets from her too made Rose feel sad, but in a way she was relieved not to have to discuss him. Frank was great fun and very attractive but he wasn't suitable. First of all, he was a doctor and Mrs Sowerby wouldn't think him good enough for Tor. He was also, Rose suspected, quite bohemian in his approach to life, an unsettled sort of character. So many men were since the war, or so her mother had told her.

Last night at supper when she'd asked him about his plans, he'd said that he was determined to go up north and join his old university professor in some research in Lahore into some ghastly sounding illness, but that he also planned to travel. He said his life was 'a work in progress', which was all very well but . . .

Then he'd turned to Viva, who he was clearly more than a little in love with, and said, 'What do you think I should do?' and she'd replied, almost coldly, 'Why do you ask me?' and turned away. It was odd, when they seemed to be spending more and more time together, that she should treat him like that, but Viva was a dark horse, no question about that, and, although it went against the grain, maybe Tor's mother was right when she'd advised her daughter to 'always keep the men in your life a little hungry'. Poor Tor, who bounded around men like a hopeful puppy, seemed to get her heart broken over and over again.

She was cross with herself for having such dreary thoughts about love and its dangers. Mummy had warned her that most brides got cold feet before their weddings; maybe this was nothing more than that. What she needed to do was to start packing and stop thinking. She should stitch the hem of that skirt that needed mending for a start.

A small cloth bag landed softly on the floor as she took her sewing case from the chest of drawers. Oh God! Here was something else she'd pushed firmly to the back of her mind: the birth-control sponge thingy that Dr Llewellyn had given her. He'd told her she should soak it in vinegar and practise using it several times before her wedding night, but the thought of touching herself down there made her squirm.

Well, here was as good a moment as any. She took the bag into the bathroom and locked the door. She lifted her dress, took down her drawers and, for the first time in her life, poked around for what the doctor had called the birth canal.

There was a moment of panic – she didn't have one, just this slippery corridor of wet skin – and then, ooh yes, she did, and it hurt trying to get the sponge into it. In fact, she thought, red-faced and panting, it was quite impossible, cramming all this into what felt like not enough space. When she parted her legs a little wider and bent down with an unlady-like grunt, the little sponge flipped out of her hand and hit the mirror. And then she sat down and cried with shame and something close to rage.

Why hadn't her mother, or someone, told her about this? All that advice raining down on her from friends and family before she left – about dresses and cholera belts and shoes and snake-bites and party invitations and who it was correct to call on – nothing, not a sausage, not a word about this.

She was washing the sponge under the tap when she heard Tor walk in with Viva. She pushed it back into its coy little gingham bag, hid it in her pocket and walked casually back into the cabin.

'What's the matter?' said Tor. 'You look mis.'

'I'm absolutely fine.'

'No you're not,' said Tor. 'Don't be silly. You've been crying.'

'Well . . .' Rose, glanced at Viva. She was about to say something general and philosophical about the ship arriving soon and it being quite a big moment for all of them when she burst into tears.

'Do you want me to leave?' Viva asked.

'No, stay,' said Tor, although Rose would have rather she'd left. 'All for one and one for all.'

Rose smiled politely. 'I'm sorry about this,' she said to Viva. 'I'm being such a fool.'

And then because there was the faintest chance that Viva would know about it, and it was really her last chance, she took the bag out of her pocket and showed them the sponge.

'It's this birth-control thing.' Her face was twisted with the effort of trying not to cry. 'Do you have any idea what I'm supposed to do with it?'

'What is it?' Tor picked it up. 'What a dear little thing.'

'Oh shut up, Tor!' Rose snapped. 'It's not. It's awful.' She snatched it back and held it towards Viva, swallowing hard.

Viva leant over and looked at it. 'I'm sorry,' she said, 'I haven't the foggiest. Hang on.'

She raced back to her cabin and returned with a thick book in a plain brown wrapping, titled *Ideal Marriage*.

'I found it in a bookshop near the British Museum,' she explained. 'I hate being in the dark about anything so I bought it.'

All of them sat down on the bunk, Viva in the middle with the book.

'Do you want me to look up sponges, darling?' said Tor, who was looking contrite. She took the book from Viva's hands. 'It's bound to be in there – budge up. Now, index, where are you?' She turned the pages. 'Here we are: love as abstract concept; love as personal emotion; the language of the eyes; sexual efficiency of small women – what on *earth* could that mean? Bodily hygiene, mental hygiene, afterglow. There must be a sponge section if we look hard enough.'

'Don't bother.' Rose's eyes were focused on a pretty Persian rug between the bunks. 'I'm sure I'll work it out eventually.'

'Look, Rose,' said Tor sternly. 'This is not the time to back out. What are you going to do in Poona when Viva's not there? It's awful feeling stupid,' Tor went on. 'When I started my monthlies, nobody had told me a thing so I was sure I was bleeding to death. My mother was away in London, so I told my father, and he practically died of embarrassment; he walked in with some old rags and his regimental tie and never spoke of it again.'

Rose got up. She hated this kind of talk, but Tor wouldn't let it go.

'Rose, sit down,' she said. 'Viva, we're going to have a glass of Drambuie and read this book.'

'But it's morning, Tor,' chided Rose.

'I don't care,' said Tor, 'drink this.'

Rose took a sip of Drambuie and then another, grateful for the blurring effect of the liqueur.

'This book is hopeless,' Tor said after a while. 'You promised to tell us, Viva, and you're the oldest. Start with kissing and work up. I mean, I've obviously kissed men, even Rose has, but how do men like it best?'

'I am honestly no expert.' Viva looked longingly towards the door.

'Viva! Speak!' Tor commanded.

'This is what I know about kissing,' said Viva at last, 'but bear in mind I've only had one love affair, not thousands. The first thing to remember is that if you stand close enough to practically any man he will almost certainly want to try and kiss you. If he does, when a man angles his head towards you it's better to go the other way in order to avoid the nose bang.' Hoots of laughter here. 'Also, although I didn't exactly experience this, I understand that some kisses are a bit like music, sometimes passionate and probing, sometimes soft, and I think the general idea is to sort of let the man conduct them so you're not kissing away like mad when he's trying to do a butterfly kiss or something like that.'

'I did kiss Jack,' Rose dragged her eyes away from the rug, 'but I'm sure I didn't do any of that – it all sounds very scientific. But how lucky for you,' she added tactfully, 'to have someone bother to teach you what to do.'

'Was I?' Viva looked down. 'Maybe . . .' She fiddled with her drink for a while. 'He was not really a teacher, or at least,' she added mysteriously, 'not someone I wanted to learn from.' Viva was almost stammering. The memory of this man seemed to make her sad.

'Finish this.' Tor poured about quarter of an inch of liqueur in each of their glasses. 'I have a big question to ask Viva too.'

'Ask away,' said Viva, draining her glass, 'but I am honestly not the font of all wisdom, simply the owner of the book.'

'Well, I'm going to ask anyway, because you *might* know.' Now Tor looked embarrassed. 'I think I did a very stupid thing with Jitu Singh the other night.'

Rose gasped.

'No, it's all right, nothing like that,' Tor assured her. 'Oh, darling, you should have seen your face – you went *white*.'

She told them about how she'd called him over and flirted with him and asked him to dance and then his pounce.

'The thing is,' Tor ended, 'I suppose in a way I was stupid, but are ll Indian men absolute beasts like that? Should one be really much more careful with them?'

'Of course they're not beasts,' said Viva. 'But I do think we confuse them.'

'How?'

Viva paused for a while, before saying, 'Well, someone like Jitu has probably seen for himself that some white women are easier than their own countrywomen to get into bed. They see us mingling freely with men who are not relations and dancing in public places. In India, only prostitutes and dancing girls can do that. I don't mean you, Tor, but in their own country, Indians see the mems having affairs, or flirting quite openly in a way none of their women would dare, so why shouldn't we confuse them?'

'So, they're mad for us?' Tor was agog.

'I don't even know if that's really true,' said Viva. 'The lady writer I used to work for who had once lived in India for years said that most Indian men don't find European women particularly attractive. They think we look like uncooked pastry. But still, they are men and we are women, and a white woman is a curiosity and for some a status symbol.'

'But are they more hot-blooded?' Tor wanted to know.

'Probably,' said Viva. She was almost blushing as she said, 'I'm not sure.'

All of them breathed out together as though they'd inhaled some intoxicating gas, and then laughed a little shamefaced.

'So we should be more careful,' said Tor.

'Yes.'

'How thrilling.'

'Darling, please,' said Rose, 'I really do think we should go up and have some lunch.' Rose wanted to stop thinking about this now. The cabin was too hot and she felt a little sick.

'Let's drink a toast to, I don't know, *afterglow*.' Tor pulled a silly face.

'You are such a twit.' Rose pinched her, thinking, *I'm going to miss you so badly*.

When they got to the cabin door, Rose said, 'Viva, will you come to my wedding in Bombay?'

Viva said yes.

Chapter 19

POONA

Many things had frightened Jack during the six years he'd been a cavalry officer. Four months after his basic training in Poona he'd been sent to a remote hill station, near Peshawar, on the north-west frontier, to help patrol one of the most dangerous and unstable borders in the world. After nights spent on horseback on mountainous roads where you waited for every shadow to kill you, the muscles on your neck stood out like organ stops.

Pig-sticking, a regimental passion and one of the most dangerous sports in the world, had terrified him for a while. You rode across rough country at a racing gallop, often unable to see further than five feet ahead of you the dust was so thick.

On the day his best friend, Scuds, died pig-sticking, he'd seen Scuds' horse put its foot down the foxhole, watched him catapult through the trees and then heard the sickening crack of his neck breaking.

India frightened him. He'd once watched a Bombay crowd drag a motorist from his car, cover him in petrol and turn him into a shrieking funeral pyre because the man had accidentally knocked a child down.

But this was a new kind of fear. It clung to him like black netting. The thought that Rose was hours away now; the idea that in ten days' time he'd be married. *I don't know you.* He'd sat up in bed this morning with the words booming in his head. He'd tried for months now to hold on to her in his mind – that shy schoolgirly peck in the reading room at the Savile Club, a picnic at her parents' house – but she'd suddenly gone, like a pleasing scent or one of those vague dreams that hangs around the edge of your consciousness when you wake. And now the whole thing was starting to feel like a hideous prank, a bad dream that wouldn't end. And soon this living dream would be a matter of public spectacle.

The memsahibs at the club had already told him how excited, how *thrilled* he must be feeling, which made him feel like an awful fraud. The *Pioneer Mail* had phoned him yesterday to find out the correct spelling of her maiden name – Wetherby? Whetherby? – and where exactly she came from in England, and he'd actually had to disguise an embarrassing pause while he marshalled these most elementary facts about her. The marigolds the servants now placed regularly in front of her photograph only served to make him feel more wretched and fraudulent.

The improbability of it all was making him feel light-headed and for the first time in years he yearned for his father. He wanted to go for a ride with him as they had a few times in the old days when there was a problem to thrash out; to hear him speak bluff, sensible words about all chaps getting windy in the weeks before they were married. But this was daft and he knew it: the old man had made a pig's ear of his own marriage and they'd never really discussed feelings anyway.

He'd also thought of confiding in Maxo – Lieutenant Maxwell Barnes – the stammering, humorous man who was one of his best friends in the regiment. He and Maxo had made friends during the riding-school period of his training at Secunderabad, they'd camped out together and once been held at gunpoint by a mob near Peshawar; or maybe Tiny Barnsworth, the six-foot gentle giant he played polo with four days a week during the season and who he got on well with. But the moment never seemed to come and besides, there was a rule in the mess about not talking about women.

He checked his watch. In twenty-two hours' time the ship would arrive; the fear spread from the muscles in his neck to his stomach, which was growling. At six o'clock that night, he would drive to Cecilia Mallinson's house in Bombay to have what she'd called 'drinkies' with her before the girl arrived.

He'd met Cecilia, 'Call me Ci Ci', twice during the past month, and found her disconcerting with her bright stream of clever chat and her hooded, knowing eyes. She'd asked him over to the club to have what she called a little 'gup' about wedding invitations and dresses and to talk over dates and plans for the hectic round of pleasures she'd planned for the girls in the ten days before the wedding.

'Of course, you don't have to come to all of them.' She'd crossed her legs and blown a plume of smoke in his direction. He loathed women smoking; the bright stain of her lipstick on two cigarette butts disgusted him.

'I shan't be able to,' he'd said bluntly. 'I'm afraid the regiment is on partial alert with the Awali Crisis. It's even possible we may have to go up north again soon.'

'Oh gosh.' She'd waggled her head and smiled at him. 'Does the little woman know about this?'

'What little woman?' It was rude of him to snap at her, but honestly, what a cheek.

'Rose, of course.'

'No,' he said. 'Not yet. I thought we should get to know each other first.'

Twenty-one hours to go. To calm himself he went down to the stables and walked into the stable of his favourite horse, Bula Bula. The name was Urdu for nightingale and the horse had been a miserable runt when they'd first met. Then it had no name and had never been out of its stable. Now, Bula's hard muscles shone with his daily grooming. Jack could pluck a handkerchief off the ground from his back at full gallop. He'd taught Bula to lie quiet under a pile of straw while other riders ambushed a raiding party, all good training for men and horses.

'Bullsy, old chum.' He found the spot in the hollow of the jaw that made the horse almost stop breathing with pleasure. 'My B.B. My Bullsy boy.'

He moved his hand to his horse's mane, kneading it between his fingers, and felt his horse lean against him in bliss. It was so easy with horses if you took the trouble to get to know them – the stabled ones particularly were so hungry for touch.

'Morning, sahib.' His groom popped out from underneath the horse, saluted and went back to his order of grooming: five minutes for each horse's back, ten for the belly and five for the face. Then on with the gleaming bridle, the blue and gold saddlecloth, oil Bula's shoes, dust his face, squeeze his glossy neck again. He was feeling better already. Clatter of hooves, Maxo and Tiny had ridden into the yard and were calling for him. He watched them for a moment from the stable, against the dazzling sky. Tough young men in their prime. His best friends.

He saw them smile at him the way people smile at funerals. Everybody knew in the tight world of the regiment that when you married things changed.

Five minutes later they were coated in red dust, shouting, galloping like savages up the long side of the polo pitch, where they played a boys' game of polo pretending to clock balls to each other, and then they took the long red path that led up to the racecourse where the horses leapt forward again, their hooves pounding the red dirt, their sides sopping with sweat.

And it was here that he found himself shouting and crying at the same time, grateful that nobody could see him. It felt like the last day of his life.

Three hours later Jack was sitting in Colonel Atkinson's office. He was shaved, bathed, uniformed, subdued.

His commanding officer was a cheerful red-faced man who spoke fluent Urdu and loved amateur theatrics. Jack liked him and admired the way he hid his more steely qualities, but today Atkinson was fiddling distractedly with the horseshoe that was his paperweight and soon Jack understood why.

'We had some rotten news last night from Bannu,' he said. 'Three of our men up there were ambushed and have disappeared. I'm going to make an announcement this morning. Reynolds, who's the senior man up there, is almost certain more attacks are planned.'

'I'm sorry to hear that, sir.'

'We all are, but the point is, it's not going to stop and it's almost certain we're going to have to take some more of you up there, and we'd like you to command a company. The timing, I know, is wretched.'

'When, sir?'

'Couple of weeks, maybe sooner. I'm sorry if this throws your wedding plans but my hands are tied.'

The colonel's look, more exasperated than contrite, said it all. Everybody knew he didn't approve of his men getting married until they were at least thirty.

'Not your fault, sir. It's an honour.' And it was, normally he would have been excited.

'Will your wife cope?'

The dry mouth, the pounding heart began again.

'I'm sure she will, sir.'

'And Chandler.'

'Yes, sir?'

'Good luck.'

'Thank you, sir.'

Chapter 20

Tor and Rose's trunks had been packed and placed outside their cabin, when Nigel knocked on their door.

'Message from the captain,' he stammered. 'Last service at sea will be at four-thirty this afternoon in the grand salon. Message from me, I have a large bottle of champagne that needs attention in my cabin at one o'clock.'

'Oh, Nigel.' Tor put her arms around him and hugged him. 'Do you honestly think you can live without us?'

He hugged her back, pink with embarrassment.

'Nnnnot sure,' he said. 'I'll write and tell you.'

Tomorrow, she knew, he'd take his train back to Cherrapunji, en route to the remote hill station he'd told them was one of the wettest places on earth. He'd mentioned in his offhand, jokey way that three of his predecessors had committed suicide there, driven mad by isolation.

'But at least I shan't have to listen to your damn singing any more.'

For Tor and Rose had taken to singing, 'Oh de painin', oh de pain', in negro spiritual voices when Nigel got low. They sang because they were not ready to listen to bad things being said about India.

'I must fly, I must pack,' he said, 'but don't forget the champagne and tell Viva to come too.'

'I'll ask her but I don't think she slept a wink last night,' said Tor. 'The Glover boy's in a complete tizz about meeting his parents.'

'I feel very sorry for him,' Nigel's clever face grew serious, 'and for Viva – life won't be easy for her in India.'

'Oh, she'll be fine, she's quite grown-up and she's going to be a writer, you know,' Tor boasted. 'And she'll be picking up her parents' things – they've probably left her plenty to live on.'

'She may not be. Fine, I mean. She's too original, too free.'

'Nigel! I hope you're not spoony on her too.'

'Oh, shut up, Tor,' he said sharply. 'You can worry about someone without being spoony about them.'

'But Viva's our font of all knowledge about India. She was born there. She says she feels more at home there than she does in London.'

'She was a child when she left,' he said. 'India's grown up. It's getting more frightening. They don't want us there now, and I don't blame them.'

But Tor's fingers were stuffed in her ears now and she'd started to hum, 'Oh de painin', oh de pain,' until Nigel stopped and howled like a little dog, pretending it was all a joke anyway.

Viva, looking pale and jumpy, turned up later for the drinks party.

She, Tor, Rose, Frank, Jane Ormsby Booth and Marion, another new friend, squeezed into Nigel's cabin.

'Oh delicious, divine.' Tor closed her eyes and held out her champagne flute. 'What a good idea this is.' She was trying with every fibre of her being to show Frank how jolly and excited she felt in spite of their upsetting conversation the night before.

'Not so fast, my child.' Nigel put down the bottle and picked up a book. 'I'm going to read you all a very short poem first. Oh hush! Wretched philistines,' he silenced their groans and cries that they'd all been brought here under false pretences. 'It will take two minutes of your time and you won't regret it. The poem is called "Ithaka", but it might just as well be called "India".'

He sat down close to Viva and started to read.

> 'As you set out for Ithaka,
> Hope your road is a long one,
> Full of adventure, full of discovery.
> Laistrygonians, Cyclops,
> Angry Poseidon – don't be afraid of them:
> You'll never find things like that on your way
> As long as you keep your thoughts raised high,
> As long as a rare excitement
> Stirs your spirit and your body.

> *Laistrygonians, Cyclops,*
> *Wild Poseidon — you won't encounter them*
> *Unless you bring them along inside your soul,*
> *Unless your soul set them up in front of you.'*

'Sorry,' interrupted Jane Ormsby Booth, 'I don't do poetry. What's he on about?'

But Viva and Frank shushed her. Nigel continued:

> *'Hope your road is a long one.*
> *May there be many summer mornings when,*
> *With what pleasure, what joy,*
> *You enter harbours you're seeing for the first time;*
> *May you stop at Phoenician trading stations*
> *To buy fine things,*
> *Mother of pearl and coral, amber and ebony,*
> *Sensual perfume of every kind —*
> *As many sensual perfumes as you can;*
> *And may you visit many Egyptian cities*
> *To learn and go on learning from their scholars.'*

'Did you go ashore at Egypt?' Jane asked Tor. 'The shops were— Oops! Sorry!'

'Carry on, Nigel.' Tor put her hand over Jane's mouth. In the silence that followed Tor heard the rush of the sea.

Nigel began again. For some odd reason he didn't stutter when he read poetry.

> *'Keep Ithaka always in your mind.*
> *Arriving there is what you're destined for.*
> *But don't hurry the journey at all.*
> *Better if it lasts for years,*
> *So you're old by the time you reach the island,*
> *Wealthy with all you've gained on the way,*
> *Not expecting Ithaka to make you rich.*
> *Ithaka gave you the marvellous journey.*
> *Without her you wouldn't have set out.*
> *She has nothing left to give you now.*

'And if you find her poor, Ithaka won't have fooled you.
Wise as you will have become, so full of experience,
You'll have understood by then what these Ithakas mean.'

There was a silence after he'd finished. He popped the champagne cork and filled their glasses. 'To marvellous journeys,' he said. 'To all our Ithakas,' and Tor saw that his eyes were bright with tears.

'Bravo, Nigel,' said Viva quietly. She put her hand on his arm. 'Who wrote it?'

'Cavafy.' He looked at her. 'I knew you'd like it.'

'I do,' she said, and they looked straight into each other's eyes.

'So here's to Phoenician harbours and to Bombay.' Frank took Tor's hand in his and made her giggle nervously.

'To fabulous journeys,' said Viva.

'And to all of you for making this one so ripping,' said Tor with such fervour that they all laughed, except Rose, who was looking pensively towards the horizon.

A little over an hour later, they put on their hats and sat in the upstairs salon, which had been made into a temporary church for the last service at sea. A Union Jack had been draped on a temporary altar, and from the windows they could see the faint blurred outlines of the coast of India.

A large, sweating woman plunged her fingers into the harmonium, and then one hundred or so voices floated out into the clear blue yonder. Tor glanced at them: the long rows of memsahibs, all dressed up today, the colonels, Jitu Singh, the missionaries, the red-faced man who was something in jute, the little children who knelt with their mothers and whose ayahs you could see outside the door in their brightly coloured saris.

The hymn ended, they all knelt down, Rose, who was sitting beside her, was praying so hard her knuckles shone.

Viva walked in late with the boy. He was wearing his outsized suit and looking mole-like and dazed.

Frank came late too. He stood on the other side of the aisle from them, looking so handsome in his full uniform that Tor had to dig her nails into the palm of her hand.

Last night, she'd had a conversation with him that had hurt her very much, although he would never have known it.

They'd taken a turn together around the deck, and it had seemed so romantic with the silky breezes, the ship all lit up like some fabulous glass castle against the starlit night, that she'd thought, *If he's ever going to kiss me properly, it will be now.* But instead he'd looked out in the blackness and given such a heartfelt sigh that she'd asked in what she hoped was a casual tone, 'Frank, what *are* you going to do when you get to India? You've been very sphinx-like about the whole thing.'

He'd looked at her blankly. 'Have I? Well, I'm a sphinx without a secret because I'm pretty much certain now that I will stay in Bombay for a few weeks and earn some money, then I'm going up north, to do some research.'

'Into that blackwater-fever thingy?'

'Yes,' he said gloomily. 'I think I mentioned it before – horrible disease, nobody knows much about it yet.'

Under other circumstances she might have tried harder to draw him out. *All men love talking about themselves – take an interest in his work,* but he'd looked absolutely mis and had fallen silent, and Tor, trying to cheer things up, had said, 'I can't believe we'll be in Bombay to-morrow morning – it really is too thrilling.'

'How sweet you are,' he'd said sadly. 'So eager for everything.'

'Well, aren't you? Come on, Frank, you must be. This is such a big adventure for us all.'

'Not really,' he replied. He'd lit a cigarette and exhaled moodily.

And then in the next five minutes she learnt that she was a brick, a lovely girl, etc., and under normal circumstances just the sort of girl he should be spoony on, but that he was in love with someone else.

Tor had forced herself to nod and smile.

'Anyone I know?'

He'd turned away.

'No. I don't think anyone does.' He'd said something else into the wind which she hadn't caught. And then he turned to her and said with real desperation in his eyes, 'I've tried so hard with her, too hard probably, but she's frozen, all locked up, and now I won't be able to get her out of my head. Oh, Tor, why am I telling you all this? It's too sweet of you to listen.'

'Not at all. What are friends for?' She'd even added a little joke. 'It's what my mother calls doorknob secrets. The things you blurt out suddenly just as you leave a room. And this is the last night on board after all.'

Nobody had been around on deck, so he'd kissed her lightly on the tip of her nose. An uncley sort of kiss.

'And what do you want, you sweet girl? Romance? Babies? Parties?'

'No.' She'd been stung by this. 'More than that.'

'Don't be offended,' he said. The tranced look in his eyes had gone and he was staring at her. 'So what is it?'

'I don't know, Frank.' She'd felt a kind of unhappy mist cloud her mind and then it cleared, and as she looked at him, she felt for one moment that he was her enemy.

Make him feel the important one. And so on and et cetera from all those soppy women's mags, but suddenly she didn't care.

'Something solid. A job. Something that stays with you and can't be taken away.'

'Gosh, are you a suffragette,' he'd said bitterly, 'or has Viva been getting at you too?'

'Darling,' Rose gave her quite a jab in the ribs, 'do stop staring.'

'I wasn't,' said Tor, dragging her eyes away from Frank.

'You were,' hissed Rose, 'simply *gawping*.'

They snuggled closer to each other, friends to the end.

They were singing 'To Be a Pilgrim', and then 'I Vow to Thee, My Country'. Nigel, who was on her other side, tried to make her laugh by singing the descants.

Dear, gentle, clever, funny Nigel. The sort of man she should marry. The stutter put him into her league. She squeezed his arm. Poor Nigel.

And then the music faded and when the captain stood up she was conscious again of the great hum of the ship's engine slowing down, and of the water rushing by. The captain, solemn in his braided uniform, asked them all to put their hands together. He prayed for peace at a difficult time in India's history. He prayed for the peace and welfare of the King and for the glorious British Empire of which they suddenly seemed such a tiny, temporary fragment.

Chapter 21

BOMBAY

Viva spent the morning sorting out the rancid-smelling clothes Guy had refused to send to the wash and generally keeping a wary eye on him. It was partly a way of avoiding herself, for they'd almost arrived. Earlier in the day, standing on the deck and watching Bombay's skyline take shape, she remembered holding Josie's hand on another sunlit day like this. Her father, young and athletically handsome, walking out of the crowd to claim them; her mother, flustered and happy, talking nineteen to the dozen to disguise the slight shyness they always felt at first until they became a family again.

Later, there had always been a celebration lunch in the restaurant on top of the Taj Hotel with its view that filled the eye, with blue skies and boats and birds. This lunch had its rituals: the fresh mangoes craved for at school, then a fiery curry for her father, biriyani for herself, ice cream, sweetmeats, fresh lemonade – all such a treat after school's shepherd's pies and suet stodge. All the days marked off the calendar in her school dorm, gone, all that longing made flesh. She and Josie with the pees again.

Opening her eyes and seeing the skyline shimmer, she felt for a moment almost nauseous with pain, like someone who's tried too early to stand on a broken leg. They were gone, *they were gone.* She'd had fifteen years to get used to it, but this morning the wounds were open and bleeding.

Chowpatty Beach was just across the thin strip of land that was Bombay Island. It was here on their last afternoon in India before going back to school that she and Josie, numb with misery, dived and dived again into the warm turquoise water. Their mother stood on the beach watching them.

'Time to come in, darlings,' she'd called eventually. Josie, thirteen months older and more responsible, headed for shore.

Viva had dug her toes in. 'I'm not coming in,' she'd shouted. 'You can't make me.'

She'd sobbed then, turning her face towards the horizon, so Mummy couldn't see. But she'd come out in the end, what choice did she have?

'Silly old sausage,' her mother had said, and bought her an ice cream.

'Miss Holloway?' The purser's assistant was at her side with a handful of bar chits for her to sign, for herself and the boy. Her stomach knotted again. They were thirty pounds over the twenty-five-pound allowance his parents had sent her. She'd be meeting them in less than an hour.

His father she'd pictured as a taller, beefier version of Guy but with more menacing teeth. *I'm sorry*, she'd imagined him saying, *but let me get this straight. You allowed a boy of sixteen to drink, and then you went ashore and left him on his own in Port Said?*

Who, apart from Frank, would back her up when she tried to tell them how strangely Guy had behaved, and how difficult her position had been. The ship's doctor – having handed her the few pheno-barbitones he called 'emergency rations' – seemed to have lost interest in him entirely. *Well, we've never had any problems with him before*, they'd say and, if the Glovers refused to pay her fare, the result was not quite penury but close.

She had a grand total of one hundred and forty pounds left in the world, wired ahead of her to Grindlays Bank in Bombay, some for emergencies and accommodation, the rest to get herself to Simla to collect her parents' trunk. If she didn't find work almost as soon as she arrived, she had, she estimated, about a month's worth of funds to live on.

Now she could smell India from the ship – spices, dung, dust, decay: elusive, unforgettable. From the harbour came the sounds of cracked trumpets and drums and shouts from the chana wallahs flogging peanuts and gram.

'Madam! Please!' An old man was standing on the deck of a paddle steamer that had drawn up alongside the *Kaisar*. He was holding up a skinny old monkey in a red hat and making it wave at her. 'Hello, madam! Mrs!' Nobody in England would smile at strangers so joyfully. As she put the palms of her hands together and made the

Hindu greeting of namaste, tears came into her eyes. Beyond him, a rainbow-coloured crowd stood on the pier now waiting for them, with one or two khaki-clad Europeans poking up between them like field mushrooms.

She looked at her watch and advanced it by one hour to eleven-thirty – five and a half hours ahead of London. In Earl's Court at this hour, she'd be watching through her basement window the usual parade of ankles, sloshing their way towards the omnibus and the tram.

In Bombay, in early winter, she felt her skin opening like a flower to the sun.

'Viva! Viva!' Tor, looking large and excitable, bounded towards her. 'Isn't this thrilling?'

'Is Rose all right?' Viva asked quickly.

'No, of course she's not, she's downstairs having kittens. She's decided against meeting him on the pier as all the mems will stare. Nigel's gone ahead to find him and to take him down to our cabin.'

'What will he be wearing? Uniform or mufti?'

'Haven't the foggiest, nor has Rose. Isn't that the sort of thing you need to be married to know?' Tor's eyes bulged humorously.

'God, how frightening.'

'Oh, Viva.' The clutch on her arm tightened. 'Please promise not to ditch me the moment we arrive. You can show me around and I'll ask you to parties.'

Viva smiled but said nothing. How could she possibly explain her financial terrors to someone like Tor to whom a monthly allowance, however small, was as natural as blood pumping into veins?

'We're all having drinks tonight at a place called the Taj. Do you know it?'

'Yes.'

'Don't you dare bolt once the ship's landed.'

'I won't.' Shyly she returned Tor's squeeze. She wasn't good at this kind of moment. 'I'd better go down and get Guy up,' she said, looking at her watch.

'Is he all right?'

'Not really. I'll be glad when today's over,' she said.

He came to the door, yawning and bad-smelling and affecting a nonchalance she knew he didn't feel. He was still in his pyjamas and had a chin full of stubble.

'Please, Guy,' she said, 'it's nearly twelve-fifteen. Wash your face, do your hair, get cracking.' Impatience flared up in her again. 'You're sixteen years old, for God's sake,' she wanted to tell him, 'not six.'

'I can't yet,' he'd said. 'There's someone in the bathroom who is on my crystal set again.'

On the night before – they'd been packing and in the middle of what seemed to her a perfectly normal conversation – he'd shaken his head and given a gargling groan, like a soul in hell, that had made her hair stand up on end.

'Why did I do what?' He'd looked at her as if she was the one going mad.

'Look, if you're worried about something, tell me,' she'd said. 'I don't like frightening noises.'

And sure enough, a few moments later, he'd said in a casually offhand voice, 'When my parents arrive tomorrow, will you stay with me? They'll probably ask a lot of very boring questions.'

He'd taken off his glasses, looking naked without them.

'Yes, Guy, I'll stay,' she'd said, 'but give it time. You'll soon feel like a family again.'

'They're complete bloody strangers,' he'd said. 'But thank you for the advice.'

'I know I'm right,' she'd lied. She and Frank had agreed it was important to keep him on an even keel, and he had been given two of the bright pink pills the night before just in case.

And now, they had definitely arrived: she felt the final bump and shudder of the *Kaisar* landing and then a loud roar from the pier.

'Go outside. Go outside and find the blighters.' Guy's voice crackled with nerves. 'Switch off the dratted wireless on your way out.'

Chapter 22

Rose had decided to come up on deck after all. She was holding hands with Tor, digging her nails into the palm of her hand.

'Where is he? Have you seen him?' she said to Tor, who was jiggling up and down.

'Not yet, but I can see Viva.' They looked down towards a blur of faces and watched her work her way through the crowd. A few seconds later, Tor grabbed Rose's hand. 'Oh God!' she said. 'Look!'

Nigel stood next to a tall blond man in a khaki suit holding a bunch of scarlet Canna lilies in his hand. When he saw them, Nigel gave them the most casual wave possible, a mere flick of his wrist. They'd known they could rely on him to be discreet.

Rose's hand tightened into an iron grip.

'I'm going downstairs again,' she told Tor suddenly. 'I don't want everyone staring. Can you wait here and bring him down?'

'Of course I will, darling,' said Tor. 'He's handsome, Rose, isn't he?' Although she'd seen the stern look on his face, his rigid posture.

'Yes,' said Rose faintly.

'When you see him, Rose, don't forget to smile,' said Tor. 'Smile and look relaxed. Oh God, I'm turning into my mother.'

Rose didn't respond. She was staring down again.

'You'll soon get to know him, Rose.'

'Yes,' she said. 'I know.'

Another quick look then Rose ran back down to the cabin again and arranged herself in a casual pose on a wicker chair between the bunks. Feet were pacing above her head, the squeak of shoes running along the corridor. She waited for what felt like an age, listening to the dull thumping in her heart, and then at the knock on the door she sprang to her feet.

'Rose,' said a deep voice. And there he was, standing in the door-way, topi in one hand, flowers in the other. He was taller than she remembered and not as handsome, or maybe that was because his face seemed somewhat contorted.

'Well, hello!' he said. She hadn't remembered him being so hearty either. He handed her the lilies. 'These are for you. They grow like weeds out here.'

When he put his topi down on the bunk, she thought he might kiss her but instead he said, 'May I?' and sat down and spread his muscular legs wide as if he was posing for a rugby photograph. He cleared his throat.

'They're lovely, Jack.' She buried her nose into the scentless flowers. 'Thank you.'

'Nice of that fellow Nigel to come and find me,' he said. 'He seems a decent chap.'

'Yes, he's a civil servant, he's off to – gosh, I can't even remember, how silly. I can find out for you,' as if he was desperate to know Nigel's whereabouts. 'These are really *so* pretty.'

Smiling at the flowers again, she felt a disagreeable blankness where her heart was supposed to be.

'Bit dusty, I'm afraid,' he said. How large he seemed with his big legs spread like that. He seemed to have filled up the whole cabin. 'They've been driven on a motorbike between here and Poona. I hope you don't mind that I haven't got a car yet. I forgot to tell you that.'

'Of course I don't mind,' she said, and he cleared his throat again.

She wished her mother was here with her ready laugh and knack with strangers.

'Tor and I had such a jolly trip,' she said after a while. 'Real life is going to be absolute hell!' The smile died on his lips.

Oh no! What a perfectly idiotic thing to say, she thought. *Now he'll be quite sure I regret the whole thing.*

'Well, you're going to be rushed off your feet here,' he started, and then stopped.

The fan had gone off; her hand resting in his felt embarrassingly sticky.

'Look, there's a slight change of plan about the wedding which I wanted to tell you about before anybody else did.'

When he said this she felt an immediate lightening of her spirits: the whole thing was off, this was a dream.

'Yes, there's been a spot of bother up on the north-west border recently; I can explain it all in more detail soon.' He was sweating, she noticed, and had a dimple in his chin. 'My CO has asked me to join a company up there but I don't know when yet. If there is any change to the date, Ci Ci Mallinson says you can move in with her for a while. The season starts in November, so there'll be masses of parties.'

She laughed a little wildly for a moment. 'Darling.' It felt so strange to be using the word. 'Whatever you think is right.'

Relief flashed across his face like sunlight.

'I appreciate you not making a fuss,' he said. 'I'm afraid the one thing you can rely on in India is that no arrangement ever quite works out.'

Ten minutes later, as they walked down the gangplank together, a thin woman wearing lots of lipstick and a cloche hat stepped out of the crowd to greet them.

'Darlings,' she said. 'Romeo meets Julietta at long last. I'm Cecilia Mallinson, call me Ci Ci.' When she kissed Rose lightly on both cheeks, she smelt strongly of cigarettes and perfume and some pepperminty smell like mouthwash.

'Everything all right?' said Tor in a low voice as they headed towards Ci Ci's car.

'Fine, thank you,' breathed Rose without moving her mouth. 'Simply lovely.'

But then she stopped suddenly. 'Oh, how awful, I forgot to say goodbye to Viva. I can't believe it!'

'Don't worry,' Tor said, 'she knew you were in a state and so was she – the boy's parents had arrived. I gave her our address.'

They followed Mrs Mallinson's smart little hat through the crowd with a team of native porters walking in front of them holding their luggage on their heads. A small girl with a dirty face and matted hair scampered up and tugged at Rose's sleeve.

'No mummy, no pappy, lady must buy.' She clawed at her mouth.

'Ignore, ignore,' their hostess instructed. 'Walk straight on; it's a swindle.'

Rose felt her senses spinning – there was too much to take in: the dazzling sun, the stink of drains and incense, the brilliant saris and dark faces. On the corner of the street, a man stared into a cracked mirror, trimming the hairs inside his nose with a pair of scissors.

Halfway across the road they stopped: a small crowd had appeared to the deafening accompaniment of penny whistles and cornets; they were carrying a papier-mâché elephant on a gaudy throne.

Mrs Mallinson put scarlet nails over her ears, wincing as they passed. 'Simply ghastly,' she said.

Tor was jumping up and down with excitement.

'It's Ganpati,' Jack shouted, 'the Indian god of commerce.'

Rose, squinting at him shyly through the sun, decided he was handsome after all. Very strong, very manly looking.

They drove home in Mrs Mallinson's snazzy little car – a bottle-green Model T Ford. Tor sat in front, exclaiming and laughing at everything, Rose was behind with Jack, absurdly aware of where his square brown knees ended and her pink silk ones began. When Ci Ci swerved to avoid a skinny horse, she fought to keep her legs separate from his – it was all too sudden, too soon.

Ci Ci turned to look at them. 'So, tour guide speaking,' she sang out. She seemed determined to be fun, which made Rose feel even shyer. 'Big pukka palacey-looking place on your left with the dome on top is the famous Taj Mahal Hotel, where we'll be having a party on New Year's Eve. Funny story attached to that,' she drawled. 'It was built by an Indian, offended because he wasn't allowed into another European hotel, and then his architect, some French oaf, put the swimming pool in the wrong place – behind the hotel instead of in front of it and he committed suicide as a result.'

All of them laughed uncertainly except Jack, who didn't laugh at all. He had hairs on the backs of his hands, Rose noticed, fine blond hairs and, now that she had had a little time to think about it, she admired the way he hadn't made a flowery speech to her on the ship. It would take time.

'Coming up on your left, Bombay Yacht Club, where we sail, another favourite watering hole, and beyond that— Oops!'

A sudden stop jammed Jack's leg against hers. A man carrying bananas stepped in front of them and crossed the road.

'And beyond that,' Ci Ci already seemed bored with showing them around, 'India. Full of pagan gods and nothing like Hampshire.'

Rose saw her eyes gleam at them naughtily in her car mirror. She blushed and felt her heart racing. Jack was holding her hand again.

Chapter 23

9 November 1928. YWCA, Bombay. Extract from Viva Holloway's diary.

I mst. write down what happened before it fades. Guy Glover is a rat, he laid a trap for me; he begged me to stay behind with him to meet his parents, who had taken a four-day train journey from Assam where Mr Glover is a tea planter. Given Guy's state of mind (incredibly erratic over the last few days: he says he hears voices through the wireless, or some such nonsense; hasn't slept, smells, no washing, etc.), I felt this right thing to do. Also wanted to collect the balance of the money agreed towards my fare.

Frank had agreed to stay behind to give his professional medical opinion on Guy (Dr Mackenzie having washed his hands of the whole thing), in case things got sticky for me, but at the last minute was needed urgently in san. So I was left to deal with things on my own.

Ten minutes before they arrived, he started to chain-smoke and, at one point, got up, went outside, and banged his head against the wall. When I went to see him he said, to my utter amazement, 'I tried to love you, but you've made things very difficult for me.' All I could think of to say was, 'Guy, why don't you sit down and have a cup of tea.' How ridiculously English!

Eventually, thank God, they came. She, Gwen Glover, drab, tearful little partridge of a woman; Mr G., a red-faced blusterer who immediately shook Guy's hand and clapped him on the shoulder.

'Well done, old boy, you got here in the end,' etc., etc. 'Nice and hot, isn't it?' to me, and 'Have you both had fun?' Fun! wld <u>not</u> be my word for it.

For the first five or ten minutes, Guy played the part of the prodigal son quite well, but when we started to collect his things, Guy suddenly left the room, slamming the door behind him.

While Guy was out of the room I handed over the two letters the school had given me for them. Mr Glover stuffed them in his pocket. He said he didn't have time to read them now, which made me wonder whether he didn't know already about the thieving, the exam results, etc.

I tried to explain (v. quickly, and perhaps, in my anxiety, not v. well) the nervous strain Guy appeared to have been under on the voyage out, and how he'd been under doctor's orders, and then – it only seemed fair to tell them – about how he'd been seen banging his own head against the ship's railings.

'But this is preposterous,' Mr Glover said, turning redder. 'Are you suggesting my son is not mentally sound?'

'Yes, I think I am,' I said. Perhaps I should have been more non-committal.

Mrs Glover started to cry and said something like, 'I knew something like this would happen,' and, 'It was only a matter of time.'

Mr Glover said, 'Shut up, Gwen,' and then, to me, 'How dare you.' He then marched outside and got Guy.

'Sit down on that bed, Guy,' he said, very much the black and white man who would sort this silly mess out in no time at all. 'Miss Holloway claims you got involved in some fisticuffs on board. Thumped a fellow or got thumped or something.'

Guy seemed to have forgotten his declaration of love a few moments before. He looked at me very coldly and shook his head. 'She's a liar,' he said. 'And she drinks; she said to put it all on your bill.'

At that precise and hideous moment, Guy's steward came in with another armful of chits, still unpaid from our bar bill. Mr G., with the air of one handling contaminated mouse droppings, spread them out on the bed. (Mrs G. by this time whimpering and plucking at her dress.)

Mr G. got out a pad and a silver pencil: 'One bottle Pouilly-Fuissé, one bottle Beaumes de Venise . . .' By the time he was finished, the bill was nearly ten pounds – the little rat had been drinking on the sly.

Mr G.'s head seemed to swell with rage like a puff adder's. I was accused of being a drunken, irresponsible liar. If I hadn't been drinking so much I would have been more sensitive to the finer feelings of a boy who hadn't, due to circumstances beyond their control, seen his parents for ten years and was understandably nervous. In conclusion, he had no intention of paying me my money, I was jolly lucky not to be handed over to the police.

Perhaps there was some fear behind his bluster: when I invited him to talk to the ship's doctor to verify my story, he didn't reply, but instead offered magnanimously to pay off the bar chits, provided I signed a note saying I would pay him off in instalments. While all this was going on, Guy, who is either very mad or very clever, stared grandly at the wall as if he had no part in it.

They left on the night train to Assam. One of my last gestures to Guy was to put the packet of phenobarbitone in his pocket. He walked off between his parents, and then ran back and tried to hug me, whispering, '*Non illegitimi te carborundum* – don't let the bastards get you down.' How dare he!

And then I was on my own in the middle of the Apollo Bunder, with dozens of porters swarming around me. I asked a tonga driver to take me to the YWCA, which Miss Snow had told me was a cheap, clean, respectable safe place to stay.

I'm paying two rupees a night here for a single room. The double is three but I simply couldn't stand the idea of sharing, not after what happened. My room, though small (about twelve foot by ten), overlooks a huge and beautiful tree (must buy tree book). It has a single iron bed, a table and a cupboard in the hall where I can hang clothes.

The clientele, as far as I can make out, consists of a mixture of working Englishwomen and Indian women, most working in Bombay as missionaries, students or teachers. The management seem friendly tho' authoritarian. LOTS OF RULES.

I can just about afford the *per diem*, but even this small amount frightens me. I HAVE NO MONEY, or practically none, and if the cheque for my first article does not come through, must try and start any kind of paid work right away.

Later
The lights-out bell here goes at 10.30 p.m.; doors are locked at 11 p.m.

Towards dusk, I went out into the street where the air felt warm and silky. At the corner of the street, an old man was sitting on his heels making *bhel puris* in a frying pan. The taste of them overwhelmed me. *I'm home*, I thought. Ridiculous, really, because Bombay was never home to me. The *puri* seller was delighted by my custom – and my groans. When I was finished, he washed my hands in a bowl of water he kept beside the frying pan. Then he produced a melon and peeled it and sliced it expertly. It was delicious, but I felt I had to pay him extra. I am very worried about money.

The next morning
Woke to cries of water man in street, a cow mooing, motor car, somebody laughing next door.

After breakfast – I ate chapattis and dahl, delicious – I went to look at the noticeboard where three jobs for 'respectable English girls' were advertised.

1) Teacher wanted at a local missionary school. Query. Do you have to be very religious (hypocritical in my case) to teach in such a place?
2) Lady companion to a Mrs Van de Velde, who lives near the Jain Temple on Malabar Hill and wants reliable person to organise correspondence, and hopefully play bridge with her. Unless absolutely desperate, I think I'll avoid being anyone's companion for a while. G.G. has scarred me for life.
3) Advertising agency: J. Walter Thompson seeks English secretary, good typing and shorthand skills. Laxmi Building, the goddess of wealth. Promising. Pity about my non-existent shorthand. I'll write anyway.

When I asked the lady at the front desk about rents for flats in Bombay she alarmed me very much by telling me that no self-respecting Englishwoman on her own would live anywhere but either Malabar Hill or in the Colaba district, where the rents are high. But she then told me that some daring souls – mostly social workers and teachers – had moved out into less salubrious suburbs. One Daisy Barker, apparently a 'damn fine egg', has come out here to teach at Bombay University Settlement, an organisation based in England that has come to India to teach Indian women at university level. I want to meet her.

Another Englishwoman has also recently passed through, en route to teach at an English school up north. The lady at reception seemed anxious to point out that she was a close friend of governors and could have stayed anywhere but had come here to meet a friend. Although these women are probably exceptions, this conversation gave me courage. So not all women out here are of the Gin and It, pig-sticking crowd. It also gave me an idea: why not a series of interviews (perhaps for *Eve* magazine) on these maverick souls? Will write outline tonight.

Work will – *must* – come.

Chapter 24

BOMBAY, FOUR WEEKS LATER

A week before Rose got married, Tor sat on the verandah of Ci Ci's house in Malabar Hill with her feet up, her face gently stroked by blossom-scented breezes. She was writing a long-overdue letter to her mother, who wrote lengthy letters full of unanswered questions every week. The weather in England was, her mother said, beyond dreadful; Mr Thaw, the gardener, had been laid up after slipping on wet leaves and breaking his wrist in the drive; it was impossible to find decent hats in Winchester. But anyway, how was Tor, having a wonderful time? Lots of parties and so forth? How did Rose feel about the wedding being put off for two weeks? Jolly cross, she imagined.

Tor, her pen dithering over the page, didn't quite know how or where to start, for as a matter of fact, far from being cross that the wedding had been delayed Rose had seemed relieved. 'It's given me breathing space,' Rose had explained in that rather careful way that Tor found worrying. And from a perfectly selfish point of view, Tor had felt thrilled to have two extra weeks with Rose in this fairy-tale house.

The house. Well, how to tell her mother, without sending her completely mad with jealousy, quite how perfect this place was and how well her cousin had done for herself, for Mr Mallinson – whom Ci said had done clever things in cotton – seemed to be stinking rich even by the standards of Malabar Hill.

From where Tor sat she could see a curved sloping lawn that led down to the Arabian Sea; a terrace bursting with bougainvillea and jasmine blossom; a dazzling blue sky; and everywhere houseboys, maids, gardeners, sweeping and tidying, raking, washing, picking up and generally making things perfect.

At this precise moment, six servants were putting up the spectacular maharajah's tent that Ci had planned as the centrepiece at the wedding reception next week.

The tent – flamenco pink and inlaid with pieces of glass and rich embroideries – was typical of Ci's famous 'touch'. While the other large houses in this exclusive and largely European part of Bombay had plodding names such as Mon Repos or Laburnum, Ci's was called Tambourine. Inside its marbled hall, a huge glass bird was suspended in a west-facing window where it glowed and spun at sunset as if it had caught fire. Ci's drawing room was full of sherbet-coloured silks and low sofas. In the upstairs guest room, which Tor and Rose shared, there were thick towels in the bathroom and jars of bath salts with wooden dippers in them; a silver-topped biscuit barrel with imported French wafers in it; a leather stationery folder full of thick cream crested writing paper. She and Rose had hardly been able to believe their luck when they first landed here.

The food was heavenly too – not all those warmed-up leftovers – or *réchauffée*s as her mother preferred to call them – you got at home: nest of warmed mince and tapioca puddings and suchlike. Here, there were fresh pineapples in the morning and mangoes and oranges warm from the trees. And no one ever nagged about bathwater or turning lights off or starving people in Africa.

Thinking about it, as Tor was now, chewing the end of her pen, the only real fly in the custard was Geoffrey, a large florid man with caterpillar eyebrows, who did go on a bit about the state of the cotton industry in India, which according to him was about to collapse. But even Geoffrey conveniently disappeared each morning, puttering off in his chauffeur-driven car to God knows where, reappearing each night at the chota peg hour.

Tor unscrewed the top of her pen and sighed. This was agony; there were so many things her mother seemed to want to know. Clearly, her main question – 'Are you meeting lots of nice young men out there?' – hid the cruder sum of 'Has our expenditure on frocks, tickets, etc., made the overall investment worthwhile?' And the simple answer to this – given the non-stop round of parties and picnics Ci had organised – could easily have been: 'Mother, it's looking promising.'

In fact Ci, one morning while they were drinking coffee on the verandah, had spelt out in clinical, and to Tor slightly shocking, detail exactly the sort of young man she should look for during her time here.

'The civil service is usually absolutely top drawer,' she'd drawled, 'and a very good catch dead or alive – you get three hundred a year as their widow, so in some ways,' a big wink here, 'better dead than alive. I'm joking of course, darling.'

Tor had already forgotten the other categories of people Ci had suggested, but remembered cavalry officers being high on the list – preferably members of English rather than Indian, which was a bit of a slap in the eye for Jack.

Her hostess had also given her dire warnings about the Chi Chi girls, the half-Indian, half-European girls, some of them, according to Ci, impossibly glamorous and 'real predators – they have absolutely no scruples about moving in and breaking up engagements. But don't worry, my petal,' this disturbing little chat ended with a pat on Tor's knee, 'they'll be falling over you soon, particularly if we . . .' but the sentence had ended vaguely in a haze of cigarette smoke, and this time anyway Tor was determined to err on the side of caution. Although several men had taken her telephone number, no one had actually made a pass at her yet, and she knew enough about her mother now to know that when she got her hopes raised high she was dangerous.

27 November 1928

Dear Mummy,
I'm afraid this will have to be a very short letter because I have got to go out soon. We are all getting very excited about Rose's wedding, which is in a week's time. Today we plan to do some last-minute shopping at the Army and Navy Store in the Fort part of town. I am very sorry to hear that Mr T. has hurt his wrist. I will write a much longer letter tomorrow and tell you about everything. I am very well and thank you, Mummy, for the dress patterns. I will see if I can get them made up for you cheaply here.

Love to you and to Daddy,
Victoria

When Ci suddenly appeared wearing a lilac-coloured kimono and ballet slippers and trailing Arpège, her favourite scent, Tor had to fight the temptation to fall over her page like a child in primary school. Her letter suddenly felt so dull and pedestrian.

During Tor's first days at Tambourine, almost everything about Ci

– the bright red lips, the slouchy walk, the chic clothes – had made Tor feel huge and slow-witted and obvious. But now awkwardness had grown into a kind of hero worship. Careful examination of Ci, Tor felt, could teach her how to be sophisticated and fun and not care so much about what other people thought about her.

'So how's our little orphan this morning?' Ci ran her long finger-nails through the parting in Tor's hair.

This orphan tag was a new joke between them, for Ci actually had two children of her own – a boy and a girl at boarding schools in England – ghostly figures in silver frames on the mantelpiece. She rarely spoke of them, except in jokes, 'my rug rats', she'd say, or 'the ghastly creatures'. Sometimes she read out their faltering communications in piping voices.

Neither child seemed to have made deep imprints on Ci's life or imagination; all Ci had said about Flora, who seemed on the evidence of the photo to have inherited her father's rather doggily devoted eyes, was that twelve was a dreadful age and that she hoped by the next holiday she would have become 'halfway human'.

'Well!' Ci was glancing through a pile of invitations that had been placed near her chair along with morning coffee. 'We are *so* in demand today I don't know if I can bear it.'

She sliced open the first letter. 'Chrysanthemum show. Jan. tenth, Willoughby Club, with tea on the lawn afterwards. Thank you, Mrs Hunter Jones, but no.' She made the letter into a dart and skimmed it into the wastepaper basket. 'The most boring woman I've ever met.'

Tor giggled.

'Could I trouble you for half a cup more?' Ci ran her red nails along the next envelope. 'No sugar . . . *this* sounds more like it: a moonlight picnic on Chowpatty Beach with the Prendergasts. They're very good value and have a handsome son. Put it on our possible pile, darling.'

Tor propped the card on the mantelpiece in front of Flora's hopeful face, now obliterated by a stack of invitations to supper parties, picnics, polo matches and shoots.

The phone rang. 'Malabar 444,' said Ci in her thrilling drawl. She rolled her eyes and handed it to Tor. '*Another* man,' she said audibly, handing the phone to her. 'He says his name is Timothy.'

This was a small red-headed man Tor had met the week before at a party at the Taj. Something in forestry. He wanted to know if he could take her out to dinner that weekend. Sorry about the short notice and all that.

'How sweet,' Tor replied. 'Do you mind awfully if I phone you back in ten minutes?'

'I'm not sure I want to go,' she told Ci.

'Then don't, darling,' said Ci. 'Plenty more *poisson*.'

This was true in a way, already at the club and at the Taj, where she'd been to cocktail parties and dances, she'd met young naval officers, yummy-looking in their white uniforms, and cavalry officers, businessmen in Bombay to make some killing in jute or cotton, and even though her brush with Jitu had made her more cautious on this count, some high-caste Indian men, some very seductive with their liquid eyes and perfect skin. And although it was true that no one had exactly seized her yet, there'd been plenty of flirting. After the many small humiliations of her London season Tor could hardly believe that now she had some choice in the matter.

'Oh, marvellous!' Ci Ci was opening a large scarlet envelope with a gaudy crest on the back. 'Oh, what fun.' She was reading the letter inside. 'Goofers will love this. Cooch Behar has asked us to go shooting with him in three weeks' time. He's got the most wonderful place.'

Three weeks' time, Tor thought. *By then Rose will be married and gone. How strange that's going to feel.*

' "Sadly places are numbered," ' Ci read on, ' "so please write back at early convenient." *Early convenient*. I thought he'd been to Oxford. We'll have to find a babysitter for our little orphan, won't we, darling. I'm assuming you'll still be here?'

As she swept her eyes upwards, Tor experienced a moment of panic. Where else would she be? At the moment she had no other plans.

'I'd love to stay on for a bit more, if you'll have me,' she said humbly.

'We'll see how you behave,' said Ci. 'Oh damn.' She had opened another letter and was looking cross. 'The Sampsons can't come to Rose's wedding, what a bore, which reminds me, I meant to ask you this earlier. Your advice. Last week,' Ci took a quick sip of her coffee, 'I had a slightly tense discussion with old frosty knickers, Captain Chandler or whatever his name is, about the reception. I thought it was a bit of a cheek actually, because he seemed to be saying he only wanted about five people he knew really well to come to the party afterwards, but our lawn looks completely wrong like that – naked and sort of golf coursey – and I am the hostess, so I've invited a few amusing chums of our own to swell the ranks. I don't think Rose will give a damn either way, do you?'

Tor, flattered that Ci Ci should ask her advice, said without thinking, 'No, of course she won't mind, why should she?' At the time she was rather pleased to hear herself add, 'We'll need a few extra caps and bells,' because it was the kind of confusing but clever remark that Ci might have made. In fact, when she thought about it later, Ci had said it in the club a few nights previously.

And now – how the week had sped by – there were only twenty-four hours to go before Rose's wedding, and Tor had woken up covered in sweat. The first thing she saw when she opened her eyes was Rose's ivory silk wedding dress, hanging up outside the wardrobe; Tor's bridesmaid's dress hung beside it like a fat sister.

Tor lay in bed for a moment brooding about the reception. All through the week, the phone had rung more or less continuously, and every time Ci had said, 'Darling, do come, you'll swell the ranks,' Rose had looked pensive and Tor had kept her mouth shut because when she'd relayed the information about the extra guests to Rose, she'd left out the bit about Jack minding, because it was too late to do anything about it and Rose was already in a state and had got quieter and quieter as the wedding day drew nearer.

When Tor went to the window she saw that, outside in the garden, Pandit and his helpers were putting the finishing touches to the maharajah's tent, which looked magnificent. She watched an ant-like stream of servants moving from the house into the garden. They were putting kerosene flares around the edges of the lawn. They were polishing glasses, and hauling tables from the house into the garden. Lots and lots of tables.

At eleven o'clock she and Rose went to have their hair arranged in the salon at the Taj Mahal Hotel, where Rose's gold silk hair was exclaimed over, as it always was. Both of them were tremendously aware of time that day, remarking on how the hours crawled by in the hot dead afternoon, and then, oh God, only nineteen hours to go and then eighteen hours and so on.

When darkness fell and it was time for their last supper together, they went downstairs, quieter than they usually were and awed by all that was ahead. Rose had been firm about wanting a quiet evening with Tor, and for once, Ci (now upstairs and changing for dinner) had let them decide.

Tor and Rose sat side by side on the verandah listening to the thump of the sea in the distance. In front of them, the shoreline was dotted like fireflies by thousands of tiny pinprick lights from the kerosene lamps and the open fires of the native quarters.

They sat in silence for a while.

'I'm petrified, Tor,' Rose's voice came through the darkness. 'Isn't that silly of me?'

'You'll be all right.' Tor took her hand, hoping she'd say the right thing. 'You'll look so beautiful.'

Such a trivial thing to say, but the truth was, she hadn't a clue whether she would be happy with this Jack person, whom she personally found quite hard work.

'It's not the wedding so much, it's everything else. It feels so peculiar without Mummy and Daddy being here. I—' Tor heard her inhale softly and let out a puff of air. 'I mean, of course I understand why they couldn't come. I'd have hated Daddy to get any more ill, but—'

Then Ci came dancing into the room, followed by two servants holding drinks trays and some jazz record that had arrived from London that day which she wanted them to hear.

She turned two lights on and told Pandit she'd like a very large gin. 'You girls look like Greek widows tonight,' she told them. 'Cheer up.'

Four hours until the wedding. Rose was still asleep. Tor went for an early morning walk to calm herself down.

In the distance, the sea glittered like sapphires, dazzling her eyes. At the bottom of the path, a gardener who was watering geraniums smiled radiantly and bowed deeply. *How jolly*, Tor thought, *all the servants who work for Ci seem compared to English servants*. Mother's hateful char Doreen and their resentful ancient gardener were always moaning about low wages and how hard they worked, and making one feel like a perfect pig if you asked them to do anything for you.

Ci, who treated her staff with a kind of amused contempt, seemed adored by them. *And why not?* reasoned Tor, walking back to the house.

Well, perhaps the little huts they lived in at the back of the house were *un peu* dog kennel-ish, but the climate was *so* different here and they had plenty of food, a beautiful place to work in, a chance to learn how to do things properly and reasonable wages. But having said all this, Tor wanted to hug this little man for looking so genuinely joyful on the morning of Rose's wedding. He looked as if he cared.

*

When she got upstairs again, Rose was not only awake but had bathed and was standing in pale stockings and her new silk underwear before the mirror.

The first thing she said was, 'D'you know, I really *am* glad in the end Daddy didn't make the trip; I'm sure it would have been much too much for him,' as if this was what she'd wanted all along. But the pale skin above her petticoat was covered in the rash Rose got when she was frightened. She'd dabbed a few spots of calamine lotion on it.

After a breakfast that neither of them could eat, they went upstairs again together and washed, and then Rose put on a breath of powder and a dab of Devonshire violets behind her ears.

'Are you ready?' said Tor, determined to be motherly and protective even though she felt completely overwhelmed.

'Yes.'

Tor took the silk wedding dress off the hanger and let it slide over Rose in luscious waves. Rose stood stock still and stared at herself in the mirror.

'Gosh,' she said. 'Caramba.'

'Now the veil.' Tor held out the fine lace.

She pinned it gently around Rose's face, thinking how innocent she looked, how young and hopeful and how the last time she'd done this they'd been dressing for the school play. Rose had been the Virgin Mary; she'd been the innkeeper at Jerusalem and worn two garden sacks stitched together.

'There.' She stepped back. 'Let's have a look at you. You'll do for most known purposes,' she said to make Rose smile, for her eyes were full of terror.

There was a knock on the door.

'One hour until show time,' Ci Ci sang out.

'Oh blast!' Tor, who was struggling into her own dress, was having trouble with the poppers. 'Oh God.'

'Here.' Rose did them up for her, and then planted a kiss on her forehead. 'You look beautiful, Tor,' she said. 'The next time we do this, it will be for you.'

At ten-thirty, Pandit in a red silk turban, drove the Daimler around to the front of the house. Geoffrey, gleaming with sweat in his morning coat, sat beside him in the front. Ci, wearing a purple cloche with a large scarlet feather in it, seemed distant and snappy, and when

Geoffrey started a monologue about some company headquarters they were passing, and how it was going through lean times too, she said, 'Shut up, Geoffrey – she doesn't want to hear all that on her wedding day.'

But Rose didn't seem to be listening to anyone anyway; she was looking towards the dusty streets, her lips moving.

When they arrived at St Thomas's everything speeded up. The garrison vicar, who seemed put out because he'd had to drive all the way from Poona specially, after their arrangements had been changed, almost bundled them out of the car and in to the vestry, the 'Wedding March' played and Rose and Tor walked up the aisle between a crowd of hats. When hats turned round to sneak a look at the bride, Tor didn't recognise anyone except Ci Ci, standing yards apart from Geoffrey, who had taken umbrage because she'd told him to shut up and he thought that wasn't on in public.

When Jack, stern and handsome in his blue and gold uniform practically covered in brass buttons and braid, suddenly appeared and stood beside Rose at the altar, Tor longed for him to turn and gasp at the sight of Rose, who really did look so ethereal and princess-like, but he stared stiffly ahead, clearing his throat once or twice. The garrison vicar galloped through the ceremony, mispronouncing Rose's surname. Rose's *I do* was almost inaudible even to Tor who was standing right behind her.

When the service was done and they walked out into the harsh sunlight, a dozen or so men from Jack's regiment appeared, making an archway of crossed swords down the path. Rose blinked at them for a moment and then at Ci's friends pouring from the church, some of them already gossiping and laughing. And then, in a moment that wrung Tor's heart, Rose scampered like a startled rabbit underneath the crossed swords and out the other side again. Tor stood waiting for her, blinded for a second by sunlight bouncing off a sword.

'Don't abandon me at the reception,' Rose muttered to Tor before she disappeared with Jack in the Daimler.

When Tor saw Rose again at Tambourine House, she stood looking pale and much too young to be married, on the edge of a roaring mass of partygoers: Ci's friends had turned up in force. She searched for Viva, who had promised to come, but couldn't see her.

Ci stepped from the throng, put a glass of champagne in their hands and shouted, 'Now comes the fun bit.'

Tor gulped a glass down and then another. The whole morning had been such a strain and she was glad it was over.

After more drinks and delicious things to eat, Ci stood on a chair shouting, 'People! People!' through a megaphone. She announced to roars of laughter that Geoffrey was going to make a speech early before they all did *A Midsummer Night's Dream* and collapsed on the lawn with their glasses because it was so hot and everyone had a lot of gossiping to catch up on. The speeches would be in the pond garden.

The guests carried their glasses underneath the arch of wisteria blossom that led into the shady part of the garden where two stone nymphs gambolled under cascades of water. Ci tried to lead the wedding party by holding both Jack and Rose's hand and scampering down the path, but Jack, who still looked shocked and who was, Tor thought, not a natural scamperer anyway, dropped her hand and walked stiffly down the path on his own.

When everyone was assembled Geoffrey Mallinson stood up with a glass in his hand, the nymphs splashing water behind him. 'A lot of you will know me only as the head of Allied Cotton,' he began prosaically. 'We've met at the club, at the racetrack, at the gymkhana, until—'

'Oh for God's sake, Geoffrey, trot on,' Ci said distinctly.

'But today,' Geoffrey ploughed on, 'I'm here in lieu of Rose Wetherby's father, who I have not had the honour of meeting but who sounds like a very fine man. And what an awfully proud man he would be today to see this beautiful young girl who stands before us like a freshly plucked flower.'

Tor was so pleased to see Rose smile at him and then shyly at the crowd of strangers, some of them murmuring, 'Hear, hear.' Tor finally spotted Viva in the crowd, and thought that it was beginning to feel more like a proper wedding, but then Geoffrey spoilt it all by booming, 'To Rosemary.'

Nobody ever called her Rosemary. It wasn't even her name.

By four o'clock that afternoon the sun reached its zenith in a perfect blue sky and some of the guests had, as Ci had predicted, collapsed in the heat.

When Rose appeared from the house again in her going-away outfit, Tor stepped up to say goodbye. She wanted to say something that would fill in the blanks of that strange and unreal day. To thank

Rose for being the best friend a person could ever have, to wish her kisses and babies, but at the last minute her mind went blank with misery, and all she did was peck her on the cheek like a maiden aunt, and say gruffly, 'Off you go then,' as if she couldn't wait for her to leave, which in a funny way she couldn't.

After Rose and Jack's car disappeared in a cloud of dust down the drive, she went up to her bedroom. It looked different already – the servants had been in during the reception, straightened the eiderdown on Rose's bed, polished her table and tidied all traces of her away. Tor lay down in her bridesmaid's dress on Rose's bed. She closed her eyes, and slept fitfully for about half an hour, dimly aware of the shouts and laughter of Ci's guests in the distance, the clatter of dishes being taken away.

When she woke up, she went to the window, and watched the sun go down over the sea, and felt homesick for the first time since she'd arrived, a sense of the vastness of India all around her, of millions and millions of people not known to her out there having babies and dying and living and of herself being an unimportant little speck living on the wrong side of the world.

She took off her damp bridesmaid's dress and went back to bed in her underwear. She pulled the sheet over her head and was almost asleep when she heard Ci shouting at her from the bottom of the stairs.

'Tor, come and play with me. I'm having a drink on the verandah.'

'Coming,' Tor shouted back reluctantly. She didn't dare say no, but she still felt shy on her own with Ci Ci.

She got dressed and went downstairs. Ci was lying in the half-dark in a kimono on a wicker lounger.

'I'm a rag,' she said. 'How are you?'

She must have noticed Tor had been crying for she pushed a glass of brandy towards her. They sat drinking together while the servants cleared away the wreckage of the day. Then Ci Ci said out of the blue, 'Most Bombay weddings are damp squibs, darling. But she'll be happy by now.' She smiled at her slyly. 'He's a wonderful-looking man.'

Tor looked at her. 'I don't like him,' she said. 'I think he's—'

'Think he's what?' Ci sounded impatient.

'Cold,' said Tor bravely. 'I kept wanting him to look happier.'

'What a silly thing to say, darling,' Ci protested. 'None of us even know him.' As if that proved anything. 'And besides,' she added, 'most people aren't exactly childhood sweethearts when they marry out here.'

An awkward pause followed, they both took sips of their drinks, and then Ci took Tor's hand in hers. She ran her fingernails along the palm of Tor's hand, and said lightly, 'Might a chap say something? This is probably as good a time as any.'

'Of course.'

'Don't be too fussy, darling; I'd hate to have to send you home a returned empty.'

Tor winced. Ci laughed as if she was half joking, but Tor knew she wasn't.

Ci put a fresh cigarette in her holder, lit it and as the smoke cleared, gave her a long appraising look.

'Darling,' she said after a longish pause, 'would you mind if I was incredibly frank with you? Because I think I could help you if you'd let me.'

'Of course.' Tor steeled herself for the worst.

'You're a big girl, aren't you, but you don't have to be if you don't want to be. All it would take would be no cake for two weeks, lemon and water in the morning, and I rather think,' Ci stretched out and held a lump of Tor's hair in her hand, 'we need a hair conversation with Madame Fontaine. With half an inch off this, you'll be fighting them off with a stick. Do you want to fight them off with a stick?'

'Yes,' said Tor, and even though at this precise moment she felt she could have died of shame, she made herself smile. 'I rather think I do.'

But then, the following night, something amazing happened. Ci Ci walked into Tor's room with Pandit behind her, his arms piled high with bright silk dresses, beaded shifts, shawls of shivery softness, headbands, feathers, necklaces, even earrings. Ci took the clothes from his arms and flung them carelessly on the bed.

'Darling, do me a favour and keep these,' she said. 'I need an excuse to buy some new clothes.'

'I couldn't!' Tor, still smarting from the conversation the night before, felt both thrilled and shamed.

'Why not?' Ci Ci said. 'New toys are much more fun, and some of these are just *un peu mouton*.'

For the next two hours Ci, smoking and squinting, watched Tor try on the clothes. Apart from the few hems that needed taking down and waists out, some of the dresses fitted perfectly and Tor couldn't wait to wear them: she'd never felt such silky silk, such soft cottons, or for that matter, had a woman with Ci's flair show her where to place a brooch for maximum effect, or how much better three long ropes of pearls looked than the skimpy row she'd been given by her aunt Gladys for her eighteenth birthday, which she'd been instructed by her mother only to wear for best and never in the bath.

The following morning Ci drove her to the Taj Mahal Hotel, where the clever little Frenchwoman Madame Fontaine, a closely guarded secret who saw only a few cherished customers, held up a lump of her hair and said, 'What is this!' which made Ci laugh. For the next hour, Madame, who Ci said was an artiste, danced around her snipping, regarding, adjusting, while the pile of hair on the floor grew and Tor, watching herself in the mirror, saw a different kind of girl. Madame showed her how to apply kohl to emphasise what she said was her best feature. 'Those *wonderful* eyes.'

An hour or so later, Tor sat with Ci in the bar of the Bombay Yacht Club awed by her transformation. She hadn't had her hair so short since Doreen of Basingstoke had cut the disastrous shingle, but this felt so different, so suave and silky and modern.

Across the bar, two young naval officers drinking together had actually stopped talking as she'd walked in. One of them was still sneaking looks at her now.

'I'm going to buy my little Cinderella champagne.' Ci looked at her for the first time with real approval. 'Lots of glass slippers from now on, I think.'

'It feels like magic.' Tor couldn't stop herself grinning.

'It is magic,' said Ci. She winked. 'And it's all done with mirrors – you'll see.'

Chapter 25

7 January 1929. YWCA, Bombay. Extract from Viva Holloway's diary.

Down to Thos. Cook's, one letter from William. Regretting his absence on the quayside when the *Kaisar* had left, due to 'unexpected court appearance', and hoping my future will be 'a happy and profitable one'. And that we may meet again on my return.

William, I wanted to tell him, we will not meet again. My biggest mistake yet. Yes, mine – old enough to know better now, clutching at straws, or dry sticks in this case – mustn't blame others, but we will not meet again.

Today: write to Tor and Rose, go to Grindlays to see if postal order there. Budget for today five rupees, do not exceed. Learn ten new words of Marathi.

Her original plan had been to go straight to Simla to collect the trunk so she could tick this painful task off her list, and then get on with the rest of her life. But the plan had gone out of shape, because she had no money or almost none now; and also, her mind seemed to be playing tricks with her: one voice saying, 'Go ahead,' another hesitating, a third creating nothing but fear.

'You utter fool,' this last voice said, 'to think you could come back here on your own and make a life for yourself without the others.' Or sometimes, 'A writer, what a joke – you're a complete failure in love and life.' In this mood her mind slid down the snake of the darkest memory of all. She was standing aged ten with her suitcase on the railway platform at Simla. Josie and her father were dead. Mother had shown her their gravestones. Mother bundling her on the train. Why didn't she want her to stay with her? Why was she slamming the doors and turning away? What had she done wrong? *Did she kiss me goodbye?*

When these voices pounced, they made her almost hate Mrs Driver for telling her you could do practically anything you wanted if you set your mind to it in the right way. What if this was sentimental tosh, the cruellest lie of all?

She'd battled with these feelings for several days now, but this morning, for no reason she could fathom, she'd woken feeling more optimistic. She opened her eyes and heard for the first time birds singing in the banyan tree outside and the choice seemed almost laughably clear: she could sink or she could swim, and she was ready to swim again.

A job. That was the first thing she needed: a tent pole around which everything else could fall. She got out of bed and consulted her notebook. Before she'd left, Mrs Driver had scribbled down in her dashing hand the names of a few people in Bombay who might help her. Top of the list was Miss Daisy Barker, the same name she'd seen on the YWCA's noticeboard when she arrived. Underneath, Mrs Driver had written, 'Mr Woodmansee, retired correspondent *Pioneer Mail* (ancient, but sound, loves giving advice).'

Viva picked up her pen and underlined Miss Barker's name twice. She'd phone her after breakfast. Pleased to have made at least one decision, she walked down the hall and into the communal bathroom where the wooden pulley above the bath sagged with the weight of wet stockings and yellowing camisoles and knickers. She filled the basin with water, stripped naked and washed herself vigorously, hair, face, teeth. How good it felt to wash like this again as if you believed in yourself. She put on her red dress and plunged a silver comb in her hair. Poor she may be but she could still look good.

The dining room at the Y was a bright room on the first floor overlooking a dusty park. Each morning, two kinds of breakfasts were laid out: for the English girls, scrambled eggs, sausages, bread, marmalade and tea that was weak and never quite hot enough; for the Indians, the small buns they called pavs, eggs and *poha*, pounded rice.

Three Bengali girls whom Viva knew by sight but not by name, smiled as she walked in. They'd come to Bombay, she'd been told, to train to be schoolteachers – a momentous step for them too, to leave home and live like this. They were friendly enough, joined in the prayer meetings and so on but kept themselves separate, probably,

161

Viva thought, because they were Hindus at heart, and preferred not to eat with non-Hindus.

They stopped talking when they saw her, and waggled their heads from side to side.

'Your dress is nice,' one told her shyly.

'Thank you,' she said. 'How is your training going?'

'I am loving it,' said the girl, smiling. 'We were saying just now we are like birds outside the cage.'

Viva suddenly felt ravenous. During the days of her nerve storm, she'd eaten practically nothing.

She put some eggs, a sausage and some rice on her plate, and sat down on a chair near the window. From where she sat she could see, down in the park, a small boy chasing a kite. The wind lifted it out of his chubby hands; he was running, laughing. From the kitchens the sound of singing and the hot sweet smells of the lunchtime curries being cooked. She ate until her plate was clean.

After breakfast she telephoned Daisy Barker before she lost her nerve.

'Hello?'

The cut-glass voice at the other end of the line was brisk but friendly. Viva asked if she could see her today. Miss Barker said she was teaching a class at the university that morning, but they could meet after lunch at her new flat in Byculla. Did she happen to know the area? No, well, it was somewhat off the beaten track, but she would give precise directions for getting there. 'Bus or rickshaw?' she added, which Viva found a relief; taxis for the time being were out of the question.

Viva, dressed in her chaperone suit and best pair of shoes, ventured out into the street. With the four hours she had to kill before her appointment with Miss Barker, she decided to go first to the Thos. Cook office in Hornby Road to collect her post, and then to Grindlays Bank to check on her dwindling account balance and, if necessary, talk to the manager there.

It had rained overnight, and the pavements were steaming as Viva crossed the road. She felt the city stretch out all around her: the rumble of bullock carts, the screech of brakes from the gaudy new lorries, a donkey somewhere braying, an incredible crush of bodies, living, dying, getting to work.

'Morning, missy,' said the palm-juice seller who sat cross-legged on a charpoy at the corner of the street. She'd started to buy a cup of juice from him each morning, the sweet taste reminding her always of Josie, who'd loved palm juice and begged their ayah for it. Since she'd been back, Josie, for so long pushed to some place in her mind where she wouldn't hurt, was real again: she could see them both running – skinny-legged – in the rain, cackling with laughter, or riding in the hills, sitting on the deck of that houseboat in Kashmir.

Dear Josie. She took her first sip. *My sister.*

As the palm juice touched her lips, the juice man opened his own mouth by a fraction like a mother bird. She'd watched him sometimes from her window at the Y, sitting on this dusty street corner, for ten, twelve, sometimes sixteen hours a day, until the stars came out and he lit his kerosene lamp and wrapped himself in a blanket at night. She had no right to think of her life as being especially hard.

'Delicious.' As she handed the glass back to him, he smiled as if they were the oldest of friends.

She struck out towards Hornby Road, stopping at the next corner to let three women in saris pass like brilliantly coloured birds. Their murmuring voices, their easy laughter, made her think of Tor and Rose; how strange to find she really missed them. First, they'd been her meal tickets, nothing more, now something else – she hesitated still to use the word friends, she who had always felt on the outside of things (or was this the fate of all expatriates?), but she did miss drinking little nips of crème de menthe with them and hearing their stories; Tor winding up her gramophone and teaching her the *Kaisar* stomp.

And Frank. This was too silly for words. She'd watched him walk away on his own, down the gangplank. That jaunty, slightly bandy walk, hiding, she now knew, a more complicated and thoughtful person. He was wearing his civilian clothes again, a linen suit, a hat with his butterscotch-coloured hair showing underneath it. *A bird of passage*, like herself, she thought, jumping quickly on to the pavement, for a bullock cart had almost knocked her over. She could have called out on that last day on the ship, but she was standing with the Glovers, and the atmosphere was so fraught and confused she'd lost her nerve. She felt an ache inside her when she thought of this, and then irritation with herself. Why should it matter that they hadn't said goodbye? He was probably somewhere else by now, charming a whole new set of women. Some men did that without even trying:

it was a freak of nature, the right kind of smile, an air of easy confidence that few women could resist. She'd made up her mind not to see him again.

The uniformed staff at Thos. Cook & Sons were stuffing letters into the small brass boxes when she arrived. Her box, number six, was near the door; as she took its brass key out of her purse she felt frightened again.

There were two letters in her box – one an advertisement from the Army and Navy Store advising her of special offers that week on 'silver sardine tongs' and 'double terai felt hats in nigger beige and other shades'. Nothing from Mr Glover; *Jail sentence suspended*, she joked with herself, and she was locking the box again when the clerk handed her a scarlet envelope with Tor's large, loopy, schoolgirl writing on it.

Dear Chaperone,
Exciting news for you. I will be all on my own in this house for two weeks from 20 Jan. onwards. A car too!!! The Mallinsons are going shooting. So please, please come and keep me company, for a night even if you can't manage the whole two weeks. Plenty of spare rooms for you to write in. I'm trying to get Rose to come down too, so we can have a bishi. I'm having a ripping time, hardly time to breathe, let alone write.

xoxoxoxo
Tor

P.S. What news of the ghastly Guy?

As she walked back up Hornby Road, Viva could feel herself being torn this way and that by Tor's offer. The wedding reception at the Mallinsons' house had been ludicrously grand. There'd be servants there and copious hot water, wonderful food, plus the fun of seeing Tor and hearing all her news.

But could she bear to stay in the dreaded Ci Ci Mallinson's house? She really couldn't stand the woman. At Rose's wedding every time she and Tor had tried to exchange a few words, she'd swooped down on them like some terrible bird of prey telling them to circulate, or making strange remarks about how 'short of new blood' Bombay was.

'Where do you hang your hat in Bombay, friend of Tor's?' she'd said at one point in her affected drawl when they met near the champagne tray. When Viva said, 'The YWCA,' she'd gasped audibly and plunged her nails into Viva's arm and said, 'How ghastly for you, darling – I hear the women there are *absolute* heart-sinkers.' She'd turned to one of her friends and added, 'It's not India at all, you know.'

Well, maybe Ci had been a little tight, or over-excited at the time, for the reception had been such a bun fight, but the desire to pour her drink very slowly over Mrs Mallinson's daringly coiffed head had been strong. Even thinking about it now made her seethe.

How dare she mock the midwives, social workers and school-teachers who stayed at the YWCA? She had *no idea* what they were like, or how hard they worked.

She was the kind of woman who thought all Indian women were dim and downtrodden. She was an idiot.

And where was this *real* India that Ci Mallinson went on about, and, if she was part of it, why the two armed guards, the Alsatian at her gate? At one point in the day, they'd been talking about some recent riots near the esplanade; she'd told them the natives had never been so restless.

Viva ate a mango for lunch at Crawford Market, sitting on the side of a fountain, carved with snakes and tigers, with birds and red dogs. And now she was on the bus, heading for Daisy Barker's house at Byculla. The hair of the woman sitting next to her smelt of coconut oil, and the feeling of her soft pillowy body next to hers made her feel hungry, for what she couldn't remember. The woman had a baby across her lap. While it slept, its eyelashes sweeping on almond cheeks, she gently batted away the flies. Another man, hanging on a strap in a sleeveless vest with wet hair underneath his arms, was telling a story to some men at the back of the bus. When he reached its conclusion, there was such an explosion of giggling and thigh-slapping she found herself laughing too, even though she didn't understand a word of it.

After ten stops, the conductor said with a wave of his hand, 'Byculla is here. Alight, madam. Thank you.'

She stepped down, and after looking at her map walked down a narrow street that led into a series of sinister-looking alleyways. The pavement was full of potholes and rotten vegetables and a few puddles left over from the night before when it had rained. Across the street a small boy was squatting on the kerb defecating, his ragged shirt pulled up to his waist. When he looked at her curiously, she looked away.

Daisy had said her house was near the Umbrella Hospital, but all she could see were ramshackle shops built like dark cages in the wall. She poked her head inside one of the shops where an old man sat on his haunches ironing a pile of shirts.

'Where is the . . . ?' she asked in Hindi, and then she put an imaginary umbrella up above her head.

'It's over there.' He pointed towards the next corner where there was a crumbling block of flats with wrought-iron balconies on the front, most of them broken. She walked across the street and was about to ring the bell when a shutter opened above her head.

'Hello, hello,' a voice that might have welcomed visitors to Buckingham Palace floated down. 'I'm assuming you're Miss Holloway.' A small round woman wearing a sun hat squinted down at her from the balcony. 'Hang on, I'll come down and get you.'

Shoes clattered down the stairs and then the door burst open on a woman who Viva guessed to be quite old, at least thirty-five. She wore rimless glasses and a simple cotton frock and had a lively intelligent face.

'Forgive the shambles,' Daisy said. 'I only moved last week; half my stuff is sitting on a broken-down bullock cart in Colaba.' She hooted with laughter like a girl.

The corridor smelt of old curries, and fly spray, but when they stepped into Daisy's flat, Viva liked it immediately. It had high ceilings and whitewashed walls and was airy and somehow purposeful-looking with its neat piles of books and bright cushions. On a desk in the sitting room, there was a typewriter and stacks of what looked like examination papers.

'Come and look at my new view.' Daisy led her through the sitting room and out on to a large balcony with a white mosaic floor and a view of roofs and a mosque. 'It's going to be a perfect party place,' she said, sunlight bouncing off her pale skin. 'We played badminton there last night. Now tea? Sandwiches? Are you absolutely famished?'

Over tea, Viva decided she liked Daisy. Behind the kindly eyes she sensed a practical energetic mind that knew how to get things done. In some way she couldn't yet define one felt safe with her. Over a second cup of tea, Daisy told her how she was part of a movement called the Settlement, formed by Oxbridge women graduates who'd decided 'we were so spoilt and privileged that we'd come to India and teach the women at the university here.'

Much later Viva learnt that Daisy, with her dowdy dresses and cut-glass accent, had a titled father who owned estates in Norfolk; but that wasn't how she wanted to live her life. She had an urge to do things for other people, and was much derided for it amongst the smart set.

'Indian women, at university?' Viva was amazed – nobody had ever gone to university from where she came from. 'Forgive me, but I thought most were illiterate?'

'Well, a lot of village people are, it's true.' Daisy looked pensive. 'But Bombay is very advanced in certain respects and we have female lawyers here, poets, doctors, artists, engineers. And they're a splendid bunch: bright, questioning, full of beans. If you're interested, you can meet them.'

Apart from her teaching, Daisy said she was doing a six-week course herself at the university so she could brush up on her Urdu. 'Do you know the language? Oh, such richness! If you have any interest in poetry at all, you must allow me to lend you some. Such a discovery!'

'I'd like that very much.'

'And you?' Daisy beamed at her from behind wire spectacles. 'Have you lived in India before?'

'Until I was ten. Both my parents were killed in a car crash up north.' The lie slipped out so easily now. 'And I went back to England; I've come back partly to pick up their things. They've left a trunk for me in Simla.'

'Poor you, that will be sad for you.'

'Well . . .' Viva never knew what to say.

'Any work planned?'

She cleared her throat. 'I want to be a writer.' When things weren't going well she felt so fraudulent saying this. 'I've had one or two things published in England.'

'Gosh, how exciting.'

'Not very, I'm afraid, at the moment. I wish it was. In fact, I'm looking now for any kind of work that can support me.'

Daisy poured more tea into both their cups.

'But you've only just arrived.' She broke the silence. 'And this is such an extraordinary time to be in India – everything's changing: ideal, I would have thought, from a writer's point of view.'

She'd told Viva about the Indian National Congress Party who were now more determined than ever to wrest the country back from the British, about the moves to boycott British goods, and how Gandhi, 'a true inspiration', was quietly mobilising Indians.

'Do you think Indians are starting to really loathe English people then?' said Viva, confused as usual about which side she was on.

'No, I don't,' Daisy said. 'Indians are very forgiving – they're the warmest and friendliest race on earth, until they are the most violent, and it can change like that.' She clicked her fingers. 'A few hot heads really fan the flames. So be warned,' she said. 'And be careful. But let's go back to the task in hand.' Daisy had her pen and notebook out. She was concentrating fiercely. 'How long do you want to stay in India for?'

'For at least a year.'

'Do you speak any Hindi?'

'A little.'

'Splendid. But do try and learn some Marathi too – it makes such a difference.'

Daisy said that she knew Lloyd Woodmansee too. 'He used to be features editor at the *Times of India*, as well as working for the *Pioneer*. I'm not absolutely sure they use many female writers, and if they do it's probably only to write about frocks and chrysanthemum shows, but he's worth a try. He's terribly old now and a bit down on his luck. Take him a chocolate cake.'

She took a piece of paper from her workmanlike handbag and wrote down his name and address. 'He lives opposite Crawford Market.'

'What sort of money might one expect if I was lucky enough to get a story to write?' Viva's heart thumped.

'Oh, practically nothing, I'm afraid, unless, you know, you're someone like Rudyard Kipling. I wasn't paid at all for the couple of things I did for them recently.'

'Ah.'

'Oh dear . . . sorry.'

'It's fine.' Viva turned away. 'It's been really kind of you to try and help me.'

Daisy put the cups back on the tray, lining them up carefully.

'Are you very short of money?' she said.

Viva nodded, mortified by the tear she could feel rolling down the side of her cheek. 'I have about twenty-five pounds left,' she said at last. 'My passage out was supposed to have been paid for, but my employer had other ideas.'

'That's not fair.'

'No,' said Viva, 'it was not.'

'Look, *do* sit down for a second longer,' said Daisy. 'I have another idea, nothing very grand but it may tide you over.'

In the next half-hour she told Viva that apart from their educational works the Settlement supported two children's homes in Bombay: one in Byculla called the Tamarind, which served a midday meal to street children and gave them rudimentary lessons in reading and writing. They had a few children living there as temporary boarders and were missing one assistant at the moment. The pay was poor – one rupee a day, but the hours were flexible and might suit a writer. The job came with a small room, nothing grand, in a house nearby which was owned by a Parsi, Mr Jamshed, whose own daughters were at the university.

'The children will tell you enough stories to fill a lifetime of books,' she added, 'and surely that's better than chrysanthemums and frocks.'

Viva thought for a bit. She put down her cup. 'I'll take it,' she said.

'Splendid.' Daisy shook her hand.

While they'd been talking, the sky beyond the balcony and above the city had burst into flames, and somewhere down the street she could hear the water man shouting, '*Pani.*'

'Maybe,' Daisy said, 'we should find you a bus home. It'll be dark soon.'

And for the first time in days, Viva didn't dread the empty hours ahead. None of this was in the least what she'd expected, but it was a start.

Chapter 26

POONA, JANUARY 1929

On the day that Viva started her first job in Bombay, Rose sat silently in the window seat of the *Deccan Express*. She and Jack had been married for three weeks and were on their way to Poona, where they were about to move into their first married quarters. Three weeks was long enough for her to know that he was a man who did not wish to be spoken to while he was reading the papers and that his plans, from now on, would generally be considered more important than hers.

This point had been made, patiently but firmly, in the bedroom of the old-fashioned guest house in Mahabaleshwar, where they had spent the four days of their belated honeymoon.

'What fun,' she'd said, clapping her hands with delight when he'd explained that they'd stop for a day or two in Bombay on their way back to Poona. 'I can go and see Tor, and maybe Viva.'

She was longing to catch up with them and hear their news. He'd frowned and she'd seen that pulse flicker in his cheek that she was beginning to register as a slight warning.

He'd explained that he had to go and look at a horse, and then they'd need to do some shopping for the new house. She'd felt quite ridiculously disappointed, but tried hard not to pout.

'There will be plenty of time once we're settled,' he'd softened immediately and put his arm around her, 'but we do need to get mobile.'

Getting mobile was a favourite expression of Jack's. As was 'let's crack on', or, if he was feeling playful, '*avante*', or '*jaldi*', which was Hindi for hurry.

Sometimes she caught him looking at the locals in amazement. Many of them seemed able to spend long dreamy hours simply sitting and staring. He could never be like that.

Quietly, so as not to jiggle Jack's arm, Rose got out the maroon leather writing case and the gold fountain pen her father had given her before she left.

'Well, my darling parents,' she wrote, 'this old married lady is on the train now. We left Bombay over an hour ago, a journey of about one hundred and fifty miles, and I'm very excited at the prospect of seeing our new married quarters this afternoon. My new address, by the way is 2 The Larches, Poona Cantonment. From my window I can see wild-looking wooded slopes and everything getting more open and more romantically Indian!'

Actually, rather dusty and brown-looking too – although Jack had assured her tersely, between reading the sporting section and minutely scrutinising the advertisements in the *Pioneer*, that come the monsoon it would be greener.

Rose broke off here and thought of the less romantic view they'd both seen – it still made her blush to think of it – earlier in the day. In a large dusty field on the edge of Bombay, they'd seen dozens of natives going to the lavatory in broad daylight. Number twos.

'Don't look,' Jack had commanded her, but she'd seen out of the corner of her eye all these bottoms, hideous and shocking, looking like field mushrooms at first glance.

'We had a ripping time last weekend,' she continued. 'I was taken on my first tiger shoot at a hunting camp near Tinai Ghat. At dusk, we saw a pack of red dogs cross the road. (Jack told me later that they are one of the cruellest and most terrifying of all animals around here.) A few seconds later, I saw my first tiger. Our *shikari* (guide) had left a dead deer lying in the path; the tiger was walking towards it. When he saw the dogs, he halted in his tracks as though utterly disgusted and walked slowly away. The red dogs must have seen the tiger but they threw themselves on the deer anyway. While fourteen or so animals ate, five or six acted as guards. The sounds of rending flesh, the soft whinings of satisfaction, were absolutely horrid and fascinating all at once. When Jack flashed his torch towards them, we saw that their tummies were so gorged it was impossible to eat any more. They left at 2 a.m. as silently as they'd come.'

Her parents didn't want a whole page on red dogs, Rose knew this. They wanted more about the wedding, about Jack, to know she was happy, that she wasn't sobbing in her pillow every night for Park House and them, but some things were too hard and too private to put into words.

The honeymoon had not gone well. On their wedding night in

171

Mahabaleshwar, she and Jack had eaten a quiet supper together in the guest house, which had smelt of damp, in a badly lit room, with another couple at the next table, who didn't say one word to each other throughout the meal, which made Rose's attempts at conversation sound even more stilted and ridiculous. She'd talked a bit about Middle Wallop and her ponies. She'd asked him to tell her about the history of the Third Cavalry, which he had at some length. His face had glowed; she'd never seen him so animated as he'd talked about how it wasn't one of the grandest or even the oldest regiments, but how he was glad now he was in an Indian Cavalry regiment, rather than with a snootier English regiment, because he'd worked side by side with Indians and seen at first hand how able and how brave some of the local chaps were.

After she'd finished her glass of wine – which was horrid and bitter and made her feel blurred and disconnected because she hardly ever drank wine – Jack gave her a funny look and then leant across the table and whispered, 'You are beautiful, do you know that, Rose?'

And she'd bobbed her head and looked at her plate. Then he'd said in the same low voice, 'Would you like to go upstairs ahead of me and get ready for bed?'

The other couple swivelled their heads and watched her leave the room. She saw the man and woman exchange a secret smile because they'd seen the confetti on her coat as she arrived. They'd probably hear her as she walked across their bedroom floor, which was directly over the dining room. In the bathroom, she felt her fingers tremble as she tried to get the sponge thing in place. Twice it had pinged out of her fingers, once landing under the bath. She'd had to crawl underneath it, terrified she'd find a snake or a scorpion there. While she was washing it again, she had heard the door to the bedroom open and close.

'Are you all right in there?' Jack called.

'Fine . . . thank you,' she'd replied.

'Come on, darling,' he'd called five minutes later.

She had her foot on the bathroom stool and was still desperately trying to get the thing in. Sweating and trying not to cry, she finally felt it pop into place. The peach silk negligee seemed absurdly too much in this spartan room, and she almost tore it when she put her foot in the hem.

When she'd stepped into the room, he didn't say anything. He was lying underneath the mosquito net in a paisley silk dressing gown, pretending to read the paper. A fan whirred overhead.

When he drew back the covers, she saw that he had put towels all over the sheets. He looked at her without smiling. 'We don't have to do this if you don't want to,' he said.

'I do want to,' she'd said without looking at him.

Tor had told her that if you did lots of riding it didn't hurt, but it did. Both of them were sweating with embarrassment when it was over, slithering and sliding in each other's sweat and unable to look each other in the eye. No, it had not been a good start, and in the two nights that followed, it hadn't got much better. In fact last night, it was he who had stayed in the bathroom for nearly an hour, with, oh horrors of embarrassment, an attack of gippy tummy. He'd run the tap and done a lot of coughing so she couldn't hear, but it was mortifying for both of them.

At four o'clock in the morning he'd said in a snappy voice, 'Goodnight, Rose, I know you're awake.' And she'd lain wide-eyed with dismay in the darkness listening to some winged insect bashing against the netted window, and his breathing get hoarse and then more and more even, until she knew he was asleep.

The train was passing through some parched-looking scrubland. The chai wallah had stopped at their seats to offer them first brick-coloured tea, then fruit cake and a pile of hectically coloured sweets. 'I wouldn't eat any of this, darling.' Jack had set aside his paper. 'I bet Durgabai is cooking enough for an entire regiment this morning.'

Durgabai was the name of one of the four new servants she had yet to meet. Oh Lord, she was nervous; maybe Jack, who was quieter even than usual, was too. How long could one man read one paper for?

Six hours later they arrived. A taxi picked them up at Poona Station and whisked them down through manicured tree-lined streets, past the club, past the polo ground. And now they'd arrived at a non-descript little bungalow, and Rose had her eyes closed and was beaming. As Jack lifted her over the threshold, the thin part of her calf caught quite painfully on the lock, but she appreciated the romantic gesture and kept on smiling.

She opened her eyes to see a dark ring of sweat under Jack's arm as he put her down.

'How lovely to be here,' she said, tilting her face up for a kiss.

She hoped he couldn't see how disappointed she was. She'd pictured, what? Well, something more like one of the many beautiful and spacious-looking bungalows they'd passed on their way here, with their wide verandahs and majestic trees. Not quite such a small dead-looking garden or this dark pokey corridor smelling a bit of damp. But he had warned her that theirs was a junior officer's house, that they'd get something bigger when he was promoted.

'So, this is it,' he said brightly. 'Is it all right?'

'Darling, I love it, honestly,' she said. 'Why, do you think I don't?'

It was starting to embarrass her how often she used that word lately. *I love it; lovely to see you! lovely to be here; yes, I'm having a lovely time; that was lovely!* There must be other words to describe so much newness.

He took her into the sitting room, which was small and unfurnished, apart from a bamboo sofa facing a single-bar electric heater. There was a picture on the wall of what looked like Scottish moorland, with a stag in the foreground with many branched antlers looking plaintively in her direction. A bird squeaked through the window, and then it suddenly felt so quiet, as if the whole house waited for her to pronounce on it. She looked at the picture again with exaggerated curiosity.

'Oh, that poor little deer,' she said, 'it's too sweet.' She blushed again; what a ninny she sounded.

'Look, we can get more furniture,' Jack told her hurriedly, his mouth went very small when he was cross, 'and bits and pieces from the bazaar.'

'I adore arranging houses,' she said. But in fact, apart from lining up dolls on her bed at home, or pinning up her rosettes in the stables, she'd never really done it.

'We will have to watch the pennies for a bit.' Jack turned his back to her. 'But lots of people hire furniture, particularly now.'

'Hire? Gosh, I've never heard of that before.'

'Well, things change very quickly here. People move all the time and – look, I'll tell you all about that later.' He was looking at his watch again.

She gazed at him silently; he looked huge, too big to be contained by this small house. They walked back into the hall together where a collection of calling cards sat on a small brass table.

'These came for you,' he said, handing them to her. 'The ladies at the club can't wait to meet you. One or two are battleaxes, but most are very nice. And two letters.' He read from one of the envelopes, ' "To Mrs Jack Chandler." '

'One's from Tor.' She smiled properly for the first time that day. 'I'm not sure about the other.' Rose didn't recognise the writing or the address of an Indian hospital written on the top left corner.

Jack told her to read them later. He only had half an hour for lunch and wanted to show her the kitchen first. 'Of course, darling,' she said. 'I wouldn't dream of reading them now.' She put them back in her pocket, but part of her did mind: it was the second time today he'd kept her from Tor.

The kitchen was a dark room at the back of the house. Jack seemed pleased that the servants of the previous tenant – a captain in the Third Cavalry who'd broken his neck in a polo accident – had left a collection of mismatched glass jars with small amounts of lentils and sugar in them on a wooden shelf. He said it would save money. Rose saw a pot of rice bubbling on its own on the stove.

'Where are the servants?' she said suddenly.

'Are you up to meeting them yet?' he said gently. 'I told them to go to their huts until you'd had a chance to look around.'

'Of course, of course!' she said although she felt like hiding. 'But can I see the rest of the house first?' She managed to make this sound like a treat.

'Well, there isn't all that much left.' He smiled at her, a bashful smile that wrung her heart. This was such a big change for both of them.

It would be so much easier next week, she consoled herself, when Jack was back with his regiment again and she could roll up her sleeves and get on with something.

And after that he'd hinted he might be away for two weeks doing something secret in a place she'd forgotten, the name of which sounded miles away from Poona. He'd already told her that she must go and stay with Tor while he was away. Was it a bad sign, she'd wondered, that she was already looking forward to this so much?

They'd finished looking at the kitchen and now he put his arm around her and led her down another short corridor, whispering, 'Our room.'

'I've never slept in a downstairs bedroom before,' she told him gaily, making this sound like a treat too. He opened the door on a small room criss-crossed with bars of sunlight falling through the latticed blinds. In the middle of the room was a double bed with a white candlewick bedspread on which somebody had placed twigs to form the word GREATINGS.

'Durga and Shukla must have done that,' he said softly. 'How sweet they are.'

She bobbed her head and blushed. The bed side of things still made her feel rigid with embarrassment and strangely giggly.

'Where are our clothes?' she said quickly, because even though it was daytime he was looking at her in the gleaming way that made her heart sink.

'Here.' He moved away from her and opened the door into the next room. 'It's a bit of a shambles, I'm afraid, but I wasn't sure you'd want the servants touching your things.'

Her wedding dress lay in a cotton bag on the floor like a dead body. Beside it was her cabin trunk, now scratched and covered in labels, her tennis rackets, a pile of dresses, the riding clothes she'd worn at school, all in a messy pile with his polo mallets, uniforms and a heap of old regimental magazines.

'I'll sort all this out,' she said. She was determined to be efficient like Mummy, to take charge of domestic details without fuss. 'It's my job now.'

'Don't forget you have four servants of your own now,' he said. 'You actually don't have to do a damn thing if you don't want to.'

Ci Ci had already warned her that the idea of servants cutting down on work was a common myth all husbands had out here. She'd made Rose hoot with laughter with her tales of some straining soup through their turbans, and one (she swore this was true although with Ci Ci you could never tell) using his toes as a toast rack.

'They'll be your biggest test out here. Rule one,' she'd raised her finger and bulged her eyes for emphasis, 'they are children in everything but name.'

'I know,' Rose told Jack, 'but I'd like to do some things myself.'

'Well, do them then,' he said. And did he sound a bit peppery at that moment, or was she simply starting to read too much into everything?

'But I am looking forward to meeting them,' she said just in case he was cross again.

So now, one by one, the servants came out of the shadows to be introduced to her.

First came Durgabai, the maid and cook, a fine-looking Maharashtrian woman with jutting cheekbones and large luminous brown eyes;

then Shukla, her seven-year-old daughter, a beautiful replica of her, hiding behind her skirts.

Next came Dinesh, stick thin and immaculate, who bowed without smiling. Jack said Dinesh had been his bearer for the past three years. Next came Ashish, the wash man, the dhobi wallah, who had a withered leg and milky eye and was as shy as the little girl. Durgabai was sweet to her, smiling and wobbling her head and saying, 'Greetings, memsahib,' as if to make up for the awkwardness of the others.

Over lunch – pea and ham soup and a dry lamb chop – Rose confided to Jack, partly as a joke, that she found it awfully tricky remembering Indian names, even the faces bewildered her, so many of them looked the same.

He put down his knife and said, quite sharply, that she'd better concentrate because it wouldn't do at all to offend them. He told her some story about an Indian major in his regiment who had known the names of every man within a week.

She stared miserably at her chop. What a stupid thing she'd said. When she looked up again, two pairs of dark eyes were staring curiously at her from around the door.

Jack barked out some Hindi words and Rose heard staunched giggling as the door closed suddenly.

'What did you say, Jack?' she asked him.

'I told him if he didn't stop staring at the memsahib, I'd come to his house and stare at his wife.'

'Jack!' she said. 'You are naughty.'

'Memsahib,' Durgabai was back again and talking to her directly. 'Sorry for interrupting your vital but the dhobi wallah is at the back door.'

Rose looked helplessly at Jack. 'What shall I say?'

Jack put down his knife and fork again. 'Tell him to come back when we've finished lunch, that we do not want to be disturbed. Good practice for you.'

'We are eating our lunch,' she said in a quavery voice to the man. 'We do not wish to be disturbed. Sorry.' The door closed.

She swallowed and looked at her hands. 'I don't know if I'm going to be any good at this,' she said. 'There's an awful lot to learn.'

'Give it time,' Jack said. He scratched his head and sighed.

*

After lunch, Jack took her out to show her what he called 'the grounds' – a stretch of concrete with a tiny lawn in it and some clay pots with roses inside that looked as if they could do with a water. All of it would have fitted into their vegetable garden at home.

At the end of the garden was a trellis beyond which she saw a woman sitting in the dirt outside a hut feeding a baby.

'Do you normally have lunch at home?' she'd asked him politely, as they crunched up the gravel path together.

'No, at the mess, or on the trot usually,' he said, flooding her with relief. 'But it's lovely to come home and see you here.'

'Thank you.' She shot him a swift glance. 'Heavens,' she squinted up at a cloudless blue sky, 'can this really be winter? It's so beautifully hot.'

'Yes it is, isn't it?' he said. 'But nothing like as hot as summer.'

'I love hot weather.'

'Good.'

He asked her to excuse him for a moment, and he walked back into the house. She stood in the sun in her new sola topi, which felt rather tight, listening to the tinkle of water in the water closet and him clearing his throat. When he came back he seemed pleased to remember something new to tell her.

'Rose,' he said, 'Mrs Clayton Booth may call on you tomorrow. She's an absolute mine of information about where to shop, servants and so forth. I hope you don't mind me fixing this up.'

'Of course I don't mind,' she said. She stood on her toes and had more or less decided to kiss him when she heard leaves rustling behind the trellis.

'Darling,' Jack pushed her aside, 'don't do that in public any more. It doesn't do in front of the servants.'

'Oh.'

'It offends their modesty.'

'I'm sorry, Jack.'

'Oh, Rose, don't look like that, there *is* so much to learn.'

What was she supposed to look like? Oh drat, she wanted to run into the house now and cry. 'Sorry,' she said again in a breathless voice.

When he went inside to collect his things, she stayed in the middle of her new garden, wondering if she'd made the worst mistake of her life.

*

When she woke up the next morning, Rose remembered she hadn't even bothered to read Tor's letter yet – it was still in her pocket along with the other one.

She'd been dreaming about marmalade, such a strong dream she could almost smell it. Every year, about this time, her mother and Mrs Pludd made a great to-do of buying the oranges and washing dusty jam saucepans, rinsing jelly bags and writing the labels, and finally unearthing from the cutlery drawer the special spoon, stained from decades of jam, to stir it all up with.

For days the house would smell of oranges. Strange what made you homesick. Stars were another thing, or at least the thought that the same stars that twinkled down on you were above her sleeping parents half a world away. Or yesterday, the sight of two young girls jumping over a hose at the club had made her homesick for Tor, not the grown-up Tor, whizzing around Bombay in Ci Ci's Ford, but the old one who used to go riding with her, or lie on the lawn, dress tucked around her battered knees, sucking daisies and looking for four-leafed clovers and nattering about nothing much in particular during those summer days when time stood still, and there was precious little to worry about.

She got out of bed quietly and felt around in her dress pocket for the two envelopes. So Viva was working, she had a place to stay of her own, how amazing, and then Tor's invitation to stay making a trickle of tears fall down her cheeks. She ached to go, but knew it would all depend now on so many new things. She sat down at her dressing table, brushing her hair in long rhythmic strokes, and wondered if Jack even liked Tor. Probably not. It bewildered Rose how most men seemed not to see how absolutely wonderful she was – funny and kind and open-hearted and all the things you'd think they'd want.

She put her brush down quietly on the dressing table and turned round to look at Jack. He was fast asleep, one long brown leg over the sheet.

While she was watching him, he made a soft smacking sound with his lips; he raised his arms in a bow above his head and put them down on the pillow. She could see the tufts of damp blond hair showing in his armpits; the fingers that had touched her, there and there. *Oh, for goodness' sake, you silly woman*, she chided herself, feeling an earthquake of sobs waiting to come out of her. Whatever was the matter with her? She mustn't cry, not again.

Chapter 27

It was starting to get hot in Bombay, a soupy, steamy kind of heat that weighed down on you and made you long for a cleansing burst of rain.

Tor, who had prickly heat, was sitting in a bath of Jeyes Fluid when she heard the phone ring.

A few moments later Ci, who was getting increasingly snappy about phone calls, shouted through the door, 'Someone called Frank, ship's doctor, wanting someone called Viva. Don't know what in the hell he's talking about.'

Tor still felt her heart flutter.

'Hello, stranger in a strange land,' she said when she telephoned him back twenty minutes later. 'So, what brings you here?'

Frank said they must meet up and he would tell her all his news later, but in the meantime, did she have any idea where Viva was. He had some urgent news for her.

'Well, that sounds rather exciting,' Tor had drawled. 'Might a chap know what it is?'

Maybe he would have explained and maybe not, but Ci Ci had appeared at that moment smoking furiously and pointing at her watch so there was only time to give him Viva's address and get off the phone.

Tor had honestly only felt a brief twinge after she'd hung up. In her heart of hearts, she'd always known he was keener on Viva than he was on her. And besides, she had more than enough on her plate now. She was in the throes of what Ci Ci called an '*amour fou*', a mad passion.

The affair had begun on 21 December 1928, at about ten-thirty at night, when she'd lost her virginity to Oliver Sandsdown in a hut on Juhu Beach. She made a careful note of it afterwards in the little leather diary which her mother had given her for traveller's tales, 'Juhu. Thank God,' later drawing a yellow line around the date and adding some stars. The only casualty of the evening was Ci's silk Chinese jacket, which got tar on its sleeve.

Ollie had turned up at the Christmas party she and Ci had given at the Bombay Yacht Club. He was a twenty-eight-year-old merchant banker who loved sailing and who had been burned brown by the sun. He was short and dark, and even though Ci didn't particularly approve – he was too far down her categories – Tor thought him fearsomely attractive because he was so confident. When they'd first met, he'd danced with her and said with a very social smile plastered on his face, 'I'd really like to go to bed with you,' which she found both funny and naughty. On the way out to the beach they'd sung 'Oh, I Do Like to Be Beside the Seaside' in the car which he'd driven at a reckless speed. When they'd got to the beach they'd taken off their shoes, and the sand felt warm and heavy between her toes. The moonlit sea had surged on to the beach in a mass of silver and blue lights and on the horizon they had seen the silhouettes of fishermen setting their nets. And then he'd kissed her – not a boy's let's-see how-far-I-can-take-this kiss, but a man's kiss that seemed to claim and demand. Her knees had literally buckled.

The hut itself, which smelt, not unpleasantly, of seawater and dried fish, had a low string bed in the middle of it where he'd taken her efficiently but without any particular ceremony. Afterwards, he'd made her stand still in front of him while he arranged her pearls against her nakedness and then he'd chased her into the sea. What her mother would have said about pearls in seawater wouldn't bear repeating, but she hadn't given it a thought. Swimming in sea as warm as milk, she'd felt savagely happy. A feeling she'd never had before. And she'd been glad, at that moment, that he wasn't the thoughtful type who needed to put everything into words. He'd held her again in the water; they'd trailed phosphorescence with their fingers turning the water into ropes of diamonds, and she had felt absolutely exhilarated and released. It was done! Wonderful! Perfect. She didn't have to worry about it any more and she was sure in time she'd get to like it very much indeed.

After they'd swum, he dried her with an old towel, kissed her quickly and buttoned her up clumsily into the silk jacket, getting all the buttons wrong. She'd hoped then he might turn a bit poetic and that they'd stay on the beach and watch the fishermen come home and talk about life, but he said some pals of his were in town and he wanted to have a nightcap with them in the Harbour Bar. They'd ended up in the water splash at the Taj Mahal Hotel.

And Oliver wasn't the only man interested in her. There was Simon, an ex-Etonian, out in India for the season, mainly for the shooting, who'd taken her out for dinner at the Bombay Yacht Club, and Alastair de Veer, a rather bloodless young civil servant, with whom a foxtrot on the verandah had led to a bombardment of calls which she'd found off-putting. Things were moving in the love department, often, if she was to be honest, faster than she felt she could control, so Frank's phone call hadn't ruffled her feathers at all.

Since the night at Juhu Beach, she and Oliver had had several afternoon assignations in his flat at Colaba Beach. For several days she'd had to powder over the faint bruises he'd left on her neck and right shoulder.

Ci had noticed. 'Don't let him mark you like that.' She'd raised one plucked eyebrow at Tor's shoulder. 'It's common.'

Which was when Tor, who had gone beetroot red, had tried to change the subject by asking Ci for a huge, *huge* favour. Would it be an awful bore if Rose came for one or two days the following week and had a what-the-hell day?

Ci Ci had introduced Tor to the whole idea of what-the-hell days when she'd first arrived in Bombay. These were days of pure hedonism when you weren't allowed to be a grown-up and only drank cocktails and saw amusing people and did exactly what you wanted to do for once. She said there was far too much seriousness in the world.

When Ci smiled and replied, 'Darling, what a good idea,' Tor's heart lit up. The Mallinsons' trip upcountry had fallen through, and Tor had felt the need to defer the invitation to stay that she had extended to Viva and Rose. It had been a shame, as she was longing for a good heart to heart with Rose. There really were times, like now, when so much was happening so fast, when nobody else would do. Rose really listened, really cared, whereas Ci, well, she was fun and wonderful and many things, but not someone you felt you could safely confide in. She was too impatient for that; also Tor was beginning to think it was rather mean of her to talk about other people so wearily as if they were nothing but a bore, or to read out her children's letters in the squeaking voice she used for them. The girl Flora, who'd been in the san recently with some horrid-sounding thing called impetigo, seemed so homesick, so desperate for love.

Also – or was Tor imagining this? – Ci was changing in other ways. Before, as soon as Geoffrey's car had puttered down the slope, she'd been full of plans for them both; now she seemed more secretive, more aloof. She'd shouted at Tor the other day for hogging the phone.

The servants seemed to have noticed too. Yesterday, when Tor had asked Pandit where the memsahib was, he'd given her an odd sneering look, then opened his palms to show how empty they were. Very disrespectful. Afterwards, she'd heard the servants laughing in the pantry.

It made Tor wonder if everybody here knew something she didn't, or if she was outstaying her welcome, which would be such a shame because she was still having the most wonderful time.

Anyway, Ci had been instantly enthusiastic about Rose coming; she'd even offered to lend her the car. If she hadn't had wet nail varnish, Tor would have kissed her.

'Are you sure about the car? Why are you so nice to me?'

Ci Ci, who wasn't a great hugger, had popped a kiss into the air. 'Because you're fun and because your days are numbered. I got a letter from your mother this morning asking me to book your ticket home after the season ends in February.'

It had taken Tor at least a couple of hours to absorb the full impact of this bombshell, and even then she refused to believe it was true. Surely someone would propose to her, or something would turn up. At any rate it now seemed absolutely and crucially important for her to see Rose as soon as possible.

Jack had answered the phone.

'Please can Rose come out and play with me?' she'd said in her whiny-child voice. 'I'll scream till I'm sick if you don't.'

And, oh, what a stuffed shirt he was, he'd replied as though she'd been completely serious.

'I'll have to check diaries, but I think that will be fine.'

He'd droned on about a visiting colonel and company orders as if she was asking him too, which she definitely wasn't. Then there was a brief whoompf down the line and a thump.

'Tor, oh, darling Torrie,' Rose sang. 'I'm so happy to hear you.'

'Rose, this is an emergency,' she said. 'You have to come and see me. You can take the *Deccan Express* and we'll have a what-the-hell day and a good gup.'

'A what?' Rose's voice faded through the crackles.

'Play truant, drink champagne, eat chocolates. Rose. I'm bursting, I have so many things to tell you.'

'Hang on a tick.' Subdued murmurings in the background.

'That's absolutely fine, darling.' Rose was back. 'Jack says the ladies' carriage is perfectly safe.'

Tor didn't need Jack to tell her that.

But then Jack had surprised Tor by ringing back an hour later and whispering, 'I want to give Rose a surprise. Will you buy her a bottle of champagne when you go out to lunch? Tell her it's from me.'

She doubted whether Ollie would have thought of that.

But then all men found Rose irresistible. Tor had accepted this long ago; she knew she'd always have to work harder.

On Thursday the following week, Tor was sitting crouched forward in Ci's car sweating with fear. Rose's train was due in half an hour, and now she was at the wheel flying solo, wondering if she hadn't slightly exaggerated her competence as a driver. She'd had three lessons in her father's Austin, lurching up a muddy farm track, and a couple of drives in quiet lanes, but nothing that even remotely prepared her for the seething chaos of Bombay traffic.

Also, Ci's car, the bottle-green Model T Ford, had been shipped out to India in the hold of the *Empress of India* the year before and was as much revered as a household god at Tambourine. Every morning, Pandit polished the rims of its chrome headlights to an eye-piercing shine. He tenderly washed the running boards, using an old toothbrush to get between the cracks, and filled up its water tank with fresh water. He put beeswax on the leather seats, and refreshed the mints that lived in the glove box alongside Ci's kid gloves and little onyx lighter. Tor was sure he would have put garlands of flowers around the mirrors and offerings of rice on the seats had he been allowed.

Bug-eyed with concentration, she turned right into Marine Drive. The traffic wasn't too bad here. At the traffic lights she stopped and took a deep breath. As she flipped out the little orange indicator and turned left into a whirling maelstrom of rickshaws, bullock carts, bicycles, horses, donkeys and motor cars, her heart was thumping so loud she could hear it.

'Help,' she cried, veering around the thin form of a rickshaw boy who'd casually drawn out in front of her.

'Oh no!' at the bullock ambling across the street.

'Sorry,' to the banana man who had, bent double under his load, made his way barefoot across the street.

Ten minutes later she drove through the gates of the huge and majestic Victoria Terminus Station. She swerved to avoid a beggar and came finally to a head-banging halt in a parking space underneath a palm tree.

She parked the car and ran through the crowd just in time to see the Poona train pull in and Rose, looking almost bizarrely pink and gold in the middle of so many brown faces, step out of first class. She was wearing the pale blue dress they'd chosen together in London. Porters were fighting to carry her case.

'Oh, Rose.' Tor flung her arms around her. 'Dearest Piglet. I've missed you so.'

As they drove back into the city again, Tor couldn't resist showing off. 'Cigarette, please, young Rose,' she said. 'They're in the glove box on the left. Oops!' She had to swerve to avoid a man selling peanuts at the gate. 'Sorry!' she sang out gaily.

'So,' said Tor when they stopped at the traffic lights, 'here's the plan: first stop, Madame Fontaine's to get the hair done. There's a girl there called Savita who is a wonderful cutter. Then, lunch and a good gup at the club -- I haven't properly told you about my party yet – and then I'm going to drive you home to the Mallinsons' for a chota peg and then some friends may call, and we might go out dancing.'

Rose clapped her hands. 'Oh, Tor,' she said, lying her head lightly on Tor's shoulder. 'I can't believe you're allowed to do all this.'

'Well, I am,' said Tor, breathing out smoke in a film-starry way, 'but for God's sake, don't tell my mother. The silly woman already wants me home.' She said this so lightly that Rose said nothing and Tor was glad – the last thing she wanted Rose to feel on a day like this was sorry for her.

When they turned down Hornby Road they both shrieked at the sight of a small boy and his father urinating against a wall.

'Isn't it awful how they just let fly here,' said Tor and they started to laugh. 'I thought we'd outlawed it. So rude!' she said in the voice of their old headmistress.

'Oh, that reminds me.' Rose took a shopping list from her handbag. 'One minor request. Would it be a frightful bore if we looked at net curtains at the Army and Navy? I've seen some plain white muslin ones in their catalogue for twelve and six. I need some for my spare room.'

'*Curtains.*' Tor was appalled. 'Absolutely not. This is a what-the-hell day; you know the rules. Nothing but good times.'

'Bully.'

'Well, if you're very good, by which I mean bad, you might be allowed to buy curtains on the way home.'

Tor made them sound like a disease.

Tor was just telling Rose that Frank had phoned last week when she had to brake hard to avoid a man with a cart full of oranges who was crossing the road. As the car stalled, the young man's face suddenly appeared in the window on Tor's side. His eyes were large and contemptuous, his purplish lips twisted. He was close enough to touch them.

'Leave India,' he said distinctly.

'What?' Rose was gaping at him.

'Leave India,' he said again. He looked at them as though they disgusted him.

'I don't want to,' Rose said, and as they drove off the man stood in the middle of the road shaking his fist at them and shouting something they couldn't hear.

When they were at a safe distance, they both laughed shakily.

'"I don't want to,"' hooted Tor. 'That's telling him. He won't sleep a wink tonight.'

'I hate being looked at like that.' Rose had stopped laughing. She wound up her window. 'Do you think things are hotting up here?'

'Oh, well, Geoffrey and Ci say it's getting worse,' said Tor. 'Trade thingamabobs, you know, sanctions, Gandhi stirring them all up, but they say most of the natives would be horrified if the British went home. What does Jack say?'

'Not very much about things like that.' Rose dragged her gaze back from the crowded streets. 'In fact, nothing at all.'

Now they were in a room full of steam at Madame Fontaine's salon, their necks stretched over basins. They could smell sandalwood and pine, and coffee brewing.

'Memsahib.' Savita, a fragrant presence in an oyster-coloured sari, had just slipped into the room. 'Shampoo with olive oil or with henna?' she whispered.

They decided on olive oil with rosewater and four young girls washed their two heads. Twenty fingers apiece massaging their heads and necks with sweet-smelling oils and then wrapping them like babies in warm towels.

'Vera could pick up a few tips here,' said Tor. Vera was the owner of a draughty hairdressing shop in Andover where they'd both had their plaits lopped off, and later their hair put up in elaborate whorls for the London season. Vera had hands like a navvy's, she bashed your head on her taps as she rinsed.

'Memsahib,' one of the girls whispered at Tor's elbow. 'Refreshment.'

The coffee tray was garnished with fat hibiscus flowers.

While they sipped coffee, the girls came back. They were fascinated by Rose's long blonde hair, which they combed reverently.

'People here are such good cosseters.' Rose smiled at Tor's reflection in the mirror. 'They really seem to enjoy looking after one.'

'Are your servants like that?' Tor leant forward, squinting at her eyebrows. 'God, these caterpillars, I must pluck them.'

'Well, not yet. We're muddling along at the moment,' said Rose sensibly. 'But I'm sure I'll get them sorted out in time.'

Tor gave Rose a look. There were times when Rose sounded quite tragically grown-up for a nineteen-year-old.

'Now, Rose,' said Tor a few seconds later. 'To return to the big question of the day. They charge eight rupees here for the first-time shingling, and this is the place for it. But don't let me talk you into it and stop saying it won't suit you – you'd look good with a cow-pat on your head.'

And they were giggling again, seven-year-old stuff really, but such a relief.

'You have wonderful bone structure, and it's going to get jolly hot soon. Just a thought,' Tor added innocently. 'Your life, your hair.'

Rose looped her hair under and turned her head experimentally in the mirror. 'We've already got water restrictions up at the cantonment.'

'Will Jack mind?'

Rose hesitated and thought about this.

'He's never actually said he likes all this.' Rose lifted up her hands under her hair and let it fall like spun silk to her shoulders. 'So I honestly don't know.'

Tor was glad to hear Rose sound even faintly rebellious about him. If it was possible to be too good-natured Rose was, and it worried Tor sometimes.

The Bombay Yacht Club was full at one fifteen when they arrived for lunch the next day. As Rose, shorn and a little shy, made her way with Tor across the room, the conversation dipped for a moment and one old man screwed his monocle in and opened his mouth into a gaping hole as he openly stared at her.

'Rose,' muttered Tor, 'the hair is a success.'

Their waiter led them to a table in the corner of the room that overlooked the harbour. As he adjusted the shutter so they could better see the yachts below, a shaft of sunlight lit up their silver cutlery, the spotless glasses and the finger bowls each with a slice of lemon in them.

'Very lovely menu for today.' The handsome Italian maître d' flicked large linen napkins on to their laps. 'Fresh lobster from the harbour, sole Véronique, guinea fowl and pheasant à la mode. Champagne is on ice, madam,' he murmured near Tor's ear.

'Tor,' Rose whispered in a sudden panic, 'I don't want to be a killjoy, but I can't aff—'

Tor held her hand up. 'Hush, child. The champagne was ordered by your husband, Captain Jack Chandler, probably grovelling because he made you miss my party.'

'Jack!' Rose looked amazed. 'Are you sure it was him?'

'Quite sure.' Their eyes locked for a moment.

The waiter poured the champagne; the bubbles made Rose's nose wrinkle.

'Can you believe how sophisticated we are nowadays?' she said after drinking a glass. 'How incredibly grown-up.'

'Rose.' Tor put down her glass. 'I've only been here for three months. I don't want to go home. I can't—'

'Please don't,' said Rose. 'I can't bear it either. I—'

'Let's not talk about it yet,' said Tor quickly. 'It's too serious for champagne.'

'Quite right,' said Rose. 'Anyway, I'm sure half Bombay is already madly in love with you.'

Tor opened her huge humorous eyes very wide and silently held up three fingers.

'Oh, Tor! You beast!' Rose clapped her hand over her mouth. She was the best person to tell your secrets to. 'Anyone special?'

'Well. There's a boy called Oliver, he's a banker and we're having quite a jolly time of it.'

'Tor, I believe you're blushing. Is he husband material?'

'I don't know.' Tor pulled her bread roll to bits. 'Probably not – how can you tell? He's good fun and very manly, but—'

'Tor, please can I say one absolutely serious thing?' Rose said. 'Don't, whatever you do, rush into it. It's such a huge change in your life, and Middle Wallop isn't so very awful. And you've got to know at the very least that you can, or I mean, that you do love the person.'

They exchanged another quick look. And Tor got a stabbing feeling in her heart seeing how quickly Rose's face had flushed with emotion. She wanted to ask, 'Is everything all right, Rose? Does he make you happy?' but you didn't ask Rose things like that. She was a soldier's daughter.

'Of course I am,' she would have said. 'Everything is lovely.'

What else was she going to say now unless it was absolutely hell and he was beating her every night?

After two hours of talk, the waiter brought them coffee and sweet-meats. Tor leant back in her chair and appraised the room in a genial way.

'Oh God!' She suddenly froze. 'Am I going completely mad or can you see what I see?'

A group of around eight people, Indians and Europeans, were gathering up their things and preparing to leave, two tables down from where Tor and Rose were sitting.

'Oh no!' Tor's grip tightened. 'It's him.'

Rose followed Tor's gaze. 'Who?'

But Guy Glover had already seen them. He had a camera over his shoulders and when he saw Tor he got up, did an affected double-take and swaggered over to see them.

'Good Lord,' he drawled, 'what a surprise.'

'What are you doing here, Guy?' Tor did not return his smile. 'Viva said you were ill and had to leave rather suddenly.'

'I was ill.' Three people at his table, a Westernised-looking Indian and two very beautiful Indian girls, stood up. They were waiting for him to leave. 'But I'm much better now.' He swallowed hard, his Adam's apple bobbing up and down. 'In fact,' he said, eyes darting, 'I've got a job. I'm a photographer now.'

'A photographer?' Tor was amazed. 'Who for?'

'For a film company here,' he said. 'They're bringing talkies to Bombay, and some English actresses and they need— Look, this is awfully boring of me but I've got to go. Everyone is waiting for me outside.'

'So you're better now.' Tor's tone was unusually icy. 'Viva will be relieved to know that.'

'Yes, much better, thank you.'

When he started to pat his pockets, first his top left then the right, Tor noted he still had dirty fingernails.

'Damn,' he said. 'I've left all my cards at home. But if you see Viva tell her I haven't forgotten her, she's due a little windfall. And by the way,' he stepped back and gave Rose a prissy little smile, '*love* the hair. It makes you look like a beautiful boy.'

Chapter 28

Love the hair. When Guy left, Rose and Tor made each other laugh by imitating him, but now Rose felt less sure about her dashing new look.

Last night, as she'd stared at herself in the Mallinsons' bathroom mirror and tried to see it through Jack's eyes, she'd felt that seeds of terror had been planted in her. Twisting and turning in the half-light she could see how fashionable she looked with it, but so different too, like another kind of person, and here her nerve had failed and she'd felt angry at herself: it was only a stupid haircut for heaven's sake, but she had no idea whether Jack would like it or not; there was still so much about him she couldn't predict, in fact, when you got right down to it, whole slabs of him she didn't know.

Recently, at the club, Maxo, Jack's best friend, had told her – he'd been a little tight at the time – about some of the fun he and Jack had had together and she could almost hear him thinking, *Before you came.* Something about pinning a friend's uniform to the door on the night before an inspection, also a mad guest night with the Fourteenth Hussars when they'd all drunk the Emperor's health out of Napoleon's jerry. 'They'd captured it at the Battle of Waterloo.' Maxo was almost speechless with laughter at the memory again, and Rose had smiled politely, but the story made her feel sad. It seemed to her that he was describing a completely different person – someone schoolboyish and a little wild, someone she might have enjoyed knowing.

As the train approached Poona Station the sun poured down on the tubs of Canna lilies and the sky above them was pure turquoise. She could see Jack standing in his riding clothes on the platform, his head moving rhythmically from side to side as he looked for her. *My husband*, she thought, *my spouse.* As if changing the word could jolt her into feeling something.

She thought about how in films when young brides met up again with their husbands, they wrestled impatiently with door handles;

they gasped with happiness as they flew down the platform on wings of love. So why the knot in her stomach as she watched him get bigger and bigger? She didn't want to feel frightened of him like this; she wanted to love him with all her heart.

The train was slowing to a squeaking halt. She stuck her head through the carriage window and mouthed, 'Jack!' She showed him her hair. 'Do you like it?'

His expression froze, then he shook his head.

Jack didn't tell lies. She knew that already – he'd pointed it out to her as a matter of pride. But wasn't it better sometimes to be kind rather than to be absolutely truthful – particularly about things that really didn't matter?

The train screamed and stopped. Porters in bright red jackets came rushing towards them, but he waved them away. He pecked her cheek and put his hand into the small of her back and pushed her through the crowd.

'Well, I like it,' she said out loud, although he couldn't hear her, 'I really do.'

But walking towards the car, his hand guiding her like the spoke of a propeller, she felt the same kind of queasy apprehension she used to feel at the end of the summer holidays when Mr Pludd drove her back to school.

She'd had such a wonderful time with Tor in Bombay – swimming and riding, good laughs and long easy talks – but as he drove her home she felt all her happiness draining away.

She tried talking for a bit: she said she'd bought him a shirt at the Army and Navy; he said that was good of her. He told her about some dinner party they'd have to go to next week, a polo match he'd be playing in on Friday, but his voice was so flat she knew he was livid.

When they were home again, she looked around her dusty new garden. Nobody had bothered to water the geraniums while she was away and their leaves were brown and wrinkled, but now was not a good time to bring that up. Dinesh, looking fierce and warrior-like, helped carry her suitcases in, and he seemed to greet her stiffly too. She thought, *He resents me for being home again; he'd rather be with Jack on his own.*

Durgabai padded in and handed Rose a cup of tea. A horrible cup with the usual bright globules of fat swimming on it, but she felt absurdly grateful for it and could have kissed Durgabai when she pointed towards her new hair and said, 'Nice, memsahib.'

Dinesh, sensing the storm approaching, glanced towards Jack to see what he thought of the hair, but Jack turned away quickly and said he'd like a wash before he went back to work. In the same constricted voice he said he had a meeting with the polo club committee after work. Rose didn't believe him.

'Big baby,' she muttered to herself. 'It's not that bad.'

Shortly after that Jack walked out of the house. He slammed the door hard, and left without patting her arm or smiling or anything. When he was gone, she ran into the bathroom to look at her hair again and saw how gaunt and pale her face looked in the mirror. She ran her hands through her bob. She liked the feeling of air on her neck, the freedom of it, but now when she looked at it again, she wasn't entirely sure the new cut didn't have just a touch of the Friar Tuck about it, which was how she and Tor always discussed other people's bad bobs. But how mean of Jack to react like this. How utterly childish.

When she walked into the bedroom, a cluster of dead insects lay inside the glass light above the iron bed, one still buzzing in a half-hearted way. In the corner of the room lay a pile of their dirty clothes – his shirts, her jodhpurs – the dhobi had forgotten to collect them.

How futile she felt, flat as a pancake. She took the spotted cravat she'd bought for Jack in the gift shop at the Bombay Yacht Club from its wrappings. It lay in her hands, limp and foolish. He'd probably hate that too, and tell her it was too expensive.

Aching from the train ride, she thought a bath might pass the time and calm her down. She walked into the garden to find the water man and saw Shukla sitting on the steps outside her mother's hut, chopping onions. The girl leapt to her feet; she tried to close the door but Rose caught a glimpse of some cheap-looking statue garlanded with flowers. The smell of incense made her nose wrinkle.

Rose felt a surge of impatience. Where was the water man, and why did the simplest things here lead to exasperating complexities? At home when you wanted a bath you turned on a tap; here Durga-bai, who didn't like Dinesh, would have to ask him to find Ashish, the wash man, who lived in a squalid hut on the edge of their compound and who daily emptied their commode and fetched their bathwater. The water would then have to be heated in the two-gallon oil cans that stood in a row outside the bungalow and hauled inside.

Poor Ashish, no wonder he was skinny as a ten-year-old boy. He was an untouchable, Jack had explained, the lowest of the low in the Indian caste system.

While she waited, Rose sat on a chair in her bedroom leafing without enthusiasm through the recipes at the back of *The Complete Indian Housekeeper*. Marmalade pudding, sago and tapioca jelly; that sounded a bit school-dinnery.

Jack had recently begun to hint that after the round of dinner parties welcoming Rose to Poona, they'd soon be expected to ask people back. This seemed reasonable, but because cooking was so new to her, her mouth went dry at the thought of giving a whole dinner party by herself. She'd heard already how ruthlessly catty the women at the club could be to those who failed. *My dear, tough as old boots. A horrid sauce, why have three cheeses in this heat?*

She'd been trying to remember the kind of puddings Mrs Pludd had cooked: apple crumbles, blancmanges – simple stuff – but the authors of *The Complete Indian Housekeeper*, authorities on everything from tapeworms in children to lizard traps, made it all sound so hard. First they said she must decide what kind of sweet: those made with farinaceous substances or cream, those stiffened with gelatine or clear jellies, or cakes and puddings. The chocolate blancmange came with a stern warning: 'Indian cooks never boil this enough. They use too much flour and leave it with a raw taste.' Rose, who didn't have a particularly sweet tooth anyway, sighed.

'Memsahib.' Ashish knocked on her door. 'Water is here.'

Watching his skinny shoulders straining across the floor, she felt weary of it all: this man with his shifty look; the servants outside whispering and waiting; Jack and his bad mood, the ladies at the Poona Club, most of whom would know by lunchtime tomorrow that she'd had her hair cut.

When the big tin bath had been filled, she got down on her hands and knees to check there were no scorpions or snakes hiding in the plug or underneath it.

'It's fine,' she told Ashish. 'Thank you.'

And exactly one hour after she had first thought about it, she took off her dress and stepped into the bath.

She cried for a while, silently so the servants wouldn't hear, and when she opened her eyes again she told herself she was behaving like a brat – snivelling in the bath and feeling so wretched. No wonder Jack could hardly be bothered to talk to her. She picked up her watch and rubbed steam from its face. Four o'clock. Four hours between now and Jack coming home for supper. Firming her jaw under her bath hat, she told herself to buck up now and behave like someone of nineteen, not nine. After she'd washed, she'd do what Mummy so often advised and pretend nothing nasty had happened: she'd put on a pretty dress, a little scent. She'd cook Jack his favourite supper, which was steak and kidney pudding and should, surely, be easy enough to cook.

Fired with enthusiasm, she sent Dinesh out to Yusuf Mehtab's, the best butcher in Poona. Dinesh's austere expression had softened when she'd explained that this dish was Jack's favourite; he'd even laughed when she'd mooed elaborately and made her fingers into little horns and said with the aid of her phrase book, 'I would like rump steak, please.'

Next, she took down a selection of pitted Bakelite dishes from the cupboard. She unscrewed the flour jar, slightly damp and clogged but surely serviceable, and remembered she'd forgotten to ask Dinesh to buy the two tablespoons of fat, Mrs Pludd had said, for the suet crust. Well, ghee would have to do.

Shukla went out to see if there were any vegetables they could use; the spring greens she returned with looked a little yellow about the stalks, but they'd have to do too – the vegetable wallah only came twice a week.

Flowers. Rose, followed by Durgabai and Shukla, went into the garden, where the only flowers in bloom apart from the parched geraniums were bougainvillea. Durgabai held the trug, Shukla the scissors.

'It's all right,' Rose said. 'I can do this on my own.' She snipped away at a few dusty stems.

'Please, memsahib.' Durgabai's glorious eyes had pleaded as she took the flower basket with the two flowers in it. Durgabai's husband was an invalid. He shrank back inside his hut whenever he saw Rose. The entire family, Jack said, lived in terror of losing the job and the shed that went with it. Rose understood, she sympathised, but she still wanted to cut her own flowers with her own scissors. It was one of the few jobs around here she was allowed to do.

When Dinesh brought the steak home, she could have cried. She'd smelt it coming through the door, and when he set it down on the table in the kitchen, she saw the muscles in his arms bulge as he tried

195

to cut it. Also, she'd indicated kidneys by pointing under her ribs, but Dinesh had brought a string of evil-looking sausages instead.

'Thank you, Dinesh.' She'd pocketed the change. She'd been told, by more than one mem at the club, to punish lapses like this by fines, but she must have asked for the wrong cut and Dinesh had tried his hardest and, who knows, she might have said sausages by mistake or he'd thought she meant intestines. She'd confused him as she seemed to do a million times a day.

Before she started cooking, she tried to recall Jack's routine at work, so the pie would get into the oven on time. Usually, he worked until three in the afternoon and then went to the polo ground to practise with the Third Cavalry's A-team, or the Crackpots as they called themselves. Rose, a good rider herself, liked to go and watch him if she could.

It cheered her to see him thundering up and down the field on Bula Bula or Topaz or Simba, his favourite mounts: the way he tuned himself to them, listening to their breathing, anticipating their turns – for his horses were so well trained they spun round with the merest movement of his head. More than once, watching him on the polo field, laughing and dirty as a boy, she'd thought, *This is Jack at his happiest*, and wished that she could make him look like that.

After polo practices, they often went to the club, where she was already on first-name terms with half a dozen or so junior wives, and was occasionally nodded at by Mrs Atkinson, the colonel's wife, who she found glacial and condescending.

Before Jack had taken her there, he'd told her cautionary tales about junior mems who drank too much or who got too familiar with senior officers' wives. He'd pretended to joke but she'd known he was serious. He'd encouraged her to drink weak whiskies drowned in soda as a chota peg, which made her feel frightfully adult.

'It's not considered common here,' he'd assured her, 'it's almost medicinal.' He warned her about gossip. 'The same old stuff goes round and round because they don't have enough to do,' he'd said, meaning the wives.

Well, that was certainly true – last week, she'd heard twice about a Major Peabody's wife who had got tight on the dance floor and danced very suggestively with a junior officer, and about the inedible meal someone else had cooked at a dinner party, which had given everybody a gippy tummy for days afterwards.

Twice already, Jack dressed in full uniform with miniature medals, had clanked off in his spurs for regimental dinners at the mess where, according to the indulgent gossip from the mems, boys behaved like boys. She'd heard the gup about a pony being brought in to jump a sofa at four o'clock in the morning. Jack had told her how he'd broken his wrist last year during a midnight steeplechase.

And again, these tales conjured up another, wilder version of Jack unknown to her yet, or only partly glimpsed, when he staggered home after mess nights, half-tight and smelling of brandy and usually wanting to make love. The last time he'd done this was awful: he'd gone all red-faced and blustery and hadn't even bothered to take off his shirt.

'Relax, relax, relax, let me have at you,' he'd said angrily and intently, and for some reason this cry had reminded her of his urgent bellows of 'Leave it! Leave it!' on the polo pitch when he wanted to score the goal. So horrible, so embarrassing – she'd hated every minute of it.

'He's late.' Rose was looking at the clock above the dining-room table, trying not to mind about the acrid smells coming from the oven, or the fact that the candle had just shed its waxy load over the polished candlesticks. *Where was Mrs Pludd when one needed her?* she thought, trying to jolly herself into a better mood, because she'd put the pie in miles too early and had to turn the oven off and on twice since seven-thirty.

She moved into the sitting room and sat in the armchair nearest the front door. She'd put on a pale peach print floaty dress, something feminine, she'd reasoned, to offset the new hair. She'd put her prettiest pearl earrings on – they'd been inherited from her grandmother, a famous beauty with the same fine skin as Rose's – a dab of Devonshire violets behind her ears. And now she sat feeling foolish and alone, an actress with no audience. She kicked off the silk shoes that she and Mummy had bought that day in London. The sight of them brought a pang. How childish that girl seemed to her now that she drank whisky and slept every night with a man and knew about five different kinds of pudding.

When the car door slammed at a quarter to nine, she leapt to her feet. Jack walked in smelling of alcohol. When he looked at her hair again he winced – or was she imagining this? – as if to tell her in code that he still minded and she was not forgiven.

'Hello, darling,' she said in the same sensible voice her mother used when her father was fractious. 'Would you like a drink before supper? It's steak and kidney pie.'

'No, thanks,' he said, 'I'm very hungry.' He looked towards the smoke billowing out of the kitchen.

Rose was trembling as she drew the curtains on the blackness of the night and lit an oil lamp. Earlier, she'd tried to make their dining room look special, which wasn't easy with its rush matting and mismatched furniture. She'd got Shukla to polish the cutlery and put the last three sprays of bougainvillea in a vase on the table.

Jack picked up the vase. 'D'you mind if I move these?' he said. 'The smell puts me off my food.'

Well, bougainvillea didn't smell but never mind.

'Not at all,' she said serenely. 'Put them on the sideboard.'

Then Dinesh, proud as a show pony, burst from the kitchen holding the steak and kidney pie; he was thrilled to be serving Jack's favourite dish.

Shukla, too shy to meet their eyes, scuttled in carrying the vegetables. The spinach had disappeared into algae like pools of slime.

'Shall we start?' There was an explosion of crumbs as Rose plunged her knife into the pie. Sawing through the crust, she talked brightly and emptily for a while about what fun it had been seeing Tor and how she'd like to have her to come and stay and that maybe they could all go hunting.

'Well, ask her then,' Jack said without any particular enthusiasm. She knew for sure now that he didn't like Tor much, and to be fair to Jack, although she didn't much feel like it at this moment, Tor did ham it up a bit in front of him – teasing him too much and becoming a little artificial and loud – but then you had to know Tor to realise that this was what she did when she felt shy or out of her depth.

'I'm sure we can find her a horse.' *If we have to*, he may as well have added.

There was another scattering of crumbs as he put his knife into his pie.

They chewed in silence for a while. Rose was humiliated: the pie was so disgusting – the meat high, the gravy full of white lumps where the flour had been carelessly stirred.

Jack took a sip of wine and looked away from her. The servants stood at the kitchen door waiting for his reaction. She put her knife and fork down with a bang.

'Don't eat it, Jack,' she said. 'It's absolutely revolting.'

She felt a huge tear roll down her cheek. He kept on eating.

'It's edible,' he said. 'Just.'

'It's vile. Please would you send the servants to bed?' She stared at the tablecloth and more tears fell. It was torture to her being seen like this.

Jack stood up and sighed heavily. He walked to the kitchen door. '*Jao! Jaldi*, Durgabai, and Dinesh, memsahib and I want to be alone.'

When the door was closed, he sat down beside her.

'I'm sorry,' she said at last. 'I'm behaving like a perfect fool.' She gave a whoop of misery and wiped her eyes on her napkin.

'Whatever is the matter, Rose?'

'You hate my hair, don't you?' she cried out bitterly.

'Well,' he looked dumbstruck, 'since you ask, no, I don't like it much, but for God's sake, Rose, don't ever cry in front of servants like that.'

'I'm sorry,' she said.

He stood up and walked towards the window. She looked at his back, suppressing an urge to shout that of course it wasn't just her stupid hair.

Her chair scraped as she got up. 'I think I'll go to bed if you don't mind.'

'Not at all,' he said. 'I think you should.'

'I don't normally behave like this,' she said at the door.

'Good,' he said, without a smile, before she closed it.

Crying, she discovered that night, this sort of comfortless, adult crying, made your eyes swell and gave you a ravenous thirst.

But just before dawn, when she'd all but convinced herself the marriage was a disaster, he'd come to her from the spare room where he'd been sleeping. He got into their bed, put his arms around her and muttered, 'Oh, my poor Rose, please don't.'

Which had made it worse. She'd said with a spluttering laugh, 'You must think you've married a madwoman.' She'd put her hot cheek against his chest, and hugged him blindly.

'But this *is* different.' His voice boomed out from his chest. 'It's hard. I do forget that.'

She wanted him to keep holding her like this. It was all she wanted. But then she felt him lift her nightdress and stroke the inside of her thighs and do all the other things that still made her feel so embarrassed.

'Don't fight me, Rose,' he said. 'Let me—'

And for the first time, she felt a definite something, not the overwhelming thing she'd dreamt of – the absence of which had so disappointed her on her honeymoon – but a glimpse of some animal comforts being given and received, something better than words.

'Now, stop that, you silly creature,' he'd teased her afterwards. 'That's quite enough of that.'

'I never cry,' she'd reassured him again. 'Ask Tor.'

'I will, next time I see her.' He'd stroked her breasts.

And they'd slept for the first time in each other's arms.

Chapter 29

When Frank phoned Viva to say that he was back in Bombay and wanted to come and see her, Viva didn't answer at first.

'Frank from the ship,' he prompted her. 'Do you remember me?'

'Of course I remember you,' she said. She was smiling and felt a flush of heat.

'I'd like to come and see you and talk to you about Guy Glover.' Frank sounded guarded. 'Something's cropped up which I think you should know about.'

'Oh no, not Guy,' she said. 'What's he done now?' She heard him breathe down the phone, a kind of sigh.

'I'll tell you when I see you, but don't be alarmed.'

'I'm not,' she said. 'I try never to think of him.' There was a thump at the other end as if he was about to hang up.

'How are you, Frank?' she said. 'Where are you living? Did you manage to find a job?' Why was she sounding so formal, almost as if she was interviewing him, when in fact she was grinning because it was good to hear his voice again even though he sounded a little strange himself?

'I've been doing some research up north,' he said. 'We've been running clinics out in the country near Lahore, mostly with children, but our grants ended so I'm back in Bombay for a few months. I'm at the Gokuldas Tejpal Hospital.'

'Where's that?'

'Not far from the Cruickshank Road. How about you?' The brisk tone in his voice had softened.

'I'm very well, thank you.' She'd made up her mind not to tell anyone about how awful those first few weeks had been – the closest she'd ever felt to a nervous collapse. 'It was hard at first, but now I'm working at a children's home and I'm writing a bit and I have my own room in Byculla – nothing fancy but mine.

'Does Guy know my telephone number?' she said, when he didn't respond to this. 'Has something happened I should know about?'

'Not for discussion over the phone.' Frank's voice had lowered almost to a whisper. 'Can I come and see you? What time do you get back from work?'

She worked out quickly how long it would take her after work to wash, to dress, to do her hair and look presentable and then was annoyed with herself. What on earth did it matter what she looked like?

'I'm busy tonight,' she said. 'How about tomorrow?'

He said tomorrow was fine.

She gave him her address and he rang off. When she took her hand away from the phone her fingers were wetly imprinted on it, like a starfish in the sand.

After she'd spoken to him she stood and looked at her room, trying to see it through his eyes. When she'd first arrived, less than a month ago, she'd thought the tiny room horrible, even frightening, a true sign that she had come down in the world and would probably go down further.

The room was free, as Daisy had promised, and its location, above Mr Jamshed's shop on Jasmine Street, was central, but with its badly painted walls against which lizards darted at night, its one naked light bulb, the thin rush matting and the curtain with the gas cooker behind, it had reminded her of the meanest kind of London bedsit, only sticky and hot. On her first night here, she'd sat out on her tiny balcony smoking a cigarette and looking down on the nondescript street, wondering what madness had brought her here.

The next day, she'd scrubbed her room until it was spotless. She'd burned a stick of sandlewood incense to take the smell of old food away. She'd put her parents' quilt on the bed; its squares of red, green and purple silk lit up like stained glass when the sun rose, throwing patterns of light on the floor.

Daisy came on the second night with an embroidered cushion, a Persian poem and a bunch of hyacinths in her hands.

> *When of thy worldly goods*
> *Thy find thyself bereft,*
> *And from the goodly store*
> *Two loaves alone are left.*
> *Sell one, and with the dole*
> *Buy hyacinths to feed the soul.*

Viva had framed the poem and hung it above her bed in a carved frame.

The following weekend, she and Daisy had gone to the Chor Bazaar – the Thieves' Market – and bought cutlery and a kettle and a fine-looking chair which she'd re-covered in an old Kashmiri shawl. She'd found an old blue and green enamelled mirror, which she'd put above the sink. At last, the room felt like hers.

On her first night, Mr Jamshed, a well-educated Parsee, who was large and jolly and noisy, had beckoned her impatiently over the threshold of the household as though she was some tardy prodigal daughter. He'd made her sit in a chair near his window so she could see his racing pigeons fly through peach-coloured light and brought her chai to drink. He'd introduced her to his daughters, Dolly and Kaniz, beautiful confident girls who bobbed their hair and wore lipstick and evidently ran rings round their father. 'They are very much for teasing me,' he'd told Viva, his eyes shining with pride and delight.

Mrs Jamshed, plump and shy at first, had insisted she stay for dinner and they'd sat around a long table in the courtyard and piled her plate with a stuffed fish covered in a leaf, and rice and vegetables, and then, later, a sweet custard pudding, until she felt she would burst. It was Mrs Jamshed who later introduced her to the Indian word *russa*, a way of cooking and serving food with love, and who warned her that unless she left some food on her plate she would go on and on being served in an Indian house until she felt like bursting.

That night, full and happy, she'd lain down in her new bed and looked at the stars shining through her scruffy curtains, and thought with shame of the hospitality she had so grudgingly meted out to anyone who'd turned up at Nevern Square, even wanting a cup of sugar. Particularly if she was writing. She squirmed to think what a frosty welcome the Jamsheds, so well educated and courtly in their manners, would receive in London, where few landladies would give them a bed. The kindness they'd shown had humbled her. She had so much to learn.

Her job at the Tamarind Home in Byculla began two days later. She'd taken the job with the quite cynical intention of earning enough money to write, perhaps get some good stories and then go up to Simla, and get what she now thought of as 'that damned trunk'. It hadn't worked out like that.

She got off the bus full of trepidation that first morning. The Tamarind Home, which looked dark and dilapidated from a distance, had once belonged to a wealthy flower merchant. Up close its elegant windows, half-eaten carvings, elaborate iron railings now rusting, showed a faded beauty in decline.

She'd been shown around its dark corridors and spartan dormitories by Joan, a cheerful Scottish midwife who said she was going upcountry soon to do a survey on village midwives and their mortality rates.

Joan told her they had room for fifteen to twenty girls here, and that they were mostly orphans, some abandoned at their gates and some found by a team of volunteers who went out three times a week in search of children who might need a temporary roof over their heads. A few boys were allowed in, but they preferred to keep the sexes apart. 'Makes everybody's life easier,' she said with a cheerful wink.

The home was open to Muslim and Hindu alike, and the aim was to eventually return children either to their families or to suitable homes.

'Don't get the idea we're doing them some great favour,' Joan said. 'If they're starving, they're grateful for the food, but some hate being dependent on our charity, particularly the older ones. Some would actually prefer to stay in the meanest slum than come here.'

Joan said that Thursday was an open clinic day when the general public could come in and be seen to by a splendid team of volunteer doctors, some European, some Maharashtrian. Children who needed more specialist attention could be seen for free at the Pestonjee Hormusjee Cama Hospital for women and children, which was up the road.

It was clear from the peeling plaster on the walls and the lack of furniture that the whole enterprise ran on a shoestring. What money the charity could raise was spent on clinics for sick children. While they were walking across the courtyard, a fluttering, cooing troop of small girls in brilliant saris suddenly landed beside them, touching Joan, and smiling and laughing at Viva. 'They want to sing you a song,' Joan explained. When they'd burst into song, Viva thought, *You never see Europeans with their eyes this bright, their smiles so wide.* Poor they might be, but they burst with life.

At lunch, eaten at trestle tables in the courtyard with the children, she was introduced to Clara, an Irish nurse who was large and pale and freckled and struck her as being a bit of a sourpuss. She slapped the dhal on to plates, and while the children tucked in, said in a resentful aside that she'd worked in another orphanage in Bombay and 'sure, this place is the Ritz compared to that'.

Joan explained how some Indian orphanages were terrifying places where children got severely beaten or the girls sold off to old men. 'It's taken us a long time to gain the trust of the local people. We always have to be very, very careful, don't we, Clara?' but Clara had refused to smile. She'd given Viva a funny look as if to say, 'You don't fit in here,' and every time, in the days to come, that Viva was put on a shift with Clara she felt like an apprentice misfit and very self-conscious in the part.

What *was* she doing here? She wasn't a nurse, she wasn't a charity worker, she wasn't even sure she liked children very much. What she mostly felt in those early days was a sense of being on the run, mainly from herself.

Things changed. On her second day, Clara took her to see the row of children waiting to be assessed by the visiting doctor. The children stood behind locked gates, barefoot and ragged, one or two of them had looked at her with a wild desperation in their eyes. They'd salaamed her, made small chewing gestures with their mouths, tried to touch her through the railings. Every single one of them seemed to be saying, 'Help me.'

One of the girls broke into a wild torrent of words to Clara. 'Her mother died a few months ago,' Clara explained to Viva. 'She's walked here from a village seventy-five miles away. Her father is dead too, and her relatives don't want her.'

And Viva had felt a shaming, a husking of the soul – the task of helping seemed so overwhelming and she was trained for nothing.

They gave her easy things to do at first. Joan told her to sit at a table in the courtyard and when the children arrived she, with the help of a Maharashtrian woman who worked as an interpreter, recorded their names in a large leather ledger. She noted the date they came in, their address, if any, and who assessed them, what drugs they were to have and whether the doctor wanted them back. They hardly ever did.

There were never enough doctors to go round. Joan, Clara and occasionally Daisy did what they could with limited medical supplies and referred really sick cases to the hospital.

On her first day at this job, halfway through the morning, the wonderfully reassuring Daisy Barker had bounced through the gates, completely at home here and followed by a line of chirping little girls who fought to bring her a glass of water. She sat down beside Viva. 'Surviving?' she'd asked.

'I'm fine,' Viva had said, but she'd felt shaken to the core.

For that morning, a crowd of pleading children had become individuals. She'd met Rahim, an intense, angry-looking Muslim boy, pockmarked and lean, whose father had been doused in petrol and fatally burned in what Clara thought was a gangland dispute. Rahim had wanted to leave his six-year-old sister while he went away and tried to make some money. He could no longer feed her: she'd been ill with flu and he was frightened to keep her with him on the streets. When they parted, the boy had touched his sister gently on the arm; she'd watched his thin child's body walk back down the street before it disappeared into the crowd.

'Couldn't he have stayed too?' she'd asked Joan.

'He was ashamed,' she had answered. 'He wants to get her out as soon as he can.'

She'd met Sumati, aged twelve. After her mother had died of tuberculosis, she'd tried to support a family of four younger brothers and sisters by taking rags from a rubbish dump, but was now worn out.

Around lunchtime an explosion of noisy boys, naked except for loincloths, had run in on their tough bare feet – for the home also ran a lunchtime soup kitchen, mostly staffed by local women. Most of the boys slept rough, Daisy explained, in cardboard boxes near the railway line. They walked for miles each day to have this one small bowl of rice and dhal and piece of fruit, and to use the cold tap in the courtyard to clean their teeth with their fingers and wash themselves which they did with great thoroughness and modesty. Daisy said they thought themselves the luckiest fellows alive to be allowed to do this.

'It makes you think, doesn't it?' she said. It certainly did.

'You know, one day,' Daisy said before she left, 'you might write more than their names in a book. You could write their stories.'

On the Monday of her second week there, things changed again. Fat Joan, breathless and scarlet in the face from running across the courtyard, came with news that 'all hell had broken loose' in a nearby slum behind the cotton factory.

A water pipe had burst, twenty had already been drowned. Half an hour later a stream of slum dwellers arrived on foot, in rickshaws, in old taxis, in carts, plastered in a foul-looking mud; many crying and pleading for help.

The adults were sent to a local hospital where there was a temporary shelter; children who appeared to have no adults were to stay. Tin baths began to appear in the courtyard, some kerosene stoves were lit to warm up food.

'You'd better put that away and help us.' Clara had shut Viva's ledger with a spiteful look and handed her an apron. 'You're in at the deep end now.'

A girl called Talika was plucked from the crowd of children cowering near the school's iron gates. About seven years old, she was pitifully thin with huge brown eyes and matted hair and wore a floral dress several sizes too big for her. She had a label round her neck that read, '*Hari kiti*' – help me.

When Talika prostrated herself before Viva, her small rag doll fell in the dirt beside her. And Viva, feeling the child's matted little head butting her shoes, had felt so many different things. Sorrow for this pathetic scrap; anger at her plight; revulsion, for the child, who had a bad cold, had left a snail's trail of snot across her stockings; and fear that she was the one now expected to do something about her.

A line of temporary cloth cubicles was swiftly erected in the courtyard. Daisy and Clara ran around putting tin baths in each and distributing bars of soap and towels.

Viva had led Talika behind one cubicle. Without brothers or sisters she'd never done anything like this before; both of them were embarrassed.

'Take this off.' She'd pointed towards the child's muddy dress and the child had looked at her with huge appalled eyes, put her doll down on the cork matting and stepped out of her clothes. She shuddered as she stepped into the cold water, but soaped herself obediently all over, her little fingers working busily but her eyes downcast. From the next-door cubicle she could hear that Daisy was already singing and laughing with her child; Viva felt frozen.

She'd poured water over the small head, repelled by the dirt that flowed out of Talika's hair. She'd rubbed in the special carbolic soap Daisy had given them for head lice. Talika hadn't cried at all, even when some of the soap ran into her eyes. She'd stood there, numb with shock. When she was dry, Joan came and gave the child a new dress and a new doll – the old one was taken away to be fumigated. She was taken to the dormitory on the first floor she'd share with ten other girls for as long as it took for her to be either claimed or abandoned. They gave her a mattress and a cover, her own pencil.

At the end of that day, Viva had been standing near the gates, light-headed with shock and fatigue, when she'd seen Talika again. She'd been given a brush twice her size, and as she swept up leaves that had fallen from the tamarind tree in the courtyard, her expression was disciplined and grave. She had a job to do; she would do it well. And the thought that passed through Viva's mind was, *Well, if she can hold her life together, so can I.*

Frank was coming tonight, and as she walked to work that day she wondered why he'd sounded so serious, so different. It was perfectly possible, she thought, stepping off a cracked pavement and on to the street again, that Guy wasn't the only thing he wanted to warn her about, he himself might have formed another attachment with some other woman in Lahore. Not that they'd ever had anything like an attachment themselves, she reminded herself, waving at the man in the chai shop who waved at her each morning. It was the Guy situation that had forced them into a curious openness, as if, during their vigils in Guy's cabin, they'd been stranded together on a desert island. This had led to the curious, maybe illusory feeling of knowing him and having been seen by him in some true way.

It was market day and the crowds on the street were starting to thicken. The man who had just passed her had two live chickens in his arms – she returned his smile. 'Halloo,' he said, 'missy girl!' On the next corner, one of the boys she'd met at the home broke into a jerky spontaneous dance when he saw her.

Frank. If he did turn up tonight, she decided, walking up the last block of pavement before Tamarind Street, she would have a drink with him, maybe supper, nothing else. William had written to her that week, a cool letter in his careful script, advising her strongly to come back to England after she'd picked up the trunk.

'I'm quite sure it's what your parents would have wanted – I certainly cannot imagine they would want you gallivanting around India on your own.'

She shook her head silently when she thought about this: how dare he act as her parents' puppet, when really his interest in her was mostly physical. When she thought about him – his black socks, his white legs, his tight smile as he levered himself into bed beside her – her soul writhed. What a hideous muddle the whole thing had become. She didn't even blame him much any more, the mistake was hers; loneliness was not love, and only now could she see how lost and unstable she'd been during that time. 'It'll never happen again,' she muttered as she walked.

By the time she got to the home, heat was rising off the pavement in tarmacky waves. It was Thursday, the day when the Tamarind opened its door to the locals, and a long line of patients waiting to see the doctor spilled on to the street. A young mother sat on the kerb under a broken umbrella, her baby splayed out on her lap like a pressed leaf. Beside her, a man fanned his wife who was propped against the railings. On and on it seemed to go, this shuffling line of people bringing with them all the diseases of the poor: worms and boils, TB, gastroenteritis, typhoid, cholera, even leprosy – all laid at the feet of two long-suffering volunteer doctors who examined patients behind curtained cubicles on the verandah.

Eight hours later, after bathing children and making beds and helping in the office, Viva walked home again through the pink dust of sunset. Frank. The thought of him had grown in her mind all day, but now, with her feet throbbing and her dress stuck to her back, she dreaded him coming too early. She needed time to wash, to sleep, to stop feeling so vulnerable.

She climbed the stairs, wearily hoping Mr Jamshed wouldn't pop out as he sometimes did, and insist she come in for a drink and 'all kinds of chinwag'.

Normally at this time after a bath and a small meal, she put on her lamp and started to write, but tonight she lay on the bed, closed her eyes and found herself planning what she would wear to greet him. The red dress – too festive, too expectant of an event. Well then, the blue skirt and top – too boring. When she came to, she was cross. It didn't matter what Frank liked, was her last thought before she went to sleep.

She sat up in bed when she heard the knock and looked towards her door. Behind the frosted glass she saw a dark silhouette bobbing. She put on a silk kimono and tried to put the lights on.

'Wait a second.' She fumbled with a candle. 'Power cut.' They were always having them.

'Viva.' His voice was muffled behind the glass.

'Frank, wait.'

When she opened the door, he was standing in the yellow light of an oil lamp Mr Jamshed had put on the stairs. He was thinner than she remembered, less boyish, but with the same shock of butterscotch-coloured hair, the same smile.

'I'm late,' he said. 'There was an emergency at the hospital and no one could cover for me.'

He was staring at her as if he couldn't quite believe she was there.

'Can I come in?' he said.

'Give me a moment.' She clutched her kimono around her. 'I fell asleep. I—'

She hated the thought that he would take her state of undress as some sort of sign. 'Oh, wait a second.'

She closed the door on him and flew around in the shadows, bumping into her bed as she put on her red dress. She stuck a silver comb in her hair and lit two more candles.

'Right,' she said, opening the door again, 'you can come in now; it's a frightful mess, I'm afraid.'

He stood at the door as if reluctant to come in. She could feel his eyes taking stock of everything: the charpoy, the typewriter, the picture Talika had made her that hung on the wall above her work table.

'Don't you lock your door?' he said.

'Sometimes, not always. My landlord has a bolt on the front door.'

When he looked unconvinced, it annoyed her. Her room had nothing to do with him.

'D'you have many blackouts?'

'All the time,' she said. 'But Mr Jamshed says now the weather is hotter, the rats that eat the electric cables will start to die. It sounds far-fetched. Is it true?'

She was talking too much. Blathering.

'Could be.' The way he bunched up his mouth and pretended to think about this made her think he was feeling shy too, and for some reason this irritated her. The old ease between them had gone, and she wasn't sure yet whether she wanted to get it back.

The flickering lights made the atmosphere between them seem

hectic, unstable, and when they went out again entirely, it was a relief. 'I can't think in the dark,' he said. 'Let me take you out to dinner.'

It was a warm night in Jasmine Street, squares of yellow light fell from the higgledy-piggledy houses on either side of them, and the streets were full of robed people walking slowly home as the bazaars closed for the night. A few street girls – all gaudy jewels and huge painted eyes – hung around on the street corner.

'If you don't mind walking for ten minutes,' she said, 'there's a place called Moustafa's a few streets away. He makes the best *pani puri* in Bombay.'

'Sounds good to me,' he said. He smiled at her almost bashfully, much of the cocky self-assurance of the ship seemed to have gone.

On the next corner, a group of men sat in a café playing draughts in a fug of smoke. When one of them turned to look at her, she felt Frank's grip tighten on her arm.

'Do you walk alone here?' he asked her.

'Yes,' she said, 'I'm not frightened.'

'Maybe you should be.'

'What's the point of being frightened about things you can't control?' she said. *When the worst has already happened*, she thought to herself. 'And anyway, I can't believe how kind most people are here,' she said out loud. 'They put us to shame.'

'You're on your own,' he said, 'don't take too much for granted.'

This remark annoyed her. He had no right to talk to her like that, she thought, walking two steps ahead of him now towards the restaurant. She was tired of men pretending to be solicitous – William had done this – when what they were really doing was throwing their weight around, or wanting other things.

'Look,' he said when he caught her up, 'I am worried and you will understand when I tell you why. Has Guy Glover tried to contact you?'

'No.' She stopped under a lamppost gauzy with flying insects. 'But Rose wrote to tell me that she and Tor bumped into him at the Bombay Yacht Club. I think he said something about paying back the money he owed me.'

Frank turned to her.

'Don't take it,' he said quickly.

She looked at him. 'Why not? I worked for it. He owes it to

me. And he can probably afford it – Rose said he's working as a photographer now on the talkies.'

'Don't take it,' he warned her again. 'Promise me you won't. If you need money, I'll lend it to you or you can ask your parents.'

'I don't have parents,' she said. 'They died years ago.'

'I'm sorry.'

'It's not your fault,' she said, her usual glib response.

'I know it's not,' he said, but she'd made him look sad. He was about to say something else, but she stopped him. 'We're here,' she said. 'This is Moustafa's.'

She'd grown to like Moustafa's café with its scuffed tables and old chairs and curling pictures of the Acropolis. Its owner was an unshaven Greek, a warm, humorous man, dressed this night in a long Kashmiri tunic. He beamed at them, brought them a bottle of wine, polishing the glasses carefully with his cloth before he poured. He brought olives and nuts and mezze.

'If you ever wanted to tell me about your family, I'd feel glad you felt you could,' Frank said when they were alone again.

'Thank you,' she said. She was sorry she'd made him look so wary. 'But there really is nothing more to say.' She remembered with a sickening jolt the time when she had told William everything, and what had happened afterwards. Her clothes on his floor, his suit neatly hung, the false sincerity.

'Tell me about Guy,' she said. 'I thought that was why we were here.'

Frank was silent for a while. 'All right,' he said at last, 'I'll tell you what I know.'

He poured her a glass of wine and waited while she drank.

'Guy's parents threw him out last month – I think they were starting to get frightened of him. His mother wrote to me, a pathetic letter, and a sort of apology in a way. She said they'd had no idea about the state he was in. After he left, she started tidying his room and found all sorts of odd things: diagrams, diaries. She said there was quite a bit about you in them – something about a dark avenging angel.'

'Oh God!' She felt a kind of weary distaste. 'What does that mean? Is he mad?'

'I'm not sure. I've been reading up on some literature on mental states since I met Guy because he interested me. The voices he heard and so forth. There is this new thing called schizophrenia, a chap called Freud has been writing about it. It means split mind. Before, all the treatment for people like this assumed they were either depraved or wicked, but they're starting to think it might be a proper sort of disease of the mind. All this may be rot of course, he may simply be a chameleon, but the point is, well, I don't want to scare you, but I think he could be dangerous either way. The man he beat up on the ship was not a pretty sight.'

For a moment she looked at him suspiciously, wondering if he was beefing up the danger in an effort to impress her.

William had been good at this: bundling her on to the inside of a pavement out of the path of a non-existent car or horse, or lecturing her about men and what cads they could be – a bit of a joke in retrospect.

'Do you mind if I smoke?' said Frank, looking back at her.

'Not at all,' she said calmly.

'Nothing may come of it,' he said. 'I'm simply passing on the facts.'

'Do you think the parents knew he was a bit mad?' she said.

'It's possible. It solves the problem of why they thought he needed a chaperone at his age.'

'All right,' she said after a pause, 'but I still don't quite see what I can do about this.'

'Lock your doors for a start, be careful about who you ask back to your room. One of the diagrams his mother found was of the house in Jasmine Street. She has a hunch he may have got himself a room nearby. There's a distinct possibility he has a sort of fixation on you.'

'Oh God.' Viva shook her head. 'What a mess. But I don't ask people into my room,' she said, looking at him.

He looked straight back at her.

'Good,' he said.

'Is that all?' she said.

'No, not quite. There's one more thing. The police came to see me. I have no idea how they found me, but they asked if I knew anything about the All-India Muslim League. They're a political party actively campaigning for a separate Muslim India.'

'Why would Guy be involved in that? He never said a word about politics.'

'No? Well, he may not be but there are a number of young Englishmen out here actively working for them – some see themselves as radicals, others see it as a way of blocking India's independence. Some of his new chums on the fringes of the film industry are not what they seem: they're revolutionaries, political hot heads, it suits their purpose to infiltrate a world where many Europeans and Indians mix more freely. Some of them are violently against Gandhi's policies of non-violence, if that makes any sense to you.'

'Not much.'

'Well, what it means is that when the time comes to boot the British out some of them think we should leave with a bloody nose.'

'I still don't see what I've got to do with all this,' said Viva.

Frank blew out a plume of smoke. He looked worried.

'I don't know yet either, and I might be wrong about all of this, but he's an obsessive and you are on his list and my fear is that if he starts coming round to see you, he won't stop and then the police will think you're involved too.'

While they'd been talking, she could see Moustafa out of the corner of her eye, hovering with menus, and now he broke into their conversation, chiding them for looking so serious, and insisting they ate tonight's best dish, which was spicy meatballs and naan bread.

'He's right, you know,' smiled Frank. 'Let's eat and forget the ghastly child.'

So they ate and afterwards they took their coffee out on the streets where the air felt warm and heavy. 'Somebody's singing,' he said softly, and then she heard it too, from the house across the street: the jostling sound of Indian drums, and then the sound of a woman's voice, nasal and sad, swooping up and down the register.

'I'm starting to love it here,' she told him. 'It's really got under my skin again.'

'Me too,' he said. 'And I don't know why.'

It didn't seem to matter what she wanted – some of the shyness had gone between them. Over their liqueurs, when he talked to her about Chekhov, whose short stories he had just discovered, his face lit up with pleasure and it had occurred to her again that she may have misjudged him. He was intelligent and passionate about life. She liked the way you could see him working out a thought in his head, processing it like a philosopher before he spoke. The sight of the loose button on his linen suit made her feel she would like to sew it back on again, a feeling of tenderness she tried to squash. So many girls had had crushes on him on the ship that not being bowled over by him had given her a different kind of feeling, almost, you could say, a thrill.

She wanted to hold on to it.

In order to get back to this, she asked him what it was like to work at the hospital.

'It's like Blake's vision of heaven and hell,' he told her. 'Some parts of it are so primitive, but it's so interesting too. I've been given more responsibility there after two months than I would in twenty years in England.'

Then he did something William had almost never done: he stopped talking about himself and asked her about her life.

'Have you been up to Simla yet?' he said.

With a shock, she remembered she must have told him at some point about the trunk without telling him about her parents. It was hard sometimes keeping all her evasions clear, even in her own mind.

'No,' she said. 'Not yet.'

'Ah,' he said. 'That was where your parents lived.' It was more of a statement than a question, and she could feel him thinking again behind that intelligent gaze, trying to put it all together.

'Yes,' she said. 'Years and years ago.'

'Ah.' When he held her gaze for a moment, she felt cornered and a little panicked so she told him about the children she was meeting at Tamarind: their gaiety; their incredible bravery; how determined they were to survive.

'Will you write about them?' he asked. He'd remembered that too, and she could do nothing about the quiet spurt of happiness that followed. 'That was what you said you'd come to do. To write.'

'If I could do that, well,' she said, 'that would be something.'

'You'll do it,' he said. 'I can feel you will.'

That was all. And when he didn't even try to kiss her on the way home, she was not disappointed.

He's right, she thought, *I will do it.*

Lying in her bed an hour later, having drawn her curtains briskly against the stars, she was surer than ever it was a job she needed, not a man.

Chapter 30

BOMBAY, APRIL 1929

April came in like a fire-breathing dragon and Viva and Rose both got a telephone call from Tor. The Mallinsons, finding the heat unbearable, had taken themselves off to a hotel in the hill station of Mahabaleshwar for three weeks. Tor had the house to herself. She needed them to come and stay with her. Simple as that. She was tempted to add, 'It's an emergency,' but hoped if she had enough baths and drank enough gin, she could keep one mortifying secret to herself.

Rose – the reliable – had phoned immediately, saying of course she would love to come, for a week if that was convenient. Jack was all for it (*Oh, hooray for Jack*, thought Tor sarcastically) because the weather in Poona had been almost as hot as in Bombay, and he knew she'd be more comfortable in Ci Ci's house.

'If we swim,' she warned, 'it has to be in private and you're not to laugh at my cossie – I look like a baby whale in it.' She was four months pregnant.

Viva, to her considerable surprise, had also responded quickly. She said she was working at some children's home, and could stay only one night or two at the most. She'd work during the day but they could spend the evenings together. Tor could hardly wait to see them.

On the day before they came, Tor woke, as she had on every one of the mornings since her monthly period had failed to arrive, sweating with fear and pleading with God to put her out of her misery. For the rest of the day she made the *bhisti*, the water man, run up and down the stairs, bringing hot water in relays to her bathroom. She'd already taken five miniatures of Gordon's gin from Ci Ci's drinks cabinet and hidden them underneath her bed in the guest room. She'd almost fainted after her second bath and stubbed her toe painfully on her bed, but nothing had happened. Between baths, she'd stumbled around in the glare and scorching heat of the garden.

As she wobbled down the path, one of the gardeners had stopped her to show her a row of dead mynah birds, their beaks sticky with blood. He'd demonstrated to her with a graphic flapping of arms how the heat had burst their lungs, and then laughed as if this was a tremendous joke. And then, as if this wasn't enough, when she'd sat in the pond garden in a state, all she could hear through the shimmering air was the cry of the brain-fever birds that got on everybody's nerves at this time of year with their monotonous cries of *It's getting hotter! It's getting hotter! It's getting hotter!* as if anybody needed reminding.

Thank God Rose and Viva were coming, she thought. She was definitely going mad.

By three-thirty that afternoon, when the mercury in the thermometer was hovering at 107 degrees, she was determined to try one more time. She called Balbir, the water man, up to her room, and when she ordered him to fill up another bath with the hottest water he could find, she could feel the man – whose brown skin was already slick with sweat – practically rolling his eyes in disbelief at her folly. What kind of mad madam sahib took boiling-hot baths in weather like this?

Someone, Ci Ci's ayah probably, a sharp-faced little woman who padded around noticing everything, must have found the empty gin bottles. She'd pulled them out from under the bed and arranged them in a neat row on top of the dressing table as if to say, 'I know what you're up to.'

Rose was due at four, and while she waited for her, Tor padded around the house barefooted and leaving footprints on the wooden floors, trying to decide on the coolest bedroom to put her in. She settled eventually on a shuttered room at the back of the house that had pretty chintz curtains and a huge fan. She told Dulal, the boy who worked the tatti mats, that when Madam Sahib Chandler came he must work extra hard to keep her cool because she was – and she'd sketched the outline of a large tummy with her hands – like that. Dulal, who was young and handsome and rather impertinent, had stared at her and laughed out loud, bringing on a fresh burst of insecurity.

Why was he laughing at her like that? Did everyone know about the gin bottles now?

Rose was here. Plumper but still pale and beautiful – even with her bob half grown out. She was wearing a blue maternity dress and when she flung her arms around Tor and said, 'Oh golly, I've missed you,' Tor felt the hard bump of Rose's tummy against hers and had to bite the inside of her lip to stop herself crying. Why did Rose always do things so well, and she always get things so wrong?

Rose looked so happy to see her, and Tor, not wanting to spoil things immediately, took her out to the verandah for tea and cakes.

Rose sank into a deep chair. 'Oh, thank the Lord,' she said, crossing her still perfect legs. 'What bliss to feel halfway cool again.'

They gossiped for a while about this and that, and after tea, Rose fell asleep in her chair in the dormouse way Tor remembered from their childhood, when after a day's hunting Rose would eat her boiled egg and collapse in a heap over the kitchen table.

Tor looked down on her while she slept. What a wonderful friend she was, coming to see her immediately and making it sound like the only thing she wanted to do. She put a cushion behind her head and crept upstairs again.

There was just time, she estimated, for one more bath before supper. Pandit, who had to go off to find the water man, who was probably in his hut having supper, stomped off downstairs and made no secret of his irritation this time. He was bound to tell Ci when she came back.

Quarter of an hour later, she sat in her bath, naked and weeping. *Please, God, please, God, please, God. Please don't make me have this baby.* She drank another tumbler of gin from her toothbrush glass, crying, 'Urggh hideous!' as it went down. Even at the best of times she hated gin. After a few more minutes, feeling dizzy and sick, she got up and saw her lobster reflection in the steaming bathroom cabinet. She got out of the bath, dried herself slowly and cleaned her teeth, still waiting for the miracle to happen. Nothing – just that damn bird still mocking outside the window: *hotter, hotter, hotter* . . .

Time to get dressed. To cheer herself up, she put on a favourite midnight-blue dress, and then one of Ci's embroidered jackets – too tight now that she was putting on weight again – a double row of pearls, 'one row far too timid' was one of Ci's maxims, and went downstairs. She was determined not to spoil the evening yet.

'Tor, are you all right?' Rose said, as she walked into the living room. 'You look puce. Are you sickening for something?'

At that moment, Chanakya, the lighting man, walked in with a glowing taper to ignite the oil lamps on the verandah, and then another servant with a plate of cheese straws. Tor shot them a significant look. 'We had one but the wheels fell off,' she said casually to Rose – their warning code to each other for as long as they could remember for 'Can't talk now.'

Pandit arrived in his snowy evening uniform, his moustache bristling and officious, to ask them what time they would like to dine. He'd brought soda fountains and glasses with whisky in them, and small bowls of olives and cheese canapés.

Tor, who always ate more when she was worried or upset, ate two canapés quickly. What was the point of following Ci's ridiculous diets now?

'Come on, Piglet, out with it,' Rose said when Pandit had gone. 'Something's up.'

Tor took a deep breath and was about to answer when the doorbell rang. Viva had arrived, on the back of a motorbike driven by one of her friends from the children's home. She burst through the door, her hair wild and dusty, and carrying her clothes in an old satchel.

'Sorry I'm late,' she said. 'There was a huge demonstration opposite the VT Station. They were burning Union Jacks; there were fire engines, policemen. I didn't actually think I'd get here at all.'

'Oh, they're at it all the time now,' said Tor. 'It took me a whole hour to get to the races the other day; the road was blocked by Gandhi supporters sitting down. They may call it a peaceful demonstration, but it blocked the traffic for hours. Do you think they'll stop it soon?'

It was a relief to have something sensible to talk about, for she was aware of the worried way Rose was looking at her.

'No, I don't,' said Viva. 'Quite a few of the children we see at the home are already Gandhiji's girls. I think he'll change everything for ever.'

'Oh well, politics.' Tor dismissed the subject with a wave. 'Geoffrey Mallinson's so obsessed we actually fine him now for mentioning Gandhi – I mean, what a bore sitting there in his nappy spinning. Look, would anybody like a wash before dinner. V?'

*

Tor followed Viva up to Ci's elegantly marbled bathroom. She poured water into the basin so Viva could wipe the dust from her face. 'Thank you for coming, Viva,' she said.

'Well, you said it was an emergency.'

'Oh, that,' Tor said lightly. 'Just an excuse to get you here.'

Viva gave her a searching look. 'Sure?'

'Let's have dinner first and talk later,' said Tor.

The gin had made her feel pleasantly blurry around the edges and sentimental. All she really wanted was to forget all about her problems and have fun with these girls, her precious friends.

'Whenever you like.' Viva plunged her face into the basin. 'Oh, water, *water*,' she murmured. 'How divine. All I get from my tap at the moment is rust and dead flies. Would it be a nuisance if I had a quick bath before dinner?'

Pandit stomped up the stairs again with the water man.

When Viva came downstairs, she was wearing a simple coral dress which emphasised the slenderness of her waist, the dark abundance of her hair, which tonight hung loose around her shoulders. Her only adornment was a pair of long silver earrings she said she'd bought from a local market. Tor, looking at her, thought, *Why are some people just born impossibly glamorous without ever seeming to try?* Beside her, she felt fat and over-dressed, like a child who had raided Mummy's dressing-up box.

Dinner was served early in a long candlelit room, kept bearably cool by fans whirling slowly overhead. The French windows were open; the air was saturated with the scents of mimosa and frangipani. Beyond the dimming outlines of the garden, the lawns and the terraces, a vast yellow moon was sinking into the sea.

Rose's blonde hair shone like a child's in the candlelight. When they asked about her new baby, she said, yes, it was a lovely surprise, wasn't it? Neither of them had really expected it, but Jack was delighted, and so was she.

'This is so grown-up of you, Rose,' Tor said, her eyes vast and scandalised.

'Yes, it is, isn't it,' Rose agreed, but the only fly in the custard was that Jack's entire regiment might be moved soon to Bannu on the north-west frontier, which was very dangerous, but they'd cross that bridge when they came to it, she said serenely. 'Gosh, do look at that moon,' she said. 'Isn't it the most beautiful thing you've ever seen?'

All of them had looked up obediently, but then Tor put down her soup spoon. 'Hang on, Rose, what does this mean for you? Will you have to go too?'

'I've no idea yet – it hasn't been decided if wives are wanted on the voyage.'

Rose said this calmly and cheerfully as if it was a joke, but Tor recognised the small muscle that was twitching in Rose's cheek, just as it had when she was eight years old and steeling herself for something frightening.

'But don't you have *any* say in this at all?' said Viva fiercely. 'I mean, you're having a baby.'

'No, I don't,' said Rose. 'I'm an army wife now, and it's not exactly Jack's fault.'

Tor could suddenly feel her own heart pounding.

How precarious all our lives are, she thought. Night had suddenly fallen outside and she could see the leaping reflections of their candles against black windows. Rose, nineteen years old and pregnant, miles from home; Jack away, possibly in danger; Viva living in her hideous-sounding flat with dead flies in the taps; and herself, well, that didn't bear thinking about, not until after pudding.

'Pandit,' she rang the small bell at her elbow, 'is there any of that wonderful ice cream left, and maybe some millefeuilles?' Why not enjoy what they could while they could.

'Viva.' Rose put down her ice-cream spoon. 'What about you? What about this job of yours? You're always such a woman of mystery.' She punched her softly on the arm.

'Am I?' Viva said. 'I don't mean to be.'

'Well,' Rose was struggling with this, 'you're so different from most of the girls we meet and so sort of changeable. In quite a good way I mean,' she added hastily.

'You are,' Tor agreed. Ever since Viva had walked through the door that evening, Tor had been trying to put her finger on a feeling Viva brought out in her: something like hunger or dismay.

'You make your own plans,' said Rose, 'you earn your own money. Doesn't that embarrass you almost?'

'Embarrass?' Viva smiled. 'What a funny word to use. I've never even thought of it like that.'

'Are you still going to be a writer?' Tor asked.

'Well, I am, or at least I hope to be. I've just sold my first proper story, a small piece about the children's home to *Blackwood's Magazine*.'

Threads of excitement ran like electric currents through Viva's voice as she said this, even though her expression was carefully impassive.

'*Blackwood's*. But that's amazing, wonderful,' said Rose. 'Why didn't you say immediately?'

'Because I can't quite believe it myself,' said Viva. 'My first few weeks here were so dreadful. I could hardly afford to pay my bill at the YWCA, but then I got work at the children's home. I've been writing at nights.'

'Gosh, how ripping.' Tor heard the flatness in her voice and tried to smile. She sipped her drink. 'What now?'

'Well,' Viva hesitated, 'I'm going to try and get the children at the home where I work to tell their own stories in their own words.'

'Heavens,' said Tor. 'That does sound interesting.'

'But do admit,' said Rose, 'it must be horribly depressing at times – those poor little orphans.'

'That's exactly the point,' Viva's eyes were blazing now, 'and that's exactly why I'm glad I'm working there because almost nothing about it is how I expected it to be, so many clichés, so many misunderstandings. Those children are poor, but they're full of life, of hope. They laugh far more than most of us do, more than English children even.

'And yes, I'm white and I'm supposed to be helping them, but sometimes I almost hate them too – their poverty, their neediness, their complete lack of anything. And this is what I'm trying to think out for myself: all the lies, all the ways we have of trying to make life simple for ourselves by putting people into boxes marked black, white, good, bad, when all of us are victims of our own prejudices. To give you one example: there are two women of high caste at the home who never want to eat lunch with me. In their eyes I'm the dirty one, I'm the untouchable. To give you another, there's a little Muslim girl at the home right now being sent to Coventry because of her religion, and there's nothing we can really do about it. It runs so deep.'

'Gosh.' Rose folded up her napkin and put it carefully into the silver ring. 'I do admire you. I don't think I could do it.'

'Yes, you could,' said Viva bluntly. 'My life is probably a lot easier than yours. It's a question of choice.'

Ah, choice, thought Tor. She'd been too distracted to pay attention to all of Viva's speech, but the part she'd heard had brought on the sinking feeling again. What had she done, really done in the last four months? Absolutely nothing apart from getting thin and then getting fat again and losing her virginity and going to lots and lots of parties and now getting herself into this hideous mess.

'So, what about you, Tor?' Viva was looking at her over the rim of her wine glass.

'Oh, I've had masses of fun here,' said Tor distractedly. 'Masses – it's been balloon.'

She really couldn't talk about it yet – particularly now.

They had coffee on the verandah and some crème de menthe for old time's sake, even though it made Tor feel a little drunker. While they'd been eating, one of the servants had lit a flare path of small lamps whose flames flickered down the garden path right down to the sea. From their chairs, they could hear the soft flopping of waves falling down at the bay, a silky sound.

'Tor, you're so lucky to live here,' said Rose. 'I think it's the most wonderful house I've ever been in.'

Tor burst into tears. She felt in the pocket of her dress and handed a piece of paper over.

'"*Empress of India*,"' Rose read out. '"Miss Victoria Sowerby, 25 May. Single."' Rose had examined the ticket, turned it over and over. 'Oh, damn it, Tor,' she said quietly. 'I can't bear it. And you've been so brave all evening.'

Tor's mother had often warned her that crying in public was a complete non-starter, but Tor had cried properly then – great heaving, gulping sobs – she'd made such an awful mess of things.

They sat on either side of her holding her hands. 'I'm sorry,' she said eventually. 'I'm being the most awful wet, and spoiling everyone's evening, and I knew I had to go home eventually, but I'd so hoped my mother had forgotten about me – I was supposed to go back in March.' She gave a strangled gulp and wiped her eyes.

Rose said they should go upstairs to Tor's bedroom, for the night servant had stirred in the shadows, they'd seen the whites of his fascinated eyes, and this was private.

'Goodnight, Pandit. Goodnight, Arun,' Tor called out gaily on her way upstairs as if she hadn't a care in the world.

It was too hot to sit in her bedroom, so they went out on to the balcony and sat down on three rattan chairs, Tor in the middle, Viva and Rose on either side. They took their stockings off, and the sea breeze on their bare legs felt good.

'So what happened to Ollie?' Rose asked. 'I know for a fact,' she told Viva, 'he was absolutely mad about her.'

Tor felt so grateful to Rose for saying this.

'You see,' Tor explained to Viva, 'I was almost engaged to a man called Oliver. He works for a stockbroker out here. We met at a party at the Taj and fell madly in love.'

The madly in love bit was a bit of an exaggeration, but there was only just so much pain you could let out all at once.

'I'd been on this very strict diet and lost absolutely pounds,' Tor assured them as if they needed to understand this first before they could believe. 'We had a wonderful few weeks – you know, picnics, parties, moonlit swims. He brought me presents: flowers, jewellery, a tin of red shoe polish.'

'Red shoe polish!' both girls said in unison.

'Well, you know how I love red shoes,' Tor explained to Rose. 'And I don't know if you know this but you can't get proper polish here and Ollie knew a man. Oh, he was so much fun,' Tor wailed inconsequentially.

She sighed again and blew her nose. Part of her had always known of course that Ollie, with his tousled hair and his dinner jackets stuffed with cigarettes and betting tickets, was a bad boy, that was part of the fun. Who wanted one of those district commissioner types with white legs and wiry hair on their knees? But the problem with Ollie was that the fun never stopped, or, as Ci had put it, the dinner jacket never went back in the cupboard – a bit rich coming from Ci who had never worked a day in her life.

'So what happened then?' asked Rose. A cluster of green insects had come to a sizzling end on the bulb of a lamp near Tor's chair. Rose picked them up and threw them neatly over the balcony railings.

'Well, we went to this marvellous party at the Taj Mahal, a full-moon party, a wonderful night. The terrace was lit up with candles. The moon was huge. He told me I was the most beautiful girl there and that he loved me.' Tor looked at them defiantly: this was her story and she could tell it any way she wanted, and besides, there was plenty of humiliation to come.

'Ci left me there. She said Ollie could take me home, and anyway, I'm not absolutely certain she's not having an affair herself, she left with another man. Anyway, Ollie and I got into this tonga. It was so romantic, clip-clopping around the streets at night. We went along the seafront and we could see all the lights from the ships. When we got to the esplanade, near the crossroads that turns into town, he turned to me and he asked me to marry him.'

What he'd actually said, or mumbled because he'd had rather too much to drink, was that she was the sort of girl he should marry if he had any sense, but sitting there with Viva on one side and Rose on the other, she felt for a moment proud and sad and very badly done by, like a proper heroine.

'I don't suppose you'll be too shocked to hear that I went back to his flat that night.'

In fact, he'd been sick on the stairs. She'd put him in silk pyjamas, he'd crashed first on the floor and then into bed.

'I only meant to stay for a cup of coffee,' Tor continued, 'but he begged me to stay, and then . . . well, I'm not ashamed to say that I have been to bed with him several times, because he did say he loved me.'

And, even now, Tor remembered the brief but blazing triumph of that moment – girls like Rose and Viva could never understand it. He had said he loved her – sort of. But once again, the following morning while he was asleep, she'd looked at him and her mind had raced foolishly ahead: children had been named, letters mentally composed to her mother saying, in essence, 'See! I did it! I'm going to be married! Married! Married! I'm never coming home.'

'And then what?' Rose and Viva were agog.

'Oh.' Tor's story went down like a burst parachute. 'Well.' She gave a deep sigh. 'The next morning, when I got up and went to the bathroom, I found some face creams and half a bottle of White Shoulders in his medicine chest. I shouldn't have looked but I had a headache.

'When I asked him if he had another woman, he flew into a terrible rage.'

In fact, it had been worse than that, he'd said, 'God, you're boring, Tor. What did you expect?' As if it had been her fault all along.

'Oh, what a *rat*,' said Rose. 'What a complete *toad*. So then what happened?'

'Nothing.' Tor had no energy left for embellishment.

Nothing was right. No tearful apologies, no late-night phone calls professing undying love. Nothing.

'But maybe the White Shoulders belonged to a visiting aunt or something,' said Rose.

'No,' said Tor.

Three days later, using a fake Scottish accent, she'd phoned his office and asked to speak to him. 'Is that Mrs Sandsdown?' the voice at the other end had said. 'No,' she'd said, 'it's Victoria Sowerby.'

'Oh heavens! Sorry!' the voice had said. As she hung up she heard people laughing.

'Married!' Rose was appalled.

'Yes,' said Tor flatly. 'Wife in England. I suppose everybody knew but me. Not only married but with lots of other girls too. Trust me to pick him.'

'But lots of other people can't have known,' said Rose, 'else Ci would have warned you off him.'

'Well, it doesn't matter now.' Tor picked another dead insect off the lamp globe and put it in the wastepaper basket. 'Back to Middle Wallop and my mother. Spoiled goods,' she said bitterly.

'Oh, Tor, please don't call yourself that, it's horrible,' said Rose.

'That's what the old biddies at the club call girls like me,' Tor told them. 'Ci Ci will, of course, dine out on it after I've gone. She's not very nice, you know.'

'Oh, for God's sake, I can't bear this.' Viva had stood up. Her eyes blazed fiercely in the moonlight. 'You can't let this happen to you. Not like this. I mean, you could work – you could go upcountry and be a governess, you could teach here. This is ridiculous.'

'No, no, no.' Tor held off this deluge with her hand. 'Shut up for a moment, there's more to come. Much worse. I'm three weeks late with the curse. I'm having a baby.'

Chapter 31

POONA, MAY 1929

Jack was out on the Poona Cantonment number two practice ground lining up polo balls and smashing them as if to smash the universe into smithereens. Bula Bula, his favourite polo pony, a willing creature who would have lain down and died for him if necessary, was panting and foaming with sweat and Jack's entire body blazed with heat, but some demon was driving him today.

Standing tall in his stirrups and perfectly balanced, Jack cantered towards a line of balls about fifty yards from the goal mouth.

Thwack. He leant down and made a fluid shot under Bula's neck that sent the ball like a bullet through the scuffed posts.

'I say, sahib! Good one, sir!' shouted Amit, his ghora wallah. He was holding the next pony for him to ride.

If only life could be this easily won, Jack thought. He hated being in such a foul mood on a horse.

He gathered Bula up with his thighs and seat bones until he had him short and bouncing like a little rubber ball, and then he hit another one, hard.

Thwack. That one for his new commanding officer, Colonel Dewsbury, cold, stuffy bastard who'd suddenly announced in the fifth month of Rose's pregnancy that leave for all junior officers had been cancelled indefinitely. After months of messing about and uncertainty, part of the regiment were definitely moving now to Bannu, one of the most dangerous places on God's earth. And *crack.* That one for that grovelling little bloke in the mess who'd suddenly remembered a bar bill from months ago from his stag party. The same month, *thwack,* he'd had to pay for the furniture he'd hired in a panic after Rose came out, not to mention his other bill from his *Darzi* for that sodding suit he'd had made for the wedding party, and would no doubt never wear again.

He galloped the full length of the polo field again, lifting himself in his stirrups and slashing left and right with his polo mallet, until his horse's sides were heaving and the veins stood out on his neck.

Calm down, man, he told himself as he walked back to the stables. *None of this is Bula's fault.*

Or Rose's. When he looked up, he saw her watching him. She was sitting on a bench about seventy-five yards away, an innocent speck of blue against a wide horizon, and the sight of her brought shame and, for one blessed moment, a feeling of tenderness.

It wasn't her fault that he'd wildly underestimated the expense involved in getting married and maintaining a wife, or that if he was sent up north, he'd probably have to sell one of the horses to pay his bills. Or that Sunita had written to him out of the blue last week to tell him she was married now. She was very, very happy, she said, and much more settled. '*I hope you are happy too*,' she'd added innocently. He'd cried when he read that.

He cantered over to where Rose was sitting. When he came to a halt, Bula put his head about an inch from the ground, his sides still heaving.

'Poor Bula.' She patted the horse's neck. 'It's much too hot for everyone, isn't it?'

She shot Jack an unhappy smile. She didn't understand him any better than he did – normally, he kept this horse in cotton wool and the big match against the Calcutta Light was coming up on Saturday.

'I've brought you some lemonade, darling,' she said. 'I was frightened you'd get heatstroke.'

'Kind girl,' he said. As he leapt from his horse, he felt the sweat squelch on the inside of his boots. The glass was up to 105 again and all of them had had a string of broken nights, particularly poor Rose who tossed and turned all night and couldn't get comfortable.

Even though the mound under Rose's blue smock was small and neat and barely discernible, it seemed to him she waddled as they walked back to the stables, her face scarlet, blonde hair escaping in damp tendrils underneath her hat.

'Are you seeing old Patterson today?' he asked.

'Maybe,' she said. She glanced at him anxiously.

Patterson was the red-faced army doctor who would, in four months' time, deliver her baby. Rose seemed to hate talking about him, almost as much as he hated the thought of the man's thick hairy fingers going anywhere near his wife. When they'd all bumped into each other at the club a few nights ago (impossible to avoid the fellow in this ant colony), Patterson, slightly tight, had said, 'So how's our bonny wee lass feeling?' and leered at her as if they both owned her now. And to Jack's shame, the anger he'd felt then – the strong desire to land one on the man's chin – had been his strongest emotion so far about this baby. Before that he'd felt nothing more than a numb surprise, a sense of unreality. For the baby was a mistake, and as his new CO had more or less pointed out, it was bad enough getting married so young, but having a 'sprog', as he'd put it, was 'really jumping the gun'.

Yes, the night at the club had been the worst. It was the day that Sunita's letter had arrived. *I hope you are happy too.* He was sitting there drinking more whiskies than usual and the thought kept breaking in on him, a spasm of pain as real as any physical pain like breaking a bone or toothache.

There Rose had been opposite him. Dumpling Rose now, for her face had definitely grown rounder, in her blue sprigged maternity dress, so cordial, so kind, so right for him, so beautiful really, and thoughts of Sunita breaking in on him like a child shouting in the middle of a carefully rehearsed concert. *I miss you, Sunita. I want you still. Those were the best days of my life.*

'Just a lime juice and soda for me, thank you.'

Rose had smiled at the waiter, who had smiled back, tenderly, lovingly, in the way Jack wished he could smile at her. One of the many things he respected about Rose was that she was so thoroughly nice to everyone. She was fair. She genuinely liked other people. *Sunita, Sunita, let down your long hair.* Rose would never become one of those monstrous mems who patronised or bullied their servants. Rose had the right sort of good manners, based on sympathy and respect, and the staff at home already adored her. Durgabai was far more excited about this new baby than he was.

And Rose was fearless too in her quiet way. Jack was the frightened one – the Poona graveyard was stuffed with English babies, who'd died of typhoid and dog bites, malaria and heat. Babies, and their mothers. Patterson, insensitive oaf, had a whole range of 'funny stories' he told new mothers.

He had told one that night, one of his favourites.

'Lovely little chap,' he had boomed, 'sitting happily in his mother's arms having a bottle, *huge* group of monkeys appeared, snatched baby and jumped from branch to branch waving it above their heads. Hwah, hwah, hwah. Hope you'll be more careful.'

Rose had laughed politely, even though she'd heard it before. She had shot Jack a 'rescue me' look.

He moved closer. 'So how was Tor?'

He had cordoned her off by sitting down beside her and putting an arm around her shoulder. She looked surprised – it was rare for him to touch her in public, still less to ask her about Tor. 'You haven't told me anything yet.'

'I didn't think you'd be interested,' she had said. And then he'd been embarrassed to see her chin wobbling. When he had glanced up at the bar, Patterson still had his eye on her. Leering. Noticing. *It must be her condition*, he decided. She'd turned the taps on a bit in the first three months of their marriage, but she hardly ever cried now.

'I'll get a rickshaw,' he had said hurriedly. 'You can tell me on the way home.'

'Of course I'm interested,' he said. 'You shouldn't keep things like that to yourself.'

He was sorry it sounded like a reproof; he was trying to be nice.

She'd just told him that Tor would be leaving on 25 May. She was leaning wearily against the soiled canvas of the rickshaw. 'I should have told you before, but it seems so—'

'So what?'

'Sudden.'

'You'll miss her.' He heard her swallow in the darkness.

'Yes.'

He touched her hand but found he didn't want to hold it. The threat of tears had put him off.

They drove through the deserted streets of the cantonment in silence. There were pools of light in the darkness near gates where the night watchmen sat and behind them smoke from fires in the native quarters. Jack, looking over Rose's shoulder, was thinking that he wished he could have liked Tor better but he didn't. There had always been some sort of rivalrous edge to their conversations that he didn't understand, but which seemed to involve Rose.

Tor had also exasperated him by not seeming to understand the rules of the game between men and women in India. Bluntly put, she wasn't pretty enough to get away with being so noisy and outspoken.

She needed to pipe down, to listen more, to be more grateful with what came her way. A cruel assessment, he recognised, but other men thought like that too and pretty women like Rose would naturally never understand it.

'But I'm surprised no one took her up.' He'd decided to be tactful, particularly since Rose was in a state. 'She's not bad-looking.'

He heard her gasp, and then an echo of it as she looked out of the window shaking her head.

'Is that all that really matters to men?' Rose's voice was low and bitter. 'Tor's funny and loving and loyal, and I think she's beautiful too. Have you never noticed her eyes? Ugh!' She broke off in frustration.

'Rose, all I said was she's not bad-looking,' he said. He could hear his voice, deep and furious, a hint of push me further and I'll really explode; he didn't like what he heard but she shouldn't raise her voice to him like that. 'And anyway, we'll all be kicked out soon.'

That was another thing the women didn't understand, how bloody tenuous it all was getting. There was a terrible brouhaha going on in Congress, the C.O. was constantly briefing them about that now. In the white corner, Gandhi urging peace; in the red, those baying for blood.

'Anyway,' Rose was not going to lie down about this, 'I'm determined to go to Bombay and say goodbye to her when her ship leaves. I've got to.'

'What about the baby? I don't think it's right for you to be seen like that.'

'He can come too. If it is a he.'

'Well, it sounds to me as if you've made up your mind,' he said.

'I have,' she said.

He was trying not to lose his temper – it wasn't up to her to tell him where she was going and when. And then he felt relieved. Earlier in the day he'd decided against all his better judgement to see Sunita one more time.

I hope you're happy too. Such banal words; they'd hurt so much. He wasn't going, he'd argued with himself, to spoil her happiness, just to see her one last time. They'd be in Bombay for the long weekend of the polo tournament and the bastard in the basement was calling out, and there wasn't much he could do about it. If Rose insisted on doing what she wanted to, well, he could too.

*

231

Later that night, unable to sleep, he got up and walked into the kitchen for a glass of water. Outside on the verandah, the punkah wallah who worked the fan had fallen asleep with the string that worked the fan still attached to his toe. He roused him and sent him to bed.

It was a quarter past three, the air felt soupy and thick, the walls of the little house seemed to be closing in on him, and he could hardly breathe. He went into the living room and was sitting in an armchair reading the letter again when Rose walked in.

Through the thin cotton of her nightdress, he could see the outlines of her tummy, her thighs, her growing breasts. Half groggy with sleep, she sat down on the armchair facing him. She lifted her hair from her neck and blew out air.

'I can't sleep,' she said. 'It's too hot.'

As he lifted his eyes to hers, he saw coloured lizards dart across the wall behind her head and felt his whole life crash before his eyes.

'Jack,' she said, 'why are you crying?'

He hadn't realised.

'Am I?' he said.

'Yes you are.'

He didn't want her to walk over to him – how unfair it was of him to think of the word waddle even then – or to sit on the arm of his chair and stroke the side of his face. If she hadn't done that he might have held it all inside, but he'd felt his guts about to explode with sorrow at the mess he had made of things, and this sweet girl trying to work it all out.

He sat there frozen while she tried to hug him.

'It's me, isn't it?' she said in a low voice, almost as if she'd been expecting this all along. 'I'm doing this to you; I'm making you so unhappy. I can feel it.'

He tried to tell her no. He buried his head in his hands so she wouldn't see how much he hated his cowardice. It would be so easy now to blame her for this.

'It's not you,' he managed to say. Two of the coloured lizards were copulating behind her head.

'Is it the baby then? You didn't seem very excited when I told you.' Her voice was gentle, there was no reproach.

Excited! No, that would not be the word. If he'd said what was in his heart that night, he would have said, *I'm angry at you for taking over my life in this way, for making me feel so out of control, for being such a duffer with your sponge thing that you can't even use it properly. I don't want my wings clipped in this way, I can't afford it, I don't know enough about you. I'm not even sure I love you yet.*

In the event he had forced out some stiff words of congratulations and gone out for a drink in the mess, bathing himself in the company of men, almost desperate at the thought of having to go home again and play the game of happy fathers when he hated telling lies.

'What's this?' Rose swooped forward suddenly and picked up the letter that fell from his dressing-gown pocket as he reached out for a cigarette.

'Don't read it,' he'd almost shouted. 'It's mine.'

'What is it?' He saw fear growing like a fire in her eyes. 'Jack, tell me. *Tell me.* 'What is it?'

He looked at her and thought, *I can't do this to her. Not like my father did. She doesn't deserve it.*

'Read it then.' He sat there like a cowering dog while she sat down again and read the letter.

'Who is this?' Rose said in a trembling voice. 'I don't understand.'

It felt like the moment when you throw yourself off a high cliff into a dark place where the sea may not be deep enough.

'Her name is Sunita. She lives in Bombay now. She was my lover.'

'Your lover?' Her voice was raised; her eyes looked wild. 'Was, or is?'

'I don't know, I don't know.'

'Is she Indian?'

'Yes.'

'A native.'

'Yes, but an educated one. Her father is a barrister.'

'Do you love her?'

'I don't know.'

'You must love her. If you didn't love her you'd just say no.'

She got up; the lizards darted away. Her blonde hair mussed from sleep looked childlike, but the look in her eye was so strange that he thought for one muddled moment that she might thwack him one around the face. In some ways he might have preferred it that way, but instead she gave him a look of such pain and confusion that he wanted to howl like a dog. What a worthless shit he was.

'Do you love her?' she'd asked again.

'Sahib,' both of them were so far gone they hadn't noticed the soft knock on the door. 'Everything all right?' Durgabai kept her eyes

233

carefully averted from her mistress, standing stricken and half naked and staring wildly at her husband.

'*Haan*, Durgabai,' he'd said. 'The memsahib *sir me dard hai*.' (The memsahib has a headache.) 'She's all right though, *dhanyavad*.' (Thank you.)

'I hate you for doing this,' Rose said when the door was closed again. 'For having this secret, and not telling me, for letting me think I was getting everything wrong. Why in God's name did you let me come?'

She held her hand protectively over her belly as if to cover the baby's growing ears.

'I'm sorry, Rose.'

She brushed the apology aside. 'Will you see her again?'

'No – anyway, the regiment's still on alert for Bannu.'

'Is that the only reason?'

He'd never seen her more furious and he shrank back from it. 'No.'

'It had better bloody well not be.'

The small part of him that wasn't frozen in shock admired the graceful way she held herself as she left the room. There was dignity in that straight young back, a refusal to sag and collapse.

It was only later, through the thin walls of the spare room, that he heard her being sick, and then the stifled moans of pain. He'd never hated himself more.

Chapter 32

It was late morning at the children's home and Viva was sitting underneath the tamarind tree in the middle of the courtyard, cutting up bits of tissue paper for the kites they were making. From where she sat, Viva could hear the hubble bubble of children's voices, talking in a bewildering variety of languages: Hindi, Marathi, English, for some, snatches of Tamil and Gujarati thrown in, all mixed with the croaky sounds of the pigeons that lived under the eaves of the home.

And through all this cut the fluting tones of Daisy, who was talking to them while they worked.

'It's a funny thing, isn't it,' she was saying, 'how few grown-up people ever really stop and look up at the sky – we scuttle around full of worries, like insects. The only ones who look up to the sky on a regular basis are madmen or children or . . . Can you finish this sentence, Neeta?'

'I don't know,' whispered Neeta, a shy girl with anxious eyes.

'Kite flyers.' Suday, the fat boy, wanted them to know that he'd had his own kite before.

'And what does looking up teach us?'

'That the sky is blue,' Neeta rallied.

'Good, Neeta. And when we look up, it widens our horizons. We see what a little speck we are in the universe, so insignificant, and we all take ourselves so seriously, but in the sky, there are no boundaries. No differences of caste – careful with that glue, Suday – or religion or race. It teaches you, "There are more things in heaven and earth, Horatio, than are dreamt of in your philosophy." A man called Shakespeare wrote that.'

Viva felt a peculiar sort of pain watching the children listening so intently. What kind of heaven and earth would they find?

Next Daisy outlined the plans for the day: when the kites were finished, Viva would take them down to Chowpatty Beach to fly them. At this news, some of the children turned to look at Viva with huge wondering eyes; some of them had never even seen the sea before. They made her feel like a magician, a conjurer.

Viva glanced at Talika. She sat at the end of the bench, completely absorbed, small hands busily working the scissors, dark eyelashes cast down, skinny little legs waving above the ground. No one would have recognised the pathetic scrap Viva had bathed a few months ago, but she was still frail-looking and much too thin.

'Watch me, watch *me*, Wiwaji,' said Talu, a tall, thin boy with a pronounced limp. None of them could say her name properly. They either called her Madam Sahib, the Bombay version of memsahib, or Miss Wiwa, or sometimes as a term of endearment Wiwaji. One or two of the younger ones called her Mabap (you are my mother and my father), a compliment that never failed to wring her heart.

'I'm cutting out my peacock's tail,' said Talu.

'I am seeing a dead rat tail,' said Suday, the joker, picking it up and whirling it about his head, and when Talika laughed it was a peal of child's laughter.

She got up from the table with her half-finished kite. 'Mine is a bird,' she said, releasing its string. 'Watch me.'

She kicked off her sandals and started to dance, stamping her feet in precise little patterns on the ground, her kite a swirl of colour above her head. Twirling, prancing, she closed her eyes and began to sing in a reedy child's voice, her throat vibrating. She was powerful in those few moments, enchanted and enchanting, lost in her dance; nobody could take their eyes off her. Viva hardly noticed that Daisy had sat down beside her.

'Well, somebody looks as if she's feeling better,' she said as Talika's sari whirled.

'Wasn't that wonderful?' said Viva. 'Where on earth did she learn to sing like that?'

'Actually, Viva, I meant you,' said Daisy. 'You look much happier than when you first came here.'

The tail of Talika's kite had trapped in the branches of the tamarind tree. Viva jumped up and retrieved it.

'I do like it here, Daisy,' she said when she sat down again. 'And I don't like children very much, or at least I didn't think I did.'

'Well, you hide it very well,' Daisy teased. 'But can I give a word of warning? It's lovely to see a child like that so free and unself-conscious, but even here we have to be so careful. There are spies everywhere at the moment, and if they saw something like that, one of them might go and tell the locals that we're training the girls here to be temple prostitutes.'

'Is that a joke?'

'No, I wish it was – it happened last year. People don't always understand what we do. Why should they?'

'Good Lord.' Viva had heard stories like this before, but mistrusted them – it seemed such a coward's game to read danger into everything. 'That was so innocent. I hate the thought of stopping it.'

'I know. One hates to see such a thing twisted, but there we are, we don't live in a perfect world.

'A few months ago, one of the older boys was taken in by the local *havildar* – the police constable – and questioned about Eve-teasing – that's what they call bothering women, you know . . .' Daisy was getting flustered. 'You know, trying to seize young girls when they don't want to be seized, or pinching their . . . you know, bosoms. It was a trumped-up charge, but there was nothing we could do about it, short of closing the home.

'And my second piece of advice,' Daisy put a gentle hand on her arm, 'is don't overdo it. Last year, half our staff went down like flies; this year we're insisting on time off. Didn't you say when you first came that you planned to go north and see your parents' old house?'

'Did I?' Viva could feel herself stiffening. 'I don't remember saying that.'

'Oh sorry.' Daisy's eyes blinked behind her glasses. 'I thought you did.' They exchanged a strange look. 'Well, here's another suggestion. This heat will drive us all mad before the rains come, so if you feel like a week off, my friends run a delightful boarding house in Ootacamund – it's a perfect quiet place to write and it's not expensive – I'd be happy to pay for you if you're short of coin.'

'How kind you are,' said Viva, 'but it's funny, I almost feel I can't leave at the moment.'

'It gets you like that at first,' Daisy said. 'For the first time in your life, you're not thinking about yourself. That's such a relief, don't you find?'

When Viva looked up, Daisy was innocently pinning the tail on a kite and did not meet her eye.

'Did you know,' she said, 'that the first kites were flown in the fourteenth century in Greece to test the sight of a blind prince? I've got an excellent book on them if you'd like to borrow it – the religious symbolism is quite fascinating.'

'I would,' said Viva, and then, 'Daisy, do you think I'm any more self-absorbed than anyone else?'

Daisy looked at her steadily through her thick glasses and said, after a lengthy silence, 'Self-absorbed, on second thoughts, is unfair, you are always watching and you *are* curious, I like that about you; self-protective might be a better word. You're very reserved about yourself, or maybe you keep that for your writing.' Daisy was teasing again.

'Maybe I do.' Viva didn't want to feel hurt, but she was. Sometimes she just got so tired of being accused of keeping secrets she didn't understand herself.

Over lunch she brooded about why she was still so neurotically private about her past and her parents. There was no disgrace about their passing.

People did suddenly die in India, it was a fact of life, the graveyards were stuffed with them. To make some special mystery out of it was to behave like those children who believe they are the secret and illegitimate heirs of kings or princesses, because they can't bear the thought of being ordinary.

If the details had been scarce – Father killed in a raid on the railway line by bandits, Mother dying a few months later (of a broken heart, she'd been told by the nuns) – it was probably for no other reason than nobody in England knew her parents that well. Her parents had been exiles for years, grown out of touch with family and friends. When the first flurry of caring was over, she'd fallen through a kind of net, a familiar circumstance to many people who decide to make their lives away from home. That was the price you paid.

When at the age of eighteen she'd been old enough to take an interest in them, she'd felt a sudden desperation to find somebody, anybody who could talk to her about them without seeming shifty or impatient. Which, of course, was where William had fitted in. What a gift he'd seemed at first, not only the executor of her parents' will, but so handsome, so articulate – he was a leading barrister after all – compassionate; he'd taken plenty of time with her. Dinners, long walks, evenings over a bottle of wine at his bachelor flat in the Inner Temple.

He'd known them very well, he'd told her on their first meeting.

Same quad as her father at Cambridge, stayed with them once in Kashmir before she was born.

He remembered Josie, so red, so funny-looking as a baby – they'd called her 'the Nawab' because of the imperious way she'd reclined on her charpoy drinking her bottle. The night he told her about Josie was the night he'd dried her tears, gently, gently, given her a little sip of wine, taken her to bed.

And then, much later, she'd made the big mistake of asking him about Mother.

She and William had been going up in the lift to his flat, when she'd said out of the blue, 'Did Mummy have a weak heart when you knew her?' This was the story she'd been told by one of the nuns.

He'd turned – she remembered all this as though it was yesterday – and said coldly, 'I was her executor, not her physician.' And then, as the lift clanked upstairs to the neat bedroom – where later he would fold his suit, put his collar studs into a box before his cold but expert kisses – he said, 'What's it really got to do with you in the end?' as though she was being nosy about some chance acquaintance.

It made her cringe, even now, to think of how meekly she'd accepted this rebuke. He had a nasty tongue and he knew how to use it, and by the end it seemed to her that she'd become so wary of him, so watchful, so feebly pliant that she'd handed over part of her own tongue as well as half her brain to him.

When she got up to shake some crumbs off her lap, Talika ran up to her and mocked the seriousness of her expression by jutting out her own small chin, and pretending to laugh and cry at the same time.

'Wiwaji,' she said in Marathi, 'don't look so sad. The sun is shining and we're going to the sea.'

Chowpatty Beach was surprisingly empty when Talika, Suday, Talu, Neeta and Viva poured off the bus later that afternoon. A few old men were sitting on the wall gazing out to sea, doing nothing but chewing air. There was a scattering of families in the distance walking slowly down the beach, a desperately thin pony walked up and down giving rides, and, underneath a stunted tree, an ancient old yogi, wrinkled and in a loincloth, contorting his body in a way designed to attract maximum attention from passers-by.

Talika and Neeta hung back at first, grabbing 'Miss Wiwa' by the arm, their eyes big as saucers. 'Ram, Ram, hello, hello,' Talika said at first in an awed voice as if the ocean would speak back, and then to Viva, 'Will it hurt me?' A few minutes later, they had their shoes off and were on the sand squealing with delight. Suday, the fat boy, puffed up with pride – he'd seen the sea before, nothing new to him – strutted for a while, kite in hand, before putting it down carefully under a stone, and encouraging the others to paddle. As the girls picked up the hems of their saris, and dipped terrified toes into the sea, the sun shone through the fabric, making them light up like flowers. How sweet they were, full of delicate wonder – they reminded Viva of young deer going down to the water to drink.

All the children struggled to get their kites airborne at first. The air was brothy and warm and there simply wasn't enough wind. Talika's flopped instantly into the water, and had to be rescued and dried out. But then Suday got Neeta to walk twenty feet or so downwind with his line while he held the kite and then, at a shout from him, it was launched into the sky, where it hung on the wind, bridled, rose and spun, making all the children cheer and shout out, as it sank and then soared off again into the vast blue sky. 'I'm flying,' fat little Suday shouted as he ran flat-footed, 'I'm flying.'

After an hour everyone got hungry. They spread cotton sheets on the sand underneath a beach umbrella. The boys went off to buy puffed rice and *chana bhaturas*, the Bombay treats, from a little stall on the beach. Back came some freshly made potato and pea samosas too, piping hot in paper cones, as well as some sticky-looking *barfi*. The food was laid out on the sheet on the sand and they sat in a circle round it, wriggling like eels with barely suppressed excitement.

There was a time when this little picnic would have stood for everything Viva feared about India: so many diseases – typhoid, jaundice, dysentery – could make an appearance in this innocent treat, but, today, surrounded by small hands darting in and out, she forgot to worry about it.

While they were eating, Talika clung to her side like a limpet. She took a tiny piece of food and chewed it very carefully, her doll sitting beside her.

'Have some more.' Viva offered her one of the sticky biscuits that she knew she loved.

Talika shook her head.

'Do you feel ill?'

'No,' she said, but after they had eaten, when Viva shook out the cotton sheet and spread it on the sand, she lay down immediately with her doll and closed her eyes.

While Talika slept, the other children ran off again, laughing and trailing their coloured kites behind them. Higher and higher the kites flew, shimmering and swooping. '*Kaaayyypoooche,*' the cry went up. 'We're best, we're the best.'

Viva ran down the beach with them. There'd been days since she'd been back in Bombay when she'd positively hated it – too hot, too crowded, too smelly, too hard – but today, how could you not love it? This beautiful beach; the sun pouring out of the sky; the madcap bravery of these children forgetting so easily that they were orphaned and poor in one of the hardest cities on earth.

A pie dog had joined them on the beach and was darting after Suday and Neeta's kites, making them squeal and dance.

'Careful, children,' she called; rabies was always a fear with the packs of dogs who roamed the cities.

When Talika woke, her eyelashes flickered with surprise at the beach, the sky, the children playing. She fitted her hand inside Viva's and went back to sleep again.

Viva, still holding Talika's sticky little hand in hers, was trying to remember something. How many times had she swum at Chowpatty Beach as a child? Once, twice, half a dozen times?

Chowpatty had been a family tradition. The place they'd come to on the last day of their holidays before leaving Bombay for the convent. Days of mourning disguised as days of fun. Or maybe not. *Children,* she thought, watching Suday in the distance, totally engrossed now in skimming a stone over the waves, *are so much better at mixing pleasure with pain than adults are.* It was perfectly possible that during those days she'd leapt over the waves too, felt nothing but joy in the shining water – perhaps this accounted for the numbness, the blankness felt when she thought about them now. She had sealed herself off too well.

She was almost asleep when another memory darted into her mind. Her mother on this beach. She was wearing dark sunglasses; she had a scarf wrapped round her face as though she'd had all her teeth out at once. Tears were dripping down underneath her mother's sunglasses like marrowfat peas. Mother was angry, Viva wasn't meant to see them. Viva was angry too; mothers shouldn't cry like this.

Viva sat up so quickly that Talika's eyes shot open too. Yes, that *was* the last time, not the other last time she'd substituted. Josie wasn't there. She'd gone. Daddy wasn't there either, she was almost certain of it: just Mother and herself, sitting on their own on a beach on the edge of India, before she went back to school. And she was frightened and very, very angry, so angry that she felt like striking her mother and that was wrong. *And if one green bottle should accidentally fall, there'd be two green bottles standing on the wall.* That song still frightened her.

When the children came running up the beach again, she was relieved to see them. Each child sat now with a kite on its knee. 'The string represents the soul's flight towards heaven,' Daisy had told her earlier. 'The person holding the string is the Almighty.' Neeta was glaring at Suday because he was boasting he had won.

'Was it fun?' Talika asked Suday.

'*Burra* fun, Missie Queen,' said Suday, who was jealous of her lying next to Miss Wiwa.

When the bus arrived at five, nobody wanted to go home except Viva, who was tired now and hoped to do some writing that night. A group of fishermen had arrived to take the salt fish off the racks where they had been laid out to dry, and the children were engrossed. They drove back to Tamarind Street through streets that the setting sun had turned red. By the time they got to the gates, all of the children were asleep with their kites beside them.

Viva was glad to hand them over to Mrs Bowden, a plump down-to-earth soldier's wife from Yorkshire, who worked two days a week as a volunteer. Mrs Bowden had lost two of her own children in India and said she did this to make herself feel better.

'Well, you lot look dirty,' she told the children. 'But no bath, I'm afraid. The bleeding plumbing's on the blink again,' she explained to Viva.

'And what about you, poppet?' Mrs Bowden said to Talika, who still looked pale. 'You look mouldy. I expect you ate too much.'

Mrs B. didn't hold with molly-coddling, they were used to children feeling mouldy here.

Half an hour later, Viva, walking down the streets towards her own home, felt full of sun and fresh air. Too tired to feel hungry, she'd picked up a mango from a street stall; she would eat it at her desk while she wrote up her notes.

On nights like this, when her feet ached and her mind felt woolly from heat, the writing was a slog, but it was also a necessity now, like cleaning her teeth, or getting up in the morning: it was what she had to do to feel like herself.

Darkness fell with its usual suddenness while she was walking, and fragile strings of fairy lights appeared around the street stalls that sold fruits and cheap clothes, palm juice and papier-mâché gods. When all the rows of lights suddenly went out, she could hear soft laughter from one of the stallholders – having electricity in Byculla was still the big surprise, not when it failed.

Opening the door of her flat, she saw that Mr Jamshed had lit an oil lamp and put it in the stairwell. As she walked upstairs, her shadow flickered and bounced off the walls like a living thing.

Her embroidered bag was full of books and heavy. She stopped for a few seconds on the landing to put it down. As she looked up the four steps that led to her rooms, a shadow passed behind the frosted glass in her door.

'Mr Jamshed,' she called, 'is that you?'

He'd mentioned that morning he might come up later to look at her broken tap. She heard the sound of running water from down below. A slash of sizzling oil and then the smell of spices.

'Mr Jamshed? It's Viva,' she called more softly.

She picked up her bag and opened the door.

She saw the soft outlines of a body lying down on her bed in the shadows in the corner of the room.

The shadow stood up. It was Guy Glover. He was wearing his black coat. He was waiting for her.

'Shush, shush, shush, shush,' he said in a gentle scolding voice when she called out in alarm. 'It's only me.'

In the half-light all she could see was the outline of her window lit up with a greenish light and a tangle of clothes on her chair – she'd left in a hurry that morning. There was a surge of music from the street outside, a wild caterwauling sound.

'What on earth are you doing here, Guy?' she said. 'Who let you in?'

Her eyes had adjusted to the light; she could see that he was wearing no shirt under his coat, and that his white bony chest was sweating.

'No one. I told your landlady you were my big sister – we all look the same to them, you know.'

When he smiled, she remembered everything she disliked about him: the thin adolescent voice that could never decide between being a baby and a bully, his weak smile. Even the smell of him, sweet and stale.

She lit a candle and looked quickly around the room to see if he'd moved anything; there was an empty hollow on her parents' bed-spread where he'd been lying.

'Look, Guy,' it felt important not to show how close she was to screaming at him, 'I don't know why you're here, but we've nothing to say to each other any more, so I want you to go away right now, before I call the police.'

'Calm down, Viva,' he said. 'I've brought your money back, that's all.'

He sounded so hurt she remembered how good he was at wrong-footing her.

When the lights came on again, they seemed brighter than usual. One of his acne spots had started to bleed.

'Aren't you boiling in that coat?' she said.

'Absolutely boiling.' He smiled sheepishly. 'But I can't take it off – ever.'

As she stared at him, her mind was split too. Was this yet another of his adolescent attempts to seem interesting, or was he completely barking mad?

'Why not?'

'Because my present for you is in it.'

He fumbled inside his coat and pulled out a scarlet and yellow cloth doll with staring eyes and fang-like teeth – the kind of gaudy thing you could buy in any cheap market stall.

Why does this boy always make me feel as if I'm acting in a really bad play? Her mood had changed to pure anger. *Why is he never himself?* She could have kicked him.

'Her name is Durga,' he said, putting the doll in her hands. 'The goddess of war – she'll take care of you.'

'I can take care of myself.' She put the doll down on the table.

'Hold her,' he insisted.

'Look, Guy,' her patience suddenly snapped, 'I'm not in the mood to play games with you; in fact, I don't know how you had the nerve to come here like this. You told a pack of lies to your parents about me. I—'

'I've got a job now,' he interrupted. 'I'm—'

'Guy, I don't care. I had no money at all when I came here, thanks to you.'

'You're lucky to have lost your parents,' he interrupted her. 'I have nothing in common with mine.'

'Look, I talked a lot of rot on the ship.' She felt a wave of revulsion at herself. Why hadn't she kept her mouth shut? 'And I'm tired. Take your doll and go.'

'Don't you even want to know where I'm staying?'

'No, Guy, I don't. I couldn't care less – my responsibility for you ended when the ship got to Bombay.'

There was a silence in the room. She could hear her own wrist-watch ticking, and then, from downstairs, the whoosh of water going down Mr Jamshed's drain.

'That's not what the police think.' He said it so softly she almost didn't hear him. 'They're bastards, but you could be in a lot of trouble if you don't pay up.'

'For goodness' sake, Guy, stop play-acting,' she cried.

'I'm not,' he said. 'I'm frightened. There's a man after me.' He sat down on her bed, put his head in his hands and then looked at her through his fingers. He swallowed and looked at the floor. 'He says I hurt his brother on the ship, but he hurt me too.'

'What does he say you did to his brother?'

Guy's voice became soft, almost babyish in its complaints. 'He says I hurt his ear and now he can't hear, but he did hit me first. That's why I think you need this.'

He bent the doll over his knee and carefully undid a row of poppers at the back of its embroidered waistcoat. He rummaged around inside.

'Take it.' He handed over a stained bundle of rupees in an elastic band. 'You may need it when they come. You can't be too careful on the streets around here.'

'When who comes?'

'The police – you see, in law, I'm your baby.'

She turned the notes over in the palm of her hand, her mind working furiously.

Was this what Frank had tried to warn her of: the dreadful,

unthinkable possibility that, in the eyes of the law, he belonged to her?

She snapped the elastic band. She could feel without counting 100, maybe 200 rupees there: enough at least to offer something to the police if they came round for bribes, but she suspected it wouldn't cover the amount she had lost chaperoning Guy to India.

'I think you should apologise to me for being so rude,' he said prissily. 'I suppose you can see now that I was only trying to help you.'

'Guy,' she said, 'I don't think I need to apologise for what is mine.'

He gave a sudden radiant smile. 'So, I am yours after all?'

'No, no, no . . . I didn't mean that. I mean this,' she held up the notes, 'the money was owed to me.'

She saw the light die in his eyes, but didn't care at all.

'Who told you I lived here?' she asked.

'It took me ages to find you.' He was like a sullen schoolboy again. 'So I rang Tor and she told me.'

'I see.'

His foot had started tapping on the floor again.

'Didn't I hear you have a job? Where are you working now?' she asked him as casually as she could.

'Nowhere,' he mumbled. 'Actually, I've lost my job. I was taking film photographs. The men who were running the company were clots.'

'So you're going home now?' Even the thought brought some relief.

'No.' He shook his head. 'I live here now: on Main Street behind the fruit market.' He stopped tapping his foot and looked at her. 'Oh, and there's one more thing. Stop telling everyone I'm sixteen when I'm actually nineteen.'

'I'm not going to fight about that, Guy. What difference does it make when you take no responsibility for yourself?'

'I do.'

'No, you don't, you're spineless,' she glared at him, still furious at this invasion of her privacy, and the loss of her evening, 'and you tell lies to get yourself out of trouble.'

He stepped back. 'That's a really beastly thing to say,' he said. 'I was always going to pay you back. I've been waiting for the right time.'

'Oh really?' She didn't even pretend to believe him. 'Well, next time, do it in the right way: ring the doorbell and wait for me to let you in.'

As she showed him towards the door, she could feel a blister on her heel break and the sticky liquid run down into her shoe.

'Don't come back again, Guy,' she said as she let him out.

'It's all right, it's all right,' he said as if she'd asked for some kind of reassurance. 'I've promised to pay you back and I'm going to.'

Chapter 33

The following morning, Viva phoned Tor in a fury.

'Tor, how could you? How stupid can you be? He's going to haunt me now.'

'Hang on.' Tor sounded sleepy as if she'd just woken up. 'Who are we talking about?'

'Guy, you bloody idiot. You gave him my address.'

'He said he had your money. I thought you'd be pleased.'

'Pleased! He frightened the life out of me. He was lying in the dark waiting for me in my room, and now he says the police are after him.'

She heard Tor gasp at the other end of the phone. 'Oh, Viva, I'm so sorry,' she said. 'But he said he had a job and money, and I thought you w—'

'Tor, you weren't thinking at all.'

Tor blew her nose and decided, unwisely, to change tactics.

'Are you sure you're not blowing this out of all proportion, Viva?' she said. 'I always got on with him rather well.'

'Oh, for heaven's sake,' Viva exploded. 'He's completely doolally – even your darling Frank said so.'

'That's mean,' Tor said. 'He was never my darling Frank. If he was anybody's he was yours.'

Viva thumped the phone down and instantly picked it up and dialled again.

'I'm sorry, that was mean of me,' she said.

'I know.' Tor was crying. 'It's just that I get everything so wrong now and I'm still so worried about you-know-what.' There was a clunk as she put the phone down and blew her nose again. 'Why is life so *complicated*?' she wailed distantly.

'Tor, are you still there?' Viva heard the click clack of high-heeled shoes on a wooden floor, Ci's sharp voice giving orders to a servant. Viva heard a rustle on the other end of the line, as Tor picked up the receiver again.

'Can't talk now,' Tor whispered. 'Can we meet somewhere for a drink? The Taj or Wyndham's or your place?'

Viva hesitated. She was working the ten-to-five shift at the home that day and had planned to write that night. *Eve* magazine in England wanted two of her sketches of India, each 1,000 words long and within a week.

'I'm not sure you'll be able to find me here, Tor,' she said. 'It's slightly off the beaten track.'

''Course I could.' Tor sounded relieved. 'I'd love to see your place, and I could bring my gramophone. Look, thanks for forgiving me about Guy,' she added as an airy afterthought and before Viva had said a word, 'but at least you've got some money now – I'm completely Harry broke.'

There were times when Viva wanted to crown her.

When Viva hung up the phone, she took the greasy bundle of notes out of the bedside drawer where she'd stuffed them the night before; she counted them again: three hundred and twenty rupees, exactly half the money she'd been promised for the voyage out. She put it in a tin, got a piece of string and tied it securely to the underside of her bed.

When she looked at her room, she saw Guy lying on her bed again: his strangely expressionless eyes on her; the imprint of his body on her parents' bedspread. Last night, after he'd gone, she'd changed her sheets, as if to exorcise him, but she'd still hardly slept a wink.

The room she had grown to love, particularly with the comforting presence of the Jamsheds underneath, felt fragile and temporary again. The walls too flimsy, the frosted-glass door too easy to break.

At times like these, she longed for an older brother or a father who would give her bluff advice, and tell her not to be frightened of some stupid boy wet behind the ears, or who might offer to give Guy a fourpenny one if he became a serious nuisance to her.

But there was nobody but Frank and asking him for help seemed to throw her back into some old and outgrown role she'd had to play with William – the damsel in distress, the silly billy, needing masculine protection, and this time with the added embarrassment of knowing she'd ignored Frank's hunch that Guy might not be just another angry displaced casualty of the Empire but someone with serious mental problems. She'd also taken the money.

Pale and exhausted, she looked at her watch. Eight-fifty. It seemed important to make up her mind what to do before she set off for work. She walked about her room hugging herself, sat down on her bed, stood up, checked her watch again and, finally, went out into a phone box in the street and dialled the number at the hospital Frank had given her.

She got through to reception.

'Gokuldas Tejpal Hospital,' said a sing-song voice at the end of the line. 'May I help you?'

'I need to speak to Dr Frank Steadman,' she said.

She heard pages rustling. 'I don't know where he is,' said the voice at the other end. 'Will you wait?'

She waited. Five minutes later, Frank picked up the phone.

'Frank, it's me. Viva. I can't talk for long, I'll be late for work. I wonder if I could ask for your professional advice on one or two of the children at the home who aren't doing very well?'

'It'll have to be after lunchtime.' The crackling line made his voice sound impersonal. 'Shall I come to the home?'

'Yes.'

'Good. Two-thirty all right?'

'Two-thirty will be fine,' she said. 'I'll see you then.'

At two o'clock that afternoon, Viva was sitting in the courtyard underneath the tamarind tree supervising a group of six children: Talika, Neeta, Suday and three shocked little girls who'd been dumped outside the gates two days before.

Only the oldest one – a fierce-looking little girl with matted hair – had spoken; the others only gazed at her with eyes numb with misery, seeming to have no idea of why they'd come or where or who they were.

It was important, or so Mrs Bowden said, to get these new girls into some kind of routine of learning to take their minds off what had happened to them, and so Viva had spent the last half-hour instructing them in what was known at the home as 'social skills' – mainly a list of 'thou shalt not's: thou shalt not put rubbish in the streets, or spit in public, or defecate into an open drain. Suday, the joker, had just said, 'And now, Miss Wiwa – please, you can teach me to wink also; that is a social skill.' She'd shown them – even though she knew that Mrs Bowden would not approve.

Frank walked in as the children were laughing. He was carrying his doctor's bag. It worried her how happy she felt to see him again.

'Now, children,' she said in Marathi, 'settle down and be quiet for a while. We have a visitor.'

'My God,' he said. He'd taken the chair beside her. 'I wish my ear for languages was that good,' and there'd been giggles and nudges as she'd blushed a deep, bright red.

'Daisy Barker's been teaching me,' she said, 'and it's not as good as it sounds. I can only say "pipe down" or "eat up" or "go to bed". Do you know Daisy? She runs this place. She also works at the Settlement in Bombay; I thought you might have been to one of her parties.'

She felt she was babbling incoherently. The children were listening agog, their eyes moving from face to face as if they were watching a tennis match.

Viva looked at her watch. 'Girls and boys,' she said, 'we can break for half an hour's play now. Say goodbye to Dr Frank.'

'Goodbye, Daktar Frank,' they chorused, and raced off to play. A few moments later Talika came back with two glasses of lemonade on an old tin tray. Concentrating fiercely, she lifted each glass with both hands on to the table.

'Stay for a moment, Talika,' said Viva. 'This is one of the girls I wanted you to see,' she told Frank. 'Her name is Talika.' Viva squeezed the child's hand, sad to see her looking so tense and fearful. She would like to have told him more about her, but was frightened Talika, whose English was improving, would pick it up and either feel ashamed or humiliated. 'She's not doing too badly, in fact, we're very proud of her, aren't we, Talika? But, as you can see, she's very thin.'

'Can I listen to her chest?'

She went to get one of the cotton screens they used for consultations in the courtyard.

'Don't be frightened, Talika,' she said. The screen was around them and the child's face bathed in its greenish patterns. 'The doctor won't hurt you.'

Frank got out his stethoscope. As he put it in his ears and listened gravely to the child, her large terrified eyes did not leave Viva's.

'Your heart is strong, your chest is clear.' He tried to smile at the child but she wouldn't have it. 'I'm sure the clinic doctor has ruled out the usual,' he added, 'TB, worms – she doesn't look rickety.'

When he released the child, she shot back across the courtyard like a frightened fawn desperate to join her herd.

'Poor thing,' he said when she was gone. 'She looks haunted.'

He looked up and held Viva's gaze for a moment. 'Do you have any idea why?'

'Not really. Her mother died of tuberculosis; at least we think she did, she still hopes that she's alive. There was a flood in the slum where she lived and she was left at our gate. Sometimes she's quite jolly now. I mean, yesterday she was even dancing, but then something happens and she is almost unreachable and I don't know why.'

'Maybe she's homesick,' he said. He was sitting close enough for her to see tortoiseshell lights in his green eyes.

'There is a whole rich life going on in a slum – most Europeans don't understand it.'

'And what about you?' He looked at her again. 'What are you doing all this for?'

The directness of his question took her aback.

'I like it here,' she said. 'I really do, and I'm still writing, in fact I've had a couple of things published.'

'But that's wonderful, congratulations.' He did have a shattering smile, that was the problem, and when he looked at her like that, she felt a tug inside her, a longing.

'I'm all right, you know.' She stood up quickly.

'I know,' he said gently. 'That's good.'

He wound up his stethoscope, packed it away in his bag.

'Except,' she could feel him about to leave, 'I may have done something rather stupid last night. Guy Glover turned up in my room. It was a shock. He said he'd come to give me my money back.'

'Did you take it?' He looked at her anxiously.

'Yes – or at least some of it.'

'I thought we'd decided you weren't going to do that.' Frank flexed his knuckles; he was frowning at her now.

'I thought I might need it.' *Because I needed to do it my way*, she suddenly recognised.

'I wish you hadn't done that.'

'I do too now, but I was . . .' She stopped herself saying the word flustered. 'I was persuaded by him that the police might want to see me and that I'd need it for the bribes. Do admit, Frank,' it was her turn to glare now, 'there is a certain logic to that.'

Frank's expression was grim. 'What he most wants is to go on pestering you. He's an obsessive and you're on his list. Why on earth did you let him in?'

'I didn't – he was in my room when I came home. He was lying on my bed.'

Frank groaned. He thought for a while and said, 'Look, Viva, I don't want to worry you but this could turn into a nasty situation. Is there anyone here at the home you can really trust?'

'I trust Daisy Barker,' she said. 'Absolutely.'

'Well, tell her right away,' he said. 'That way, when the police come round she'll be warned.'

'Do you really think they'll come here?' Viva felt a sick sinking in her stomach.

'They might. They've probably already got their eyes on you anyway, a group of European ladies running a place like this at a time like this, when everything is so uncertain.'

'Oh God.'

'Now I've frightened you,' he said more gently. 'The police have plenty of other things to do at the moment, so don't worry too much, but just be more careful, please.'

They found Daisy sitting in what was grandly called 'the back office' – a dark, humid room in the depths of the building with a large overhead fan and an elaborately tiled floor. The room had a desk, a chair, an old filing cabinet and on the wall a calendar, on which a woman in a sari floated down the Ganges in a boat extolling the joys of drinking Ovaltine.

'Daisy,' said Viva as they walked in, 'this is Frank. He's a locum at the Gokuldas Tejpal. We met on the ship.'

'Oh, greetings.' Daisy jumped up and pumped his hand. 'Well, we're never ones here to look a gift doctor in the mouth – if you ever have any spare time.' She took her glasses off and smiled winningly. 'In fact, only last night we had two street boys in with minor burns but one does worry in this heat. I wonder if you could have a quick look – could you? Oh, you are so kind.'

The boys, skinny and shifty-eyed, were produced. A brief case history supplied. Both had been residents in one of the local orphanages. They'd been beaten so badly they'd run away, finding shelter in a shed near the railway track two miles away from the Victoria Terminal, with six other boys. A fight had broken out over a pot of cooking rice, both had been scalded.

As Frank examined them, Viva became aware of his hands. They were beautiful hands, brown and long-fingered, now gently probing the wound on the boy's leg.

'It's actually healed quite well,' he said. 'What did you put on it?' he asked the boy in Hindi.

The boy, Savit, said he'd peed on it and then put ash from the fire into a paste.

'Well, God was on your side,' Frank told him gravely.

When both boys had been examined, and their wounds treated with antiseptic cream, they went away grinning as if all this attention had been a tremendous treat. Frank turned to Viva. 'I think you should tell Daisy now the other reason why I'm here.'

'I was going to,' Viva said. She took a deep breath. 'Daisy, do you remember me telling you a little about the boy on the ship? The little monster it was my misfortune to chaperone? Well, there's a new episode. He punched one of the passengers on the ship, the son of a prominent Indian businessman. No charges were pressed at the time, but it seems that the victim's family are now after some kind of revenge and I could be implicated.'

'Why you?' Daisy's clever eyes blinked behind her specs.

'Because legally, technically, we were in foreign waters and he belonged to me.'

'That sounds absolute codswallop to me. Are you absolutely sure?'

'No, I'm not,' said Viva. 'The boy loves dramas, he says all kinds of strange things to draw attention to himself, and this could easily be another, but the point is, he came round to see me the other night. He claims to have been bribing the police, and if he or they come round, I— well, Frank thought I should let you know what's going on.'

'Well, bribing the local police is hardly a big news story in Bombay.' Daisy seemed to be taking all this in her stride as Viva had hoped she would. 'But I don't at all like the thought of him turning up in your room. You must definitely tell Mr Jamshed and get him to change your locks, and then I think . . .' Daisy closed her eyes '. . . I think you should leave town for a few days to put this young man off. I've been trying to persuade her to do this for a few weeks anyway,' Daisy explained to Frank. 'I think she looks tired.'

He glanced at her impersonally, and she felt she had become, in that moment, another one of his patients.

'I'm not tired,' she said.

'It's going to get even hotter than this soon, Viva,' said Daisy. 'It's imperative to take breaks. Don't you agree, Frank?' Viva was surprised to see that her employer was almost flirting with him, certainly both of them seemed to be treating her as if she was public property.

'I do,' he said. 'I think they're essential.' He stood up and picked up his bag. 'But, ladies,' he looked at his watch, 'you'll have to excuse me. I'm on duty at four. Leave a message for me at the hospital if you want any more help.'

'Gosh,' Daisy said after he left, 'what a good-looking man,' adding more professionally, 'and how useful for us that he works at the Gokuldas.'

'Yes,' said Viva. The suddenness of his exit had registered as a slight shock to her, a feeling that there were other things she'd meant to say.

Glancing through the open door, she saw him striding across the courtyard, opening the gate, then shutting it firmly behind him.

'And I think he's absolutely right about you taking a few days off. Do go to Ooty,' Daisy urged. 'It's cool and beautiful and that guest house I was telling you about really is charming. Do you have a friend you could go with?'

'Well, I might have.' She remembered shouting at Tor that morning and felt guilty about it.

'It will do you nothing but good,' Daisy was beaming, 'hills, cool breezes, little chalets, mountain birds.' As her square practical hands sketched out the vistas, Viva felt fearful. Something about the word chalet. *Rain, a woman crying.*

'Are you all right, dear?'

When she looked up, the fan above her was clacking. Daisy was talking.

'I'm fine. I'm fine,' she said.

'Oh good.' Daisy gave her honking hockey captain's laugh. 'Just for a moment, you looked as if you'd seen a ghost.'

Chapter 34

It was Tor's private opinion that Viva had been *un peu* hard on Guy, even on the ship. Of course he could be silly and affected, and maybe he did occasionally make things up, but what sixteen-year-old didn't?

She herself had spent most of her sixteenth year in Middle Wallop imagining that Nigel Thorn Davies, her father's red-faced land agent, was secretly and painfully in love with her, and that he would seize her and declare his feelings for her at any moment – at dusk in the summer house, or on a country walk somewhere leafy and private. Sometimes it seemed to her that she'd spent her whole life imagining things would happen that hadn't.

And she still smiled to remember that moment on the ship when she'd played Guy the Jelly Roll Morton record. The satisfying way he'd yelped, how his skinny neck had jerked around like a ball on an elastic band. In that moment, he'd been what the negro jazz musicians at the Taj called 'a gone coon', and wildness was something she wistfully appreciated.

But even so, she was tremendously relieved when Viva phoned on Tuesday morning to apologise once more for her outburst. When Viva had suggested a short holiday in Ooty, she said she'd love to come.

'The timing could not be more perfect,' she'd added significantly. 'You see,' she lowered her voice to a mutter, '*it* came.'

'What came?'

'You know, *it*. The thing I was worried about. *My friends.*'

'What friends?' Viva sounded baffled.

'*The curse.*' Honestly, Viva, for an intelligent woman, could some-times be very obtuse. 'I had so many hot baths I practically dissolved, but oh, the relief. It was the worst four weeks of my life, Viva. I thought I was going to have to waddle straight off the boat and into a home for fallen women.'

'Well, thank God for that. What a relief.'

'It was and I'm sure that's what made me so switched off about the Guy thing. I couldn't sleep, I couldn't even eat, can you imagine. Also—' Tor looked around the room to see if any of the servants were in earshot. 'Ci and I have had the most appalling row. I'll tell you when I see you. I've started to hate her,' she whispered. 'I can feel her marking off the days till my ship leaves. I honestly think she's gone mad in the heat.' Tor said before she hung up, 'I can't wait to get away.'

Although Tor had tried to joke with Viva about her awful row with Ci, it had hurt so much. She thought about it when she put the phone down: which parts she could bear to tell and which parts must stay hidden inside her huge humiliations file and buried for ever.

Even Ci must have known she'd overstepped the mark. She'd tried to blame it later on the heat and the fact that Geoffrey's cotton factory was losing more and more money and maybe this was partly true: before the storm burst, the atmosphere in the house had felt positively electric.

The tension had begun building when Ci came back from her hols in Mussoree, looking more drawn and tired than when she'd gone away. She'd started to stare at the phone in a funny way, to smoke more than usual and on one shocking occasion Tor saw her smack Pandit around the face for bringing her a Gin and It without her usual ice. Pandit had stood there smiling and apologising, but Tor had heard him mutter darkly as he raced back into the kitchen with the red mark on his cheek.

Tor was almost convinced now that Ci had a lover. Ollie had told her, with typical lack of tact, that most of the mems took them.

'I could honestly walk through the Malabar Hill at two o'clock on a weekday afternoon,' he'd boasted, 'and make love to almost any woman I wanted, they're so bored, and so desperate.'

He'd also told her – at first she'd so enjoyed these thrilling gups – that a hotel in Meerut – a favourite station for trysts – had taken the precaution of employing a blind porter to ring a two o'clock bell to warn all the lovers to get back to their beds at a decent hour.

Anyway, whoever it was that had been sending Ci flowers was no longer sending them and now she no longer cooed, 'Dahhllling,' into the phone like a dove, and there was a look, almost feral, in Ci's eyes as the scarlet talons ripped through the post in the morning before she tossed the letters aside. She was in a mood to draw blood; Tor was the closest victim.

The row began quite late one night when Tor was sitting at her dressing table, half undressed for bed, and Ci had walked into the room.

'Darling,' she said, 'you know all those clothes I lent you when you first came out? I'd like them back, please.'

Tor wanted to cry at the meanness of this, for Ci had said she could keep them. Also, she'd felt so fine in those clothes for a while, so sure that everything in her life would change.

'Do you want them now, Ci?' she'd asked warily, wondering if she'd have time to give one or two of them to the dhobi who she sometimes saw cycling down to town in the morning with Ci's evening dresses sailing behind, all of them coming back in the evening beautifully ironed. She'd ripped one or two of the seams, and the Chinese silk jacket still had tar on its elbow, picked up on the night that Ollie had taken her to Juhu Beach. She'd stuffed it to the back of the wardrobe thinking she'd sort it out later.

'No time like the present.' Ci's smile was a grimace. 'Geoffrey's just announced a cut in the clothing allowance, and I doubt you can fit into them any more, can you?'

Then Tor, feeling bulky in her sleeveless nightgown, had been forced under Ci's eagle eye to lay all the clothes out on the bed.

'Good God.' Ci had picked up her Wolhausmenson hunting jacket and pushed her talons through the rips under the arms. 'Who on earth did this?'

'I only wore it once,' Tor had stammered, which was true. Ollie had taken her out on some 'nags' he'd been lent at the racecourse. 'It was rather tight.' In fact, ludicrously tight for a riding habit, but Ci always chose style over practicality. 'And we were jumping an oxer and— I was about to get it fixed.'

'About to get it fixed.' Something peculiar had happened to Ci's mouth. 'What stopped you? You haven't exactly been busy here.'

They'd glared at each other for a long moment.

'Darling, I feel I must say something to you,' Ci had continued in a new more-in-sorrow-than-in-anger voice. 'You see, nothing happens to you in life without self-discipline. I mean how much, for instance, do you weigh now?'

Her eyes had swept over Tor's plump arms, her expanding girth. *I hate you,* Tor had thought. *I hate the way you talk, I hate the way you smoke,*

I hate the jokes you make about me to your friends. For she could just imagine how Ci would soon be describing her at the club. *Huge, darling, fat as a pig again,* or *a returned empty – rather a large one, I'm afraid.*

And in that moment, it was almost tempting to wipe Ci's sad, superior smile off her face by telling her that not only was she fat but she was expecting a baby too, so she could see some things were even more important than her blasted clothes.

'Ten and a half stone,' Tor had said. A lie. She was too frightened to go anywhere near the scales. And now, because she was in such a state, Tor could almost imagine Ci saying in that same flat voice, 'You've been crying a lot lately, Tor. Are you up the spout or something?' and hated her even more, but no, Ci was holding her green Chinese silk jacket up in front of her, the claws of her nails like pegs.

'What have you done to this?' she was shouting. 'This jacket was embroidered in Paris.' Her voice rose into an undignified shriek. 'It's absolutely and completely ruined.'

'I wore it on the beach.' Tor had wondered for a second who this woman was who was roaring at the top of her voice, and then realised with a queer thrill that it was her.

'I got tar on the sleeve,' she'd shrieked. 'Clap me in leg irons, why don't you?'

'Oh yes, that's right,' Ci had roared right back, her eyes bulging. 'Oh, very grateful! I mean, all I've done for you in the past six months is to clothe and entertain you, you *great fat fool.*'

After Ci said the 'great fat fool' bit, her mouth had clamped shut. Even she knew she'd gone too far.

And only later could Tor appreciate the wonderful irony of what happened next. As she and Ci faced each other – red in the face, breathing heavily – Tor had suddenly felt the pop of air between her legs, the unmistakable stickiness of blood. Shouting had done what gin and hot baths had failed to do. She'd suddenly beamed at Ci, who must have thought she'd gone mad. 'I'm fine!' she said. 'I'm absolutely fine.'

And it was at this moment she understood that not having a baby might, in certain circumstances, be every bit as magical as having one.

After speaking with Viva, Tor phoned Rose to see if by some miracle she could come to Ooty too. Viva had said it would be fun if they could all get together.

'It's supposed to be beautiful up there,' Tor wheedled. 'Do try and come. Tell Jack I'm leaving India in the blink of an eye, that I desperately need you and you'll probably never see me again.'

'No need for any of that,' Rose said crisply. 'I've already told Jack what I'm going to do.'

Well, bully for you, thought Tor. Rose sounded so much more in control, almost steely when she spoke about Jack.

The plan was that as there was a party at Daisy's on Wednesday night, Tor would stay with Viva and they'd take the train to Ooty the following morning. Rose would meet them up there. That gave Ollie – Tor worked it out on her fingers – four days in which to phone her and tell her he'd suddenly realised he'd made a ludicrous mistake and wanted to divorce his wife in England and marry her after all, or failing that, maybe she might meet someone wonderful up at Ooty. What a good story it would make at their wedding reception. *The most extraordinary thing, I was on the very point of going back to England when I looked up in this little hotel we were staying at and I saw . . .*

Oh, what an idiot you are, thought Tor, catching herself out in her own daydream.

Dreaming was what hurt most, better to face facts now. She was fat and on the shelf, and there, barring a sudden miracle, she would stay.

Because they'd hardly spoken since their row, Tor was surprised when Ci insisted on driving her over to Viva's house the following Wednesday afternoon. She wondered if it was because Ci, who could sometimes seem surprisingly sensitive to the good opinion of others, was trying to leave a good last impression, or perhaps make up for the row the week before.

All Ci said was, 'Byculla, darling, is the absolute armpit of Bombay. I wouldn't dream of you taking a taxi.'

The drive did not start well. After getting Tor to light one of her Abdullahs, Ci had filled the car with smoke and then started in on her again.

'This is absolutely the last thing I'm going to say to you about clothes,' she said as they wove in and out of a line of bullock trucks laden with sugar cane, 'but are you absolutely sure I didn't lend you my Lanvin jacket as well? That one's part of a limited edition.'

'Quite sure.' Tor had been staring at the bullock's bottom, wondering how a creature could be so thin and carry so much. 'I tried it on,'

Tor said. 'And it was miles too small for me.' Ci often set these mean little tricks for her.

'Even when you lost all that weight? Months ago, I mean.'

'Even then.'

'How many pounds did you lose in the end?'

'Two,' said Tor. God, the woman was obsessed every bit as much as her mother.

'Do you find the dumbbells helped?'

'Not really. Look, Ci, I don't actually think I am all that fat, what I am is big-boned. I don't have a lot of flab on me, and my waist is quite small.' This was true. 'Curvy' Ollie had called her in a rare compliment. 'Statuesque' was the word one or two of her other boyfriends had used. Sometimes it felt important to fight back.

'God, look at that ghastly creature!' Ci suddenly exclaimed. A naked man covered with ash was walking between the traffic, shaking his bony fist at the car. 'Two pounds – ah well,' Ci went back to ignoring the world outside the car, 'I don't suppose it will matter too much in Hampshire.' Whatever that meant.

Then Tor, never a great one for directions, managed to get them lost.

Somehow, they'd ended up on the outskirts of the Bora Bazaar, the vast, sprawling, untidy market where it seemed half of Bombay congregated to sell their rubbish.

'Really, Tor,' Ci said as her skinny little ankle pumped the accelerator, 'you are quite hopeless. I think I'd better have another ciggie.

'So where now?' Ci's smile was a snarl by the time they got to the end of a road that led nowhere. 'All this is *terra incognita* as far as I'm concerned.'

'Stop the car right now,' Tor longed to shout. 'I'm sick of being grateful to you, sick of being your problem, sick of being wrong.' But back in the prison of politeness, she sat in the perfumed smoke of Ci's car feeling sad and unworthy and hardly daring to breathe in case she said the wrong thing again.

When they finally got to Byculla and Jasmine Street, Ci, who'd sulked for the last twenty minutes, refused to park, saying it was far too dangerous and now too late. She would drive straight home.

'I'm sorry,' were Tor's last words to her, and Ci's dismissive little shrug had hurt more than her anger.

261

Chapter 35

Tor had sounded so low on the phone that Viva was amazed to see how radiant she looked when she opened the door.

'Excuse my humble home,' Viva said as she led her upstairs. Mrs Jamshed had been cooking up her famous shrimp patio that morning and the smell of garlic and cumin in the hall was so strong you could taste it.

'Excuse it!' Tor said. 'I'm so happy to be here I could practically burst. Oh, Viva, what a wonderful place,' Tor said when she opened the door to her room. 'So bohemian. I love it!' She looked at the ceiling now covered with children's kites, ran her hand over the silk bedspread and bounced on the bed.

'It's going to be a bit cramped,' Viva said, 'but I've borrowed a camp bed. I don't mind sleeping in it, and we're going to Daisy's tonight, and we'll leave first thing, so what the hell.'

Viva got them both some lemonade, and they went out on the balcony and Tor made Viva roar with laughter when she told the story of the Ci Ci row.

'The only thing I am so grateful about,' Tor's eyes looked huge with shock at the thought of it, 'is that I didn't tell her about . . . you know . . . possible problems in the baby department. That would have been the final straw. And the club! Just imagine. That would have kept the old biddies going for months.'

'Why do you care so much what people think?' Viva said. 'You can't win them all.'

'I do care,' said Tor. 'I want everyone to love me and they won't. I wish I was more like you.'

'What do you mean, more like me?' Viva pushed a plate of biscuits towards Tor. 'Come on, dig in.'

'A cat that walks alone. Look at all this.' Tor gestured towards her room. 'I could never do this on my own.'

'Be broke, you mean, and live in a house that smells of curry? Poor Tor.'

'No – don't tease. I mean live like this and know that one has done it oneself.'

Viva didn't want to spoil Tor's good mood by telling her how lonely and desperate she'd felt here at times, or how scared after Guy had turned up. She took a sip of lemonade.

'I don't think earning your own living is as hard as it used to be,' she said. 'If it's independence you want.'

Tor heaved a sigh. 'I don't think I do.'

'What do you think you want then?'

'A husband.' Tor's big blue eyes looked absolutely serious for once. 'Some babies, a place of my own. For me the rest is just being brave.'

In her usual frame of mind, Viva might have raised plenty of bracing objections to this: have encouraged Tor to get some sort of training; offered to introduce her to the already wide variety of women that Daisy knew – teachers, archaeologists, language experts, social workers – who found dozens of other things to do in India apart from hunting for husbands. But tonight, she felt strangely disinclined to urge Tor towards serious goals.

Frank was coming to the party.

Daisy had dropped this casually into the conversation earlier.

'I thought I'd ask that nice young doctor friend of yours,' she said. 'He said he'll come if he's in town and not on duty.'

Why this piece of news should have made her feel so annoyingly hectic, she had no idea. She'd planned to write for an hour or so before Tor came, but instead had spent the time jumping on and off a chair and trying to line up her reflection with the only mirror in the room which lay in the shadows opposite her bed on top of a chest of drawers.

Wobbling on the chair, she'd tried on her best dress – it was a flame-coloured silk, its long darts emphasised her small waist and she liked the small bow at the back. Then she tried a blue embroidered jacket she was particularly fond of. She'd ripped the jacket off, tried on the only other presentable outfit she owned, a cotton shirt made of some white gauzy material. It looked pretty, she thought, against her coral and silver earrings.

She was enjoying herself when the sight of her eager, happy face in the mirror frightened her. *He's not going to come*, she'd warned herself. *And even if he does, you don't want him.*

'So what do you think?' she was asking Tor now, in an offhand voice, as if this was the first time she'd tried the flame silk dress on. 'I could wear it with these.' She clipped on the silver and coral earrings that had belonged to her mother.

When Viva saw her face in the mirror again, she saw that her pep talk had done no good. She was still horribly excited.

'I think you could wear a jockstrap and opera glasses and still look beautiful,' said Tor. 'Which is quite unfair, because you don't seem to give a damn about all that.'

Daisy's party was in full swing when they arrived. They could hear, from the street below, bursts of laughter, some jazz – the clownish kind with lots of whistles and squeaks. A row of coloured lights shone from the balcony.

'Come in! Come in!' Daisy, beaming and wearing a bright pink dress, opened the door on a roar of conversation. Although Daisy lived on a shoestring, she loved giving parties and entertained with a reckless aristocratic confidence that Viva admired. With Daisy, there was no careful mixing of people of the same kind, no placement, or particular show, instead she threw all the people she liked – children, academics, local musicians, neighbours – into the pot, fed them well, wound up the gramophone and let them get on with it. It was a real lesson in life.

'Come on!' She steered them towards the balcony, where they heard bursts of music and laughter. 'I want you to meet everyone.'

'Everyone' was the usual rich mix: Mr Jamshed and his two stunning daughters, Dolly and Kaniz – one of whom was dancing the Charleston. There was a large and stately Swedish sculptress in a caftan, on her way to study the carvings at Elephanta. Social workers, academics, writers, a fat man who was a professor of music and in Bombay to record. Some of them sat on sofas on the balcony under the starry sky, others were dancing.

Tor was immediately swept off by Daisy to talk to a Bombay advocate, Mr Bhide, who she said had bravely defied convention by marrying a Hindu widow. (The widow turned out to be twenty-five, shy and clever.) Viva stood for a few moments on her own at the edge of the roaring crowd. She was sipping one of Daisy's lethal punches, hoping to calm her nerves.

For the next half-hour she wandered through the groups of people, chatting and laughing, her senses trained like a pistol towards the front door. He hadn't come after all. Well, good in a way, she reassured herself; it made things far less complicated.

Halfway through the evening, Daisy's servants brought out bowls of steaming rice, three different kinds of curries, chutneys and poppadums. They set them down informally on the balcony on low tables with cushions around them. Someone had put 'Lady Be Good' on the gramophone and the foggy sounds drifted across the balcony into the streets below.

'Please join us.' Mr Jamshed beamed at Viva and Tor. He was sitting cross-legged beside a low brass table. His plate was piled with food; his girls were all around him. '*Chalo jumva avoji*,' he said, 'Come, let us eat. My girls are teasing me for being old-fashioned and I need you to give them stick,' he said to Viva in his beautiful English.

'You see,' Dolly appealed to Tor, who was goggle-eyed at all this, 'we are discussing education, and what my poor father fails to understand is that we have actually skipped a generation. My mother behaves as your grandmother, but I am as modern as you.'

'No, wrong,' said Tor with that peculiar intensity that Viva liked about her. 'Viva tells me that you're studying law at the university, so you're miles ahead of me. I left school at sixteen. I can barely add up.'

'I'm sure you're very clever also,' Dolly said tactfully.

'I'm not,' Tor said. 'I'm quite dim, and, by the way, none of the girls at my school went to university either. We learnt to sew and speak bad French instead. But I can dance the jitterbug if that's any good to you.'

'Yes!' Dolly and Kaniz said together. Their white teeth gleamed in the moonlight. They were entranced with their new friend.

'Absoludol,' said Tor, standing up. 'But first I need to get us all another drink and powder my nose. Will you come with me, Viva?'

As they stood side by side in the bathroom, Viva saw Tor was both tipsy and happy. She thanked Viva twice for bringing her here and walked with particular care as if she was on castors back through Daisy's sitting room and on to the balcony again, into the milky softness of the night.

'A wonderful, wonderful party,' she said on her way through. 'The strangest thing – I've hardly given Ollie a thought all evening. It's such a relief.'

'I'm glad, Tor.' Viva, who'd been glancing towards the door all evening, felt like a complete hypocrite. She checked her watch surreptitiously one more time. Eleven thirty-five – Frank wouldn't come now. Too busy after all maybe, or perhaps not busy at all but writing to some girl in England she knew nothing about, who he was madly in love with, or out at another party. There were always so many reasons for things not happening in the way you thought they might.

Mr Jamshed had appeared again. He was shouting at her over the laughter and the talk and the smoke about some concert that was coming up – some wonderful new composer, very like Bach in his symmetry – she could feel herself smiling and nodding, but could hardly concentrate, she suddenly felt so tired.

Her dress was sticking to her back, her feet hurt, she thought longingly of bed and normal life again. And then, when she looked up, Frank was standing near the door looking at her.

'Will you excuse me for a second?' she said to Mr Jamshed. 'I . . .' and she was gone.

Without a word, Frank took her arm and pulled her towards him.

'I'm late,' he said. He looked dishevelled and a little wild-eyed, as though he had been through an ordeal of his own in the past few hours. 'And I'm ravenous.'

'Are you?' She almost hated the clamour in her heart.

She got him some food, and when he'd eaten, they danced. First one dance, and then the next.

About three-thirty in the morning, Frank, Viva and Tor sat on the balcony together.

'Just like old times,' said Tor. 'We could be on the old *Kaisar* again.'

When Viva looked at Frank she saw him shake his head slightly as if in disbelief.

A faint pink flush was showing in the distance where the sun would soon be rising. The raggle-taggle rooftops were taking shape one by one.

'I've drunk too much,' said Tor, who was on her fourth or fifth gin fizz, and who was lying on a charpoy with a cushion behind her head, 'but may I just say that that was one of the best parties I've ever been to in my life. Wonderful, *wonderful*, beautiful people, such fun. I honestly think Byculla is one of the jolliest places on earth.'

'You're right, Tor,' Frank said seriously. 'It was a very good party.'

Viva liked his smile so much – it was so charming, so sudden – it lit her up. There wasn't much she could do about that, even though she was still determined to stay on guard.

Tor lay dozing on the charpoy.

'How am I going to get her up in the morning?' Viva needed to know suddenly. 'The train leaves for Ooty at ten-thirty.'

'I know,' he said. 'Tor's just asked me to come too.'

He leant over and took a strand of damp hair from Viva's forehead. He tucked it behind her ear.

'How would you feel about that?'

Viva hesitated. 'I'm not sure,' she said. The casual touch of his fingers on her hair both calmed her and made her senses blaze. She felt so out of control, and didn't like it.

'I've got some time off from the hospital,' he said casually. 'And, also, you might just be better off with a man around at the moment.'

'Is it Guy?' she said quickly.

'Yes, partly. I got a letter from the police two days ago. It sounds like something else has cropped up. They want to talk to me about him.'

'When do they want to see you?'

'Next week.'

'Why didn't you tell me earlier?'

'Because you looked happy.'

They looked at each other for a few seconds, and then Tor stirred.

'Tired,' she murmured, 'very, very tired and very, very hot. Up the wooden hills to Bedfordshire.'

And Viva returned to her senses.

'I'll be back by then,' she said lightly and cruelly. 'And Ooty is a girls' outing. Sorry.'

Chapter 36

When Viva told Tor that she'd booked them third-class tickets on the train to Ooty, Tor said that was fine with her. She was short of money too, and if they were kidnapped by white-slave traders it would almost certainly be more fun than Christmas in Middle Wallop.

But the sledgehammer heat of May, even this early in the morning, made Viva worry that she'd made the wrong choice as they boarded the train at the Victoria Terminus Station.

They'd entered the splendid building, with its flying buttresses and stained-glass windows, early in order to avoid the crowds, but already their carriage was a writhing, roaring sea of humanity: picnicking families, capering schoolchildren, grannies in saris, one man with a stained cotton bed rolled up on his lap.

Tor sat down next to a smeary window; Viva was in the middle, opposite a plump young mother holding numerous greasy packages on her knee. It was a relief to feel the slight movement of oily air as the train slowly chugged out of the station and into a shimmering heat haze.

For the first hour, Viva enjoyed watching Tor's big blue eyes nearly pop from her head at the sight of a naked sadhu who'd leapt on to the train at the first station, his skin shrunken, buttocks barely covered by a thread. Then came the chai wallahs and food merchants who sped through the train as if their trousers were on fire selling tea, omelettes, biscuits, soup, dhal and chapattis.

But now three hours had passed and the heat had parboiled the smells of sweat and hair oil, spicy food and flatulence, and the glass of the window was almost too hot to put your head on. Tor, already groggy from the gin fizzes the night before, had started to groan and say she felt sick.

Viva seemed to hardly notice it. This was the first time she'd left the city since she'd arrived, and a strange kind of exhilaration had grown in her as she stared out of the window at the tiny railway stations, at women with water pots on their heads, and then, on the edges of a scrubby plain, a small camel train appearing then dissolving in the dust.

Daisy was right; it was wonderful to be in motion again, just what she'd needed.

The train clattered down narrow gullies, across parched plains, *clackety clack*, again the murmurs of Indian voices all around her. Viva closed her eyes and fell into a vague dream in which William, not Tor, was travelling with her.

They'd never travelled well together. When they'd first met, he'd taken her away on two holidays with him. On the first – a touring holiday in Switzerland – they'd stayed in a series of predictable, irreproachable hotels, all of them known to him, and one night – near the lakes of Berne – he'd gone into a terrible sulk when their reservations had been cancelled by mistake.

She'd sat on her own on a balcony overlooking a lake; and this was the moment when she'd understood that William, underneath the intelligence and the slashing wit, was a timid man who wanted travel to provide as few shocks as possible, and to be as much like home as could easily be arranged. She hadn't blamed him for this, but had felt something inside her fighting for air, for light.

Half asleep, she imagined him across the aisle from her; the elbow of his smart suit was resting in the greasy packages of her new friend's picnic. He was angry with her for subjecting him to this, irritated by her enthusiasm. *What is the point of this*, she could feel him saying, *when we can easily afford to travel in the first-class carriage? What are you trying to prove?* And bit by bit the fun of the day would be leached away.

Frank wasn't like that. He got excited by small, unexpected discoveries – he'd loved Moustafa's scruffy café that night, told her with excitement about some of the unexpected places he'd discovered in Bombay, like the Thieves' Market, and— *Oh God.* She was awake now and looking out at stunted thorn trees. She must not think of him in this way. When they'd danced the night before, her body had felt so sweet, so light, the smell of him woody and tart like lemon trees, and something denser and deeper that drew her to him.

She shook her head suddenly. The memory of that dance was somehow imprinted on her body: his hand on the small of her back, the glow that seemed to come off his skin, the way he'd closed his eyes for one moment as if in pain as she had moved her face closer to his.

She made herself think of William again as a necessary corrective.

For months after he'd left her, she'd felt broken and dirty as if she'd been run over by a truck, and what had made it so much worse was that with her parents gone there'd been no one around to pick up the pieces. She'd lost her pride – wandering around like some stricken animal waiting for him to claim her again, to tell her that it had all been a silly joke on his part. If it hadn't been for work – for that was the time she'd started as Mrs Driver's typist and started to write herself – she would surely have gone mad.

Remember this.

The train went from light to dark; they were moving through a makeshift tunnel blasted out of rock. If Frank did come to Ooty (for Tor had woken up and overheard her saying it was a girls' outing and protested sleepily that Frank could come too), if he did come, she must understand clearly that his interest in her was protective, brotherly. Or that he'd just come to be with Rose and Tor – how conceited, after all, to think she was always the main attraction. Whatever happened, she would not lose control of herself, not in the hateful way she had before. That was a promise.

The carriage burst through into sunshine again, the train shrieked and Viva opened her eyes. The plump little woman with the moustache who sat opposite her was tapping her gently but insistently on the knee; she was starting to take food from packages on her lap. Nuts and fried chickpeas, small evil-looking fritters that had left circles of oil on the brown paper they'd been wrapped in.

'Eat with us,' the woman said in Marathi. Her clothing and sandals were cheap; her smile radiant with happiness at the thought of offering food to total strangers.

'How kind you are,' Viva replied. 'Where are you going to?'

'We came from near Bombay and we are going to Coonor, near Madras,' the woman said, delighted to find that Viva spoke a little Marathi. She said they were going to visit relatives there and also hoped to see Gandhiji at a rally. 'I got up early this morning to prepare this food.' She saw no paradox in offering them to an English person. 'They're Bombay delicacies, please try.' She unwrapped some more *bhel puris*, puffed rice flavoured with onions and coriander; she handed Viva some spicy potatoes served in a bun.

Tor had woken up and opened one eye. 'Viva,' she said with a pleasant smile towards the woman, 'if you're expecting me to tuck into that you have another thing coming.'

Viva took one of the fritters and ate it. 'Delicious,' she said to the woman, 'but unfortunately my friend is unwell. Would you like one of our sandwiches?'

She unwrapped the picnic they'd slung together that morning – cheese and pickle sandwiches on day-old bread. The woman turned away, clearly embarrassed. Maybe it was against her religion to eat the food of untouchables. *There are so many ways of getting it wrong*, thought Viva.

When they'd finished eating, the woman wiped Viva's hand with a damp flannel she had in her bag and then she pointed to the fat girl of about fifteen who'd sat beside her eating stolidly. Her daughter, she said, would like to sing for her. She had a fine voice; she could sing for four hours and hardly take a breath. The woman indicated this by placing her hand on her own chest and inhaling mightily.

'I want you to look pleased when I tell you this,' Viva said to Tor. 'This girl is going to sing for us and it is a very great honour.'

The girl fixed her huge velvety eyes on Viva, and took a deep breath. She began to sing, her voice high and clear and sad.

Viva could only pick out a few words: I adore, terrible despair, I love, I want. 'It is the love song of Sita and Ram,' her proud mother explained. 'It is her present for you.'

The girl, lost in her song and totally unselfconscious, had moved closer to Viva, so close she could see the engravings on her nose ring, even her quivering tonsils. *We're so different*, Viva thought. *You could live here for a hundred years and never really understand.*

The girl's song had swooped now into a plaintive keening sound which made her think of unhappiness and William again. Two weeks before they'd parted, he'd taken her up to a small hotel he knew near Edinburgh. There he'd told her, more in sorrow than in anger, that he found what he called her 'obsession' with her work too difficult to bear.

(It was only later she found out it had nothing to do with this. There was another woman in Bath, who had phoned Viva hysterically one night saying William had promised to marry her too.)

But on this night, at the Buchan Hotel, he had gently but firmly told her off: she was young, yes, and parentless, but life must go on and it would never go on happily for her unless she learnt not to be so self-engrossed. He was pleased she had her writing to do, but, if she would allow him to be so blunt, a self-engrossed bluestocking was unattractive to a man.

She had wept at the time, not tears of remorse exactly, more tears of anger and puzzlement. He told her he was only saying all this for her own good and later in bed, had made love to her and she had accepted him, rather than dare look into the pit of loneliness she felt waiting for her outside that cold hotel.

Three weeks later, he'd moved in with the young widow near Bath, who turned out to be rich and very boring – or so he said, six months later when he wrote to her, not to ask her to come back (he was too clever for that) but saying that as her unofficial guardian they must build bridges, stay friends, they owed it to her parents to do so.

That was when she told him about her plans to go to India, and it was only then that he mentioned casually what he had meant to say before, that her parents had left some furniture and a couple of trunks for her in Simla. 'Nothing of great value,' he'd been led to believe, but she might want to pick it up some day. The name of the woman who kept it there was Mabel Waghorn. He had her address if she wanted it.

'Why didn't you tell me before?' she said.

'Your emotions were too raw,' he said in that careful, precise way he had of making everything seem true.

And in a way, he'd been right. If he hadn't been, why was she still procrastinating about going back to Simla, and why did it still feel like the most dangerous thing she could do?

The girl eventually stopped singing. Viva said, 'That was beautiful, thank you,' and the mother, who'd been watching Viva's face, gave her another gentle pat on the arm and her mouth briefly crumpled. She was clearly in awe of her talented daughter, now eating a handful of chickpeas.

Tor lifted a corner of the damp flannel she'd draped over her temples. 'Is it safe to come out now? I seriously thought she might sing for the full four hours.'

'Lovely,' Viva said to the woman. 'Thank you, quite charming.'

'I wasn't asleep,' said Tor when they were back in their own world again. 'I was thinking about going home and then about Ollie, and that I might send him a telegram when we get to the hotel. Maybe it's true that his wife doesn't understand him any more; I mean, if she did really love him she wouldn't let him go away all the time, or maybe he's waiting for me to say I forgive him. I've got nothing to lose, Viva.'

Yes, you have, thought Viva, feeling a terrible stab of pity for her. *Your pride, your life, even.*

'Is he really what you want?' she said instead. Tor's face looked so flushed and hopeful.

'You're right, you're right.' Tor put the damp flannel back on her temples.

A few seconds later, her large blue eyes appeared again over the cloth, this time with a look of deep confusion in them. 'I don't know how anybody ever really knows they're in love,' she said. 'I mean, in books and films it seems to come to people in a blinding flash and off they rush on to boats or trains, and then the music comes up and then "The End". Why is life so much more complicated?'

'I don't know,' said Viva, and meant it.

Chapter 37

OOTACAMUND

It rained heavily on the night before they arrived, and as the tonga carrying Tor and Viva clip-clopped up the steep hill that led to the Woodbriar Hotel, the ground was strewn with dashed rose petals, and the air smelt of roses and wet grass. They breathed in deeply. After twenty-four hours on the train, their limbs ached and it was bliss, they agreed, to feel almost cold again.

At the end of a pine avenue, they climbed towards a house on stilts which seemed to float in mist on the edge of a hill. A hazy figure stood up on the verandah and began to wave frantically.

'Rose!' shouted Tor. She leapt from the tonga and, narrowly avoiding the horse, ran up the drive, up the stairs, and then flung her arms around her friend.

'Darling Rose.' She beamed, hugging her hard. 'Look at you! You're vast!'

A slight exaggeration this, as Rose's mound was small and neat and hardly showed under her blue smock.

'Oh, Tor.' Rose squeezed her eyes shut and hugged her again. 'I've missed you so much.'

'Viva's been horrid to me,' Tor complained as they walked arm in arm into the house. 'Not only did she make me travel third class, but she forced me to listen to this girl who sang like a gnat for three hours, I swear. And it was boiling and everybody smelt.'

'How dare you be nasty to my friend,' said Rose, giving Viva a hug. 'And stop that horrid noise,' she said to Tor, who was making her own gnat sounds, 'and come inside and have some tea. You're going to love this place.'

They did. The hotel's owners, Mrs Jane Stephenson and her friend, Bunty Jackson, were the merry widows of army officers. Lean and vigorous, they bred Welsh mountain ponies, adored their garden and served up the kind of food – shepherd's pies and rhubarb fools – that made their mainly British clientele misty-eyed with nostalgia. In the sitting room there were comfortably dilapidated chintz sofas set beside roaring fires, mildewed copies of *Country Life* resting on antique tables and, on the walls, Stubbs's prints and photographs of favourite dogs and 'the girls' riding winners.

Over coffee on the verandah, Rose told them she had got a lift up to Ooty from a friend of Jack's, a Colonel Carstairs and his wife. Both of them had ticked her off for travelling in her condition. ' "You're looking frightfully peaky, dear," ' Rose mimicked with a gentle smile. Rose was never mean about people.

'Nosy old biddy,' said Tor.

But Viva thought that Rose looked peaky too. There were dark circles under those formerly cloudless blue eyes. She also looked older in some way that Viva found hard to define, more wary.

'Did Jack mind you coming?' she asked. After all, it was not exactly normal for a man to allow a wife in this condition to travel alone in India, which was probably why the Carstairs's eyebrows had been raised.

'I don't think he minded.' Rose fiddled with her biscuit. 'The heat in Poona has been frightful, and he's been so busy, and this really is my last . . . and, well, it's just so lovely to be here.'

There was a silence. Rose's cane chair squeaked as she moved. 'Oh, complete change of subject, but I must tell you a terrible story that Jane told me last night about dogs,' she said in a brighter voice.

Rose's story was about a local maharajah, rich and spoilt, who went every year to England to buy the champion of Crufts dog show. Once back in the fearsome heat of his castle in Madras they were kept like discarded teddy bears in a filthy dungeon underneath the house. A friend of Jane's had been to lunch at the palace a few weeks ago and the dogs had been dragged blinking into the sunlight, thin and with their coats matted. When one of them had been made to 'die for the queen', she'd felt like crying.

While Viva and Tor expressed shock, Bunty strode in wearing a tweed hacking jacket and stood with her legs apart like a young sub-altern. 'It's absolutely true,' she said. 'I'm afraid it's a case of monkey see, monkey want. You see, they don't have the experience with animals,' she said.

'Some do surely,' Viva protested.

'Almost none of them.' Bunty closed the subject. 'Completely different attitude to ours, I'm afraid.'

Jane then asked if they'd mind ordering their supper in advance – they were doing *She Stoops to Conquer* at the club and there was a seven o'clock rehearsal. Dinner would be set up for them in a private room where they could talk in peace. Would a mulligatawny soup, local trout, a dish of pommes dauphinoise and apple amber for pudding fit the bill?

'That sounds delicious,' Rose said politely. 'But where are the other guests?'

'Oh, only four this week, and all either fishing or riding,' said Jane. 'We're very small here, and you'll hardly be aware of them, which reminds me – there's something I've been meaning to show you.' She disappeared towards the smoking lounge, returning a few moments later with a green leather visitors' book in her hands.

'One of our guests last week said he was a friend of yours, look.' She pointed at a childishly round signature, halfway down the page. 'Oh, hang on—' One of her servants had called her to say that her horse was ready. 'If I don't ride now, it will be too late. D'you mind?'

'Good Lord,' a lock of Rose's blonde hair fell over the book, 'how odd.'

'Wonderful views, excellent fare. I shall return. Guy Glover,' he'd written in the comments column. He'd left an untidy blot to the right of it.

Viva felt a coldness in the pit of her stomach.

'What in the hell was he doing here?' she murmured, looking towards Tor.

'Well, don't blame me,' Tor said defensively, 'I mean, how odd is it really? Lots of people come here when the weather's hot. Ci Ci told me she'd been here.'

'I'm not blaming you,' said Viva, although she was still irritated.

'Has he tried to contact you again?' Tor asked.

'No,' said Viva shortly.

She heard Tor ask Rose for another scone, the scrapings of curtains being closed upstairs. It would be dark soon outside.

'I expect he was up here doing some photography,' she said casually to both of them.

She was trying to remember exactly how much they had been told about the incident on the ship, about the police. Her instinct then and now had been to protect them.

'He only stayed for a few days,' said Tor. 'But what difference would it have made if he'd stayed longer?'

'None whatsoever.' Viva forced a smile. Tor was right, not everything had to mean something.

After supper, it was arranged that Viva should take the bothy – a small attractively furnished guest room separate from the house – and that Tor and Rose would share a room on the first floor in the main part of the house. After Viva went to bed, Tor and Rose went upstairs to their room. When they'd washed and put on their nightdresses, Rose went to the window and opened the shutters.

'Look,' she said.

The rain had ceased and a pale moon had stopped between their muslin curtains; it hung there in a skein of mist.

'Do you remember,' said Rose, 'how we were once completely convinced that there was a man in the moon?'

'What halfwits we were.' Tor poked her in the ribs. She wasn't in the mood to be wistful.

Rose's bed was near the window and had been made up with beautiful crisp linen sheets. They both got into it, and opened the shutters wide so they could see the outlines of the hills, vast and purple, in the distance. The rain fell again with a gentle shushing sound outside the window, and they could smell the faint lemon and honey of the old-fashioned roses that had been put on their bedside table.

Rose closed her eyes and pulled her eiderdown up over her stomach.

'Close your eyes, Tor,' she murmured, 'and tell me we're at home. Mrs Pludd will be up any minute now with cocoa. Copper is munching hay in the field outside.'

Tor shut her eyes obligingly, but she didn't like the game.

'Perfect, Rose,' she said. 'All those lovely walks up to your waist in mud, ice on your washstand water in the morning, chilblains.'

But then she felt mean. Rose was entitled to feel homesick with a baby on the way and other things, for she'd confided over supper that her mother had written to tell her that her father had had a chest infection and was 'not feeling one hundred per cent', which, in Wetherby speak, meant he was practically at death's door. It was more than likely that Rose may not see him again.

'Do you miss it very much, Rose?' In the glow of the lamplight, she could see the fluff of baby hair at Rose's temples, her flawless skin. She looked too young to be having a baby.

'Sometimes.' When Rose squeezed her eyes shut, the golden feathers of her eyebrows turned downwards. 'But I suppose there are days when everybody hates it here: the heat, the stinks, the club.'

This from Rose who never complained.

Tor fiddled with the charms on Rose's bracelets: the gold fish, the lucky horse, her tiny St Christopher.

'Do you remember you wore this on the night we sent Queen Mary to sleep?'

This was the way they always described their presentation at court.

Rose was smiling. 'I was *so* nervous,' she said. 'Do you remember Mummy gave us champagne for the first time and then the charms in the red leather box? For some reason they thrilled me more than anything. I remember her saying, "This was Granny's, now it's yours." It felt like being given the keys to the kingdom.'

'Like the beginning of everything.' Tor undid the little gold catch and the bracelet fell with a clunk in the dish on the bedside table. 'Do you remember how grown-up we felt having our own taxi to Buckingham Palace, and all those hours getting dressed? And then, what a joke: old meat pies and queuing for two hours in the pouring rain and finally! The Queen! Practically in a coma, the poor woman was so bored by us.'

'Did you ever wear your dress again?' said Rose.

'Don't,' said Tor. 'I looked like a tent in mine: all that hideous satin and that dusty tiara. How stupid it seems now. It almost bankrupted my parents, as my mother has never ceased to remind me. What was the point of it, Rose?'

'No point,' said Rose, and then more diplomatically, 'but it was sweet of our parents to try.'

'Well, hang on a sec.' Tor turned to look at her. 'Didn't you at least meet Jack at one of the parties?'

'Oh yes, Jack,' said Rose. She shifted the eiderdown off her stomach. 'I met Jack.'

The curve of her belly moved as she turned over.

'Is everything all right, Rose?' Tor asked.

'Fine,' said Rose.

'It must be jolly hot having a baby,' Tor said helpfully.

'It is hot sometimes.' Tor heard the rustle of a handkerchief. 'It's . . . odd when you feel it moving.'

'Is that exciting?'

'Yes.'

Tor inwardly rolled her eyes. Why would Rose never say when she was upset about something?

There was a sound outside the window, an almost human shriek. Tor shivered. 'What on earth was that?'

'Monkeys.' Rose held her hand. 'Jane says there's a family of them in the trees near the tennis courts. They're huge and grey and look like people, you know.'

'Rose,' Tor tried again, 'look, I know we've agreed not to talk about this, but I'm going home very, *very* soon now. When I see your mother, what do you want me to say about you?'

'Only tell her good things.' Rose's voice came hesitantly through the dark. 'Say I'm having a balloon time, that the baby is fine, that Jack is . . . that Jack is fine. But do, if you can, find out the truth about Daddy. I know this chest thing is much more serious than they're letting on.'

'Why do people skate round things so in letters home?'

'I don't know,' said Rose. 'I don't even know what the truth is yet.'

'Please tell me what's wrong, Rose.'

'I can't.'

'Why not?'

'Because I'm married now and you can't just blab – it's not fair.' Rose's voice had risen. 'It's not fair to the person you're married to: you only hear one side of the story.'

Tor flopped back on her pillow. This was exhausting. Her dearest, most loved friend. When she put her arm around her, Rose clasped her hand hard.

'Sorry if I seem nosy,' Tor said.

'Not nosy,' said Rose in a muffled voice. She'd turned her back to Tor. 'You're the best friend ever.'

Tor waited again, but nothing, and then Rose fell asleep.

Tor lay awake for the next few hours with her eyes open, listening to the wind and the monkey sounds and Rose's calm, even breaths.

She had a strange feeling in the pit of her stomach, like when you're swimming and you want to put your feet down on something solid, but the water's deeper than you think and there's nothing there.

Chapter 38

The following morning, Jane Stephenson strolled in after breakfast, with a Pekinese dog under her arm, suggesting they might have a picnic that day at Pykeva Lake. They were very welcome to take her tonga.

'Is the pony quiet?' Rose asked anxiously.

'Bombproof,' said their hostess.

'Mind you,' she couldn't help adding, 'I do think your husband's brave letting you come away like this.'

Tor, who was sitting behind Jane tucking into toast, rolled her huge eyes at this and sagged in her chair.

'Isn't he?' said Rose pleasantly.

When Viva, Tor and Rose stepped into the morning sun after breakfast, it was dazzling: every leaf and flower seemed to have been rinsed clean by the rains the night before and the air was full of birdsong.

'Do you love birds as we do?' Bunty had followed them out of the house with a large, well-thumbed book. 'If so, you are in for *such* a treat: the Kashmiri fly catcher, the blue robin, the laughing thrush – he's a frightfully noisy fellow, you'll hear him chuckling. Do take these.'

The bird book and a pair of binoculars were thrust into Rose's hands, and then their tonga arrived pulled by a smart Welsh mountain pony that Bunty said she had bottle-fed when its mother died.

Their driver, a handsome fellow in crimson turban and white puttees, salaamed them into their little carriage. A touch of the whip on the pony's fat little bottom and they flew down a winding road overlooking blue hills and lakes, and a vast expanse of blue sky beyond.

Tor was being silly with the binoculars: 'I say,' she said, in Bunty tones, 'is that the slatyback forktail? By jove, it is!' and then hearing them laugh, their driver turned round and started to sing them some wobbly songs which he said the memsahibs would enjoy, and they all joined in for a while. Viva even knew some of the words – she'd sung them with her children – which amazed and pleased the driver.

At lunchtime, their driver found them a fine picnic spot under a group of banyan trees overlooking the hills. As soon as they sat down, a group of large grey monkeys, hard-eyed and muscular, swung down from the upper branches of the trees and inspected them minutely.

Tor stood up and stared right back.

'I suppose you're wondering why I asked you here today,' she said in the tones of their ex-headmistress, Miss Iris Wykham-Jones. 'Well, from now on, no fleas whatsoever to be eaten from armpits during assembly. Do I make myself perfectly clear?'

A monkey furled back its lip and screeched.

'No staring. No bottom washing in public!'

'Don't upset it,' Rose begged. 'Tor, please, that's not funny. I hate them.'

'Calmness, Rose,' said Tor, 'they're much more frightened of us than we are of them.'

'How do you know?'

'I don't,' Tor admitted. 'It's one of those things people say.'

The driver had leapt to his feet at the monkey's cry. He showed his white teeth to the girls, bashed the tree with his stick and laughed heartily as the monkeys fled.

'Hanuman, the monkey god,' Viva said, 'is supposed to be good at answering prayers.'

But Rose still looked pale. 'They're horrible,' she said, 'I really do hate them.'

'All gone now,' said Tor, rolling out a tartan rug and opening the picnic hamper. 'So let's eat – I'm starving as usual.'

They unpacked freshly made rolls packed in blue and white checked napkins, thin slices of roast beef, curried eggs, fresh mangoes, a large bouncy Victoria sponge and home-made lemonade carefully wrapped in pages from the *Ootacamund Times* so it didn't drip.

'This is the best picnic I've ever had,' Tor said between mouthfuls of her sandwich. 'By the way, why did our driver show you that terrifying dagger in his belt, Viva?'

'To protect us from the *badmash*, the villains, on these roads. But we're safe, or so he says. This is Snooty Ooty after all and the locals like English people.'

'Just what they thought at Amritsar,' joked Tor, 'before they sliced off their heads.'

Viva said, 'They didn't slice off their heads, they—'

'Don't talk about it,' Rose said suddenly. 'I'm sick of that sort of talk. It goes on all the time now in Poona.'

'You're right, Rose,' Tor poured the lemonade, 'no gloomy talk on a what-the-hell day, so don't mention ships or home or my mother. Let's drink to us. To the bishi.'

At the clink of their glasses a huge grey monkey swung down to the lower branches of the tree, his eyes flirting at them through the foliage. He swung to another branch where he furled back his lip and laughed at them silently.

'Horrible.' Rose froze. 'My doctor tells me they snatch babies.'

She was close to tears and Tor felt worried. She'd never seen Rose so jumpy and she wished she knew why.

After they'd eaten, Viva took out her journal and started to scribble.

'Oh, for heaven's sake, Viva,' Tor teased, 'put that thing down and behave like a normal person for once.'

Viva hardly heard her. In the tonga, she'd been thinking about Talika, how, on the night before she'd left Bombay, Talika, perhaps fearful that Viva wouldn't come back, had come into the office on some pretext or other, hauled her skinny little body up into the chair opposite Viva's and asked her if, when she came back, they could go out into the streets again and try and find her mother.

Viva had said, 'We'll try.' But her heart had sunk to her boots. Daisy had already tried and failed several times.

Talika had talked about her mother, 'because I am forgetting her,' she'd said, fixing her coal-black eyes on Viva.

She showed her a picture she'd drawn of a shack, surrounded by slashes of rain.

'*My house*,' she said. There were three stick figures outside it with pots on their heads. 'This is the place where my mamji cooked chapattis.' She'd pointed to a little fire on the ground. 'This is me helping her. There's my grandmother.' She pointed to a horizontal figure on a charpoy. 'I am making dhal for her.'

Her eyes were clouded with sadness as she recalled these memories. 'They're my *bhoot kal*.' She'd folded up the piece of paper and put it in her dress pocket.

'What does *bhoot kal* mean?' Viva asked Daisy later.

'Ghost time,' Daisy had said.

Viva stopped writing for a few moments. The hills in the distance, the taste of lemonade in her mouth, reminding her of one vague strand of memory, like a gap in the mist, elusive, upsetting, through which she saw another tree of monkeys, a woman frightened of them, English voices raised, one laughing, one scared.

A thought broke through like a wrecking ball – her own mother was crying in the middle of a family picnic. Why did her father lead her away outside the rim of trees? Was he telling her off? Was he comforting her? Why did it hurt to think of these things?

'Viva.' Tor snatched away her pencil. 'You're looking serious. Have some of this.' She put a piece of cake in her hand.

Viva put a piece in her mouth. It was delicious – buttery and springy and with a tart lemon icing.

'That's perfection, isn't it?' Tor was watching her eat and smiling. 'Doesn't that make you sing all over?'

'Delicious.' Viva smiled at her. One of the many things she had come to like about Tor, and knew she would miss when she went home, was her enthusiasm for small things – lemon cakes and Jelly Roll Morton, dogs, sunsets.

Enthusiasm. Viva was half watching a line of iron-grey clouds that were moving above her head. How ironic it was that William, the least enthusiastic person she had ever met, was the one who'd told her what the word meant. In Greek of course.

'It means to be possessed by a god,' William had told her in his clear precise voice.

On that same evening – they'd been sitting at the time in Wheeler's Restaurant in Soho, eating a rather good chocolate mousse – William had just announced that suffering was at the core of human life. It was one of the few facts, he said, on which both Buddhists and Christians agreed.

When she'd said to him that she enjoyed lots of things in her life and sometimes couldn't wait to wake up in the morning, he'd all but winced at the vulgarity of it.

'I'm not talking,' he'd said in a strained and impatient voice, 'about, I don't know, dollies and ponies and the smell of coffee brewing, all those things that everyone talks about when these conversations occur: I'm talking about real and lasting happiness. I believe that if it exists at all, it comes from work, from self-discipline and not expecting more from people than they can give because they'll usually let you down.'

Now she wondered why she'd listened so obediently to these sour little lectures of his, when part of her had recoiled from them and known at the time they were only partially true. Of course having work you liked was a great thing, almost everybody in the world knew that, but it was only part of the picture. Now she thought of Talika on Chowpatty Beach dancing barefoot with her kite, in spite of all the things she'd lost – sometimes happiness really was that simple.

She stretched out on the rug, closed her eyes and let thoughts of William drift away. How lovely this was after the busyness and heat of Bombay, to doze on a rug and feel your friends nearby, to see the purplish patterns of sunlight behind your eyelids, to hear wind shushing through pines, like gentle waves on the seashore. As she drifted off to sleep, she could still taste lemon in her mouth and before she could stop it, felt the soft brush of Frank's lips on hers.

'Oh God!'

She sat up quickly, bumping into Tor, who was lying beside her.

'What happened?' said Tor sleepily. 'Were you stung by a bee?'

'I'm all right,' said Viva, hugging herself. 'I'm all right. I nearly fell asleep.'

But she lay there with her heart racing as if she'd escaped some crash or fall.

She mustn't think of him like that, she told herself, and trying to think of all the things she didn't like about him. For a start: too attractive, and some puritanical part of herself felt this might lead to conceit or carelessness or laziness, because the advantage was unfair and unearned, like being dealt a five-card trick every day of your life, or until your looks faded. She acknowledged she may have been a little unfair to have overlooked some of the pain in his life, and the fact that he clearly took his medical studies more seriously than he let on . . . and oh, he dressed rather shabbily and his hair always looked as if it needed a cut. But that smile, that wonderful sudden smile, she'd seen on the ship how it melted other hearts, and how she must keep herself aloof from it. Yes, that was definitely it; she still wasn't at all sure about him. *Charm* – William had taught her the ancient origins of that word too – charm, he'd said, was not a superficial or a glossy thing: it meant *capable of casting a spell.* So maybe that was what she'd felt in Frank's arms when they had danced, a little giddy, a little unhinged, but nothing she couldn't put right. He could cast his spells on weaker creatures, she thought, hovering on the edge of sleep. To survive, she'd need all her wits about her.

284

It was starting to rain again. When she stood up, their driver was approaching them. He was pointing towards the other side of the valley, where thick grey clouds were massing.

'Blast!' said Tor. 'We're going to get soaked.'

The grey pony cantered all the way home, but they were still drenched by the time they got back to the hotel.

They were running under umbrellas towards the verandah when Rose stopped so suddenly that Viva banged her nose on the back of her head.

Frank was standing near the door smiling at them. He was wearing the same crumpled linen suit, carrying his hat in his hand.

Viva felt her heart cartwheel when she saw him, and in the next moment, she almost hated him. What a cheek to imagine he could just turn up in the middle of their holiday as if that was all they wanted.

'Madam.' He bent facetiously over Rose's hand, and brushed it with his lips. 'There's been a spot of bother in Bombay. I thought I should come and escort you all home.'

'Oh, come on, Frank!' Tor was dripping with rain and scarlet in the face. 'You can't fool me; I know exactly why you're here.'

Viva glared at her. She dug her fingers into the palm of Tor's hand.

'Frank.' She coolly took his hand. 'What brings you here?'

'I've ordered tea,' he told her, 'in the parlour where we can talk.'

They ran upstairs and changed quickly out of wet clothes and then they walked into the parlour together where the red curtains were open still on what were now sheets of rain. Frank sat down on the fender with his back to the fire and with his legs sprawled easily in front of him.

When Bunty appeared with a tray of tea and scones, she'd changed into a floral dress – the first dress they'd seen her in – and put a faint breath of powder on her weather-beaten cheeks. Viva felt another flash of anger. How dare a man feel so confident, so sure of himself, for he must feel it? How the house's pulse rate seemed to have gone up since his arrival.

Bunty gave Frank the first cup of tea, and made a fuss about scones and jam for him. Viva heard the ticking of the grandfather clock near the window and then became aware of him looking at her over his teacup. Flustered, she turned away and made a point of telling Bunty what a perfect day they'd had. She asked her about the blue robin she'd read about in the bird book. Was it honestly blue, and was it as cheeky as an English robin?

How false she sounded, even to herself – like somebody's maiden aunt.

'Yes, they're marvellous, quite fascinating.' Bunty had heard all this, or something similar, a million times before from other guests and was clearly eager to get back to talking to Frank about his doctoring, as she rather archly called it. 'I mean, you honestly work in a *Bombay* hospital,' she said, as if he'd descended to the last circle of hell. 'How awfully brave! Are you what the natives would call a *niswarthi*?'

'What does that mean?' Tor asked bluntly. She'd been gazing at Frank while he spoke.

'It's a Hindi word for a selfless man.' Bunty beamed at him.

'Oh Lord, no, not that.' Frank stretched his legs out and smiled the smile. 'I'm only doing it for the beer and cigarettes.'

And there he was again, Viva decided, a fine young male animal surrounded by a pride of admiring females. The same Frank she'd mistrusted on the ship. Well, it was a relief at least to have got that straight.

Bunty retired after tea to supervise the clearing of the gutters and to check that all the animals' shelters were rain-proof. Sometimes in May, she said – speaking directly to Frank – they got a curtain-raiser to the monsoon, which could be frightening. Last year, during a freak storm, twenty inches of rain had fallen in twenty-four hours and a large chunk of their drive near the house had collapsed.

'Heavens,' said Rose weakly. 'Never a dull moment.'

After she'd gone, a servant entered the room. He drew the curtains, lit the lamps and adjusted their wicks, before closing the door behind him.

'So, Frank,' teased Rose, when they were on their own again, 'tell us about this spot of bother in Bombay, or was that all a ploy to come on holiday with the glee club?'

'Unfortunately not.' Frank had moved to a wing-backed chair near the window. His playful manner had gone. 'The Muslims and the Hindus have been rioting in the streets for two days now. Nothing unusual about that, but some of it has been fierce: I saw them set light to a man in the street. They poured petrol over him. He went up like a guy on Bonfire Night.'

'Oh my God.' Viva was thinking of the home, of Suday and Talika and Daisy and Mr Jamshed.

'Don't worry yet,' he said. 'It's all fairly localised in the hutments around Mandvi. Byculla's quiet, and so's Malabar Hill. It will all die down as soon as it starts. But I didn't like the idea of you travelling home alone and I had two days off.'

He looked directly at Viva as if explaining himself to her.

'We thought you should get back before Tuesday – there's a big Congress meeting then and there could be riots around the VT Station. They're certainly laying on extra beds at the hospital. Your husband phoned Mrs Mallinson,' Frank told Rose. 'He was going to take the Poona train down to Bombay to meet you, but he can't – all leave is cancelled.'

Rose's expression did not change.

'You'll be fine in the ladies' carriage back to Poona,' Frank assured her. 'After all, this has nothing to do with us, they're fighting each other, but he's naturally concerned.'

'Naturally,' said Rose drily. 'How kind of you both to think of it, but I'm sure there's nothing to worry about.'

Rose stood up, her yellow hair swinging against the lamp and almost touching the flame. She said she was very tired and thought she would go to bed. She turned at the door and said it had been a wonderful day and she would never forget it.

'There's nothing to worry about,' she said again.

'Who's worried?' said Tor, standing up. 'Anything that stops me going home is fine with me.' They all laughed as if she was joking but she wasn't.

Rain had begun to fall with a hard splintering sound like pebbles against the window.

'I'm going to bed too.' Viva stood up.

'Stay for a moment,' he said. 'There's something else I need to tell you. Sit down first.'

He reached over and held her hand.

'I'm afraid there is no easy way of saying this, so I'll say it quickly. There's a rumour that Guy's been murdered. I'm so sorry.'

'What?' She stared at him stupidly for a while. 'What are you talking about?'

'It's a rumour,' he said. 'It may all be wrong, but the police say he's not in his lodgings, and when his parents were contacted, they said they hadn't seen him for weeks. A burned overcoat with his name in

287

it was found in a street near your house. Apparently, he moved there a month ago.'

'He was up here just last week.' Viva felt her stomach tighten. 'I don't know why.'

'I don't know either.'

'Why did you say nothing had happened in Byculla?'

'Nothing did, apart from this.'

'Does Mr Jamshed know?'

'No. At least I don't think so. And none of this may be as bad as it sounds, but I thought you should know, or at least be warned.'

'Who told you?'

'A policeman, one of the Byculla locals. He's the one who's had his eye on Guy.'

'Oh no!' She felt water gush into her mouth. 'Are you saying they torched him?' She thought she was going to be sick.

Frank steered her into a chair.

'I don't know,' he said again.

She rubbed her eyes and shook her head. 'Tell me what happened.'

'Nobody really knows yet, but the policeman told me that the brother of the man Guy beat up on the ship is called Anwar Azim. He's very powerful, very political, and he is part of the All-India Muslim League, which Guy, for reasons still unclear, has got himself involved in. Azim made his own enquiries about the incident on the ship – that was probably just a case of bribing a few Lascars – and then took matters into his own hands.'

'But surely our police will do something about this?'

'Not necessarily. Quite frankly, it's all too messy. It couldn't come at a worse time.'

'Is it that bad?'

Her voice had started to judder. He put his arm around her, but she drew away.

'Nobody really knows.' He was trying to soothe her.

'No, please,' she protested. 'Don't soft-soap it. Tell me the truth. Oh, Guy!' She pictured him suddenly: like a cloth doll in flames.

'I don't know the truth yet,' said Frank. 'Only random facts.'

'Such as?'

'Well,' he watched her anxiously, 'there could be a big split soon in the party, and then anything could happen, or nothing, nobody really knows.'

'Who told you all this, about Guy I mean?' Her mind seemed to be going backwards and forwards.

'The police. They gave me this.' He handed her a thin wallet and a packet of photographs. 'They said they were his. They asked me to give them back to his parents.'

'Perhaps we should look at them first.'

'I already have. Some are of you. Look.' He pointed towards a close-up of Viva walking in the street near the children's home. She was wearing a summer dress, she was smiling at Parthiban, the man who sold her mangoes on her way to work. Underneath it, he'd written in black ink, in a childlike scrawl, *'Mataji'* – my mother.

In the second photograph she was sitting on the Chowpatty Beach, with Talika asleep on the sand beside her. Behind them was a sky full of kites. Underneath it, he'd misspelled her name, Miss Viva Hallaway, and written, *'Is she Cain, or is she Abel?'*

'He's been following me,' she said.

'If it hadn't been you, it would have been somebody else,' said Frank. 'He's desperate for someone to love, or blame.'

'How horrible.' She was starting to shake. 'I didn't love him at all, I almost hated him. I should never have taken him on.'

She felt Frank's arm around her shoulder. 'This is not your fault,' he said gently. 'He was sent back to England, alone, at the age of six. He was warped from that moment on – even he knew that. I'm also more and more convinced he has serious mental problems.'

A flame flared up in the fireplace. She saw Guy in it – his eyes staring, the teeth bared, grinning.

'I don't think we should tell Rose and Tor until it's confirmed,' she said. 'What's the point of frightening them until we're sure it's true?'

Frank screwed up his face. 'I thought about that all the way up,' he said. 'But it's a lot for you to have to carry on your own.'

'Does Daisy know?'

'Not yet.'

She got up with the vague idea of going to bed; she was dizzy and felt his arm again.

'Let me help you,' he said gently.

'I'm in the cottage across the lawn,' she said.

As they walked across the sodden grass, a gust of wind flung her coat around her and a faint, bilious wash of light lit up the hills across the valley.

'There's a big storm coming,' he told her.

'Horrible, horrible, horrible.' She was crying now, thinking of Guy's hair burning, his clothes on fire. 'He didn't deserve it.'

She felt Frank's arm around her shoulder.

'We don't know yet,' he said. 'Hold on to that – the place is alive with rumours.'

There was a boom in the distance, another flash of light, the rain unleashed itself in one sudden sheet of water and both of them were drenched.

Her hands were trembling so violently it took her ages to find her key in her handbag. When she handed it to him, she saw his wet shirt showing every rib and the hollows of his shoulders, the curve of a young man's waist.

'You're wet to the skin, Viva,' he said. When he touched her, she cried out and then he touched her very gently again, her shoulders, her belly, her arms, and she closed her eyes and put her head on his shoulder.

There was one small light burning beside the bed in Viva's room. She'd left a dress on the floor and on her desk her pens, a carafe of water, her journals.

He took a towel from the stand beside the bed, he rubbed her face dry. She had no words for the tears that poured down her face, or for the shivering that had started in her body. Tenderly, he rubbed her hair; he took off her soaking coat, then her cardigan and dropped it on the floor. He wrapped a dry towel round her.

'Stay with me for a while,' she said, feeling him about to leave. Her teeth were chattering.

When he lay down, she hugged him like a child with her eyes squeezed shut. Somewhere dimly in the background she could hear the sharp pebble-like sound of the rain falling on a tin roof. She heard the moaning of the wind, and everything became simple as she pulled him on top of her: her hunger and his young man's body on top of hers, blocking out death.

When it was over, he looked at her. He shook his head and both of them looked at each other in fear and wonder. Then he gathered her up, all of her, and groaned and shook his head again.

'Don't say you love me,' she said.

Chapter 39

For their own safety, Frank insisted they travel first class on their way home, but even so Tor felt like crying – everybody seemed so out of sorts. Frank and Viva sat across the aisle from her, as far away from each other as possible. Rose was silent and bunched up near the window, and Tor, finding nobody wanted to talk, felt all her high spirits draining away.

She brooded for a while on her weight gain. Last night, after supper, she'd sat down with a clunk on the large sitting-down weighing scales that Jane kept on the landing floor, underneath a picture of the Ooty polo team, lean fit-looking men every one of them.

Jane had boasted that these ornately carved scales were exact replicas of the ones in the Bombay Yacht Club and were accurate to the ounce, which was why her heart had sunk as she watched the needle rise towards eleven stone. Even at her heaviest, in London, she'd never been eleven stone; her mother would have plenty to say about that.

'I'm vast,' she'd complained a few moments later to Rose, pinching her flesh in front of the cheval mirror. 'I'm a baby elephant, and d'you know what's really upsetting is that it only makes me want to eat more.'

'You're not fat.' Poor Rose had heard this a million times before, but still managed to sound indignant. 'You don't want to look like a ghastly stick and you've got those great big blue eyes that one day a man is going to drown in,' she'd added in her fortune teller's voice.

'No, he won't,' Tor had said gloomily. 'I'm practically deformed I'm so hideous – and look at these spots on my back.'

'I'm not getting out of bed to look at your spots, Tor,' said Rose, who'd been propped up on two pillows at the time. 'But, Tor,' she whispered, 'do you want to see a proper baby elephant?'

And right there and then Rose had shocked her by pulling down the coverlet, and pulling up her nightdress – something Rose would never have done before her marriage – to show off the hard swelling of her stomach and her belly button, which protruded like an acorn.

'Touch it,' she said. 'Can you imagine how vast I'm going to look at nine months?'

Tor put the flat of her hand on the dome, and then cupped both sides.

'Oh God, Rose . . . isn't that' – Tor almost said horrible – 'isn't that . . .' she touched it gingerly with her fingertips '. . . peculiar. You don't look big yet, but it feels so different, and it's so funny to think of a baby sleeping inside. Has Jack seen it yet?'

'Yes,' said Rose.

'What did he say? Did he kiss it? Did he cry?'

Rose had looked at her.

'You're so romantic, Tor,' she'd said flatly. 'I don't think he said anything.'

And again, Tor felt she'd crossed a newly drawn line in Rose's life, and that beyond it lurked a world full of adult worries – worries that Rose thought she was too thick or inexperienced to share.

The train chugged on, and now Tor, her cheek pressed to the window, was brooding about India. In two weeks' time all of this – the huge blue sky, the mud huts flashing by, that donkey, that woman in a pink sari waving at the train – would be gone, and would soon become faded in her mind like pictures in an album. How bloody unfair that was when, in spite of everything that had gone wrong, she had been so marvellously happy here.

Her sigh left a circle of condensation on the window pane, and then, as the train whooshed past fields of sugar cane, a happier thought bubbled up: maybe the riots in Bombay would get so bad that nobody would be allowed to leave, and if this happened the ship would be cancelled, and then perhaps she might go and live with Rose for a while, at least until she had her baby – for she didn't imagine that Ci Ci would want her much longer.

Or perhaps Ollie would, at the last minute, fight his way through the crowds to rescue her. He would wrest her P&O ticket from her hands and tear it up on the gangplank; the pieces would flutter into the breeze. They'd dance together again like they had that night at the Taj; he'd tell her with tears in his eyes what a lucky man he was to be given a second chance.

Errrgh. What an idiot. A crick in the neck ended that daydream. When she opened her eyes, Rose was looking at her.

'Are you all right?' she asked. 'You've been twitching.'

'I don't want to go home,' Tor blurted out and then regretted it. There had been an unspoken agreement between them both on this holiday not to discuss the unthinkable: in two days' time, Rose was going to take the train to Poona, and then what? Jack was supposed to get home leave every three or four years. But who knew if he'd take it, or where they'd go. They might never see each other again.

'I'm sorry too,' said Rose carefully. She looked out of the window. 'It is going to be funny being back in Poona again after having such fun with you chaps.'

Tor glanced at her. 'Rose, I was just thinking. If I ever did come back to India, or found some way of staying, could I come and live with you for a while?'

'Gosh.' Rose looked quite thrown. 'Do you mean after the baby's born or something?'

'Yes.'

'Well . . . maybe.' Rose wasn't exactly jumping at this. 'Obviously, I'd love it, but I'd have to ask Jack. And I mean, what would you do? I mean, how would you live? Would your pees support you?'

'Oh, I don't know.' Tor slumped against the back of her seat. 'I don't know . . . It was just a silly train thought. Forget I mentioned it. I mean, I can't just dump myself on you, can I?'

'It's not that, Tor,' Rose said after a long silence. 'It's just that there's quite a lot going on at the moment.' To Tor's horror, she'd turned red and her voice had cracked.

'Rose,' Tor said, 'I'm trying so hard not to pry, but *is* everything all right?'

'No,' Rose said when she could speak, 'I mean, yes – it's just that Jack really might be sent to Bannu soon for operational experience. Most of the regiment have come home, but they've been threatening this for months and, you know, my life's not my own any more.'

'I know, Rose.' Oh, poor Rose, she looked so upset and embarrassed. To change the subject as quickly as possible, she looked across the aisle to where Frank and Viva were sitting.

'What on earth is going on there?' she whispered. 'They look so mis, like stone statues.'

'Very odd,' Rose whispered. 'This is not gossip, well, I suppose it is, but I saw him leaving her room early this morning. I couldn't sleep and was watching the sun come up. But now look at them, they haven't spoken one word to each other almost for the entire trip. Did something happen?'

Tor shrugged. 'I don't know,' she mouthed. 'Do we dare ask her?'

While Rose mouthed, 'No!' Viva half opened her eyes, looked in their direction and closed her eyes again. She wasn't very good at pretending to be asleep.

When their train arrived at the Victoria Terminus, it was raining. Geoffrey Mallinson, red-faced and agitated under his umbrella, elbowed his way through the swarming crowd to meet them. Over the roar of the station, he explained in a hearty bellow that he'd driven himself in the Daimler because walls had ears and he didn't entirely trust his servants at the moment. Frank got into the back with Viva and Rose. Tor sat in the passenger seat.

On their way out of the station, the Daimler swished through muddy puddles littered with discarded placards from the demonstrations.

'Well, you chose the right time to leave town,' Geoffrey said, half turning so he could speak to Frank. 'We've had a dickens of a time here: first the rain – seven inches in one hour – then the riots. It took me two hours to get to work yesterday.'

Tor pretended to shudder. 'Do you think they'll go on for ages?' she said hopefully.

Geoffrey didn't seem to hear her; he was one of those men who, if there was another man present ignored the women. 'I hope you're all coming for lunch,' he suddenly boomed. 'Ci's laid on a marvellous spread.'

Tor saw Frank and Viva glance at each other and hesitate. They still hadn't spoken.

'Do come.' Geoffrey glanced at them anxiously through the rear-view mirror. 'The memsahib's been cooped up at home for five days now because of the troubles; and, who knows, you might not see us again at Tambourine.'

'What do you mean?' said Tor.

'Well,' Geoffrey's eyes struggled to find Frank's, 'London's getting windier and windier about these demonstrations, and of course there's been a tremendous slump in profits since the war. I don't suppose we'll hold out much longer.'

Tor gasped. 'What?'

'How many factories have already closed?' Frank asked.

'Well, certainly five or six – mainly jute and cotton – in the past few months, and we're only hanging on by our fingernails. Tragedy really, when you think of how hard we've worked and all the years it's taken us to build the thing up.'

The car lurched as Geoffrey swung suddenly round a bullock cart blaring his horn. 'Hurry up, you blithering idiot!' he yelled out of the window. 'Get over! Get over now! But not a word to Ci over lunch,' he said when the car was purring smoothly forward again. 'This has all been far more of a shock than she lets on.'

Beads of sweat had formed across his forehead like a line of unpopped blisters. He mopped them with his handkerchief.

'And of course, it may well all be a storm in a teacup,' he comforted himself, adjusting his large bulk against the car seat. 'I mean, it's not as if we haven't seen it all before.'

'Darling sweets.' Ci pounced the moment they entered the hall. She was wearing an orange silk dress, more suited to an evening party than lunch. Her mouth was carelessly smeared with red lipstick, some of which she left like a brand on Tor's cheek.

'Lovely, lovely, *lovely* to see you all,' she said. 'And who does this divinely good-looking young man belong to?' Visibly brightening, she put a hand on Frank's arm. 'Pandit,' she shouted, 'I think we all need rather a large gin – in the drawing room, if you please.' She snapped her fingers.

'How do you think I look?' she asked Tor suddenly as they walked across the marbled hall.

Tor said, 'Wonderful, Ci Ci, quite wonderful and how very kind of you to stay in for us.'

She understood now the frantic paddlings going on beneath the polished surfaces of Ci's life – the dumbbell sessions, the daily eyebrow pluckings, the shrieks about clothes.

'*Stay in for you.*' Ci turned to look at her. There was something bird-like, frantic about her eyes. 'I haven't stepped foot out of this house *for five days.* I'm actually speaking to you from the grave. When I woke up this morning there was no colour in my cheeks at all.'

'Well, it's even more kind of you to ask us for lunch,' Rose rescued Tor. 'Were the riots horribly frightening?'

'Not a bit,' said Ci Ci grandly, 'they're two-hatted oafs.'

'Cecilia refers to the fact that Hindus often carry Muslim hats in their pockets, so they can change if they wander into the wrong area,' Geoffrey said helpfully – always happy to translate.

'And vice-versa,' Ci added indignantly, 'and it's all rot, so let's all have a very large gin and forget about the lot of them. Pandit! Where are you?'

'Well, actually,' said Frank, 'I'm afraid I can't.' He looked at his watch and frowned. 'I'm on duty at six.' He was speaking to Viva as if she was the only person in the room, but Viva shook her head and turned away.

'Oh, don't go. One little drinkie won't hurt.' Ci was almost pleading. 'I've done the whole thing for you really, to thank you for rescuing the girls. And everything's on the table. Our chauffeur will drive you both back – you won't have a hope of a taxi from here, not at the moment.'

Frank and Viva looked at each other again, and there was another awkward pause.

'How very kind,' Frank said eventually. 'But I must be gone by four at the very latest.'

He looked most peculiar, thought Tor, and again she saw that when he glanced at Viva, she turned away.

Four liveried servants, one behind each chair, leapt into life as they entered the dining room. They salaamed deeply.

The light, well-proportioned room gave out on to a terrace where there were large tubs of heliotrope and arum lilies all in bloom. The enormous crystal chandelier, switched on quite unnecessarily given the brightness of the day, floated bubbles of light over a table set with damask cloths, Venetian glasses and small bowls of tuber roses.

Ci Ci sat down unsteadily at the end of the table. 'Pandit,' she said, 'forget the gin and charge everyone's glasses for a celebration glass of champagne.'

'I've forgotten, my love, what it is we're celebrating exactly?' Geoffrey said nervously.

'Life, Geoffrey,' she said, giving him a beady look. 'Life. He's got no sense of occasion,' she told Frank. 'He never had. Come on, hurry up. *Jaldi*,' she said to the three servants who were handing around plates of salmon mousse and Melba toast. There was a pop as Pandit opened the Moët & Chandon with an expert twist.

'Now,' Ci said, when everyone had taken their first sip. 'I've been sitting here, *God help me*, with Geoffrey for the last few days, so what I need is a good gup. Tell me something I don't know. Astonish me.' She gave a curious grimace.

Tor, Rose and Viva shot desperate looks at each other; Ci swallowed another mouthful of champagne.

'Well, they say they had a very jolly time in Ooty, dear,' Geoffrey prompted helpfully.

'Oh, did you?' she asked Frank. 'Any amusing people there at this time of year?'

Rose gamely stepped in. 'Well, it was quite quiet, but it was such fun being together again, Ci Ci,' she said. 'And the Woodbriar is every bit as nice as you said it would be, and Jane spoiled us and packed us splendid picnics and we saw some wonderful flowers and it was so nice to feel cool again.'

She sipped some water and came to a sudden halt – Ci's eyes over the rim of her glass had gone perfectly blank, like a goldfish who'd come to the surface of a bowl and found no food there.

'And what about our Tor?' At last Ci had swivelled round to talk to her. 'Any decent men there, or was it all picnics with the girls?'

'No men at all.' Tor hated the faint air of salaciousness that hung around her question and was, suddenly, not in a mood to placate her. 'But lots and lots of lovely lemon cake.'

'Oh, I remember that *wonderful* cake.' Poor Geoffrey was all over the place like a man who'd invited a semi-wild tiger into his sitting room to entertain the guests.

'So Tor's been eating again, *what* a surprise,' said Ci Ci.

'Darling!' Geoffrey jumped up so quickly he dropped a crystal fingerbowl on the floor, and shards of glass and water spread over the Persian carpet. Ci looked at it perfectly expressionlessly for a few seconds.

'God, you're a clot, Geoffrey,' she said at last. 'A clumsy clot.' A shred of meat had clung to her teeth. 'Really. I mean it.'

'Ha, ha, ha, ha,' Geoffrey laughed as if this was a splendid joke; he clapped his hands. 'D'you know, she's right for once? Vivash will clear it up,' he said.

'Not for long, Geoffrey,' Ci reminded him softly.

Before Ci went upstairs for her afternoon siesta, she remembered that a man had called for Tor and she'd meant to give her the message.

'Oh heavens, who?' Tor tried to sound unconcerned. *Oh, Ollie, please, please, God, let it be Ollie.*

'Now, who in the hell was it?' Ci put down her cigarette holder while she thought. 'Oh, I know, I know. What was his name? Toby Williamson. He said we'd all met at the Huntington's; I had no memory of it. He wanted to know you were safe in the riots. He left a telephone number.'

Tor's heart sank instantly. 'How kind of him,' she said.

'Was he the one with the insect collection who wrote poetry?' Ci's expression was satirical. 'Such fun,' she told the others. 'She read some to me. "My heart is a tool/I've been such a fool . . ."' she improvised gaily. Tor felt her cheeks flush with shame.

How cruel of her to have shown his very nice poem (actually about birds and eggs or something) to Ci, who had doubtless amused her circle at the club with it too. She'd met Toby at some do at Government House. A sweet man, she remembered, who did something to do with teaching boys at a school somewhere. He'd talked to her about birds, and then, she remembered, about women's clothes and she, totally, in the grips of Ollie obsession, had hardly heard a word. All she could really remember of him was that he had a kind smile, and, oh yes, that was it, they'd had a hot-making conversation about modern poetry until she'd had to explain to him she was a complete ignoramus and he'd have to speak to her friend Viva about things like that. He hadn't sneered at her about that, but looked at her thoughtfully.

'I'm envious,' he'd said. 'You have it all to come.'

I was just phoning to see if you were all right. That was kind, but when she tried to remember what his voice sounded like, she couldn't.

When Ci had left the room, Rose said, 'Will you phone him back?'

'Not sure,' said Tor, who was suddenly feeling very tired. 'He was a bit of an egg head.'

'Nothing to lose,' said Rose lightly. 'Except your ticket home.'

'No,' agreed Tor.

'Shall we toss for it?' Rose got out a three-rupee coin. 'Snakes you do, squiggles you don't.'

She flung the coin in the air, then clapped it in the palm of her hand.

'Snake wins,' she said.

Chapter 40

When Viva and Frank got in the back of the Mallinsons' car after lunch, she pulled the seat rest down between them.

'I can't stand that woman,' she exploded as soon as they were in motion. 'How dare she speak to Tor like that?'

'Careful.' Frank looked at the chauffeur, who was driving with an ear cocked in their direction. 'Maybe she drinks because she is frightened,' he said in a low voice. 'Everything is ending for her too.'

'Well, I really do hate her,' Viva muttered. 'She's pure poison.'

She felt his hand touch hers.

'Viva,' he said, 'I'm worried about you going back to Byculla on your own. Let me stay with you for a while.'

'No,' she said. 'No. You can't come back.'

'Talk to me, please,' he said. 'There's hardly any time left now.'

'I am talking to you,' she said childishly, pulling her hand away. 'I'm talking to you now.'

'We can't just pretend nothing happened.'

Yes we can, she thought. She'd done it before and she could do it again.

The most disturbing thing of all was that she felt so intensely alive sitting next to him like this, so aware of the shape of his thigh muscles under the lines of his trousers, his hand resting casually on the seat rest. Her body was blazing with sensation in a new way, and all of this felt wrong and muddled up because Guy could be dead, and surely nicer or better people would be in mourning, not in lust.

'I've got a lot of work to catch up on, and Mr Jamshed's there, and look,' as they drove up the Queen's Road, she pointed outside the car window at the calm streets, the palm trees, the sea beyond. 'Everything looks perfectly normal again. It's as if the riots never happened.'

She heard him take a sharp, impatient breath, turn towards her and turn away again.

'I want to see you again,' he said. 'I must. What happened has nothing to do with the riots or with Guy. You know that's true.'

She said nothing because that felt safer.

She was trying to hold on to the idea that the night before had been a moment of temporary madness, a lapse in discipline. Nothing hurt as much as love, that was what she had to remember.

'Not yet,' she said. 'It's all been too soon, and so . . .'

When the words were out, she felt vaguely nauseous again. What she most wanted was to wash, to sleep, to stop thinking for a few hours.

'Are you worried about me coming up to your room?'

When he moved his head closer to hers, she could smell his hair, his skin.

'Yes.'

'I thought you didn't care what other people thought of you. I like that about you.'

When he smiled at her, she trembled.

'Well, I do care,' she said. The car had stopped at the traffic lights, near Churchgate, and on the kerb, not ten yards from them, two men were soaping themselves, splashing water from an old bucket over their heads. 'Everyone cares in the end,' she said. 'Unless they're mad or ill.'

A swarm of beggar children clustered around their car, fighting to polish its gleaming body work. When Frank rolled down the window to give them a handful of annas, his arm brushed hers and her body sang as if it led a separate life of its own.

'When will we know?' she said when the car was moving again, past the Flora Fountain and in the direction of the hospital. 'About Guy, I mean. Have the police told his parents yet?'

'I don't know,' he said. 'I expect some news at the hospital when I get back. Shall I leave a message or come over?'

'Leave a message,' she said. 'Don't come over.'

He looked at her and said nothing.

'I was horrible to him,' she said. 'If he was ill – I mean seriously, mentally ill – I should have got help.'

'Viva,' he tried again, 'you weren't horrible. Don't forget, I was there too and it wasn't your fault.'

'How far is it to the hospital?' She was longing suddenly for his confusing presence to be gone.

'Two streets from here.'

'It's beginning to feel like "Ten Green Bottles" with Tor and the Mallinsons going back.'

She could hear him trying for a more conversational tone to give himself more time. 'Are you leaving too?'

'Not yet,' she said. 'What about you?'

'I've been offered a job in Lahore,' he said. 'That research job I told you about.'

'Will you take it?' She looked straight ahead of her.

'I haven't decided yet.'

One side of her mind now watched the street sellers setting up their stalls, the lights being lit around the Flora Fountain, the wispy clouds in a rainbow-coloured sky; the other wondered if she would regret it for the rest of her life if she let him slip through her fingers like this. While the chauffeur parked the car, she followed Frank up the steps towards the main entrance.

'I should probably thank you for coming to Ooty to rescue us,' she said, 'but I don't know what to say any more. I don't think I've quite taken it in yet.'

He stopped with one hand on the door. 'About us or about Guy? Please don't forget it's only a rumour – I did tell you that.'

'Both.'

He looked exhausted, she noticed, and pale. His eyes searched her face for clues. 'Don't say anything you don't mean,' he said, 'but promise me that you won't feel ashamed.'

'I'm not ashamed,' she said. 'I feel as if I've been through an earthquake.'

He gave her a steady look. 'Ah, now that, I understand,' he said.

He was about to say something else, but she put her hand over his mouth.

'No,' she said. 'Don't. Please. Not yet.'

There were no signs of riots as the chauffeur took her back through Byculla, the same old potholed streets, crumbling houses, street markets, flower stalls.

She let herself into the house – everything the same here too: bicycles in the hall; the smell of Mrs Jamshed's curries in the air.

Mr Jamshed was in his front room in the middle of his afternoon prayers. He was facing the sun and wearing his *sudreh*, the shirt he prayed in tied three times with the *kusti* cord he wore to remind him, he had once explained, of the three principles he lived his life by: 'Good words, good thoughts, good deeds.'

She stood at the door waiting. In prayer, his normally jolly face looked guarded, forbidding, like an Old Testament prophet.

When the door squeaked, he opened his eyes. 'Miss Viva.'

'Forgive me for interrupting you, but is everybody all right?' she said. 'I've been so worried about you.'

'We are tolerably well,' he told her. He looked at her, polite, distant. 'No riots in the streets, thanks be to God, and I have heard nothing to the contrary from your school or your home or whatever it is you call it.'

'Oh good. What a relief.'

'Well, not really.' He still had that strange look on his face.

'Other things have been going on here that I am not happy with. Come.' He gestured towards the open door. 'It's better I show you myself.'

He put on his battered sandals and padlocked the front door behind him, something she'd never seen him do before.

'You see,' he explained as they were walking upstairs, 'while you were away, an unruly element broke into our house. They made a mischief in your room and did other things. At first I thought it might be hooligans, now I think it might be a friend of yours.'

'A friend of mine?'

'Wait.' He held his palm up at the threshold of her door. 'I will explain to you in a minute.'

When he opened the door, she cried out with shock. The curtains were closed, but even in half-darkness she saw her typewriter slung on the floor; her dresses, knickers, blouses, pictures lay in random heaps. A suspender belt had been draped on an empty picture hook on her wall.

'Oh no!' She ran to the little pine cupboard beside her bed where she'd kept the first draft of her book. It was still there.

Mr Jamshed drew the curtains with a scraping sound.

'That's not all,' he said. 'Look.' He pointed to the wall. Gazing into the half-light, she saw above the washstand a photograph of herself leaning against the railings of the *Kaisar-i-Hind*, next to Nigel, the young civil servant. The wind was blowing her hair, and Nigel, looking spivvy in a striped blazer, was poking her in the ribs. A photograph nailed on the opposite wall showed her leaving Daisy's party, her shoes in her hand, looking drunkenly dazed and happy. 'Whore,' was written in large untidy letters across the corner of it. In the third picture, she and Frank were leaving Moustafa's. On the bed, beside a hammer and a pile of nails, was an out-of-focus photograph Tor had taken of her and Guy side by side on deckchairs.

Moving towards it, she felt the crunch of glass under her foot. She'd stepped on a small votive pot, with a spent candle inside it.

'All these pictures had candles alight underneath them when I found them,' Mr Jamshed said. 'My house could have burned to the ground.'

She sat down on a heap of clothes on her bed and shook her head.

'I know who did this,' she told Mr Jamshed. 'But he may be dead. I don't know yet.'

As soon as the words were out, she realised how peculiar they sounded. 'You must think I'm mad,' she said.

'Madam,' Mr Jamshed spoke very formally, 'I don't think you're mad, but I cannot allow you to bring danger and other things to our house.'

'What do you mean?'

He gave a snort of disgust. 'You know what I mean. How can your father or your brothers let you live like this?'

'I don't have a father or a brother,' she said.

'I don't know anything about you,' he said. He was standing a few inches from a picture of her laughing and carousing with Tor and Frank. 'I've never really spoken to you about my beliefs, but I will tell you something now. The god I was praying to when you came in, his name is Ahura Mazda. Nothing happens in my life except through him. When I see all this,' he gestured towards the photographs, the underwear, 'I know I have let him down. I am like a child who has brought a dangerous toy into the house. No! No!' He held his hands out when she tried to protest. 'I must finish what I have to say. This is partly my fault, because my girls so want to be modern like you and I want them to be educated, but this is the danger. In our religion purity is at the heart of everything we do, and this is . . .' Words failed him and he threw up his hands, looking stricken. 'This makes my house feel unclean.'

'These are my friends.' She could feel the ground moving under her and didn't know what to do. 'You saw us at the party. You liked them.'

He shrugged. 'I don't know them. And him.' Mr Jamshed jabbed

303

his finger at the picture of Nigel. Who is he? And him?' He pointed to Guy. 'Is he another man who comes to your room?'

'He's just a boy. I brought him over on the ship. I was paid to do it. I didn't even know him before.'

'*You didn't know him*,' said Mr Jamshed. 'And you, a young girl, were paid to bring him? No, I don't believe. Even in England, they wouldn't let this happen.'

His eyes were large pools of suffering. His forehead deeply furrowed.

'Madam, I am a Parsee, we are broad-minded people, but I found alcohol bottles in your room too, and now this. And I'm very worried for my family. I already get stick from some local people for letting my girls go to the university – more shame for me. And what about those children you are supposed to help?' He smacked the side of his head to show how impossible this was.

She lowered her head. All their previously intriguing differences had suddenly become a chasm impossible to leap.

'Mr Jamshed,' she said, 'I understand how this looks, but I must ask you something as a matter of urgency. Did anyone see this boy in the building?' She pointed towards the picture of Guy.

'This boy?' Mr Jamshed examined the photo closely. 'My neighbour Mr Bizwaz described a fellow like this. He said he looked like an Englishman. He went out into the street; he took off his coat and shoes and set light to them. He shouted after him but he ran away.'

'Only his coat and shoes?'

'Only his coat and shoes.'

It took a while for this news to sink in.

'Are you sure?'

'Mr B. does not lie.' He glared at her when he said this.

'Oh God,' she cried. 'But this might be good news. We thought he might be dead.'

'You thought he was dead?' Mr Jamshed had begun to scratch his head as if bad thoughts swarmed all over him like cockroaches. 'Mrs Daisy Barker told me you were a very respectable young English lady, and now this too.' He stopped scratching and looked at her. 'Crisis for me, Miss Viva,' he said. 'I can't let you stay here. Not tonight, because it's dark, but tomorrow you must leave. You can't stay here.'

'Mr Jamshed,' Viva protested, 'I honestly can explain everything. Let me bring Mrs Barker over to speak with you tomorrow, she—'

'Madam, forgive me.' He held up his palms like a shield. 'But you are both foreigners, so you don't know everything. I can only repeat: there are men who live around here who are very fanatical. They already think women like you are—' He stopped, unable to say the words. 'Not pure,' he said. 'I have been sticking up for you with them. I can't now. It's too dangerous.'

'I understand.' She could feel the heat travelling from her neck to her cheeks. 'I'm not a fool.'

And now the words tumbled out of Mr Jamshed. 'You are not a fool, and it pains me to say such harsh words to you, but I am so worried not just for you, but for the children's home. You don't know how the ordinary people around here look at you. They may be smiling but they're completely confused. You have no family, no husband, no baby, no jewellery. What are you? Who are you? Believe me, madam, it's horrible, to say such things to a stranger in our country, but I must.' He nodded his head stiffly and walked towards the door.

'May I say goodbye to Mrs Jamshed, and to Dolly and Kaniz? You've all been so kind to me.'

'No,' he said. 'I'm sorry. Daughters are home but I don't want them to see you again.'

Chapter 41

Viva had heard of the phenomenon by which certain people – the feeble-minded, she'd always assumed – had only to be accused of a crime to feel themselves guilty of it. The next day, as she walked through the gates of the children's home, she understood it: she felt as if she was carrying a bomb with her.

After Mr Jamshed left, she'd spent over two hours pulling down the creepy photographs and putting them in the rubbish bin, and then packing up her room.

After that, she'd hardly slept at all, her mind whirling with thoughts of Guy and Frank (for she could not rid herself of the idea that her wild night in Ooty had somehow been instantly punished), and Daisy, and the home, and whether Mr Jamshed might relent and let her stay.

Somehow she doubted it, and she had no idea yet where she would go next. In the normal run of things, Daisy would have offered her a bed, but Daisy would be upset to lose Dolly and Kaniz, her prize students. And what if Daisy believed the rumours about Viva's immorality, what then? It was possible that Daisy would never want to speak to her again, in which case it would be back to the YWCA, a dreadful thought.

She pushed open the elaborately carved gate at the front of the home. It was a relief to her to see how absolutely the same everything looked. The same dim and shuttered rooms that reminded her of a large and shabby dovecote, the same birds in the tamarind tree and, across the courtyard, in the shade of the verandah, Mrs Bowden was reading to her sewing class in the same broad Yorkshire accents from a book Viva recognised – *English Poetry for Indian Girls*.

'*Little drops of water*,' the girls chanted back in their sing-song voices.

> '*Little grains of sand,*
> *Make a mighty ocean,*
> *And the pleasant land.*

Little deeds of kindness,
Little words of love,
Make our earth an Eden,
Like the heaven above.'

As Viva carried on walking across the courtyard, carrying her invisible bomb, the gardener, wearing the flat cap of a Muslim, was pushing around a few wet leaves with his broom. A row of patients sat on benches waiting quietly for the dispensary door to open at ten fifteen.

Walking down the dim corridor towards Daisy's office, she felt almost giddy with nervous tension. What if Daisy didn't believe her about Guy and the photographs, the fake suicide or why Frank had suddenly turned up in Ooty? Even she could see how far-fetched the whole thing sounded.

She found Daisy in her office. She was sitting, a small solitary figure, behind a pile of letters, scratching away diligently and fully concentrated. When she saw Viva, she gave a start, then stood up beaming.

'Oh, greetings! How nice to see you. Did you have the most wonderful time?' She'd stuck a pencil absent-mindedly through her bun.

'I did, Daisy.' Viva had decided to grasp the nettle all at once. 'But I'm afraid I have rotten news to tell you.'

Daisy listened carefully while Viva poured out her story, only punctuating the silence with a mild 'Oh golly' and 'Oh goodness me.'

'What a terrible shame if he stops Dolly and Kaniz coming to the university,' was her first reaction. 'They're brilliant students and they love their work. But what about this other business with Guy?' A nervous rash had appeared in the V of Daisy's frock, even though her face was serene. 'Do you think he'll carry on spreading rumours about us? That could be very serious.'

'Oh, Daisy.' Both of them jumped as the pencil fell from Daisy's bun on the floor. 'I am so, so sorry,' said Viva. 'None of this would have happened if I hadn't come here.'

'No, that I can't accept. That's nonsense,' said Daisy briskly. 'Mr Jamshed is right – there are spies everywhere and none of the locals really know what to make of us: why should they? They've never seen women like us before.

'Also, dear Mr Gandhi may preach non-violence, but what he's done is to show poor people and women, who have been incredibly downtrodden up until now, that they can make a difference. So there's anger at the British, the anger of poverty, and anger at our educating their women. In a sense we're stuck inside two revolutions and sooner or later, the whole boiling lot will explode, and, of course, when people like your man Guy start spreading rumours it doesn't help matters. But don't imagine for one moment he's the cause of it.'

'So what can we do about him?' said Viva.

'Good question. You can't arrest someone for setting their coat on fire.'

'But he broke into my room.'

'So what do you think?'

'I think the police should be told.'

'Maybe.' Daisy hesitated. 'But if we do that, we open another can of worms. The police, you see, have already been under pressure from certain hot-heads in the new Congress to try and close us down. So far we've resisted.'

'What about our people, what do they think?'

Daisy fiddled with her papers. 'The last time a government official came here, he admitted we were doing fine work but thought we should close down; he said that they could no longer guarantee us protection. That was before you came. Perhaps I should have told you.'

The two women looked at each other.

'When I told the staff and children, they all wept and begged us not to go. It was horrible and heartbreaking. These children, Viva, have nothing. I'm not saying they all want to be here, they don't, but if we leave them, they die or end up on the streets. Someone has to understand this.'

Daisy had taken off her glasses. There was a long silence between them.

'I'm so sorry, Daisy,' Viva said at last. 'You've worked so terribly hard here.'

Daisy's eyes, naked without her glasses, looked old for a moment, old and scared.

'I need the children as much as they need me,' she said quietly. 'That's the truth. But onwards.' The glasses went on again. 'Let's get back to the horns of this particular dilemma. Do you think that this Guy Glover person will strike again, or was this a silly prank?'

'I don't know,' said Viva. 'I wish I did, but I do know that I'd hate to be the one who closed this place down.'

At the sound of Guy's name, a whole series of contradictory thoughts passed through Viva's mind: yes, she was frightened of him and yes, if he was genuinely mad she should feel sorry for him, but what she mostly felt was rage, pure and simple. How dare this feeble-minded little poseur wreak such havoc? So he'd had a miserable time at boarding school in England, so what? He'd never gone hungry as the children at the home had, or worked himself to the bone as Daisy did to get them fed and educated. And there were others things too – much harder to admit. The fact was, he'd detonated a bomb inside her. She'd flung herself at Frank on that night in Ooty like a mad-woman or a wild animal. After two days' reflection, what must *he* think of her now?

She sat for a while. She could hear a saucepan being banged, and then, from the courtyard, children shouting nursery rhymes: '*Mary, Mary quite contrary, how does your garden grow?*'

'I don't want to go to the police, Daisy,' she said. 'There's too much to lose.'

'Are you sure?' The nervous rash had spread up to Daisy's chin. 'I don't want you to be in any danger.'

'Quite sure,' she said. 'I think he's made his showy gesture, and now he'll go home.'

'Positive?'

'Positive.' Then they smiled at each other as if they'd understood that some lies were worth telling.

Eight days after this conversation, Viva moved into a new room on the first floor of the children's home. It was bare as a nun's cell when she arrived: an iron bed, a scuffed wardrobe and a temporary desk – a wide plank placed on two packing cases – the sum total of its furniture. She liked it this way. It looked like a place for work, even for penance, and she was drawing in on herself again. When she got up from her desk and opened the battered shutters, she could see the feathery foliage of the tamarind tree. Daisy had told her that in northern India the shade of this tree was thought to be sacred to Krishna, the god who personified idealised love. That Krishna had sat underneath a tamarind tree when separated from his loved one, Radha, and experienced the fierce delight of her spirit entering him.

But Talika had told her a much bleaker tale. She said the tree was haunted. She'd shown her how the leaves folded in on themselves at night and that many ghosts lived there. Everybody knew that.

Each morning now, she heard the mournful sound of the conch shell blowing from the courtyard outside, the murmur of children's voices from the dormitory above and occasionally the muffled tinkle of a bell as some of them performed their morning *pujas*.

After her conversation with Daisy, both of them had agreed a new timetable for her. Four hours' teaching in the morning, followed by lunch, and in the afternoon she was to write the children's stories. A harrowing task, she could see that already. The day before, she'd spent two hours with Prem, a little Gujarati girl with sad eyes, who told her of the earthquake in her home town of Surat. How her whole family had been wiped out, how she'd been rescued by a kind lady who told her to call her auntie, how this auntie had brought her by train to Bombay and then made her work as a prostitute – the phrase she'd used with an unhappy smile was 'good-time girl' – and how she had been beaten and used by all kinds of men before she ran away and came here.

At the end of this tale, two hours in the telling, Viva had offered to change her name in her story.

'No,' the girl had said. 'This is the first time I have ever told this story to anyone. Put down the name of Prem to it.'

Tomorrow, two sisters who had walked from Dhulia on their own were coming to talk to her. These girls had run away when they'd been promised as child brides to two old and brutal men in their village. When they'd refused, they'd been beaten savagely by their parents.

'We are only village girls but we are changing,' the elder of the two, a proud-looking girl with a fierce nose, had told Viva. 'We don't deserve to be given away like a cow or a mare.'

A few days later, Viva was sitting at her desk typing like a whirlwind, determined to write up Prem's notes before supper, when there was a soft knock on the door.

'Lady has come to see you, madam.' A shy little orphan called Seema put her head round the door. 'Name is Victoria.'

Tor burst into her room and flung her arms around her.

'Viva,' she said, 'I need to talk to you immediately. I'm in such a state I think I'm going mad!'

'Good Lord!' Viva looked up from her work with some reluctance. 'What on earth's going on?'

Tor flung off her hat, sat down on a chair and let out a burst of air. 'Do you have a drink?' she said. 'I don't know where to begin.'

Viva got up and poured her a glass of water.

'Begin at the beginning,' she said.

'Well,' started Tor, 'do you remember that awful lunch at the Mallinsons' when Geoffrey told us they might be leaving? Well, I thought he was joking, but it turned out to be true. After you left, Ci finished the entire bottle of champagne herself and then drank some more and she basically hasn't stopped drinking ever since. It's been awful, Viva. She's been horrible to me for months really, but the other day we had the most appalling row.'

Tor drank half a glass of water quickly.

'What about?'

'Well, Ci had been to the club in the morning and she and Mrs Percy Booth, one of her poisonous friends, had had a row about a coat that Ci said she'd lent her and wanted back – typical of Ci.

'Ci stormed out in the most tremendous huff, and when Mrs P. B. phoned the following morning, Ci slammed the phone down on her. When it rang again, immediately, Pandit was told to take the message. After he'd taken it, Ci kept shouting at him, "What did she say? You're to tell me *exactly* what she said. You won't get into trouble." So then, poor Pandit thought for a bit, he went that sort of green colour the natives go when they're afraid, and said, "Mrs Percy Booth says you're a complete fool of a woman. Sorry, madam." Half an hour later, he was marched from the house between armed guards. He was crying. It was horribly unfair. I shouted at Ci, "How could you be so mean? You promised him he wouldn't get into trouble". Then she looked at me – that awful sort of hooded falcon look she gets.

'"Boring," she suddenly shouted. "Very, *very* boring," and then she said, "I gave him a week's wages," as if somehow that excused everything.

'I almost hit her, Viva – I mean, I could feel it in my right arm. So then Ci slammed out of the room, hardly spoke to me for days and had meals sent up on a tray to her room. Even Geoffrey couldn't get her down; it's been desperate.'

'But you're leaving next week! How could she be so mean?' said Viva.

'No! But yes, that's the point.' Tor was beaming. 'Now comes the most unbelievable part. Do you remember that man Toby Williamson? He phoned while we were away to ask if I was all right. I could hardly remember a thing about him, except that he was rather eccentric and badly dressed – it turned out he'd borrowed his father's dinner jacket on the night we met – so he actually looked as if he was having a baby – Viva, *don't laugh*, this is serious.

'After a few days of being sent to Coventry by Ci, I was so desperate to get out that I phoned him at the Willoughby Club. I felt I had nothing to lose, and Mummy had sent me a list of materials and things she wanted me to bring home and I knew I had to get her a present. But with Pandit gone and Ci upstairs, I needed a lift.

'He came straight over. His car was so scruffy – simply jammed with clothes and books – and Ci, who'd come down hoping someone fun had arrived, looked him over as if he was something the cat had sicked up.

'He was tongue-tied for a bit and I was almost sulking. You know what I'm like, Viva, so stupid really. I sort of compare myself to those people you read about in *Tatler* and so forth – idiots, really, in their wonderful clothes, their cars – and all this seemed so ordinary.

'He wanted to take me first to a place called Bangangla. It sounded jolly boring to me – something about burial grounds and a lake. I put my foot down and said I really had to go shopping. I explained about the materials and how I would have to buy Mummy a present and why it was important to suck up to her.

'Well, to nutshell it – he drove me to the Army and Navy Store. "Tell me what she's like," he said when we were in the hat department. "I'm good at presents." "You won't believe this," I told him, "but she's tiny, like a bird."

'And then he reached out and put one of those dreadful ostrich-feather sola topis on his head and squawked like a bird, and we both looked at each other and had complete hysterics. It's never happened to me with someone I don't know before but it was bliss – if there was an aisle we would have rolled in it. Sheer nerves probably, or else I was just relieved to be with someone of my own age and away from the Mallinsons.'

'So what happened then?' Viva was starting to enjoy this.

'We ended up buying her a teak elephant. Toby told me that the elephant's head must always point towards the door for good luck – I think that's what he said, either the head or the bottom. As soon as it was wrapped up, I knew she wouldn't like it – she's never liked any of my presents, they almost seem to make her angry. Anyway, all this is beside the point. After the shopping, he drove me to this place, Bangangla. It's such a funny place, a sort of secret lake, right in the middle of Bombay, with steps all around it. It was so peaceful.

'We ate lunch at a little restaurant near there, and afterwards, we sat on the steps and talked and talked and talked, first about his work – he's a biologist, or a bird man or something like that, but he's working in a boys' boarding school up north to make money – and then about absolutely everything: our childhoods, our parents, all the kind of ordinary things I don't like to talk to men like Frank and Ollie about because they're so good-looking and I always have people like Ci or my mother drawling in the back of my mind, "Sharpen," when I get too sincere, or when I don't think I'm good enough for them. Do you have a headache powder, Viva? Sorry, I know I'm talking too much but I will get to the point soon.'

The powder was dissolved in water. Tor lay down for a second with the damp flannel over her temples, and then she sat up.

'Here is the best bit,' she said. 'All the time we were talking I noticed what a nice mouth he had and that if he had a decent haircut, he'd be almost handsome. And then he started to say some poetry to me and I said, "Look here! I must warn you – I'm very dim and I only know one poem and it's called 'Ithaka' and I think it's codswallop."'

Viva laughed. 'What did he say?'

'He said, "Why?" and I said, "Because it's a lie. It's all about finding diamonds and pearls on your travels and coming back a richer person, but if anything, being in India is going to make me feel much poorer, because if I hadn't come, I wouldn't know how wonderful life can be."

'He didn't say anything for a while; in fact we sat in silence. A small funeral party had come down to the lake and we watched this man strip down to his dhoti, wash himself and scatter his father's ashes on the surface of the lake. That was quite sad and Toby explained how the man was saying goodbye. That was interesting, and then I told him the whole story about Pandit and he was horrified too.

'In the car going home he said that he didn't agree with me about "Ithaka" being just about the joys of setting out into the unknown, he thought it was about finding yourself, something like that anyway.

'Then he stopped the car near Chowpatty Beach. The sun was

setting and he kissed me – oh, Viva, have I finally gone mad?' Tor's beautiful big blue eyes lit up.

'Go on! Go on!' Viva was the one on the edge of her seat now; Tor was in a trance like state.

'He said, "I have a preposterous idea to put to you. You don't want to go home and I want to get married, so let's get married. It'll be an adventure, and I already know you make me laugh."'

'Oh no, no, no!' Viva put her hands over her ears. 'This can't be true.'

'It's true.' Tor folded her hands in her lap and looked down at them.

'Tor, you went out with this man for one afternoon. You can't do it, you simply can't.'

'But it's not like that.' Tor put the flannel back on her forehead. 'That's the funny thing. You know how sometimes you just know.'

'No, I don't,' said Viva. 'Not like this.'

'Toby says it's more like an Indian marriage except that we've arranged it ourselves.'

'But it's nothing like that, Tor,' Viva protested. 'You know nothing about him or his parents and they know nothing about you.'

'I know that his mother lives in Hampstead with his father, who is an architect, and that she writes poetry and that she goes swimming in a pond in Hampstead Heath every morning with a kettle in her hand.'

'Oh well,' Viva said, 'everything's understood now.'

'It's to make the water warmer,' Tor added helpfully.

'Wonderful.'

'Oh, Viva.' Tor clasped her hands together like a child. 'Try to understand. I don't have to go home to Middle Wallop this way. I shall have a house of my own. He said our life together would be a journey of exploration – like those Buddhist monks who go into the forest in order to find their ant-man or something like that.'

'*Atman*,' said Viva. 'It means inner essence, and none of this sounds remotely monk-like to me.'

'Oh, Viva,' Tor said suddenly. 'This headache really is a corker. Do you have another powder?'

Viva dissolved some more Epsom salts in a glass of water.

'How old is he, Tor?' she asked more gently. She was surprised to feel herself almost panting with alarm.

'Twenty-seven and a half, and he earns one and a half thousand pounds a year teaching at a school for Indian boys in Amritsar. It's called St Bart's or something. We'll have our own house there.'

'I thought you said he was much older than you?'

'I've told you already, he was wearing his father's dinner jacket – it made him look vast – he's really quite slim.'

'And has he actually proposed to you yet?'

Tor looked secretive. 'Well . . .'

'Come on, Tor, out with it.'

After a tremulous silence Tor said, 'I am already bethrothed.' She rolled back the cuff of her dress and showed Viva a silver bracelet round her wrist. 'He gave me this – in the Hindu religion it means "beloved".'

'But you're not a Hindu, Tor.'

'I know, and I couldn't give a fig. We went to the Bombay Registry Office yesterday and I have this too.' She showed Viva a gold band, which she'd hung on a chain inside her dress. 'We're eloping tonight. I shall leave a note for Ci Ci and I've already sent a telegram to my mother, and the best thing of all about this, Viva,' her eyes blazed with excitement, 'is that it's too late for anyone to do anything about it.'

Chapter 42

When Tor had left with the same speed at which she'd arrived, Viva sat down on her bed, poleaxed by her news. The madcap speed with which Tor had donated herself to this Toby person seemed to her to border on insanity, and the thought of her driving north in a few hours' time in his ancient car made her shudder with terror. Her friend was in a paper cup heading for the rapids. The only thing she was grateful for was that Tor had been so bound up in her own news she hadn't asked a thing about Frank.

Viva didn't want to talk about him. It was over.

She'd sent a letter to Frank a week ago informing him that Guy was still alive, and it seemed that his 'death' had been some sort of prank that had fooled them both, but as a result of it, she had had to move from Mr Jamshed's.

'It was kind of you to try to be our knight in shining armour,' she'd written, and then thinking this sounded sarcastic, she'd put, 'to escort us home, but I think it would be better for us not to see each other again.' In her first draft she'd put, 'at least for a very long time,' and then crossed that out, thinking a swift amputation was better than death by slow cuts.

'Mr Jamshed and Daisy,' she'd continued, 'have made it clear to me how important it is at the moment to do nothing that would harm the reputation of the home.' Her pen had wavered here – if they hadn't slept together, perhaps she might have told him about the desecration of her room, and Mr Jamshed's painful accusations, but now he seemed part of that shame.

'I want to finish my book now, and when it is done, I shall go to Simla and pick up my parents' trunk,' she'd said in her last but one sentence. 'Good luck to you in your future endeavours. With kind regards, Viva.'

The last bit, about travelling to pick up the trunk, had been a bit of bravado, and maybe (she hadn't thought of this at the time) a way of consoling herself because the letter, which had taken her over an hour to write, had left her body slick with sweat and her mind so disordered that, after the envelope had been sealed, she had taken down her notebooks, determined to work. When that seemed impossible, she'd walked around her room hugging herself and almost panting with distress.

Later in bed, and unable to sleep, she thought of how it had been in that little guest house in Ooty in the pouring rain and pain turned to anger at herself. She deserved everything she'd got, and now the thought of her tears, her moans, the way she'd clung to him dismayed, repulsed her, and she wished with all her heart she'd kept her distance. This keeping of distance was no mere figure of speech for her. After Josie and her parents died, she learnt – and partially succeeded, right up until the William fiasco – not to trust, not to hope and, above all, not to reveal. Life was easier that way.

Frank wrote back two days later.

Dear Viva,

Thank you for letting me know about Guy. It is a great relief to hear he is not dead. You will now, no doubt, deal with the situation as you think fit and need no further warnings from me. I have definitely decided to take the job in Lahore. I leave next week. I doubt you will, but don't try to contact me before I go.

Yours sincerely,
Frank

She was sitting on her bed in her new room as she read the letter. Afterwards, she'd crumpled his words in her hand and thrown them in the bin, and then, in a mood of feverish energy, picked up a broom and swept the floor. When the dust was collected, she scrubbed out the large wardrobe with carbolic soap, relined it with paper, and arranged her few clothes with finicky neatness inside. She'd lined up her writing paper, pens and typewriter on her desk, put her pile of notebooks in order of date on her one shelf, and finally pinned a timetable on the wall near her desk. Good, her life was back in some sort of order again. Let work begin.

Later that night, exhausted and numb, she'd lain down in her iron bed near the window. Drifting towards sleep, with her own arms wrapped tightly round her, the last thing she heard was the cry of a baby owl who was nesting with its mother in the tamarind tree. Talika had told her once it was an omen for disaster. She was glad she did not believe in such things.

Chapter 43

The telegram Tor sent home to Middle Wallop – SORRY STOP NOT COMING HOME MARRIED INSTEAD YEST STOP I'LL WRITE AND EXPLAIN STOP VERY HAPPY STOP LOVE VICTORIA – led to a fusillade of letters and telegrams passing between Ci Ci Mallinson and Tor's mother, Jonti – both convinced the other was to blame.

Jonti Sowerby fired the opening round by asking how it was possible for a girl to have been so unsupervised that she had simply disappeared into the wilds of India like this. Had Ci Ci even heard of this Toby person? Did anyone know what his father did? She asked Ci Ci to suggest what she should now do with a single ticket she had purchased for Victoria, at a time when they could barely afford it. The cost, 'in case she was at all interested', was sixty pounds.

Ci Ci – minus Pandit and in the throes of packing to go home – wrote back by return of post, asking Jonti whether she was familiar with the old saying: no good deed goes unpunished.

'May I point out,' she continued, 'that your original request was for Victoria to stay with us for the duration of the Bombay season, which runs from November until February at the very latest. Had Victoria not been "conveniently forgotten", none of this would have happened.'

Since Jonti had been vulgar enough to bring up the money question, might she also point out the money saved by not having Victoria around. 'She is, as I may have to remind you,' Ci had added spitefully, 'quite fond of hot baths and eating.'

Ci had, however, softened this blow by saying she'd made a few enquiries about 'this Toby person' locally. The word at the club was that things might not be as serious as they might have seemed. His parents, though intellectuals, had come out to India last year and stayed with the Maharajah of Baroda, who in her opinion was anti-British.

Ci enclosed with this letter a dress-maker's bill for Tor, and said she had left 'a rather old twinset' at the back of Ci's wardrobe. If

Jonti felt like sending her a postal order for the stamp, she would return same.

Jonti wrote to Rose's mother next. She asked if she could shed light on the elopement, which had 'broken a devoted mother's heart'. 'Only another mother could imagine how excited I was getting at the thought of seeing dear Victoria again,' she'd ended poignantly.

Mrs Wetherby, who had had Tor to stay for more school holidays than she could count, took this with a large pinch of salt, but promised to send the letter on to Rose anyway.

'Rose,' she wrote, 'has recently moved up north to the frontier station of Bannu. We tried to persuade her to stay in Poona, which we understand is far safer, but she was adamant. She is also, as you probably already know, nearing the last month of her confinement, so you may not get a letter back immediately!

'We, quite unusually, haven't heard from her for several weeks, in some ways a blessing in disguise, since my husband has had a serious heart attack and none of us have had the heart to tell Rose yet – she has so much on her plate already. Anyway, here is the new address: Married Quarters number 312, c/o Bannu Cantonment, North-West Frontier, India.'

Jonti's letter took three weeks to reach Bannu, the grim little town where Rose and Jack now lived in what was called by the army 'emergency married quarters'. After months of speculation, Jack and twenty other members of the Third Cavalry Regiment had been sent there to plug some gaps on the north-west frontier after a raid that had killed five members of an infantry column. His job now was to take two- or three-day treks into the hills in order to decide which areas were suitable for future operations. After the first morning's ride, the hills were so steep that the only communication with Bannu was with the carrier pigeon.

Jack had begged Rose not to come. Everybody knew this area, with its steep mountains and treacherous ravines and fierce, trigger-happy gangs, was one of the most dangerous places on earth. Some years ago, a woman, Mollie Ellis, was kidnapped in Kohat. Since then a large barbed-wire fence had been erected around the cantonment, and no Englishwoman was allowed to step outside the barbed wire without permission.

But Rose had insisted on coming. They'd expected to live in Peshawar Cantonment, where there was a reasonable military hospital, but a flash flood two weeks before they arrived had made the fifty or so houses there uninhabitable. The only other alternative, or so the duty officer had said, was that Jack move into the officers' mess and for Rose to return to Poona.

'She'll stay,' Jack had said woodenly. 'If you can find us another house.' He knew it was pointless to argue with her any more.

On a baking-hot day in late August, they'd been given the keys to this deserted-looking bungalow surrounded by red dust and scrub. Rose had felt the hammer blows of heat strike her as she got out of the car, and looking towards a shimmering horizon, she'd felt it travel up through the soles of her feet. She'd felt sweat dripping between her breasts, which seemed to her now the size of large ripe melons.

In shock, she'd walked around the house with Jack, almost unable to focus her eyes, feeling the heat radiate off the walls. In the room where they were to sleep, their iron bed had bird droppings on its straw mattress; the walls in the dusty sitting room were covered in a green moss left from the last monsoon. The last tenant – a drunk, the duty officer had told them – had left a half-eaten tin of bully beef on the kitchen table; the broken commode in the bathroom was full of dark brown urine.

Outside her kitchen window was a woodwormy verandah, beyond that the red dirt track leading to Bannu, four miles away. On the other side of the track the Kurran river ran down the valley with a light roar which sounded all day and all night. Above the river, high mountains, and on the other side of them, the great numerals that marked the end of the British Empire. She pictured chaos over there: blood and chaos and wars. She should never have come, it was her fault, not Jack's, and he'd tried to warn her over and over again.

Jack had arrived in a fearful temper – Bula Bula, who he'd brought up by train to ride in the hills and to play polo on – had come down with prickly heat and was looking miserable, and then Jack had the great fright of temporarily mislaying his rifle en route – the loss of a rifle was a court-martial offence and a great disgrace, but thankfully Rose had found it for him under a mound of clothes in the bedroom of the rickety hotel where they spent their first silent night together.

When he'd first seen the house Jack had shouted, 'Oh for Christ's sake, what a fucking shambles.' It was the first time she'd ever heard him swear, although they had had several shouting matches after he'd told her about Sunita. He'd ignored her attempts to joke about her not expecting him to carry her over the threshold this time. If she hadn't been here, his glare informed her, he could have done what he'd wanted to do all along and lived with his friends in the mess.

Ten minutes later there had been a knock on the door and a tall Pathan woman arrived, dazzling them with the magnificence of her eyes and her imperious posture. She wore a dark blue *shalwar kameez* and had a gold ring through her nose. Addressing Jack in Pushto, she said her name was Laila and she was from the next village. She would help them in the house, a statement rather than a question. Standing behind her was her husband, Hasan, as handsome as she was, with piercing green eyes. He said he would be their driver and gardener, although there was no evidence of a garden in the rocky soil outside. When Jack asked her if she had any family, children, she told him she'd had six but that three had died. When Jack said he was very sorry to hear that, she replied it was the will of God.

It had taken Rose and Laila four days of scrubbing with carbolic soap and endless pots of water heated up on a wooden stove to get the place even half habitable.

When it was clean, Baz and Imad, Laila's two sons, who worked in Bannu in a carpenter's shop, came and put up shelves, mended the bed and the hinge of the wooden box bought for the baby's new clothes.

And today, with two weeks to go before the baby came, Rose was in what was to be the new baby's bedroom trying to sort out its clothes. She'd been on her own for the last week – Jack was on patrol near the village of Mamash, an area where tribesmen had killed one of the soldiers. He hoped to be back in the next few days, but with him you never knew.

Dripping with sweat, she stood in a smock, barefoot and with her hair tied back off her face; her ankles swollen like an old lady's. As she folded the new baby's tiny shirts, the ridiculously small trousers, the flannel liberty bodices, the pile of nappies, she had to remind herself that this was one of the moments she'd so looked forward to, because now it had come the heat and the horrible house made it feel completely unreal. She felt as if she was dressing up a ghost dolly that would never really come.

On the morning Jonti's letter arrived, along with one from her mother, by mail lorry with the weekly newspapers, Rose was sitting on a chair in the sitting room, surrounded by a black and sticky carpet of stinkbugs. They'd arrived the night before, from nowhere it

322

seemed, and then two enormous frogs had leapt in from the verandah when she'd opened the door and gobbled some of them up. She left them where they were, made herself a jam sandwich and took the battered envelope that held her mother's longed-for letter back to bed with her. She read it greedily, so many questions she didn't know how to answer. She'd hardly heard a word from Tor herself except to say she was madly in love and was never going to go home again, but people made things up in letters all the time. Were you supposed to pass them on?

Since Jack had told her about Sunita, she'd told nothing but lies to her parents and she was just so sick of this new person she'd become: outwardly huge and lumbering, inwardly thin-skinned, unreliable, unsure of everything.

She got out of bed to look for her writing paper. She would have to answer it. From the shelf above her desk, she took down her box of shame, a wooden box full of letters from relatives and friends, telling Rose how clever she was to be having this baby, and how delighted she and Jack must feel. She'd hardly answered any of them yet: since Jack's revelations she'd felt bruised and disorientated and at the same time so cross with herself. At least Jack had had the courage to tell her the truth. He'd sworn he would not see Sunita again. Surely she should be grateful for that?

She was not. The atmosphere was so strained between them now that when Jack left the house, Rose experienced a physical feeling of relief like a tight hat being taken off. On the nights he was home, their conversation was so stilted she sometimes had this image of them all out to sea on a dark night in two small and separate boats drifting further and further apart.

She didn't blame him for all of it; there were so many other things bothering her now and she was cross with herself for being so wet.

Other people managed without fuss the perfectly natural business of having a child. What right had she to feel so fuzzy in the head, so lazy and feeble-minded? On the night before he'd left, Jack had ticked her off quite sharply for leaving a dish of roast goat on the sideboard, which had immediately seethed with ants, and she'd had some sympathy for him. The man was living with a halfwit.

Rose had planned her morning. If she sat at her desk near the window and didn't move until she'd answered four of her letters, that would be a start.

Dear Mummy,

Advice please! Jonti Sowerby has written to me asking about Tor, and I do understand how worried she must feel, but the problem is, I've hardly heard a sausage from Tor since she moved.

I mean, she wrote to tell me about her honeymoon in Kashmir and how she's moved into a bungalow with Toby near Amritsar, and that they're going bird-watching in the hills soon. She sounds blissfully happy, but I'm not sure how much Tor has told her mother about all this and I don't want to break any confidences. My mind has been in a bit of a fog since arriving, so please forgive, my darling mummy, if I don't write much today but I will write a longer letter soon. When you write back, don't forget to tell me how Daddy is. You did not mention him in yr last and being so far away one always imagines the worst!!!

I miss you, darling mummy, but you mustn't worry about me any more. We have defeated the ants and we are very smart now we have had a proper new commode fitted last week. Jack joins me in sending you much love. I am the size of a hippo, but the doctor says mother and baby are fine, so don't worry at all.

I'll write a longer letter soon.
Bestest love,
Rose

As she was sealing the envelope, the distinct outline of her baby's foot appeared through the side of her smock. She doubled up with pain, and then felt a whole new swarm of anxieties. She felt so ill prepared, but didn't want to make a fool of herself by admitting herself into the very basic military hospital in Peshawar too early. She'd been looking forward to seeing the garrison doctor the week before; she'd taken a list of questions with her. Was it normal to feel so much kicking in the night? She'd hardly slept for the last week. Was it all right that she felt giddy sometimes? She'd actually fainted in the kitchen two days before; she'd been talking to Laila and woken up on the sofa.

Well, maybe he was tired too, but the garrison doctor had looked over his glasses at her and made her feel as if she was being a complete fusspot – even though she hadn't admitted about the fainting. 'What a lot of things you're finding to worry about, Mrs Chandler,' he'd said in a voice of strained patience. 'It might have been better for everyone if you'd stayed close to a bigger hospital like the one in Poona.'

She'd smiled and tried to look sensible, but the truth was, she was frightened now, frightened at the remoteness of their house, frightened that when the baby came she'd drop him, or forget him or that he'd be eaten by something or get malaria or blood poisoning.

On the way out of his office, the doctor had mentioned quite sharply that he'd had to deal with a fatal stabbing that morning between two warring tribesmen, as if to say, 'This is the real world, not monitoring your baby twinges.' And in the tum-tum horse and buggy going home, she'd suddenly felt such a surge of anger she'd wanted to turn round and ask that stupid man to come with her and look at all those tiny mounds of earth, those temporary headstones. That was real life too and he had no right to talk to her like that.

Three letters to write, only three, then she could go and lie down, but the kicking had started again, regular as drumbeats, and nauseating. She staggered over to the glass to see if it was right for sweat to be pouring from her.

When the kicking stopped, Rose took a deep breath and sat back down at her writing desk, relieved to be feeling normal again, whatever normal was nowadays. She picked up her pen, filled it with ink and unzipped the red leather case her father had given her for her thirteenth birthday. At the time, its compartments marked "correspondence", "stamps", "bills" had thrilled her, made her feel so adult and capable, a person who could organise her own life.

In the stamp compartment, her father had tucked a feather, now faded to a dull beige, from the green woodpecker who lived in their crab-apple tree and two perfect little shells he'd found for her on the beach at Lymington, where they spent their summer holidays.

She rolled the feather between her fingertips. *How typical of him*, she thought, *first to notice and then to want to share this small but perfect thing with me.* If she closed her eyes, she could almost smell him, woody smells and wool, the spice of the tobacco he kept in his moleskin waistcoat. He was ill; she could feel it now by her mother's silences, maybe even dead. She put the feather back in the writing case. That was it, he was dead and her mother didn't want to tell her, because she'd been ill and was thousands and thousands of miles away from home.

Stop, stop, stop! That was another thing that had to stop soon: talking to herself like an old lady.

The top two sheets of her writing paper were damp and smelt of mildew. She tore them off and threw them away.

Dear Mrs Sowerby, Dear Mrs Sowerby, Dear Mrs Sowerby. Thank you for your letter. I am . . . If she wrote this over and over again it might propel her to the next sentence.

She put down her pen and sat listening; through the thin walls of the house, she could hear the gentle padding of Laila. She was making up the new cradle; there was a squeak as she rocked it and any moment now she'd come into the room and ask her to look at it, this empty cradle for this baby not yet born.

She'd had some bad dreams about this baby. In one, she'd left it on a countertop in London while she'd tried on hats; in another, she'd carelessly sat its little bottom on a stove – that dream was so strong she had actually smelt its skin burning like crackling on roast pork; the week before, she'd left it underneath the mountain for days while she'd gone climbing. When she came down, the ayah was screaming and the baby all blue and still in its bassinet.

Dear Mrs Sowerby,

How lovely to hear from you. I have only had one or two letters from Tor and she sounds very happy and well. Although I do appreciate what a shock it has been for you, I don't think you should worry about her too much.

Thank you for your kind words about my confinement. The doctor has told me to expect the baby in two weeks' time. I am going to have it in the cantonment hospital in Peshawar, which is not too far away and has better facilities than our local hospital. I am feeling v. well, thank you.

Our new house has been quite an adventure. In front of me I can see . . .

Rose stopped and put down her pen. The horizon shimmered and danced, the sweat had broken out on her forehead again. It was so stinking hot that if Jack hadn't been away she would have slept on the verandah the night before, but she hadn't dared, frightened of the thought of waking up covered in more stinkbugs or being licked by frogs.

'Memsahib.' Laila had brought a glass of lemonade for her.

'Thank you, Laila. I think we should unwrap the tea service today.'

She pointed towards a packing case in the corner of the verandah. 'When I've finished my letter, I'll help you.'

Laila, who didn't understand a word of this, smiled attentively. A few moments later, Rose was on her hands and knees taking china from bits of newspaper when she felt the odd sensation of a cork being popped between her legs.

Now water was streaming down her legs and splashing her shoes. How humiliating! She'd spent a penny on the floor in front of Laila. Her next thought, as she scrambled around trying to mop it up, was relief – thank God Jack hadn't seen that.

But Laila seemed to know what to do. She held up her hand and smiled widely.

'Baby comes,' she said in faltering English. 'Is all right.' She'd patted her softly on the back.

Rose, gasping from the shock of her first proper contraction, said, 'Laila, get the doctor, please. *Daktar, daktar.*'

A few minutes later she saw Hasan whipping up his skinny horse and galloping towards town.

'Memsahib, sit.' Laila had made up a nest of cushions for Rose on the cane recliner in the corner of the verandah near the packing cases.

'It's a false alarm, I'm sure of it,' said Rose, who was smiling again. 'I'm not due for two more weeks.' She pointed towards the half-unwrapped china. 'Carry on, carry on,' she said in one of her few words of Pushto. 'I'm very well, thank you.'

When Laila had finished with the china, she carried it into the kitchen. Rose lay on her own under the mountains listening to the roar of the river and the cheep-cheep-cheep of birds she didn't yet know the name of. She pulled the sheet up to her chin. She forbade herself to panic, even when another mule's kick in her stomach surprised her and made her yelp. If by some chance the baby was early, it might not be such a bad thing. The doctor would come and she would surprise Jack with a bonny new baby on his return.

Oh, how wonderful that would be, she thought, lying back on the cushions, panting slightly. They'd had such rows about her coming here; they'd raged for weeks in the privacy of their bedroom before he'd finally relented. The north-west, he'd insisted over and over again, was no place for a woman, particularly a pregnant one. There'd be no club for her – or at least no one there she knew, since most of the regiment had moved back to Poona – no companionship, and it could even interfere with his promotion.

'Why are you so determined to come?' he'd shouted on the night of their worst row. There'd been one moment then when he'd stood over her, his face looking so set and furious she thought he might hit her, and if he had, she knew she would have hit him right back; she could feel herself snarling.

'You know why,' she'd shouted. 'Because I'm having our baby, because I don't want to stay in Poona with all the gossips, and because if I lose you now I'm never going to find you again.'

That was how bad things had been between them since his confession about Sunita. She felt she was only hanging on to him by the slenderest of threads. That if she let that snap it would be over.

That night, he'd come home and told her there was a hospital in Peshawar where she could have the baby. The muscle in Jack's jaw that twitched when he was angry had twitched during this announcement; she'd ignored it but was sad because she felt in that moment that she hated him.

Rose, lying on the verandah, was getting used to the slight twinges that her contractions brought. She'd been here for nearly an hour. She was waiting for the cup of tea that Laila was making her and wondering idly why Dr Patterson from Poona hadn't told her about the spending a penny thing, nor for that matter had *The Modern Woman's Beauty & Hygiene Book*, which she had read obsessively in the months leading up until now. But what she was mostly thinking was, *Why do people make such a fuss of this? It really is no worse than the curse.*

The important thing is to stay calm, she told herself. The corkscrewing pains she was feeling inside her womb she pictured as waves, which could easily be jumped, and when they went away they left her on a smooth flat beach.

When Laila came back with a plate of biscuits, Rose felt reassured by her queenly bearing, her flashing smile. She was wearing her pale blue *shalwar kameez*. Rose would remember this for the rest of her life. She smelt so sweetly of roses and spice. Her fingernails were clean.

She drank her tea, slept for a while and then the pain woke her up again. The sun had dipped behind the mountains and she could hear the river growling and tumbling in the distance. 'Hasan home?' she said. '*Daktar*.' She wasn't sure that Laila understood her and was cross with herself for not making more effort with learning her language.

She'd started lessons with a *munshi*, a language teacher, but he was a dry old stick and the hot weather had made her so sleepy, so not much progress had been made.

Now Laila was standing at her elbow and leading her so respectfully around the verandah. When she suddenly doubled up with pain, Laila rubbed the small of her back. The sun continued its slow descent behind the horizon, Rose lay down again. The bird had stopped singing. Laila brought her a dried apricot, a slice of bread and butter, and encouraged her to sip the tea that had grown cold beside her. Rose had tried not to grunt too loudly in front of her. Hasan would come soon or Jack or the doctor.

'Oooh! Oooh!' she heard herself groaning like an animal. 'Sorry, sorry,' she said when Laila leapt to her side and started to shush her softly. 'OOOhhhh. Help!'

She looked at her watch. Seven o'clock and dark now; a scattering of rain was falling on the window panes. She'd never felt more alone in her life. 'Where is Hasan? *Daktar*? Captain Chandler?' She was trying not to shout, but Laila just shrugged, and half waved as if they were on opposite sides of a canyon.

'Help me,' said Rose, who was still trying to sound calm. 'I think it's coming.'

Laila took her into her bedroom. She helped her sit down in a chair from which she stared out at the mountains. Laila took Jack's striped pyjamas from under the pillow and put them on the chair. She removed the sheet and put a clean tarpaulin on the bed with another sheet on top of it.

'Don't worry about that.' Rose was watching her impatiently from the chair. She wasn't hurting; all she wanted was to lie down. 'Doctor here soon.'

'Memsahib, sorry, sorry,' Laila said.

Rose fought her off at first, she was unbuttoning her skirt, she was pushing her down on the bed.

She heard herself screaming. Nobody, nobody had told her it hurt this much.

'It's fine, Laila,' she said politely, when the pain went again. 'Thank you so much.' How awful to be seen like this.

And then the pain again: a bucking bronco kicking her to death from inside. When her screams stopped, she saw the purple rim of the mountain again, she smelt roses and sweat. Laila cradled her to her soft bosom, spoke soothing words. But suddenly, Laila was parting her legs and looking at her.

Laila started to mutter words she didn't understand. She put both of her hands together to indicate a circle the size of a grapefruit.

But then nothing. The baby wasn't coming. Rose muffled her screams in her pillow at first, but then she called out, 'Mummy, Mummy, help me, Mummy.' Only pain now; she was on the side of a mountain waiting to fall. She didn't care if the baby died, she didn't care if she died, she wanted it to stop.

Laila's hand was holding hers: a hard-working hand, tough, strong, skin like sandpaper. She squeezed it; Laila was her world now, the rope that stopped her falling.

An hour before dawn, when she felt she would die soon of the pain, the baby shot out and another woman, perhaps the village midwife – she never did know who – burst into the room and cut the cord.

In the chaos that followed she felt Laila put the child in her arms. She heard herself shout, 'My baby! My boy!' in a choked voice she hardly recognised as her own. Her first miracle. The pain was there but in the blink of an eye it meant nothing. She looked out of the window. She saw a red sun burst over the mountains, and a feeling of vast exhilaration swept over her, overpowering, unexpected. She wanted tea, she wanted food, she wanted to kiss everybody and everything in the world.

When Laila brought the boy back washed and in a muslin night-dress, she watched her rub his gums with a piece of date that she'd been chewing. She had no idea why she was doing it but she trusted her now.

'Give him to me, Laila.' Rose couldn't stop smiling. The sky outside the window was bathed in red light; there was a cup of tea on a tray beside her bed. On the floor was the cushion where Laila had prayed during the night, and Jack's pyjamas.

'Give him to me, give him to me.' She crooned, her eyes brimming with happy tears, and the two women beamed at each other in delight.

The baby's head had a fuzz of blond hair on top of it, soft as chicken feathers. His skin was mottled from the furious exertions of the night before, his eyes looked weary and knowing as Rose flopped him under her chin.

Then Laila put the baby on her breast. How funny it felt, but she loved the snuffling sounds he made. She had never felt so tired or so necessary.

'Sleep, memsahib,' Laila said softly when the baby fell asleep on her breast. When she turned down the lights and straightened Rose's blanket, Rose had the most incredible urge to kiss her goodnight, but she didn't, because she knew that if she had, Laila would probably have had to wash for about four days to purify herself. Indians didn't like to be kissed, at least not by memsahibs.

'Thank you, Laila,' she said instead. 'I can never thank you enough.'

Laila put the palms of her hand together. She bowed her head. She smiled at her, a smile of sweetness and understanding that seemed to convey an equal joy, a delight that she'd been there too.

At ten o'clock that night Jack went into the bedroom where Rose and the baby were asleep. He lifted up the oil lamp he was carrying and in its glow saw his son first as a tiny heap of clothes, a shroud. Creeping closer, he saw that the baby had a garland of marigolds round its neck, and it was so red, like an old colonel with high blood pressure or a very ripe tomato. Rose looked pale lying beside him, and there were dark circles under her eyes.

'Darling.' Jack put out his hand. 'Darling.' He touched the baby's hair softly, and then Rose's hair, still damp with sweat. He saw its minute fingers, like the pale tubers of a small plant, flex over the bedclothes.

When she woke up, he was standing in his sweaty jodhpurs, crying so hard he couldn't speak. She used the corner of her nightdress to dry his eyes, and then he kissed her.

'He's beautiful,' he said at last.

She put her hands over his lips, and smiled at him radiantly.

'Yes,' she whispered, holding their baby towards him. 'The most beautiful thing.'

Jack couldn't find his pyjamas, so he got into bed in his underwear and lay down beside them.

'The doctor will come soon,' he whispered. 'He's on his way now. There was a small landslide on the road, it's cleared now. I can't believe how brave you've been.'

They lay in the dark holding hands. The baby lay on top of them, a sleeping Buddha.

'I have a son,' he said out of the dark. 'I don't deserve him.'

He could feel his son's head against his arm. The soft silk of his hair.

Rose squeezed his fingers. 'You do,' she said.

Chapter 44

Viva was playing tennis with her best friend Eleanor when the nun came to tell her that her mother had died. Sister Patricia, a raw-boned Irish girl, had beckoned her off the court; they'd walked back down the path towards the school, and all Viva could remember now was how hard she'd had to concentrate not to put her feet on the cracks in the crazy paving. And how blank she'd felt inside – a muffling feeling like snow.

It was months before she had properly cried, and that was just before the Christmas holidays, which, it had been agreed, she would spend with a distant cousin of her mother's who lived near Norwich. The cousin, a tall pinched-looking woman who looked nothing like her mother, had taken her out to tea, once, in a nearby hotel to finalise arrangements. Over lukewarm tea and stale scones, she'd made it clear to Viva that this was quite an imposition, that she'd hardly known her parents. 'They spent all their time in India,' she'd said reproachfully. 'They said they loved it there.' As if dying had been an act of care-lessness on their part.

Viva had thought little of it – she didn't think much at all about her insides in those days – but two days before they broke up, the school had taken a group of girls to a production of *Snow White* in Chester. Viva, sitting in the darkened theatre with a bag of Liquorice Allsorts, had been enjoying herself, until the prince sat on a tin-selled tree and sang to Snow White 'A Pretty Girl Is Like a Melody'. Her father's favourite song. Viva had to leave the theatre with a cross, postulant nun who'd been enjoying this rare treat. The nun had loaned her a used handkerchief and watched her, standing under the Christmas lights outside Debenhams, heaving and sobbing and pretending to look at the mannequins in the windows, until she'd collected herself sufficiently to join her own group again.

Everyone had thought it kinder to ignore this outburst, and on the way home in the bus, she felt so ashamed that she'd told herself that this must never happen again. That the world would set traps and that she must from now on avoid them, and that the best way to avoid them was to hang on to the frozen feeling that had, up until now, kept her safe. It was songs and soppiness she should beware of.

This by now ingrained training persuaded her to feel glad after Frank left, relieved he'd gone, glad that he had not tried to contact her again. Daisy had told her in a casual aside that she'd heard that he had gone to work in Lahore and what a fascinating project that sounded. Blackwater fever was the most ghastly business and the quicker they could find a cure for it, the better.

He had not called to say goodbye, which was good too.

Work was what mattered now. Now at nights, long after the children had gone to bed, she would sit at her desk near the window. She would listen for a while to the gurglings of the ancient plumbing, to the owls still hooting in the trees outside or a child calling out in its sleep. And then she would write, often until the early hours of the morning, these children's stories. Children who were often described as plucky and resilient – as she herself had been once – but who mostly had learnt not to step on the cracks.

The book was harder to write than she thought it would be. Although Daisy had several times tried to warn her against such lazy thinking, somewhere at the back of her mind she had always imagined that living at the Tamarind must, for many of these children, be an amazing treat, a glimpse into a style of life most of them had only dreamt of. Now she saw that this view was both sentimental and arrogant. Some, it was true, were grateful for the food and the bed; others felt uneasy at this living between two worlds. They missed the rich, broiling, rough-and-tumble life of the slums; they worried that other people in the streets outside might think they had become 'rice Christians' and were selling their souls for a hot meal; a couple of the boys told her flatly and defiantly that they may be here for the time being but they were first and foremost Gandhiji's boys.

But whatever they said, she was determined to record it faithfully and bit by bit, day by day, the sheets were piling up on her desk. Daisy had already shown some of the stories to a friend of hers at Macmillan, the publishers, who'd said if she could produce more chapters of this quality, they might be interested.

She was now so concentrated on this work, so determined to do it and do it well, that when she opened the *Pioneer Mail* and saw the announcement that Captain Jack Chandler's wife, Rose, had had a baby boy, Frederick, she'd felt surprised and shocked at herself for feeling – well, what was it? When she tried to chase down the feeling, she wasn't sure. To say she was jealous was putting it too crudely, but certainly powerful and dismaying emotions had been stirred. By nipping the Frank business in the bud and concentrating on her book she had hoped to find a cleaner, harder version of herself, and in some ways this had worked. Long hours of concentration had brought a kind of quiet joy, a feeling of being emptied and made full by her own efforts. But sometimes, particularly when she was on the margins of sleep where everything is allowed, she felt his arms around her again, the terrible intimacy of his kisses, all the things that had shaken her to the core and made her feel so frightened.

She wrote a note to congratulate Rose immediately, and sent a pretty shawl, made by one of the girls at the school. She went back to work, for there was still an enormous amount to be done on the book before she felt confident to show it to the publishers. September passed in this way and then October, and then what passed for winter in Bombay, bringing clear, warm, sunny days and sudden sunsets, and the occasional nights when the wind swept down from the Himalayas and across the Deccan Plains and you put an extra blanket on the bed.

At the beginning of November, all the children started to get excited because the full moon would soon be in Kartika and that meant their biggest festival of all had come: the Festival of Diwali, the Hindu Festival of Lights. Held on the darkest night of the year, it marked the arrival of winter, the return of the Hindu divinities, Sita and Ram, a time for celebrating light over the forces of darkness.

For weeks now, lessons had been interrupted by local tradesmen calling in to ask for donations to help build *pandals*, the huge floats that would soon be transporting gods down the streets of Byculla. The dormitory above Viva's head had vibrated with the feet of children scrubbing their rooms from top to bottom, whitewashing walls and then making their own statue of Durga – a towering edifice of tinsel, paper and lights – which Viva had been called upstairs several times to admire and advise on.

Fireworks, set off early, stopped them sleeping, and outside the school gates, on the corner of Jasmine and Main Street, four pathetic goats, their front feet stuffed into old cardigans, had been tethered to a rusted bed head and were being fattened for the feast.

On Tuesday, 3 November, the night before the festival was to open, Vijay as Lord Ram had rushed around, cardboard sword in hand; Chinna, an orphan girl from Bandra, had played Sita.

While they were all clapping, Daisy had put her head round the door and asked Viva, Mrs Bowden and Vaibhavi, an Indian social worker, to come to her room.

'I know how tremendously busy you all are,' she apologised when they were crammed into her small office, 'and I don't think we need get too steamed up about this, but something happened here yesterday that I can't in all conscience keep to myself.'

She got up and moved a few books from the bookshelf.

'As most of you know, this is the safe. Not much coin in it, alas, but some important documents about the home. Two days ago, when I came to work, it had been broken into. Whoever it was took my address book and some lists of the children and left rather an impertinent note.

'Now I don't want to spoil the children's fun tonight,' Daisy had taken off her glasses and was polishing them carefully, 'and after the fireworks I shall be having my Diwali party as usual, to which you are all of course cordially invited, but be aware perhaps of the need for some caution.'

'What are you saying?' asked Mrs Bowden, who liked things black and white and who had already made it plain she wouldn't be going to the party.

'Only this,' said Daisy. 'Point one: be careful with your personal possessions. Point two: follow the rules about head counts when you take the children out on the streets. Diwali is a very exciting time, and although most of the locals are wonderful, not everyone likes what we do here. That's all.'

She gave them her toothy, reassuring grin. Nobody looked alarmed as they left her office. It was easy to feel that not too much in the world could go wrong if Daisy was around.

The children insisted that Viva dress up for Diwali. At five o'clock that afternoon, as she put on her red silk dress, she could already hear drums beginning to beat in the streets outside, the cracked sounds of horns, shouting and laughter, and from above her head, the vibrations of children's feet running faster and faster in their excitement.

A few moments later, there was a knock on her door. Talika stood there dressed up in her new finery: a beautiful peach-coloured sari, her skinny arms covered in glass bracelets, kohl around her eyes, her small ears weighted down with gold hooped earrings. She looked so proud and shy and radiant that Viva longed to hug her but she kept her distance. A few weeks ago, when Viva had asked her if she missed her mother's hugs, Talika had said stoutly, 'My mother never hugged me. She came back from work in her factory and she was too tired.' Another cat that walked alone.

Behind Talika was little Savit, the boy with the badly burned leg. He was wearing a brand-new kurta and had a gold crown on his head. Neeta behind him wore a purple sari with a small tiara set with jewels and fake rubies and pearls that hung over her forehead.

'How do I look?' Savit asked her.

'You look wonderful,' she said. 'Like Lord Ram himself.'

He squeezed his eyes shut, and shuffled his little wasted leg. This was almost more excitement than he could bear.

An hour later, when Viva stepped out into the streets with her little charges, they were watching her face and when she gasped, they laughed and clapped their hands. The dingy shop fronts and collapsed verandahs of the street had been transformed into an explosion of lights that shone as bright as the stars above them. Every stall, every conveyance, every inch that could be lit was ablaze; windows were filled with clusters of candles, skinny trees were garlanded and glowed like Christmas trees against the sky, and crowds of people, dressed up to the nines and dripping with jewels, greeted each other in the street.

She wandered with the children for a while between stalls sagging under the weight of sticky sweets, carrot halva and almond cakes. Savit was having trouble with his cardboard crown but refused to take it off. As he limped along beside her through the crush of bodies, he explained in a breathless shout that Uma Ooma, goddess of light, had come.

'She brings light into our darkness,' he said.

She heard drums, a discordant trumpet and then above the swaying heads of the crowd came a lopsided *pandal* with a gorgeously decorated goddess inside it, garlanded with magnolia flowers and surrounded by roses and jasmine petals.

A man holding a fat toddler on his shoulders obliterated Savit's view for a moment. The boy stood patiently waiting.

Now Talika was tugging at her sleeves. 'Mamji, Mamji,' she said. She often called her mother when she was excited. 'Lakshmi comes tonight.'

Lakshmi was the goddess of wealth. Viva knew already that tonight every single door in Byculla would be open so she would come and spread her munificence around. And then the fireworks: Catherine wheels spitting like fat in the orange night air, and then banging rockets, staining the faces of her charges with blue and yellow and pink light, and making the huge crowd gasp with delight.

Two weeks ago, when local traders had begun pestering people to donate to the Diwali fund, ringing the bell at the gate of the home, interrupting lessons, asking for money for fireworks, Viva had complained to Daisy that it seemed an awful waste letting all that money go up in smoke. Now she saw that she was wrong.

Here was the heart of the matter: tonight, on the darkest night of the year, in one of the poorest countries on earth, hope was being celebrated. And she was part of it, standing there, gaping, humbled by their undefeated joy, their faith that things would get better.

'Isn't this fun?' Daisy had appeared at her side, a piece of tinsel hanging from her hat. 'I hope you're planning to come to my party later?'

'Try and stop me, Daisy,' she'd said, grinning. After weeks of hard work she suddenly felt lit up and ready to enjoy herself.

It was midnight by the time the street celebrations started to die down and she'd got the children to bed and stepped out into the street again. Small crowds were drifting home through the haze of multicoloured smoke from the spent fireworks. A pie dog wandered around picking up scraps underneath a trestle table.

Stepping from the kerb, she heard the ping of a bell and then the whirl of wheels, the soft touch of a hand on her arm.

'Madam sahib.' A wiry little man with one eye cloudy like a sugared almond pointed inside his rickshaw. 'Miss Barker sent for you. Get in, please.'

He set off, his skinny legs pumping up and down, and she, tired from the evening, settled back against the shabby seat and dozed for a while. When she woke, she pulled back the canvas flap that separated her from the road and saw that they were bumping down a narrow dirty street with washing hanging on either side.

'This isn't it,' she said. 'Miss Barker lives near the Umbrella Hospital. Could you stop, please?'

But the wheels kept on whirling and he didn't turn.

'Stop now!' she called, but he didn't reply. The next thing she felt

337

was a jarring bump and her heart thumping as she looked around her and saw nothing that she recognised. 'Excuse me! Excuse me.' It felt important to be polite to him. 'This is not where I want to go. Wrong street!'

She tried to lean forward but was flung back in her seat by the speed with which he accelerated.

They were jolting down another narrow street where the cobbles made her teeth chatter. To the right of her she could see the slum dwellings the locals called *chawls*, a grim collection of buildings where itinerant workers could stay. They were mostly in darkness now except for small pinpricks of light from kerosene lamps. With a jerk, the rickshaw turned right; on the street corner she saw two women in saris standing in a pool of yellow light in front of a narrow building with grilled windows. Street girls, she thought.

The road was churning underneath her feet. She sensed a slowing down, a rise in the road: opening the curtain again and seeing the road so close, she thought if she chose the right spot it should be perfectly safe to jump out. She was gathering up her shawl when a turn to the left threw her off balance and scattered the contents of her handbag – lipstick, compact, notebooks and pens – on the floor.

She felt the rickshaw stop. A cloudy eye appeared round the curtain. She saw the jagged edge of his teeth stained with betel juice.

She felt the tip of a knife underneath her ear.

'Get out,' he said.

Her black notebook had flopped to her feet in the gutter. It had all the notes in it she'd planned to type up the following day.

'I want that,' she said, trying not to move or blink. 'Can I please pick it up?'

The tip of his knife settled deeper into the hollow between jawbone and ear.

'Don't move,' he said.

A scuffed shoe kicked the book into a heap of rubbish near an open gutter.

'Please,' she said. 'Take all the money in the purse, but give me my notebook back.'

The knife jumped against her throat this time.

She heard him sigh. His right leg hooked the book towards her.

Briefly, as he picked it up and handed it to her, the knife went away. 'Thank you,' she said, but he shook his head.

He punched her roughly in the back. 'Walk,' he said.

There were no Diwali decorations in this part of town, just the faint orange of the night sky above them, and shuttered dark slums on either side.

He led her down a passageway so narrow that she had to walk ahead of him. On one side of them was an open sewer that stank of human waste, and on the other heaps of rubbish, parts of a bicycle and what looked like the dreadful remains of a medium-sized animal, maybe a donkey. She caught a glimpse of fur, of staring eyes as she walked by.

Her ears strained to pick up scraps of sound behind the slum windows: a baby crying, the clink of a bottle on a table, a tangle of music. He prodded her painfully from time to time, muttering, '*Gora*,' – foreigner – and obscenities she recognised from the street boys.

At the end of the street, the rickshaw man stopped. They'd reached a high narrow house with a solid-looking studded door. The windows were covered in dirty louvred shutters; there were no lights visible behind them.

'We're here,' he said.

The door opened. She felt arms pulling her down a narrow corridor lit by an oil lamp. There was a soft patter of feet. Someone held her hair back, and before she had time to scream, a petrol-smelling rag was forced between her lips.

A door opened; she was pushed so hard into the clammy darkness that she hit her head on a solid wooden object, a chair or a window-sill. She heard a man shout, the scrape of a chair as she fell down. The last thing she felt were ropes being tied round her wrists and neck, and then a blow and a darkness that tasted of metal.

Chapter 45

When Viva woke, a man, middle-aged and wearing an embroidered cap, was staring at her. His eyes were large and protruding, their whites yellow. His breath smelt of garlic.

'She is awake.' He spoke in Hindi to someone she couldn't see.

She was cold. There were red swellings on her wrists, and marks where they had been tied tightly with rope. The piece of sacking around her shoulders smelt of hemp and mould.

'My name,' the man in the cap said, 'is Anwar Azim.'

He was a small but powerfully built man, with a large nose set slightly off centre, and a sprinkling of gold teeth set in a fleshy mouth with a ridge on the lower lip where it looked as if he'd been cut and had stitches. He had the deep phlegmy voice of a heavy smoker, but he spoke good English, though without a hint of warmth. 'I've been wanting to meet you for some time.'

He cleared his nasal passages noisily, a contemptuous sound which filled her with dread. When he'd emptied his mouth in the brass spittoon in the corner of the room, he looked at her again impassively.

Her head ached so badly it was hard to focus on him or the room she was held in, but she saw it was small, about ten foot by twelve, with stained walls and a torn carpet. In the corner, a table marked with cigarette butts held a gaudy shrine to Ganesh, the elephant god. The plaster elephant had a garland of dead marigolds round its neck and, inexplicably, a red toy car in its arms.

His eyes followed hers. 'This is not my room,' he said.

In the middle of his temple there was a dark brown mark and the slight indentation of a devout Muslim who kneeled to pray several times a day.

She must have lost consciousness then, because when she woke up again, a young man with a wispy beard and a pleasant, pockmarked face was looking at her. He was lying on a charpoy placed in front of a locked door. A bolt of pain shot through her head as she turned to look at him.

'I'm thirsty,' she said. 'Can I have a drink?'

To her surprise, he leapt up immediately.

'Of course,' he said. He picked up a carafe of rust-coloured water and poured her a glass.

He held the glass to her lips and she heard her noisy gobbles. He looked away as though she disgusted him.

'I'm sorry,' he said in a posh, precise voice, 'this place is a bit of a fleapit. I have no idea what sanitary arrangements will be here.'

She felt herself gaping at him.

'Why am I here? What have I done?'

'I can't tell you,' the young man said. 'It's not my part of the ship. Mr Azim will return later. In the meantime, do you want something to eat?'

'I want to go home,' she said. 'I've done nothing wrong.'

Her head was hurting her so badly it made her feel sick, and although one part of her knew she was in danger, a huge lassitude was creeping over her like a fog and what she most wanted was to lie down, to go to sleep and let what would happen happen.

When she woke again, she looked towards the window where a closed wooden shutter filtered bars of light across the room. The rope round her wrists had been untied and her hands lay uselessly in her lap. There was a large fluid-filled blister near her watchstrap.

A fat woman in a dirty sari stood in front of her with a tray holding two chapattis and a small pot of dhal. The bearded boy with the refined English voice who had spoken to her the night before appeared at the doorway. He spoke sharply to the woman, who removed the plaster elephant statue, tucked it under her arm and took it downstairs with her.

Viva wasn't hungry but forced herself to eat, hoping it would clear her mind. While she ate, her ears strained to hear anything that might help her: she heard a tin can knocking in the street outside, a door closing, the rumble of a handcart, a bird.

She looked at her watch – eight-thirty-five in the morning. Surely they'd be looking for her at the home by now? Daisy had expected her at the party, she wouldn't let her down, but then a bad thought came. If it was Wednesday, which she was almost certain it was, Daisy taught a morning class at the university, and the others might think she was with her. Also, how on earth would they find her here? A room in the middle of nowhere.

While Viva ate, the boy lounged on his charpoy and watched her. There was a gun on the mattress beside him and two lethal-looking knives.

When she had finished her meal, he left the room suddenly, shouted into the darkness and the woman came back with a rank-smelling bucket. As she used it, she dimly remembered someone telling her that Indian men were mortified at the thought of a certain kind of woman having bodily functions.

The woman, who had a rolling walk and coarse open pores, tied her up again. The look she gave her was curiously blank, and empty of either malice or curiosity, but at the sound of heavy male footsteps coming upstairs, both of them stiffened, and the woman's movements became jerky and rushed as though she was scared too.

Anwar Azim opened the door.

This morning, his clothes were a perfect mixture of East and West. Over his *shalwar kameez* he wore a beautiful butter-coloured camel-hair coat, the kind of coat a chap could have worn without disgrace inside the winner's enclosure at Ascot. The conker-coloured brogues he wore under soft linen trousers were expensive and polished to a high shine.

When he took off his coat and folded it carefully, she saw a Moss Bros label in the silken lining. He drew up a chair and sat opposite her, close enough for her to smell his cigarettes, the mustard oil on his hair.

'Good morning, Miss Viva,' he said softly. His eyes moved slowly from her neck to her breasts, to her legs. 'How was your night?' he asked in his plummy accent.

'Unpleasant,' she said. 'I don't know why I'm here.' She was determined to look him in the eye.

He yawned elaborately, showing gums and teeth. 'I'm sorry you were uncomfortable. Is there anything I can do for you?'

'Yes,' she said, 'I would like a blanket; I'm cold.'

'Cold by English standards?' he teased her, for the air in the room was quite warm.

He pulled up a chair. 'Don't worry,' he said. 'You have a few easy questions to answer and then you can go home.'

He turned and said something to the boy, who stood up with a square of black cloth in his hand. He pushed it over the top of the window shutters, blocking out the light, then he lit an oil lamp and put it on the table.

'Sorry about all this.' When Azim moved closer and stared at her, she was conscious again of how unhealthy his eyes looked. Their whites were the colour of over-boiled eggs.

'And maybe I should say "happy Diwali" to you,' he said without a ghost of a smile. 'Do you find our native customs quaint?'

She watched his hand stroke the front of his shirt.

'No,' she said. It annoyed her that her voice sounded so weak and trembling. 'I don't find them quaint. I enjoy them,' she said more firmly. She looked down at the patterns that the children had drawn on her hands, fading now and slightly smudged. 'As you can see.'

'I myself don't celebrate. We used to burn the bonfire on Guy Fawkes Night at our school.' She stared at him. Was this a bit of sarcasm on his part? 'Another charming custom,' he said.

He took out a mother of pearl case, put a cigarette between his plump scarred lips and lit it with an expensive-looking silver lighter that she recognised as a Dunhill – Mrs Driver had used the same model to light up her morning cheroots.

'So,' he said when his head was enveloped in a blue haze. 'I won't beat about the bush with you. It is very simple, actually. First, I want you to tell me where Guy Glover is, then I'd like to hear from your own lips what you do on Friday nights at your children's home.'

The request surprised her. 'What do you want to know?'

'Mr Glover has been keeping an eye on you there, or he was until we lost him. Anyway,' he continued mildly, 'tell me what you do.'

'Well, nothing much,' she said. 'We all have supper with the children, and then we read stories to them and then they go to bed.'

'What kind of stories?'

'All kinds: adventure stories, legends, Bible stories, Ramayana stories.'

'Anything else?'

'No. We try and make it a special night of the week, but only in the sense that we all eat with the children. We look forward to that.'

'So there is no truth in the rumours circulating that you make the boys bathe with the girls at your home?' He stopped for a moment to remove a fleck of tobacco from his lower lip. 'Or that you wash provocatively in front of the children?' His voice had become cold as steel.

She felt fear fly through her body. 'Did Guy Glover tell you that?'

Mr Azim just looked at her.

'If he did, he's lying,' she said. 'We respect the children and they respect us. If you came to look around you would see.'

'We have had people looking around,' he said. He rubbed his lips with his hands and looked at her for what felt like a long time. 'And we have seen and heard many bad things.'

'Next question. Why do *you* live in Byculla?'

She looked at him and took a deep breath. She estimated he must have had about ten or twelve stitches in his lip, it looked like a knife wound and gave him a surgical sneer even when he was smiling.

'Because I like it there. I have a job there.'

'Why do you question our children all the time and write their names down in a book?'

He pulled open his coat and from its plush lining produced her notebook.

'That's mine.' When she moved her body towards him, she heard the click of a rifle at the door. The guard stood up.

'Sit down.' He was suddenly shouting at her like a dog. 'Answer my questions.'

With a huge effort of self-control she said, 'I'm writing the children's stories.'

'Why?' His eyes snapped open.

'Because they're interesting.'

'They're nothing; they're street children, life dust.' He gave that most dismissive of all Indian gestures, a flick of the hand sideways as though to rid one's body of an insect. 'You have better things to do than that. What other books have you written?' he said. 'Can I buy them?'

'No,' she said. 'It's my first.'

'Your English is very good,' she said after another long silence. She had decided to soft-soap him, or at least to try. 'Where did you learn it?'

'I was at Oxford University, like my brother,' he said it coldly but the little side-to-side wiggle of his head showed he was pleased. 'Before that St Crispin's.'

She'd heard of it, it was one of a number of Indian public schools that claimed to be 'the Eton of India'. They delivered Western-style education and values to the sons of maharajahs, and the sons of anyone who could afford it and who felt it beneficial to have at least a veneer of Englishness.

'Was that where you celebrated Guy Fawkes Night?'

He got up, frowning. 'Don't ask me questions,' he said. 'We don't have long.'

When he left the room quickly, she assumed it was for his noon prayers. A few moments later she heard a trickle of water running and then in the silence that followed imagined him performing his salah, the obligatory prayers that the Muslim children at the home performed five times each day, at sunrise, noon, mid-afternoon, sunset and nightfall.

While she waited, the young guard at the door pointed the barrel of his gun in her direction.

Half an hour later, Azim came into the room again, this time without his coat on.

'Did you go to pray?' she asked.

'No,' he said. 'I am not a religious man. Not all of us are.'

So she was wrong about that, and looking more closely saw the mark between his eyes was a frown, not a prayer mark.

He moved closer to her. 'I am going to make it clear to you why we are holding you here,' he said, with ice in his eyes. 'What goes on at the children's home is a side issue; our main aim is to find your friend Guy Glover.'

'He's no friend of mine.'

'No?' Mr Azim flicked out his tongue and removed a shred of tobacco from it. 'You shared a cabin with him on the *Kaisar-i-Hind*.'

'I didn't share his cabin,' she said. 'I was his chaperone.'

He looked puzzled.

'I was paid to take care of him,' she explained.

Azim started to scratch, first his neck, then his chin, as if she was giving him a rash.

'Don't start by telling me lies, Miss Viva,' he warned her. 'I don't want to have to hurt you.'

A sour feeling like nausea began at the pit of her stomach and travelled up through her spinal cord into her mouth.

'He was a schoolboy,' she stammered, 'or at least I thought he was. I needed a job. I was there to look after him.'

'Well, you didn't do your job very well,' he said softly.

The photograph he took out of his coat pocket was of a smartly dressed young man with oiled black hair crimped into waves. He was sitting in a dinner shirt on a chair in a resplendent ship's cabin. His lip was swollen, his eye half closed and shiny. On the bed behind him a dinner jacket had been laid out like a dead penguin. A pair of immaculate dinner shoes lay on the floor.

'This is my younger brother,' said Azim. 'Your friend Guy did that.'

'I knew about it,' she was forced to admit. 'But I had no part in it.'

'So why not tell the police? Because he was a nignog?' He smiled at her unpleasantly.

'No.' She looked at him. 'That's a horrible word. I never use it. What I was told was there were special circumstances and that everybody wanted it hushed up.'

'What circumstances were these?'

She looked at her hands. 'I don't know,' she whispered.

'Did you know Guy Glover was a thief?'

'I did.' Her mouth was so dry she could barely talk. 'And so did your brother. Why didn't he press charges?'

He squished his mouth between his fingers and looked at her for a while.

'Because,' he said, 'we were able to persuade Mr Glover to work for us instead, and now we are very angry with him for giving us the slip. We hear he may be going back to England. He may even be on his way now. As soon as you can help us find him, we will let you go.'

After he'd gone the guard put a blindfold around her head. Through it she heard the sound of Azim's shoes clumping downstairs, then the whoosh of the geyser again, the rattle of the pipes. Straining to hear other sounds in the street outside, she caught the rumble of wheels and the cry of the water man. But she dared not shout back. She was frightened of Mr Azim now. He meant business.

Before he'd left he'd said in a voice of deadly calm, 'My brother is a fine man. A peaceful man. He didn't want me to do this. He doesn't believe in your eye for an eye, tooth for a tooth business. But your young friend left him deaf in one ear. You can still see the marks on him. I should have killed Mr Glover then, but I thought he might be useful to us. He has not been useful to us. He has betrayed us. Now, it is my duty to avenge him.'

On the fourth day, after a breakfast of dhal and chapatti, the woman arrived and allowed Viva to wash in a trickle of rusty water and then to use the bucket while she averted her eyes. Viva hated this bit. When this was done she was tied up again and heard the descending tinkle of the woman's bangles as she walked downstairs. She'd begun to associate this sound with a pounding in her heart, a dryness in her mouth – after it, Azim would appear.

He frightened her but she was beginning to see a kind of insecurity in him. He reminded her of a man who has raided a theatrical wardrobe department without any clear idea of what part he was required to play. Sometimes he'd arrive in one of a number of beautifully tailored, expensive and hot-looking English suits which he'd wear with an embroidered Muslim flat cap, twice he came to her in his soft cotton native clothes but wearing a monocle which kept popping out of his eye.

The pattern of his interrogations was just as unpredictable, and she began to think the clothes were the outward manifestations of some kind of mental crisis; sometimes he would lecture her softly on his personal beliefs: 'I am first of all a Muslim, then an Indian,' he told her one day. 'The Koran teaches us we have a right to justice, the right to protect one's honour, the right to marry, the right to dignity and not to be ridiculed by anyone.' The next day, he told her that he was a man who believed only in progress, not religion: progress and reform. It was time, he said, for the people of India to stop being grateful for every crumb that fell at their feet, and to rise up against the bloody British. To stop being their servants: 'Oh yes, sir,' he'd mimicked a minion. 'I am running, jumping, fetching for you.'

On the fourth morning, he returned to a familiar obsession of his. 'What do you do on Friday nights at the children's home?'

'Nothing very special,' Viva replied. 'We have a meal with the children who are boarders, and we sometimes have readings afterwards.'

'What kind of readings?' Mr Azim asked suspiciously.

'I've told you, poetry, Bible readings, sometimes the children will tell us a story from the Mahabharata, or some local fairy stories – it's a way of understanding each other's cultures.'

He gave her a look of deep disgust. 'So how do you explain this to the children?' He shoved a book near her face. 'Do you understand what this is?' He was trembling with barely suppressed emotion.

'I do. It's a holy book – the Koran.'

'And this.' His hands were shaking with emotion as he riffled through the pages. 'This is a great insult to a Muslim.' He grabbed her hair and shoved her face towards the book. There were torn pages in the middle of it.

'I know.' Her lips were so dry she could hardly speak. For the first time she wondered if she would get out of here alive.

'We found it in your room.'

'I— we didn't do that, Mr Azim,' she said, trying to keep as still as possible. 'None of us would – we're non-sectarian.'

'Don't try to pull the wool over my eyes, Miss Viva.' He was shouting so loud he was spraying her with spit. 'My own father died in the 1922 riots in Bombay so I know what happens when you British get involved with our religions, and you had nothing to do with that either – oh, these naughty natives.' His voice had risen to an hysterical high-pitched squeal. 'So wild and out of control, but your people started them to prove to us how much we needed you. What you have done to my brother – same thing! What you are doing at your school – same thing! And still you think you are a great wonder helping those poor Indians.'

'I didn't do it,' she screamed, and then with an enormous effort of will calmed herself down.

'Mr Azim,' she said, as he sank back into his chair, 'I am truly sorry about your father.'

'Don't talk of him,' he said stiffly. 'You disrespect his name.'

'And your brother,' she went on, knowing that this might be her only chance. 'But I didn't help hurt him, and I'm not a spy.'

He gave a soft snort and licked his lips.

'You may not believe this,' she continued, 'but we have tremendous admiration for Gandhi at our home; we believe the time has come for India to rule itself. We know we have made terrible mistakes and done some good things too.'

'I don't like Gandhi,' he told her. 'He is only for Hindus.'

'Well, there's something else I must tell you too,' she added. 'My own father died in Cawnpore in 1913. I was nine years old; he'd gone there to work on a new railway. It had nothing to do with politics. I was told he was killed by bandits, seven local Punjabi men who he worked with and respected were killed too. My mother died a few months later. Englishmen are not the only ones with blood on their hands.'

There was a silence in the room. When he looked at her his eyes were so blank she wasn't even sure that he'd heard her, perhaps he'd been thinking again about his own father.

'I have forgotten how to pray,' he said, almost to himself.

And she felt for a moment perfectly cocooned, as if she was some fly caught in amber, or a speck of matter inside a block of ice.

His chair scraped on the floor as he moved it closer to her. He closed his eyes and gathered his thoughts before he began to speak to her.

'I am a member of the All-India Muslim League,' he said. 'Some of your lot, British peoples, have been collaborating with us behind the scenes. I gave your friend Guy the chance to help us too. Your friend Miss Barker at the school is well known by us to be a close Gandhi supporter – we think it goes further than this. Can you help us?'

'I don't know what you're talking about,' she said.

'No?'

'No.'

He stood up. 'That's a shame,' he said. 'Tonight is the last night of the Diwali Festival. It's time for us to decide what to do with you.'

'I'm not a spy,' she said monotonously, although she really didn't care at that moment what happened to her. 'None of us are.'

'Don't bother to tell us your lies any more, Miss Viva,' he told her and closed the door.

Chapter 46

Viva tried to sleep to blot out the fear but woke half an hour later frozen and with a crick in her neck. The last night of the Diwali festivities must be nearing. Last night she thought she'd heard from a few streets away the muffled thuds, and then the screams and fizz of fireworks. The idea that there were people out there leading normal everyday lives – laughing, eating, hugging their children – made her feel even more alone, like someone in a boat lost in the middle of the ocean who sees pinpricks of light from a distant shore.

Now she wondered if she would leave here alive. If Guy had been blackmailed to spy on them all at the home, God knows what he might have told Mr Azim about her. *Who would miss me if I died tonight?* she thought. *Who would care?* She imagined her funeral: Daisy would be there, and maybe Talika and Suday; some volunteers from the home, maybe Mrs Bowden, maybe Clara, the Irish nurse who had never really liked or trusted her, out of some Catholic sense of duty. Tor, she was sure of it, would make the trip from Amritsar and Rose, miles away in Bannu, with the new baby and everything else. She saw more clearly than ever before what a fragile bubble they all lived in and how much she had needed their laughter and their love.

And Frank. How painful to think of him now. He would come. She was almost sure of this now. He had tried to get close. Damaged people like herself and Mr Azim were always protecting themselves, their families, their religion, their pride, their secret wounded selves. Frank had opened his heart to her, made no secret of his feelings. How brave that seemed now.

In the darkness she thought about that wonderful day in Cairo, when they'd all laughed so much, quite oblivious to the storm brewing back on the ship. The guest house at Ooty. 'Don't you dare be ashamed of this,' he'd told her afterwards.

She remembered rain falling outside the window, the dampness of their skins in the twisted sheets; how afterwards, before she'd had time to register shock or shame, they'd sat up and looked at each other and laughed incredulously at what had happened. He'd drawn her towards him, the light slatted through the wooden blinds, and held her face in his hands, and he'd looked at her. Twisting and turning in the dark she thought of how his smile began with a gleam of mischief in his tawny-green eyes, spread to the two dimples in his cheeks and then just dazzled her with its beauty. And how, as she'd felt its effect, she'd made efforts to close herself down, it was too overwhelming. Let other women fall for it; she, special old Viva Holloway, was far too clever for all that.

The thought made her grimace in disgust. What a fool she was. What had the poor man done wrong in the end, except step across some line she'd drawn too many years ago to make any sense now?

Well, there was an admission, especially since friends like Rose and Tor thought her so adventurous, so mysterious. Frank had liked what she was and tried to help her on her way. He'd made love to her straightforwardly, like a man.

Her mind was leaping around now. *Yes, yes, yes*, that was it: life unconditional. He'd stepped out of his clothes and left them on the floor, he was hungry for her and she for him. Why had she said no in the morning?

'Frank,' she whispered into the dark. All she wanted was to hold him. She'd missed her chance.

When Mr Azim arrived the following morning, she'd decided what to do.

'I've been thinking,' she said. 'There is one house in Byculla where I think Guy could be hiding.'

He looked at her suspiciously. 'Why are you are telling me this now?' He had large circles under his eyes and looked as if he'd slept as badly as she had.

'I was thinking about your brother last night,' she said. 'How much you must have looked forward to seeing him again and the shock of seeing his face like that. It must have been horrible.'

'It was,' he said. 'He didn't deserve it.'

She leant her head towards him and made herself look into his eyes.

'I've been thinking about the children's home too. I am not a particularly religious person either, so this has nothing to do with God, but I wondered how I'd feel if a group of Indian men came to our country and tried to teach our children their ways. I'd feel suspicious, angry even . . .' Was she talking too much? Azim was looking at her with deep scepticism. He fiddled with a ring on his little finger. He was waiting. 'But the real truth is, I'm tired,' she said. 'I'm hoping after I've led you to him you'll let me go.'

'He'll be angry with you. He is not a gentleman.'

'I don't care. I want to go.'

He looked at her again and pursed his lips.

'This is not in your dispensation,' he said after a long silence. 'It's mine.'

'Of course,' she said. She forced herself to smile. 'I just thought if I could help it would be silly not to.'

From the corner of her eye, she watched the smart English brogues tapping nervously on the floor. He stood up and heaved a shuddering sigh.

'Where is he living in Byculla?'

'In a flat near the fruit market,' she said. 'I can't remember the exact address, but if you take me there I will be able to find the way.'

His eyes brooded over her, hooded and suspicious.

'I'll come back at half past five,' he said.

He came back again on the dot of five-thirty, this time with a tunic and a Kashmiri shawl, which he flung on her lap. He had changed again into his *shalwar kameez*, a snowy-white one with beautiful pearl buttons through which his stomach strained.

'Time is running out.' He sat on the chair in front of her, legs akimbo.

'Where are we going?' She hated hearing her voice tremble like that.

'Out in the streets to see if your memory is jogged.'

She looked at him. 'I think that's a good idea,' she said. 'I'll try my hardest.'

He looked at her suspiciously. 'Why are you trying now? What has changed?'

'I'm tired,' she repeated. 'I don't see why I should take the blame.'

He was not convinced. 'He will make you pay for this.'

'I don't care. I want to go.'

'I keep telling you,' he said. 'This is not in your dispensation: I decide. You could still run straight away to the police. It would be my word against yours, and guess who would win.'

'Of course,' she said demurely. 'I just thought if I could help, that it would be a chance worth taking.'

He gave one of his monstrous nose snorts, as if trying to clear his head of all matter. 'Tell me again where he lives in Byculla,' he said eventually.

She closed her eyes, pretended to think.

'It was either near the fruit market or a small flat near the Jain Temple on Love Lane,' she said at last. 'I'm a *gora*,' she used the Hindi word for foreigner, 'so you'll have to be patient with me – everything looks so different during Diwali.'

His eyes swept over her coldly. 'Not that different,' he warned. 'And Byculla is not a big place. If you try and give me the slip, I am going to kill you.' He said something in Urdu she didn't understand, maybe a curse or a prayer.

'For me,' he said, 'it would not be a sin but an honour. I don't like women like you. You bring shame to us and our children.'

She tried not to flinch when he brought a vicious-looking knife towards her.

The sliced rope left three deep red marks on her wrists.

'Don't move,' he said when she tried to rub them. All pretence of friendliness had gone. He put the knife back in a leather holster he wore on his belt.

When he left the room, she got dressed, supervised by the older woman who watched her with no expression whatsoever, which was unnerving. She was given a chapatti to eat, a drink of brackish water, and then, suddenly, she was led downstairs and out into daylight again.

When they got out in the streets she was bundled into a rickshaw. She sat thigh to thigh with Mr Azim, which terrified her. Before they had left, he'd shown her a gun. He said, 'If you make things difficult for us, you will be sacrificed.' A phrase that made her think of the skinny goats she'd seen outside the butcher's shop on Main Street. It really would be that easy.

It was six o'clock now, not cold but dull and damp with all light bleached from the sky. Apart from one or two painted doorways, and lights on in some poor-looking house, Diwali celebrations seemed sparse in this area of town.

'I normally drive a car,' Azim was anxious to tell her, 'but this is better for us.' His brogues were tapping impatiently on the rickshaw floor. He clearly didn't like slumming it. He rattled off some orders to the rickshaw driver, who looked cowed and terrified himself, and then he turned to her.

'So where does he live?'

'I think it's near the Jain Temple.' She was determined not to stammer. 'Please be patient with me. I've only been there twice.'

He glanced at her sharply and she heard him sigh. He took out his gun, laid it on his lap, and then covered it with the flap of his *kameez*.

The grim street they were passing through was empty, apart from a mother kneeling on the steps, with two little girls who were drawing what looked like Diwali patterns on their doorstep.

'When we get out of the rickshaw, pull your scarf over your head,' he said. 'And if I am telling you something, answer back in a normal way. I am telling you that tonight Lakshmi, goddess of wealth, comes to Byculla. So maybe we'll all be luckier.' He gave a false laugh, and she laughed back.

This is what a beaten wife must feel like, she thought: *aware of every movement, every gesture, weighing every word.* But she must play the game: stay calm, converse with him in as pleasant and friendly a way as possible. If she let the bully out, she was sunk.

They crossed a road into Main Street where the evening sky was mottled and bruised-looking. To their right, in the middle of a row of dilapidated houses, she saw a small temple lit up like a fabulous jewellery box with hundreds of small candles around the shrine.

She took a deep breath.

'Mr Azim,' she said, 'how many more days will the festival go on for?'

His eyes flicked towards her. He moved his leg away.

'Too long around here,' he said. 'Diwali is for people who think like children.'

The street was starting to fill again with the holiday crowds. 'It's for children,' he repeated, looking at them.

Viva understood loneliness and she felt it now. He was as much a stranger in these streets as she was.

'So you never celebrated it in your house?' she asked him.

'I am telling you,' he said impatiently, 'my brother and I were educated by you British people. We learnt English history and poems. We were beaten – what's that saying? – regularly as gongs.' His voice had risen. 'Until I left that school, I did not know *one* Indian poet,' he said after a pause, 'Imagine that in your own country.'

354

Before she could reply, he put his hand up. 'Stop,' he told the rickshaw driver. 'Turn right here. Don't talk any more,' he told her. 'I need to concentrate.' His face had begun to pour with sweat.

'I was going to say that's a shame,' she said a few moments later. 'There are wonderful Indian poets.'

He sniffed loudly to signal the end of this conversation and started to shout at the rickshaw driver, who had got stuck in a minor traffic jam with a bullock cart and a group of holiday makers.

'Where is he?' he said to her suddenly.

'I'm not sure yet,' she said. 'Could you tell me where we are?'

'Fruit market is there,' he said. He pointed towards the vast sprawling building, almost unrecognisable tonight under its weight of lights and tinsel. The crowds were getting thicker and now she could hear, indistinctly at first but getting louder, the whooping, shouting noise of an excited group, the braying of a trumpet. A skinny street boy ran alongside the rickshaw trying to sell them some flyblown sweets. When Azim shouted at him the child shrank away.

Now they were forcing their way down Main Street where the stall keepers were lighting their lamps, and the skies had started to glow with the reflected light of thousands and thousands of candles. A small crowd forcing a lurid-looking papier-mâché goddess above their heads was slowing them down and making Azim angry.

'Understand this, madam.' He had to raise his voice to be heard over the din. 'I know you chaps all think that we sway in the wind of all this idol worship, but I don't. I think it's killing our country. I think it's time to fight back.'

She watched his fingers close around the gun.

'Gandhi will kill us too,' he said. 'With kindness. We've been too polite for too long.' When he turned to her she felt hate coming off him like fog.

'What happened to your brother must have been the last straw,' she said, as calmly as she could, for she knew with absolute certainty now that he would shoot her if he had to.

'I need to find Glover tonight,' he said. 'I've been told he might leave India tomorrow on another ship.' He mopped his forehead with a handkerchief. His hands had started to shake.

'Here's what I remember,' she said. 'The two times I went to his flat I took a short cut across the market and then— I'm sorry.' She shook her head. 'I'm going to have to see it again.' When he moved his head to look at her, she was sure he had seen through her lie. She saw him freeze momentarily while he thought, then his eyes blinked and he shrugged.

'I shall be walking right behind you,' he said. 'If you try and run away, I will shoot you, not now but later and nobody will ever know what happened to you. Do you understand?'

'I understand.'

He barked at the rickshaw driver. The little carriage stopped.

'Get out,' he said.

A firework went off about ten feet from her as she stepped out into the street. He prodded her in the back and they walked through the doors and into the market where she was deafened by the sound of bleating sheep and goats and the screech of caged birds.

She was starting to panic. The taste of metal in her mouth was fear. The sounds inside the building seemed to swell unbearably. She scanned what felt like a solid wall of sounds and faces with no plan yet apart from escape.

Two young girls were walking very slowly ahead of her. They were dressed up to the nines in their saris and jewellery, thrilled with their new clothes and nattering happily to each other. When they blocked her passage down the aisle, she felt she could have throttled them. Azim couldn't see them; he was prodding her in the spine with his gun. '*Jaldi, jaldi,*' he said.

'I can't go any faster,' she said.

Now she could see the vast door at the end of the market open underneath rafters where pigeons sat. Beside the door were the caged birds: each cage lit tonight with Diwali lights.

Outside the door, she saw another crowd, moving swiftly in the direction of another teetering *pandal* surrounded by musicians. In the crush of the fruit market, she felt the strong tug of the crowd, like a undertow, and then the hardness of his gun in her back warning her not to run, but she had no choice now and nor did he. She heard someone laugh and then a scream. The smell of smoke in the air, someone else shouting, '*Jaldi!*' and then she fell, and a scuffed shoe kicked her hard in the teeth and she heard a sharp crack. A jarring pain in the side of her head, thousands and thousands of feet thundered through her brain, and then nothing.

Chapter 47

She woke up with the taste of old fruit in her mouth and then thought all her teeth must have been kicked in because of the pulpy feeling around her lips. She was lying under a table, her left elbow jammed in a chicken crate with a few soiled feathers inside. A million feet were rushing by her, inches from her head – feet in sandals, bare feet, hennaed feet with complicated patterns on them, large black men's shoes, some with no laces. The sight of them made her so dizzy she fell back into the dirt, trying to hide herself in an old sack.

Moving made something trickle down her temples and brought a sharp pain. She touched the pain, looking at the blood on her fingers as if it belonged to somebody else.

More feet rushed by; voices piercing her skull and bringing sick into her mouth.

She made herself wait, first five minutes and then ten. Judging from the racket above her, the crowd that had swept her away from Azim was still thick, but she could not risk him coming back. *Wait, wait, wait,* she told herself wearily, feeling herself come and go.

It was dark when she woke again. She was somewhere else, lying on a lumpy mattress. When she touched her head it was bandaged and she had the most excruciating pain in the roots of her teeth as though they'd all been pulled. Her eyes flickered open, but the light hurt too much. A young Indian woman with a calm, gentle face was bathing her forehead.

'*Mi kuthe ahe?*' Where am I? she asked. When her eyes flickered open again she saw, in one brief bilious flash, a slatted roof, a dirty window. She was in a slum or *chawl*.

'*Kai zala?*' What happened? she said.

'You were knocked and kicked,' the woman demonstrated. 'Don't worry,' she added in Marathi, 'you're all right now, they are coming to take you home.'

Coming to take you home. She fell on the soft mattress of those words. *Home soon, home soon. Daisy will come.*

She opened her eyes again, a new ceiling: sticky, yellow. Above her was a naked light bulb, some dead insects, a low beam covered in cobwebs. When she touched the side of her head, she felt the stickiness of old blood through the bandage. The pain in the nerve endings of her teeth was still excruciating, but when she checked gingerly with her tongue, her teeth were still there.

From behind her bandage, she heard a door open, voices, the creak of wooden floorboards.

'Daisy?' she said.

Nobody answered.

'Daisy, is it you?'

When she tried to sit up, she felt a hand close round her wrist. A mouth was coming close to hers, so close she could smell something sweet and stale.

'It's Guy,' he said.

She closed her eyes so tight that more blood trickled underneath her bandage.

'Guy,' she whispered, 'why are you here?'

'I don't know.' His voice sounded jerky and hard. 'I can't help you; I don't know why I'm here.'

'What's happened to me?' When she tried to sit up bright lights went on in her skull.

'Some stupid person in the market found you knocked out. They said an English girl was hurt. I wanted to help, but now I don't – you're frightening me like that.'

'Calm down, calm down.' Her mouth felt frizzy and distended as if it was packed with cotton wool. 'All you need to do is to go to the home and get Daisy Barker; she'll help me.'

She heard his bark of frustration, the thud of his own hand hitting his head.

'I can't, they'll catch me. I'm in too much trouble myself.'

'Guy, please, that's all you have to do.'

'I'm leaving tomorrow, I told you that. Ask someone else to do it,' he mumbled.

He was drumming the pads of his fingers on a tabletop and humming in the way he had on the ship when he felt most agitated. She heard the scrape of a match. Her mind felt swollen, unreliable, but she must speak.

'Guy, why did all this happen to me? What did you do?'

No answer. While she waited she forced herself to remain conscious.

'Nothing,' he said.

'Yes, you did,' she said. 'I know you did now.'

'I wanted to get you out of the home,' he whispered at last. 'It was bad for you there.'

When she tried to shake her head, she moaned, 'No.'

She felt his mouth draw close to her again, smelt the acrid smoke on his breath. 'Listen,' he whispered. 'Listen very hard.' She felt his hand brush her temples. 'You're *my* mother. I chose you.' The faint mist of his spit on her cheek.

'No! Guy, no! I'm not her!'

'Yes.' She heard the slow exhalation of his breath. 'You saw that school. They hung me out of a window there on sheets. My other mother chose that school; she wanted me to stay there.'

'Guy, *listen* to me. This isn't right.'

'I loved you.' He was panting and she was frightened again.

Through the exploding lights in her head she thought, *He hates me now*.

'I can tell you a story about my mother,' he said. He was standing up now and his voice was throbbing with rage. 'When I was twelve years old, both of them came back to England. I hadn't seen them for a long, long, long, long, long, long time. My father said it would be a good joke to dress me up as a waiter and let me take her breakfast in. A surprise. I took the tray up to her room. I said, "*Mummy*," tried to kiss her.' His face contorted. 'She screamed for my father who was in the next room. Oh, that was a hell of a good joke. She loved me so much she didn't even know who I sodding well was.'

'That was wrong of them,' said Viva. The effort of following all this was making her sweat. When she reached out and tried to hold his hand, he pulled himself away. 'A silly trick to play.'

'I want to kill her,' he said calmly. 'She jams up my wireless. Don't look at me,' he instructed her when she hauled herself up on her elbow. 'You're frightening me. I don't like you looking like this.'

'Listen to me,' she said. 'Turn your back on me if you don't like the bandage but listen hard. I know exactly what you've got to do.'

'Um.' He'd turned his back on her; his shoulders were slumped, the toes of his shoes turned inward. He clicked an invisible switch behind his ear. 'What?'

'I know you've been worrying about a lot of things for a very long time,' she said. It was hurting her to speak this clearly but she made herself do it. 'And you need to stop for a bit, to rest.' She watched his body sag.

'I can't,' he said. 'They're after me, and you. That's why I have to go back to England again.'

'What did you tell them about me?'

'That you couldn't go on working at the home. That I needed you.'

'There were other things too,' she said.

'I can't remember them, they've all got muddled. Mr Azim was trying to hurt me – he was frightening me.'

'All you have to do is go back to the home now; tell them where we are.'

'I can't,' he said in a muffled voice. 'They'll find me and hurt me.'

'Well, find someone to take a message there,' she said with her last ounce of strength. 'It will be much better for both of us in the end. Tell them to come get Viva, Guy, and then, if you like, you can come back with us and we'll find people who can look after you until you're better again too.'

He got up and walked around the room hugging himself. 'I'm not so bad, you know,' he said. 'I didn't mean to mess up your room.'

'I know, I think you've just got tired.'

'Not sure, not sure,' he said. 'There are too many people on my airwaves at the moment. My father's looking for me too,' he said. 'He's angry as well. He gave me a thrashing after I got off the ship; he said I was rude to him.'

'Here.' She leant forward and turned off his invisible switch. 'Turn them off if you don't want them. Nobody outside of you can control you. They can say things, they can ask you to do things, but you can say yes or no. All I'm asking is for you to let me help you. I won't let you down.'

'Everyone lets me down. No one likes me.'

'I know you think that, but it's not true and there comes a point in your life when you can't go on getting so angry with other people.' He was listening to her intently, but he looked perfectly blank, and she had the strangest feeling as she looked into his eyes that there was nothing behind them. But she could still hear herself almost like a separate person – quite lucid, determined to survive this.

'A point in your life when you've got to take up your bed and walk, otherwise all you'll do is spread unhappiness. I know about this, I've struggled with it every day of my life since my own parents died.'

'Don't talk about that,' he shivered. 'It's horrible.'

'People will love you if you let them,' she continued.

His head was turned away from her, but she could feel one ear cocked and listening.

'You can't,' he said. 'I've asked you.'

There was a silence. 'I think we could be friends,' she said at last.

'And walk into the sunset,' he was sneering at her again. 'Holding hands.'

'No, don't be silly. What I mean is, I'll listen to you. I think you're tired of running and you need some rest.'

She prayed to God she had hit some sort of target, but the effort of talking had worn her out. Her head slipped down the pillow and she was fast asleep again before she heard his reply.

Chapter 48

ST BARTHOLOMEW'S, AMRITSAR, DECEMBER 1929

Sometime before Christmas, Daisy wrote to Tor out of the blue saying that Viva had been hurt in an 'unfortunate accident' during the Diwali celebrations but was well enough to travel again now. She herself was going home to England for an indefinite period, and the home was virtually closing down; was there the slightest chance that Viva could come and stay during the Christmas holidays? She needed a change of scene, she said. All would be explained when Viva saw her.

Tor was surprised that Viva hadn't written herself, but then Viva never did things in quite the same way as other people, and although she was upset to hear she'd been hurt, Tor was excited at the thought of seeing her again. She wanted Viva to explore her wonderful new life in Amritsar, to see the new bungalow, but mostly, she wanted her to meet Toby and see what a prize she had bagged.

An idea gradually snowballed in her mind: if Viva was coming for Christmas, why not Rose and Jack too, but because her own mother had always made such an incredible fuss about guests, she broached the idea to Toby nervously at first.

'Why are you sounding so Tiny Tim about it?' he'd said, surprised. 'There's tons of extra rooms in the school if our house gets too small.'

'Our house', how she loved to hear him say the words. Their three-bedroomed bungalow was a miniature version of St Bart's, as everyone called the school, which was a large and eccentric hotchpotch of a building that boasted Mughal arches, Tudor beams, Victorian windows, elaborately carved verandahs and steep roofs shaped like witches' caps.

The bungalow itself sat in a glade of mango trees between the school's cricket pitch and a wild garden. The previous occupant had retired some five years ago and vines had grown like wild hair over its windows. Damp and mildew had left large mossy areas on their verandah floor.

It still made her heart swoop with pity and love to remember that when she'd first seen the bungalow, Toby's bedroom was the only properly lived-in room. She'd looked at its iron bed, the thin, green chenille bedspread, yellowing mosquito net and framed insects on the wall, and thought it looked like the room of a boy left behind for the holidays in a deserted school.

Fortunately, the damage to the handsome little bungalow proved quite superficial. After a day set aside for unpacking, Tor, in an enormous rush of energy, set about redecorating it with the help of two new servants: Jai and Benarsi, bright good-looking boys from the local town who adored Toby because he spoke fluent Hindi and made them laugh.

Then to her astonishment, her mother had sent a cheque for fifty pounds, stipulating that it must be spent on furnishings. The money came in handy – Toby was only teaching part-time at the school this term while he finished his book, *The Birds and Wildlife of Gujarat*. In a fever of excitement they'd gone out and bought their first double bed, then a bedspread from the local bazaar embroidered with birds and flowers. A new sisal rug went on the floor. Next, Tor had supervised whitewashing, carpentry and floor scrubbing.

The garden had been cleared and replanted. Their little sitting room had fresh coir matting, an old sofa and the two cane chairs Toby called Bombay fornicators. She had a proper table at last for her gramophone, and Toby had spent five nights designing and putting up what he called the Châteauneuf-du-Pape of shelves for his books and her records.

'So, I really can ask them?' She'd looked at him suspiciously. It was sometimes so hard to believe she had this kind of freedom. He kissed her on the tip of her nose.

'Last Christmas,' he said melodramatically, 'was so awful I almost went home and drank arsenic.' He'd spent it in the club in Rawalpindi, drinking port in a dusty paper hat with a drunken tea planter and a missionary. 'I can't believe how my life has changed,' he added quietly. That was one of the best things about being with Toby: so silly and playful one moment, and in the next, so able to say what mattered most.

Anyway, Rose had written back almost immediately to say she'd love to come and that Jack – whose regiment was off doing something frightening in the mountains – would try and come, at least for a day or two. But would it be too stinking fish of her to stay for longer? She was dying for Tor to get to know Freddie.

In early December, Tor told Toby to stop being a boring swot and have a what-the-hell day with her. For the past three weeks, he'd been working feverishly on his book trying to get it finished before Christmas. He pulled her down on his knee, squeaked, 'Sorry, dear,' in his hen-pecked-husband voice, then kissed her and said, 'What an excellent idea.'

They made love early the following morning, underneath their mosquito net, leapt out of bed ravenous and suddenly rowdy, and spent the next few hours working together. They moved Toby's telescopes and bird books, his sitar, his piles of wild-life photographs from the guest room into the main school. Then Tor looked up Christmas pudding recipes in Margaret Allsop's *Christmas for Colonials*.

Toby went into the woods to look for a Christmas tree. He came back with a gnarled-looking baby monkey puzzle tree, which he planted in a pot and said he would water until Christmas and then plant outside again. After supper, he put on some Beethoven and they painted the tree's tips with gold and then they turned off the lights and danced together through the moonbeams that fell through the windows of their sitting room.

The next day they went to the bazaar in Amritsar to buy the ingredients for Christmas cakes. Toby chatted to the stallholders, and then she'd got out her list and he'd ordered heaps of sultanas and raisins. Cinnamon and nutmeg were plucked from huge, brilliantly coloured mounds of spices, weighed on large medieval-looking copper scales and put into tiny twists of paper.

They were on their way to have a chota peg at Murphy's Bar on the main street when Toby stopped and put on his glasses, and from a chaotic stall bursting with old coins and broken glasses, plucked a box with four glass globes in it, each one about the size of a duck egg and exquisitely patterned. 'As good as Fabergé,' he said, blowing dust from them, and then as he lifted them up to the light, their colours, red and purple and green, swirled against his face.

'They're perfect,' he said. 'Aren't they, darling?'

'Can we afford them?' she said. He'd warned her already that the bird book was never going to make them rich.

'Yes,' he said at once. 'For our first Christmas, we can afford them, and champagne.'

And looking at him, she felt her senses suddenly blazing with happiness.

Pure love.

She had Toby, who she waited for eagerly each night, she had a house of her own – well, almost – a whole thrilling life ahead of her, and as if all this wasn't enough, Rose and Viva were coming for Christmas.

This glorious mood did not last: five days later, she was in the throes of a full-scale domestic crisis. Bloody old Margaret Allsop had written in ridiculously small print in her recipe book that she should have had her Christmas cake wrapped in greaseproof paper and in a tin by mid-November.

'I was supposed to be feeding it all month?' she lamented. 'Why on earth would you feed a cake? I thought it was the other way round.'

Toby, who'd been working in the summer house, had just wandered into the kitchen, his fingers covered in ink, his hair endearingly on end. He said he was sure it didn't matter a damn. He was practically certain that his own mother had made her cakes on Christmas Eve.

Tor was soothed by this. She tied up her hair, lashed on an apron, lined up her ingredients and, after telling Toby she felt like the sorcerer's apprentice, began to weigh out the flour, the cherry and the raisins and then throw them into a big bowl on the kitchen table.

Jai and Benarsi watched her intrigued as she stirred it all up, adding a pinch of cinnamon, a dab of mace, then the eggs and butter, and only grating a little bit of her knuckles into the orange peel, all the while keeping up a running commentary. Miss Allsop said it was important to show the servants new skills, and really, Tor was thinking, as she poured the whole fragrant mess into a cake tin, why had her mother made such a fuss about it? Cake making, she explained to Toby when he put his head round the kitchen again, was an absolute doddle. Mudpie making for grown-ups.

The cake was smoothed down and wrapped in brown paper. Jai carried it ceremoniously towards the wood stove and stoked up the fire. Toby went back to work; his typewriter click-clacking from across the lawn, such a comforting sound. With three hours to go before the cake came out, Tor thought she'd go for a ride. It was such a beautiful morning and maybe her last chance before Christmas.

After the ride, she'd stopped for a natter with Elsa Chambers, one of the school secretaries. Elsa, a stout girl from Norfolk who'd come to India originally as a nanny to a high-caste Indian family, said that she was thinking of flying home next year on an aeroplane, which Tor thought was amazingly brave. Then Tor had been called back to the stables by a groom to look at a lovely little filly that had just arrived for one of the young maharajah pupils. Tor was rubbing its ears and chatting to it when she let out a piercing yell, sprinted back across the quadrangle and into the kitchen.

'Good God, what's happened?' Toby appeared at the door looking shaken.

Tor fixed her huge eyes on him and then on the cake lying in a cloud of evil smoke on the table.

'Oh dear, oh dear.' Toby dropped a shower of blackened currants on the floor as he cradled the cake in a towel in his arms. 'Mr Kurtz, he dead,' he exclaimed dramatically.

None of them had the faintest idea what he meant – it was his tragic look that made laughter explode like air from a balloon. First Jai and Benarsi squeaked, and then Toby was whooping and wiping his eyes. 'Sorry, darling, sorry!' he spluttered. 'I'll help you make another one tonight and then we can write a poison-pen letter to Margaret Allso—' He couldn't finish. Tor was laughing so hard she had to sit down and clutch her sides. Wave upon wave of laughter until finally she'd shaken her wooden spoon at them. 'You are a silly lot,' she said in a weak voice, wiping the tears away. 'Absolute oafs the lot of you. *Memsahib tum ko zuroor kastor ile pila dena hoga.*'

Tor so hoped that when Viva and Rose came to stay they would see Toby like this: silly and full of life, and incredibly clever too – he'd read all kinds of books. Naturally they were suspicious of him. He'd proposed so quickly they probably imagined that he was either desperate or criminal or unappealingly over-confident. He was none of these things. He could be terribly shy and awkward with people he didn't know. He had been with her at first.

The day after their registry office wedding in Bombay, her mood of reckless euphoria had sunk like a blancmange. They'd driven north in his battered Talbot, and he'd talked for what seemed like hours and hours in a monotonous drone about shops and clothes. He told her later his mother had once said the way to a woman's heart was to take an interest in her, so he had at least tried. But on that day, when he'd asked her whether she preferred a cloche to a flowered hat, what colours she liked best, pinks or greens, Tor had sat in growing panic. The man was a crashing bore! She'd made the worst mistake of her life.

On and on the car had chugged, further and further away from Bombay, through miles of desert, then tiny, increasingly deserted-looking towns and dun-coloured plains, until it got too hot to talk, and she drifted off to sleep.

When she woke up and saw the gold band on her finger, she thought she should at least ask him to explain in some detail what he did. He'd perked up immediately. He had already told her that he taught history and science at St Bart's but then he said that he was also writing his life's work, a book on the thousands of extraordinary birds there were in India, many of them sacred. He'd then glanced sideways at her across the car and asked if she'd mind if he told her a secret.

'Not a bit,' she'd said, glad that things were loosening up between them. 'I like secrets.'

Then he told her how one morning he'd been walking across the school playing grounds when he'd found a small bantam's egg lying on its own in the grass. It had lost its mother, so for the next six weeks he'd held the egg under his arm until it had hatched. He'd felt the shell crack, the fluffy little head emerge, not ticklish at all but so soft. 'So now I know what it feels like to have a baby,' he'd said softly and she'd glanced at him in the darkening car.

'Gosh,' she'd said, 'how sweet of you.' But really thinking, *What if he turns out to be barking as well?* 'What a marvellous story,' she'd added, thinking she sounded exactly like her mother.

On that night, she'd tried to tell herself that she must think of this marriage as a more or less practical arrangement: in the same way one might think of, say, laying out money for a last-minute holiday or buying a piece of furniture in a second-hand shop: if you didn't expect too much, how badly wrong could it go?

Now it pained her to remember she had ever thought of him in such a cold and practical way. The bantam story, so typical of his kindness, melted her heart. She also loved the way his hair felt silky when she ran her hands through it in the morning. The way he went to sleep with his arms around her. His jokes, the cups of tea he brought her in the morning with some special treat to eat. The way he pursued his work with energy and passion, the way he read to her at nights: Joseph Conrad, Dickens, T. S. Eliot – all the books she'd once thought she was far too dim for.

Mind you, she still hoped he wouldn't tell the bird-under-the-arm story too early on in his acquaintance with Viva and Rose. It did take time to know a person.

Later that afternoon, after the Christmas cake was given a decent burial, they decorated the house. Two hours later, there was barely a space left in the bungalow not covered with tinsel or candles or lights.

'D'you think we've overdone it?' Tor asked. Ci Ci had suddenly leapt into her mind, frowning and saying, 'Less is best, darling,' one of her style rules.

'Absolutely not.' Toby was winding pieces of tinsel round the knobs of their hideously ugly radiogram. 'The rule at Christmas is that nothing succeeds like excess.'

She hugged him and kissed his ear.

'So what do you think?' she said, as they stood back arm in arm to admire their room.

'Quite magnificent,' he said. 'An abode of bliss.'

And her heart had simply swelled with love again, for it was Toby who she was really celebrating this Christmas: the greatest gift of her life so far. She so hoped the girls would like him too.

Chapter 49

After her parents' death, Viva had often spent Christmas in the houses of people she barely knew: cousins, and once, when nobody else could be found, with her school's head gardener, whose childless wife had made it clear, during a sullen Christmas lunch, that she expected to be paid for the privilege of serving her turkey.

So when Tor's invitation came – in the form of a lurid cardboard elephant on which she had written, 'Christmas at Amritsar – do come!' – her immediate response was to say no. She loathed Christmas with a passion, and even without Christmas, she was feeling awful.

Her escape from Mr Azim had left her with a cut eye that needed five stitches, a cracked rib, headaches and insomnia. It had shaken her confidence profoundly. She'd been interviewed at length by Sergeant Barker, an irritable Scot who'd sat sweating in his uniform and implying that if she, a single woman, chose to live in one of the less salubrious suburbs of Bombay and to ignore the advice of the British Government, she'd had it coming to her and was lucky not to have been killed.

But at least she and Daisy had managed to find Guy a room at a Bombay rest home. Dr Ratcliffe, the gentle, gaunt-looking man who ran the home, had once been a victim of mustard gas and was both sympathetic and successful with patients with nervous disorders. He too was of the opinion that the form of dementia Guy appeared to suffer from might be a kind of schizophrenia. He loaned Daisy and Viva a paper on the subject written by a Dr Boyla, which stated that the condition once thought of as the symptom of an over-active, even a degenerate mind should be treated with more compassion. 'It's not enough,' Ratcliffe said as he'd shown them round, 'to simply write "gone bonkers" over a patient's notes as some of my colleagues do. We've got to find a lifeline if not a cure.'

Guy was put in a tranquil sunlit room on the edge of a courtyard.

They'd put him on a regime of nourishing foods and exercise. His room overlooked a small garden that Guy enjoyed working in.

When she was well enough, she went to see him. They sat together in the courtyard drinking lemonade, and the last time she'd visited, he'd actually said, 'I'm sorry I hurt you. I didn't mean to.' It was the calmest she'd ever seen him, the most happy and in control.

But four days after that, Guy's father had arrived from Assam. He came to the home especially to tell Daisy and Viva that he didn't hold with trick cyclists, and that the last thing Guy needed was women fussing over him. He said he'd brought a one-way ticket for Guy to get back to England again. An old pal of his was in the army there and they felt sure he would find a place for him in his regiment. In spite of everything that had happened, when Guy, looking pale and shaken, had come to see her for the last time, she'd felt the old tug of guilt and responsibility and a kind of quiet anguish that he was being thrown to the wolves again. Guy had asked Dr Ratcliffe to drive him over to the children's home especially so he could say goodbye. They'd been sitting on a bench outside Daisy's office when he'd suddenly put his arms round her and buried his head in the side of her neck like a child.

'I don't want to go,' he'd said. 'Can't you do something?'

'No,' she'd said, and realised, finally, that this was true. She wasn't his mother or his guardian. His parents didn't trust her or Dr Ratcliffe, who they thought was a quack. Guy was outside of her control. There was nothing she could do to mend his life.

He'd hugged her again.

'You're beautiful,' were his last words to her. 'I'd like to marry you one day.'

The incongruity of this had made her head reel.

Afterwards, Daisy, who was going back to England for Christmas, had more or less insisted that Viva went on holiday too. She said there would be only six children at the home over Christmas, and Mrs Bowden and Vaibhavi were happy to stay.

'Take two weeks off, you need it – and you are positively banned from worrying about that boy any more or from doing any more on that wretched book of yours. Go!'

When the train arrived in Amritsar two weeks before Christmas, she was relieved to see Tor was on her own. She didn't feel up to meeting anybody new.

'Viva!' Tor's face broke into a huge welcoming smile. She hugged her hard then looked under her hat.

'Good heavens!' she said. 'Your eye! What happened?'

'Oh, nothing, *nothing* really.' Viva had dreaded this. Her eye still felt like a badge of shame and, although she still lived in fear of Azim, she tried her best to gloss over the incident. 'I had a little adventure, and then a fall. It looks far worse than it is. I'll tell you all about it over supper.'

'Oh, Tor, I can't quite believe I'm here.' She took hold of Tor's arm for support. 'And what a day.'

It was: the sky clear as glass, a perfect untrammelled blue.

'Well, Toby and I are determined not to let a nasty little bit of sunshine spoil Christmas,' Tor joked as they walked arm in arm towards the car park. 'He says he's going to drop blobs of cotton wool from the attic, so everyone feels at home.

'Viva, I can't wait for you to meet him.' Tor tightened her grip on Viva's arm. 'You're going to love him. You really are.'

Viva hoped so. Did he know how vehemently she'd tried to talk Tor out of marrying him? Viva – the great expert on love and marriage! But she'd been so frightened for her.

While Tor drove the Talbot back to the school, Viva gave herself a stern talking-to. One of the results of being locked up with Azim was that she now suffered from a form of claustrophobia. She'd felt it on the train: the pounding heart, sweating palms, a swirling sense of suffocation. As she looked out of the car window, it was stealing over her again like a grey mist. She made an effort to focus on a dusty village they were passing, the man with his thin white horse, the old woman walking down the road with a bundle of twigs on her head.

She scolded herself as if she was her own whining child. *Shut up for a day or two! Go to the corner and sit down! Forget yourself.* This was Tor's turn to shine. When she'd glanced at her a few seconds ago, she'd thought how beautiful she looked – pure and shining in her new happiness. Her own problems could be shelved for a few days. Was that too much to ask?

Half an hour later, Tor stopped near a gate with a huge coat of arms above it.

'This is it,' she said. 'Home sweet home.'

They drove up a short drive, towards the flamboyant main school building, all flourishing carvings and mini turrets, and a properly green front lawn where two peacocks strolled picking up seed. Behind them was a sign saying, 'St Bartholomew's College for the Sons of Gentlemen and Maharajahs, aged seven to fourteen.'

'Not our house, so don't get too excited,' Tor said gaily. 'We're the poor relations.'

The car bumped along a gravel path beside a cricket pitch, which announced that the score between St Bart's and Rawalpindi was 179 for 6, past a quadrangle of whitewashed stables and a polo field where a lone figure in breeches and a turban was playing stick and ball.

'Now,' Tor glanced at her as they headed towards a circle of trees beyond the cricket pitch, 'close your eyes, we're getting warm.'

It still hurt Viva to close her eyes. The doctor said she'd been lucky not to have lost her sight.

'Are we there yet?' Sunlight flickered in underwater patterns inside her eyelids.

'We're getting warmer.' Tor swung round a corner; gravel swished under the wheels.

'Now!' Tor took her hand and squeezed it hard. 'Open.'

Viva heard herself laugh out loud for the first time in a long time. She'd stepped into a child's fairy tale. There was a fat Father Christmas sitting on the chimney; every window twinkled with candles; icicles made of string hung from the bougainvillea pots; scrolls of brightly coloured paintings drawn with childish abandon had been hung to fill the empty squares of the verandah. One showed a plump wise man wearing a jewelled turban, another tobogganing children joined by tigers, cheetahs, snakes.

Above the door, in silver letters a foot high, a sign said, 'Happy Christmas.'

'We've put them up miles too early,' Tor said, 'but we couldn't wait.'

'It's wonderful, Tor,' Viva laughed. 'What genius lives here?'

'Well, genii actually – if that's the plural.' Toby had appeared with two servants behind him all dressed up and carrying glasses, champagne and cheese straws.

'Hello, friend of Tor's,' he said, awkwardly stretching out his hand.

'No, no, wait! Wait!' Tor raced ahead of them, cranked up the gramophone and soon the room was filled with Ivor Novello singing 'Ding Dong Merrily on High'.

'I've had to restrain her from lighting the fire,' Toby said. 'The temperature's only sixty-five in the shade.' Seeing him beam at his new wife, Viva thought how young he looked – tousled hair, slightly inky fingers, a shirt tail that hadn't quite been tucked in – and innocent: she'd imagined he'd be smoother and far more devious-looking.

'Darling.' Tor put her arm round his waist. 'Darling, a quiet moment before we get silly. This is my friend Viva. About whom you already know so much. She's going to tell us about her eye later, so don't ask now.'

'Greetings, Viva.' He shook her hand warmly. 'How about a glass of champagne?'

'I'd love one,' she said.

'Oh drat!' When he poured the bubbles straight over the glass, Viva thought, *He's as nervous as I am.*

When they'd got her a new glass, she took a deep breath, and then a sip. *See!* she addressed the part of her that was always frightened. See – there were already three things to celebrate: that she'd travelled here on her own; that Toby didn't look like an obvious drunk or wife beater; that nobody had yet mentioned Frank, whom she didn't want to talk about. So, even though the whole thing was kicking off earlier than she would have chosen, let Christmas cheer commence. No whining, no brooding, no dreading, no looking backwards or forwards.

She raised her glass towards Tor. 'Happy Christmas,' she said.

Chapter 50

When Rose turned up the following day with four-month-old Freddie in her arms, Toby teased the girls for going gaga. But he was such a beautiful baby, with Rose's silver-blond hair, a perfect little chiselled dimple in his chin and intelligent and only slightly crossed blue eyes. When Viva held him in her arms, she was once again shocked that she felt – not exactly jealous, what would she do with a child? – but in awe of Rose for producing something quite so perfect, so powerful.

Even when he was only chuckling in his bath, or lolling around having his nappy changed, Freddie seemed to increase the emotional temperature of the house, as if he was a little fire burning away.

'Oh Lord,' Toby complained to the girls when he was at last allowed to hold him. 'The memsahib is going to want to be in foal right away now,' and then, just as Tor had feared, he launched into his story about keeping the egg under his arm and what that had meant to him.

'So what happened to your bird?' Viva enquired gently.

'Two months after it had hatched, I trod on it. I was running to get the post. Sorry, darling,' he said to Tor, 'didn't tell you that bit. I've only just been able to talk about it.' He was not joking.

'That's dreadful,' said Viva softly. 'You must have loved that bird.'

'You're right,' he said. 'I did love that bird.'

When Rose and Tor went off to supervise the bathing of the baby, Viva stayed on the verandah to watch the sunset and try and unravel her curious and unsettled mood. She was happy for Rose, but babies did change things for those left behind. Having one was definitely a mark of facing a physical terror – rather like those teenage boys flung from trees with a rope round one ankle in Borneo during initiation ceremonies. It was one badge of being a grown-up and, even now, there was a new quiet confidence about Rose – who'd admitted it hurt and had promised to tell them all about it when Toby wasn't around. And, even though Rose hadn't said much about Jack yet, a baby also meant you'd put your trust in someone else, become a family.

Tor would have a baby soon. No question about it. That thought shouldn't make Viva feel lonely, but it did: their friendships would change; everything would change. There was only so much energy to go round and babies seemed to suck up love and attention like giant magnets.

Some bad thoughts flew around Viva's head. What did she have to show after her year in India? Clever old Viva, once regarded as the wise and worldly woman of their group. A nearly finished book that probably nobody would want to publish, no fixed abode, very little money and no concrete plans for the future.

Why hadn't they all seen right through her from the start?

The sun was shedding a lavish apricot-coloured glow over the playing fields and the woods beyond where, from time to time, a flock of dark birds rose and wheeled around in the sky, settling in the tops of trees. A few seconds later, it was dark and a scattering of stars had appeared on the horizon. Toby came out on to the verandah and sat down beside Viva.

'Are you all right there?' he said gently. 'I mean, is this a private think, or can anybody join in?'

'Not private at all,' she lied. 'It's so lovely to have the luxury of not racing around like a mad thing. Tor seems so . . .'

'So . . .'

They both laughed.

'You first,' he said. 'You're the guest.'

'Well, I just wanted to say I've never seen Tor so happy.'

'Oh, I do hope so! I still can't quite believe it.' He looked about eight when he said that. 'I understand you had some doubts?' His grin in the dusk was mischievous.

Viva laughed, embarrassed. 'Well, do admit – even by Indian standards it was pretty speedy.'

'I know,' he said. 'We took the most gigantic risk, but they're always the best, don't you think?'

'I don't know. I'm not very brave like that.'

'Oh, come on, Tor's been telling me about your work, your book. You sound very brave to me.'

She didn't reply.

'Have a chota peg with me,' Toby urged, 'and tell me about it. I don't meet many writers up here.'

So they sat and drank and talked and Toby was so enthusiastic it encouraged her to tell him in more detail than she normally would, the story of Talika, and then, because he'd insisted, about two new inmates at the home, Prepal and Chinna, how they'd brought up seven brothers and sisters on their own after their parents' house was burned to the ground.

'These children are so brave,' she said. 'They laugh, they sing, they tell jokes. They refuse to go under.'

He was gazing at her intently. She could hear a bird rustling in the trees and the croaky cry of what sounded like a jackal in the woods beyond.

'They must trust you,' he said. 'If they didn't, they wouldn't tell you these things.'

'Don't most people like telling their stories?' she replied.

'It depends what you mean by stories. I think the English are neurotically private as a race – we're the Western Orientals. Oh, I mean if you meet some old buffer at the club, he'll tell you what regiment he fought in and what a shambles the government is, but most chaps won't tell you what really hurts them or what they most love. Don't you agree?' He looked at her directly and drained his glass.

'I do,' she said.

'So,' he said after a pause, 'do you have a publisher yet?'

'Not yet,' she said. 'Only an introduction to a man at Macmillan who liked a couple of chapters.'

'My publishers are called Stott and Greenaway,' he said. 'I'd be happy to introduce you. You won't get rich, but their books look beautiful.'

A peal of laughter coming from the baby's room made them both look up. There was a loud splash and then Rose and Tor singing 'Daisy, Daisy, Give Me Your Answer Do'.

Toby took a polo mallet from the corner of the room and thumped on the walls. 'Pipe down,' he cried. 'We run a respectable establishment here.' The girls sang louder; the baby chirruped like a small bird.

A few seconds later, Freddie appeared in Tor's arms flushed from his bath and smelling of soap and talcum powder. 'Say goodnight to Uncle Toby and Auntie Viva,' she said.

Viva kissed the baby's forehead. His skin smelled like new grass. He waved his pink little fingers at her and struck her softly beside her eye where her scar was healing. She flinched, but kissed him again. 'Goodnight, Freddie darling,' she said. 'Sleep well.'

After Tor left the room, Viva felt cross with herself for starting to feel low again. If she was going to be the ghost at the wedding, she should at least have had the decency to stay in Bombay.

'Have one of these.' Toby had returned with a plate of sturdy-looking mince pies. 'Tor made them.'

She wanted him to stop being so nice to her now, to be left alone with her own dark thoughts.

'Um, delicious,' she said, scattering crumbs all over her lap. 'You know, it's awfully good of you to have us all.'

'The more the merrier as far as I'm concerned,' said Toby. 'Shame, though, that your doctor friend couldn't make it. Lahore's really no distance at all from here, and I would have liked to talk to him about blackwater fever. It's the most dreadful thing. We lost a couple of boys to it here last year.'

'What doctor friend?' She stared at him. 'I didn't know he'd been invited.' She put down her drink. 'Who invited him?'

'Oh Lord,' he said. 'I've put my foot in it?'

'No, no, no, not at all,' she said with a lightness she did not feel. 'He was everybody's friend on the ship. I hardly think of him but . . .' She looked at her watch. 'I'm going to go to my room and freshen up – it's nearly supper time. I enjoyed our chat, thank you for it.'

'Oh damn it!' Toby looked stricken. 'I've blabbed, haven't I? What an idiot.'

Upstairs, she locked herself inside her room, and sat doubled up at the foot of her bed. So this was the end of it: he'd been asked; he didn't want to come. How much more clearly did she need to be told? And then she felt pain blooming inside her and there was nothing she could do about it. A winding kind of pain as if she'd been dealt a blow in the solar plexus. *This is the end of it*, she told herself again. *He'd been asked, he'd said no.*

Get this into your fat head, she raged at herself, *and don't you dare cast a cloud over Christmas because of it.*

Five minutes later, she crept into the spare room across the landing where Rose and Tor stood in the glow of an oil lamp tucking the baby's mosquito net around him.

'Tor,' she said in as natural a voice as possible. 'Did you ask Frank to stay for Christmas?'

Tor's face told her everything she needed to know.

'No, not really.' Tor turned for help to Rose, who was concentrating hard on the baby's sheet and refused to meet her eye.

'Well, I suppose I might of, a little bit,' said Tor. 'It was actually such a coincidence: we met up at a party in Lahore, it was such fun to see him, and I thought we all should, you know, meet up again.' She looked uncertainly towards Rose.

'Gosh,' said Rose, 'I don't believe you told me that.'

'And?' Viva tried to keep the wobble out of her voice. 'What did he say when you asked him?'

'Well,' Tor couldn't meet her eye, 'it was such a shame. He's working this Christmas, and had other plans.'

'Did he know I was coming?'

Tor fiddled with the mosquito net. 'Yes.'

'It really doesn't matter,' said Viva, who hated their sympathetic looks. 'I hardly think of him now.'

'That's good,' said Rose and Tor together, which meant that everybody in the room except Freddie was lying now.

Over supper, Toby, who said he was learning to carve and usually did it like an axe murderer, managed a decent job on a joint of roast beef. Jai came in and lit a flare path of oil lamps around the verandah, and then they opened a special bottle of wine Rose had brought with her and they toasted each other.

The talk was jolly and open, and Viva did her best to join in.

Over pudding – a very good treacle tart – they had a conversation about the difference between a friend and the kind of chap you'd choose to go into the jungle with.

'I'd never choose you for the jungle,' Tor teased Toby. 'You'd be crawling around on your hands and knees looking for the greater spotted titmouse or the meadow waxcap or some such and we'd never get out. No, I'd take Viva with me.'

'Why me?' she wanted to know.

'You're brave and you don't go on about things. I mean, take this mysterious thing that happened to you in Bombay that you were going to tell us about later and never quite got round to. If I'd had stitches in my eye, or been knocked out, I'd dine out on it for months.'

'Oh, these.' Viva touched the side of her eye lightly. *Trapped.* 'Well . . . it was nothing really; well, it was *something* but not as bad as it will sound.'

She had rehearsed this moment on the train on her way here, but even her light-hearted version of her kidnapping, starring her as terrified maiden in red dress, Azim as pantomime villain, drew gasps of horror from them.

'But you could easily have been killed!' said Tor.

'Why didn't the police come?' said Rose.

'Well, they did. But you know how these things get swept under the carpet here,' she said.

'Not usually when they concern English people,' Toby said drily.

'Don't forget,' she reminded him, 'that the governor has warned us twice to think about closing the home, but no one can bring themselves to. It's a complicated situation.

'By the way,' she was keen to turn the spotlight away from herself, 'Mr Azim went to a very pukka English boarding school near here, I think. He told me he was flogged there, that the games master broke his little finger, and that he never once celebrated Diwali there – it was called Guy Fawkes Night – can that possibly be true?'

'Yes,' said Toby simply. 'It's all horribly mixed up and we do walk a tightrope. Some of the upper-class Indians who leave their children here will not stand for their children being beaten by anyone but themselves; others seem to want a proper old-fashioned Western-style boarding school: fags, bad porridge, beatings, cricket, the lot.'

'But Guy Fawkes? Surely not.'

'Yes – they have it here. Even worse in some ways is how we cram Wordsworth and Shakespeare down their throats and ignore great Urdu poets like Mir Taqi Mir or Ghalib. It's a great shame.'

The conversation ended when Tor put her finger to her lips and looked towards Freddie's room. 'Listen,' she said. The baby was crying, in a rickety sort of way that didn't sound very serious. They all stopped and listened intently until they heard the click-clack of the baby's cradle, which was being moved by a piece of string tied to the ayah's foot, and then her crooning lullaby.

'What is she singing?' Viva asked Toby.

' "Little master, little king, sleep, my darling, sleep," ' said Toby. 'Nice to know women somewhere respect their damned men folk.' He gave them a brigadier's glare.

Viva relaxed for a second as he filled up her glass with red wine. The story about the kidnapping had been successfully negotiated, and no one need ever know how much it had hurt her or how much of a fool it had made her feel, how it had taken away the kind of arrogance you need in order to feel you can make a difference to other people's lives in a country so many miles away from anything you properly understand.

'But, Viva,' Tor suddenly turned to her, 'finish your story. What happened to that little rat Guy?'

So she told him about Dr Ratcliffe and his home. How well he was doing there until he was whisked away.

'He's gone back to England now. It's the saddest thing. His father got him a commission in the army. He'll be a fighting man soon. Can you imagine anything he'll be less suited for? What do they see when they look at him?'

'We do not see things as they are, but as we are,' Toby said quietly. 'That's from the Talmud.'

'I've been guilty of that,' she told him.

'And, Viva,' Tor could be remarkably persistent when the mood took her, 'sorry to ask all these questions, but you'll be gone soon and I need to know. Where will you move to if the home does have to close?'

'I don't know,' she said. 'I'm pretty sure they will close us down soon.'

'Heavens.' Tor's eyes were like searching headlamps when she turned them on you like this. 'Won't that be a disaster for those children?'

'Not for all of them.' She hated the way her voice had started to tremble. 'Some of them can't wait to leave. The status of orphans in Indian society is so low, you see. Oh, they'll stay if they must, but we're not always their salvation. Some of them pine to live out on the streets again.'

'Any idea where you'll go?' Tor asked.

'Heavens.' Viva felt trapped again. 'I hadn't really thought about it. I—'

'Have one of these.' Toby pushed a box of chocolates in her direction. He seemed to be trying to come to her rescue again. 'By the way,' he said, 'I've been meaning to ask you, whereabouts in India did your parents live? Wasn't there something about a trunk you're supposed to pick up?'

Thinking that she wouldn't notice, Tor put down her pudding spoon and mouthed, 'No,' to Toby. After a brief moment of panic he went on smoothly, 'When I was a boy we moved all the time too – my father was a scientist, but he worked for the Forestry Department in India for years, so I never really knew where I lived either. Quite fun in a way, but the only problem is' – Viva saw him glance at Tor as if to say, 'How am I doing?' – 'the only problem is, one's inner globe is always slightly spinning.'

'Mine isn't,' said Tor. She stood up and put her arms round him. 'I absolutely love it here.'

Viva watched them with hunger. How at Tor's touch he squeezed his eyes shut and laid his head against hers.

And when Rose left to check on the baby, Viva, sitting surrounded by empty wine glasses, felt a wave of desolation sweep over her. She shouldn't have come; she wasn't ready yet.

'Viva,' Rose had come back, 'how would you feel if we asked Frank again, not to stay but just for Christmas lunch? He was this very good-looking ship's doctor,' she explained to Toby. 'We were all very spoony on him.'

Viva felt a spurt of anger – how trivial she made it sound.

'Toby would like him,' Tor added.

They looked at each other, and Viva swallowed.

'I'd rather you didn't,' she said. 'He's said no once.'

They left it at that.

Chapter 51

The following morning, Tor said that Viva and Rose should go for a ride on their own together.

Toby drew a map for them. The school, he said, had twenty acres of riding tracks, one of which led to a lake which was a lovely spot for a picnic. To make it even more fun, Freddie could go with them on the school's Shetland pony. He could go on the leading rein. They had a special little basket chair with straps for babies, called a *howdah*, which he could loll around in like an emperor. Toby said the groom could walk beside Freddie for five or ten minutes and then lead him home so that the girls could have a really good gallop.

A really good gallop. Viva felt her stomach tighten at the idea.

An hour or so later, she and Rose were trotting between an avenue of poplar trees that led into the wood. Viva's pony, a grey Arab wearing a scarlet bridle, was delicate and frisky and made bug eyes at everything that moved: parrots, leaves, spots of sunlight on the path.

Every muscle in her body was starting to clench with fear.

Over breakfast, when Toby asked whether she could ride, she'd said, almost without thinking, 'Oh, lots as a child.' But one of the problems of having no parents or brothers and sisters was that you said things like that without ever really knowing what was real. Did 'lots' mean four or five times in total? Every week? She hadn't a clue really.

A few seconds earlier, when both ponies had shied at a quail, she'd almost fallen off while Rose sat poised and queenly as though she and the horse were one.

One clear memory she did have was riding with her father in Simla. She must have been about three, maybe four. He'd come thundering up the track on his horse, leant down from his saddle, plucked her from the ground as if she was a toy or a feather, sat her in front of his saddle and cantered off again towards the horizon and she'd felt the horse explode with energy beneath them, felt the firmness of his hands holding her to him like the still centre of a spinning wheel.

Her best memory.

'What were you thinking about?' Rose must have been trying to talk to her – she was squinting at her from under her riding helmet.

'Nothing much.'

'Oh!' Rose gave her a sceptical look. 'Well, look, I'm going to give Freddie a kiss and send him home with the *syce* now.' She leapt down and adjusted Freddie's bonnet over his scarlet face and righted his soft little body, which had slipped down into the basket. 'The poor little chap looks done in.'

Rose tenderly watched him go until the tiny Shetland was swallowed up by trees.

'Right.' She swung up into the saddle again. 'Now you and I can have some fun.'

'Lovely.' Viva's stomach was in knots.

They rode through an open wicker gate; a flock of green parrots flew off into the woods. Ahead of them Viva saw a long winding track that led up a short incline between misty trees. Rose said it was the perfect place for a gallop.

'Ready?'

'Ready.'

Rose disappeared in a cloud of dust.

When Viva let go of the reins, her pony took off like a rocket, fighting for its head, and then all Viva felt was some pure form of terror. *The closest you'll ever get to flying*, with the wind bashing your face, horse's feet thundering underneath you. On and on they sped, the scrub whizzing by and then through a muddy track past cinnamon-scented trees; a couple of logs had to be jumped, and then, when they halted at the top of the track, the ponies were slick with sweat, and they were laughing and far more relaxed with each other.

'Oh, what bliss!' Rose, cheeks flushed and with her blonde hair let loose, suddenly looked about twelve. 'What absolute and utter bliss.' She and her dark bay horse danced in unison with each other for a second, two handsome creatures in their prime. *She is beautiful*, thought Viva, *and she is brave*.

When they stopped talking, they could hear the burblings of the stream that followed the track, the thud of their horses' hooves on red dirt. When they'd got to the stream, they let the horses drop their heads to suck up a few greedy mouthfuls, and on the other side of the bank a heron flew away. Viva felt the light touch of Rose's hand on her sleeve.

'You look so much better, Viva.'

'Do I?' Viva picked up her reins. Something about Rose's worried smile made her feel defensive.

'Are you really all right, Viva?'

'Yes, yes, this is perfect.' Viva put her hand on her pony's neck. 'I'm glad you suggested it.'

'I didn't actually mean that.'

'Oh,' she said, 'well, whatever it was, I am fine. What about you?'

Rose gave her a strange look. 'Truth or flannel?'

'Truth.'

Rose said, 'I don't know where to start. So much has changed in this year.'

'Really! How?'

A hank of blonde hair had fallen down around Rose's face. She thrust it under her hat.

'Coming here. India. Everything. I came without giving it a second's thought.'

'Rose! That's not true; you are easily the most sensible of all of us.'

'Oh, come on, Viva. You must have noticed what a baby I was.' Two beads of sweat had started to fall down the side of Rose's face. 'Such a baby.'

Viva felt wary. Rose seemed suddenly very wound up.

'D'you think anything really prepares you for India?' Viva said. 'It's like a vast onion: every layer you unpeel shows you something else you didn't know about it, or yourself.'

'I'm not just talking about India,' Rose went on doggedly. 'I'm talking about getting married to Jack. It was so awful at first.'

Viva was so shocked her scalp prickled. She'd always assumed Rose was silent about Jack because she didn't want to gloat about her handsome husband in front of Tor.

'Absolutely ghastly,' Rose insisted. 'I felt so shy, so homesick, so completely out of my depth with him and everything.'

'Gosh,' said Viva after a while. 'How is it now?' She was hating this almost as much as Rose was.

'Well,' Rose fiddled with her reins, 'some of it got better – at least the bedroom side of things – at first it seemed so *rude*.'

They burst out laughing and a partridge flung itself croaking out of the undergrowth.

'But it's better now?' Viva asked cautiously. 'You know, the other things.'

'No – well, only partly . . .' Rose was faltering. 'You see, it got worse. Much worse.'

'How?'

'Well,' Rose gave a deep sigh. 'Do you mind me talking like this?'

'Of course not,' Viva lied. This was awful and she knew that Rose would regret her confidences later.

'Something happened. A horrid thing.' There was a long silence before Rose found her voice again. 'In Poona. I went to the club by myself one day. Jack was away at camp, so it was just me and a few of the usual old biddies in the sort of ladies' area of the bar. One of them, a Mrs Henderson, a notorious old gossip, was being generally nasty about almost everyone: how bad they were with their servants, or how little they entertained and so forth. It was all very, very boring and I hardly listened to a word of it, but then she seemed to quite deliberately bring up the subject of men and how they could be such animals. I felt this sort of special silence fall and everyone trying not to look at me and feel embarrassed. It was such a funny moment, and then Mrs H. said, "Gosh, have I put my size sixes in it?" She really was about as subtle as a ton of bricks. And everyone changed the subject.

'I was so wet behind the ears I might have forgotten about it, or put it down to Mrs H. being a clot, but then a few nights later, I went into the sitting room and Jack was sitting there reading a letter. He was weeping. When I asked him why, well, you know Jack, well, you don't really, but he's sometimes *hideously* honest.' Rose heaved a big sigh. 'He confessed straight away.'

'About what?'

'About his other woman.'

'Oh no.' Viva put her hand on Rose's arm. 'How horrible. Was it true?'

She didn't have to ask – Rose's lovely profile was all bent out of shape at the thought of it.

'Yes, it was. He didn't have to tell me; in some ways, I still think it might have been better if he hadn't. Even though it finished when he married me, all the time when we were on the ship he was seeing her. He said he'd found it hard to say goodbye. I was so shocked at first I prayed the baby would die and then I thought I would probably have to kill myself. I know that sounds dramatic but I felt so far from home and so awful.'

'Was it somebody you knew?'

'No.' Rose took a deep shuddering breath. 'Her name is Sunita. She's Indian. She's a beautiful, educated Bombay girl. When I asked him if he loved her, he said he felt immensely grateful to her, that she'd taught him so much, and that she was a fine person. In other words, he loved her.'

'Oh, Rose, what a thing.'

'It was.' Rose was stroking her horse's mane and breathing in and out hard. 'It was the worst thing ever and I was too proud to tell anyone.'

The horses moved through a line of trees, sunlight dappling Rose's face.

'That was why I insisted on coming up to Ooty that time with you. But when I got there, I felt such a fraud. I was crying so much I'm surprised I didn't wash the baby away, and you were both so thrilled for me.'

'Oh, Rose.' Viva felt sick. 'You should have told us. That's what friends are for.'

'Viva,' Rose gave her a straight look, 'that is a little rich coming from you.'

Viva ignored this for now. 'So what did you do?'

'Well, I've really never felt so mis. I felt I loathed him for a while and I've never loathed anyone in my life before, apart from one awful girl at school who was nasty to everyone. One of the most infuriating things was the way he apologised to me; it was so stiff.' Rose did his voice. ' "Look, sorry, Rose, but men are men and these things happen." And then he went all sulky as if somehow this was my fault. Oh, I was livid. It wasn't that I wanted him to grovel, but I was so hurt and the worst thing was that I had actually started to really love him. Not like in books, or in plays, but small things: like having his arm around me in bed, caring about what he ate, even worrying about his constipation – he's one of the few people I know in India who get it – don't laugh, Viva, it's true.' She wiped some of the sweat off her horse's neck and flopped some of it on the grass.

When they reached the lake, three herons flew away with a light flapping of wings.

'I hope you don't mind me telling you all this.' Rose looked pale as they sat down together on the rug.

'I think you've been very brave,' Viva said. She could never talk about herself out loud like that.

'There was nothing a bit brave about staying.' Rose took off her helmet and shook out her hair. 'What were my alternatives? To go back to Hampshire, divorced and expecting a baby? It would have broken their hearts, and besides, I'd been telling them in letters what a whale of a time we were having here. So much has gone wrong for my mother since the war, my brother dying and then Daddy being so ill, I feel she needs things to go well for me.' Rose closed her eyes in pain. 'Jack didn't mean to be cruel.'

'Does he talk about her?'

'No, well, yes, but only once when I insisted on it. He could think of nothing bad to say about her. I rather admired him for it. I only needed to look at his face to know he still loved her, maybe still does.'

Viva looked at her in astonishment. Rose was so fair.

'I felt horribly jealous – if it hadn't been for Freddie, I can't say what would have happened. The actual birth was awful – I'll tell you and Tor about it later, not now. It happened at home by mistake and we were miles away from hospital. Jack came back that night, and when he saw me from the door with Fred in my arms, he broke down and cried. He got into bed and said he was sorry and that he would protect us until his last. It was such a funny old-fashioned thing to say but it meant so much – but by then,' Rose batted the apology away like a fly, 'I didn't need it. Everything had changed again. He got into bed and put his arms around me and Fred lay on top of us, and when I looked outside and saw, I don't know, how huge the world was – the moon, stars – I knew I'd never felt more in my life. I can't even properly put it into words. I also knew that if I'd left him, I would leave half of me behind.'

'Heavens.' Viva was bewildered, for Rose was actually glad, or so it seemed. She would have left him like a shot.

After lunch, Rose fell asleep on the rug with a biscuit in her hand. Her confession seemed to have exhausted her. Viva went to check on the horses, who were tethered and munching grass, and then she went back and lay beside Rose, thinking how self-engrossed she must have been in Ooty not to have spotted that Rose was in such distress. She often got this wrong, she decided, this idea that there were lucky people in the world, like Rose and Jack – blessed with good looks or money or parents – who somehow glided through life and didn't have to go through the same things other people did. But it wasn't true. Everyone seemed to suffer, but differently.

She was struck too by how Rose had told her own story simply and from the heart. How Rose had assumed Viva must know about this catastrophe if they were to be properly close. *And the truth shall make you whole.* But could you only know another person to the extent that they were prepared to show their true selves to you? That thought gathered at the edge of Viva's mind like a cloud.

She could easily, at that moment, have told Rose about what had happened at Ooty, about Frank, and Guy. Rose, who'd proved rather unshockable, would have understood, and maybe have some sensible advice for her. But her door seemed jammed – opening it too frightening – there might be a howling wasteland beyond.

A more painful thought followed: that all the energy Rose had spent on trying and, by all accounts, succeeding in loving a flawed man, Viva spent in not caring, on a kind of willed heartlessness. She did it – at least this was her excuse – so she could work and survive. Who was right?

Viva's scar was beginning to throb; it was all too complicated. If only she could reduce what Rose had told her to a manageable thought – something she could believe in, applaud, feel sorry about.

When she was a child, her father's scientific mind had often perplexed her by answering a question with a question. She remembered asking him one day, 'How do you make an aeroplane?'

He'd said, 'What is the purpose of an aeroplane?'

She'd said, 'To fly,' and then he'd made her work out what it would need to fly: wings, lightness, speed and so forth.

So what was the purpose of men and women together – apart from the obvious baby-making thing? Shelter? Protection? Women's suffrage was already changing the rules. So was it to help you make love? To increase your understanding of love by branching out beyond yourself? But that sounded hopelessly high-minded and romantic – some people clearly did terrible damage to each other – but how could you possibly really know before the damage was done? This was surely the greatest gamble of all.

She was trying to think of it in purely abstract terms when Frank's smile – his dimples, the sudden sweetness of it – made her squeeze her eyes tight shut. She mustn't think of him again like that. Her chance had gone. It was over.

Chapter 52

When Rose woke up, Viva was lying next to her with her eyes wide open.

'What are you thinking, Viva?' she said.

'That we should ride home soon; Tor will think we've been eaten by a crocodile.'

Rose suddenly felt furious with her. Both she and Tor had been shocked at how ill Viva looked. It wasn't just the bruised eyes, both of them had agreed; all her fire seemed to have gone. Even her hair seemed less shiny.

'Say something to her while you're riding,' Tor had said. 'I would but I'll only put my foot in it, and you know how prickly she can be.'

So Rose had tried, and because Viva was a good listener, she'd said far more than she'd meant to. It had been so long since she'd confided in anyone – and now she felt angry and stupid, because Viva had just stood up and brushed the crumbs off her jodhpurs and was smiling at her in a superior, chaperone-ish way, as if she felt sorry for her. Any moment now, Rose could almost feel it, she would bring out that blasted notebook and pencil of hers and then she would definitely want to crown her.

She took a couple of deep breaths. 'So aren't you going to say anything?' The words were out before she thought of them.

'About what?' In the sunlight you could still see yellow and green bruises around Viva's eyes, and the row of small holes where the stitches had been.

'About yourself?'

'But I thought we were talking about you, Rose. I'm so sorry.'

She pulled a pencil out of her pocket and rotated it between her fingers – a nervous habit of hers.

'You don't understand, do you?'

'I don't know what you're talking about, Rose.'

'About saying things.' Rose moved a couple of feet further away from her. 'You know, friendship. I tell you something that's import-ant to me and then you say something about you that's important to you. It's called letting your guard down.' Rose was shocked to hear herself practically shouting.

'Rose!' Viva moved away from her so quickly she knocked over the hip flask. 'I do tell you things. Sometimes.'

'Oh, rubbish,' shouted Rose. 'Absolute rubbish.'

'This is not a game of tennis,' Viva roared. 'Why do I have to confide in you just because you have?'

'Well, drop it then, Viva,' Rose bellowed back. Two swans flew across the lake, their wings flapping like sails, and the horses' heads shot up, but she couldn't stop herself now; it was such a relief not to be pretending. 'Just drop it. I'll overlook the fact that you've lost about a stone in weight; that you look absolutely done in; that someone tried to murder you in Bombay and you don't want to talk about it; and that Frank, who is clearly mad about you, has been sent away with no reason, or none that you want to talk about. Let's just talk about ponies and Christmas pudding. I'll pretend not to notice any of that – it's just silly little Rose who has all the problems and makes all the mistakes, and Viva, the magnificent, is still divinely in control.'

'How dare you say that.' Viva's fists were balled.

'What do you want me to say?'

They glared at each other.

'Well, you could start with Frank. Most friends would at least tell each other what happened.'

'Nothing happened,' said Viva. When her jaw set like that, Rose was almost scared of her. 'We had a brief whatever it was, but I needed to work, to finish my book, to get on with things, to try and earn my own living. I don't have a mummy and daddy in the background to help me along.'

'No, you don't,' Rose admitted. 'But that doesn't mean you can tell lies about yourself.'

'What lies?' Viva's voice was cold.

'About how you feel.' Rose felt her sandwich starting to congeal in her stomach. She'd never had a proper row with a friend before.

'Don't you dare judge me.' Viva's eyes had gone as black as coals.

'I'm not trying to judge you, I'm trying to be your friend. Viva, please,' she touched her gently, 'sit down.'

Viva sat down at the far end of the rug and glared towards the lake.

'Look,' Rose tried again after a long silence, 'it's absolutely none of our beeswax, but we do care. We were with you in Ooty – we saw you with Frank, you seemed mad about each other.'

Viva shifted her legs, moved her head rapidly from side to side, then said, 'All right, if it makes you feel any better, I made a bloody great mess of the whole thing. Now do you feel better?'

'No, of course I don't', Rose said quietly. 'That's mean.' She stretched out her hand, but Viva ignored it.

She stood up suddenly. 'I'm sorry. But I'm hopeless at this sort of thing. Thank you for trying, really, but I think we should go home now.'

'Say something, Viva,' Rose pleaded.

'I can't. There's nothing really to tell; it's all such a muddle in my mind.'

Viva's sigh sounded like a dry sob from deep inside her. There was another long silence.

'All right.' Viva had turned her back to her and her voice was muffled. 'Do you remember the night Frank came to Ooty, to warn us about Guy? After you went to bed, he came to my room. He stayed the night. Are you shocked?'

'Of course not.' Rose gave her a soft punch on the arm. 'Things happen in India that are different from home, and besides, it was so blindingly obvious!'

'Was it?' Viva looked up reluctantly.

'Yes, it was.'

'How awful.'

'Why awful?'

'Because it's so secret.'

'You both looked so different, sort of spellbound. I remember feeling jealous, thinking that's the way I hoped I'd feel on my honeymoon.'

'I didn't feel spellbound, I felt, well, it doesn't matter now. It was so confusing.'

'But,' Rose was perplexed, 'forgive me, but did something go wrong?'

'No.' Viva's voice was almost inaudible. 'That part was wonderful.' She gave a soft squeak of pain.

'So you sent him away because it was wonderful.'

'I felt so guilty – because he'd come to warn me that Guy might have been killed in the riots. I was sure he was dead.'

'It wasn't your fault that Guy did what he did.'

'Look, Rose.' Viva's face was white. Her bruise had lit up like an angry flower. 'I said I didn't want to talk about it and I don't, so can I stop now?' She stomped towards the horses so fast she almost stumbled on a rock. 'I really do want to go home now,' she said.

Tor was standing in the kitchen when Viva walked into the house. She shut the door so hard that a wreath fell on to the verandah. She heard her shoes click up the corridor and then the door to her bedroom close.

Rose was hanging up her riding hat in the corridor and looking towards the closed door.

'Rose, what happened?' said Tor. Her heart sank.

'Disaster,' whispered Rose. 'She's absolutely livid. She really does hate talking about things.'

'Shall I go?' Tor mouthed. 'I could take her a cup of tea.' She lifted an imaginary cup to her mouth.

'I'd leave her for a bit,' said Rose. 'I really do think she wants to be on her own. Is it all right if I give Freddie a bath?' she said loud enough for Viva to overhear. 'He could probably do with one after his ride.'

A row of paper chains had fallen from the hall ceiling; Tor picked it up and wore it round her neck like a stole and felt her spirits plummet. While the girls had been out riding, Jack had telephoned to say he was back temporarily in Peshawar, but it was looking unlikely that he would make it for Christmas. He'd started to explain but the line had sounded like a forest fire. Rose would be upset. Viva was hardly the life and soul, and with eight days to go before Christmas, Tor now envisaged quiet meals with herself overdoing it as usual, an exhausting hostess. All the decorations that had thrilled her a few days ago now looked silly and childish – an unwelcome dig in the ribs reminding them to have fun.

Toby (oh, how sweet and uncomplicated he suddenly seemed) would wonder why she'd been so excited about asking all these tricky people to stay.

These gloomy thoughts were interrupted by bird-like chirrupings coming from the direction of Freddie's room and then a gurgle of laughter. Tor opened the door to his room. Fred was being lifted from underneath his mosquito net by Rose. He opened his eyes when he saw her, smiled and wiggled his fingers.

She followed Rose into the bathroom, where Jai had filled up the old zinc bath with water. Freddie's nightdress was unbuttoned, and Rose lowered him into the water after testing it carefully with her elbow.

'Freddo, darling, Mr McFred, who's a pretty baby boy,' she crooned lapping water up his fat, creased little legs. The baby gave a reckless, gummy smile and then kicked his legs out. How nice it was, reflected Tor, rolling up her sleeves and kneeling on the other side of the bath, to have at least one jolly person in the house.

'Do you think Viva's going to be all right?' she asked Rose, in a low voice.

'I hope so,' whispered Rose. 'But she is infuriating sometimes. I mean, we did talk about Frank a bit, but it really was like pulling teeth, and then she got – well, you saw her stamp in.'

'So what to do?' Tor hissed back. 'It'll be so awful if nobody speaks over Christmas.'

'That's unlikely,' said Rose in her more normal voice. 'Here, pass me the flannel, Tor. Fred's got cradle cap. If you put that towel on your knee, I'll pass him to you. Careful, he's slippery . . . Wheeee!'

The dripping baby was held up in the air and passed from friend to friend, landing up on Tor's knee.

'You are a *burra* baby,' Tor told him, kissing his toes, 'and a fine horseman.' She clicked her tongue and bounced him up and down on her lap. 'This is the way the ladies ride, clip-clop, clip-clop, clip-clop.' When she bent down to kiss him again, he shot a jet of urine into her eye.

And suddenly they were in hysterics, doubled up and shrieking breathlessly, aged about six, seven at the most again. While they were laughing, Viva walked into the room and sat down on the cork-covered stool beside the bath.

'This sounds fun,' she said.

'It is,' Tor choked. She put a towel on Viva's lap and passed the baby to her. 'That child has a lethal aim. He just pee-peed into my eye.'

Viva smiled and played with his fingers for a while. She looked as if she wanted to laugh but was too worn out.

'Tor,' she said at last, 'how far is Frank's hospital from here?'

Tor beamed, she couldn't help herself. 'Oh, it's nothing, absolutely nothing – half an hour, maybe three-quarters at the most.'

She could see Rose behind Viva's back making 'keep calm' gestures with her hand.

'Well . . .' it was the first time Tor could ever remember Viva looking shy, '. . . Toby's been telling me about his last Christmas at the club, the dusty paper hats, the old wine, it sounded horrible – of course Frank may have other plans by now,' Viva ploughed on, 'but I don't think it would do any harm to go over and wish him a happy Christmas – even if he can't come.'

She drew Freddie deeper into her lap and wrapped her arms round him.

'What do you think?' She looked at Rose and then at Tor. She was trembling.

Tor walked over to Viva and kissed her gently on the head. 'I think it's a wonderful idea,' she said.

Chapter 53

They left for Lahore the following day. Tor at the wheel of Toby's ancient Talbot, Rose with the map on her knee beside her, Viva in the back seat.

The car was too noisy for Viva to join in the hum of conversation, a relief since the idea of arriving unannounced at Frank's suddenly seemed completely preposterous and she was half annoyed with the girls for talking her into it. The very thought of him less than an hour away from here – shaving or getting dressed, seeing patients, drinking tea – made her mouth go dry with anticipation.

To distract herself, she thought about Toby and his birds. He'd talked about them at supper the night before. At first she'd found Toby reassuringly kind, but rather too garrulous, the kind of man who, if he was a woman, you might say burbled prettily, but now he'd relaxed with her she'd discovered his dry sense of humour, and that his conversation was studded with gems. For the past few weeks, he'd been studying the migratory birds, the Arctic terns and some garganey ducks who, like the Fishing Fleet, came to India for the winter months. He'd told her how orphaned birds would sometimes accept the most pathetic substitutes for their mothers – a pullover, a hot-water bottle, an armpit or even a paper aeroplane – anything rather than nothing, but preferably something that moved.

With her head resting against the back seat, she decided that as a mother substitute William had more of the paper aeroplane than the hot-water bottle about him. He'd appeared in her life during her first bewildered weeks in London when she'd been lonely and desperate for any kind of companionship. He said he was a good friend of her parents; and that he would take great pleasure in taking her to a production of *Turandot* in Covent Garden. In the restaurants he took her to, she'd waited hungrily for stories about her parents, about Josie, but the feeling had grown that their names were a kind of taboo.

And William hadn't turned out to be a storytelling kind of man anyway: he liked facts, certainties. He'd given her lots of advice about how to manage her money, where to live, the kind of people best avoided. And when, finally, he'd taken her into his bed his love-making had felt like a sleight of hand, something that both of them were trying to pretend was not happening, which had left her feeling empty and confused. He'd never been really curious about her either, except as a kind of project, a puzzle that he could solve.

How different Frank was. She could see this now. That night at Ooty, he'd taken her like a man, with no apologies or wincing smiles, no sense that this was anything but natural, but what had really thrown her was the discovery of how interested in her he had been, and this had not been her experience with most men to date. Frank seemed to want to understand her as a separate human being. So that was frightening – in fact, everything she'd been running away from for years – but amazing, too.

Viva glanced at her reflection in the car window. So now she was about to humiliate herself in front of him, for he was also a handsome and impatient man who was used to women liking him and she'd treated him dishonestly, shabbily. He'd probably made other arrangements for himself by now.

A wave of nausea swept over her. *You think too much*, she told herself, staring out of the window.

The day had perked up a little. A pale sun was shining on land, which from the distance looked like an overcooked omelette. She watched two vultures swooping and diving in a long wavering line, then foraging inside the remains of what looked like a goat's carcass. How hard life looked from here.

Now they were passing an old man and woman toiling along the road, almost obliterated by dust. Stone figures from a prehistoric age. Both barefoot, him leading a donkey, she carrying firewood on her head. Their car puttered by; the woman put her wood down beside a hovel the size of a coal-hole and stared at them.

In the front seat Viva and Rose were arguing about double de-clutching.

'No, Rose. Wrong,' Tor said, roaring up the engine and making the car leap forwards. 'This is how you do it. Foot down, foot up, foot down, forwards.'

'It's a car, Tor, not a pogo stick,' said Rose, rolling her eyes in the mirror, 'but suit yourself.'

'Viva,' Tor flung over her shoulder, 'attention, please. When we get to Lahore, do you want us to stay with you or shove off? Moral support and all that.'

'No,' said Viva quickly. 'Don't stay.' She couldn't bear the thought of anyone watching this debacle. 'Come and fetch me at four o'clock; that should be plenty of time. I'll just walk around if he isn't there,' she added as if, after all, this was nothing more than a sightseeing trip. 'It'll be fun. And of course, it's quite likely he's had lot of invitations for Christmas by now,' she said. 'But at least we'll have asked him.'

She saw Tor glance at Rose, and then shake her head very slightly. She watched Rose give a soft sigh.

They'd reached the outskirts of Lahore, a flat city dominated by one high hill. Tor stopped the car and consulted the careful maps Toby had drawn for them. She could see now the Shish Mahal, the Palace of Mirrors, against the skyline, which meant that now, according to Tor's calculations, they were a few miles away from the hospital.

It took half an hour and lots of frantic hootings on Tor's behalf to force their way through the narrow teeming streets, and then all of a sudden they were clear of the bazaar area and lurching up the drive towards a grandly dilapidated mongrel of a building with Mughal arches and vast shuttered windows, and a row of dusty-looking cactus plants leading up to its steps.

'This is it.' Tor's foot pressed the brake. 'We're here: St Patrick's Hospital, home of Frank. Now are you quite sure, Viva, you don't want us to stay?'

The two of them gazed at her anxiously.

'Absolutely certain,' she said, even though her heart was jumping in her chest. 'You see, it really is all right either way.'

'Of course it is,' Rose said evenly. 'We know that.'

Tor turned round and planted a fervent kiss on top of Viva's hair. 'It's just a lark,' she said. 'But good luck anyway.'

While the girls were staring in the direction of the hospital, Viva sneaked a mirror out of her handbag. Her face looked pale and startled. She drew the mirror closer to her eye and peered at it closely: the faint crosses where the stitches had been removed were fading but you could still see the bruises. But surely in the right light, she tilted her face, you would hardly notice them.

When she looked up, Tor was smiling at her. 'You'll do for most known purposes,' she said.

Viva opened the car door and put one foot on the ground. 'Well, here we go,' she said. 'This should be character-forming.'

'Yes,' said Rose obediently. 'That's an awfully good way of putting it.'

'It doesn't matter,' Viva longed to add, 'I'm perfectly fine, I enjoy my life. I can happily live without this,' but they'd disappeared in a cloud of dust, leaving her alone.

Inside the hospital, a uniformed man with an enormous waxed moustache was sitting at a desk cordoned off by a length of rope. Her shoes clicked down the marble floor towards him. When she stood in front of his desk, he stopped writing in his appointment book and looked at her.

'How may I assist madam? I am supervisor here.'

'I'm looking for a Dr Frank Steadman,' she told him, but he was shaking his head before her words were out.

Weary with the weight of his responsibilities, he consulted the book. 'No one here hails by that name,' he told her and then, just for good measure, rubber-stamped an empty page. 'You must go somewhere else – maybe St Edward's: British peoples are there.'

She should have given herself more time – everything in India always took longer than you expected it to.

'I know he works here,' she said. 'He's been studying blackwater fever.'

'Wait here, please,' he said. 'I will look.' He led her into a dark, muggy room crowded with patients; as she walked in, all of them stopped talking and stared at her.

When her eyes had grown accustomed to the gloom, she saw an old man sitting on the bench opposite her. He was fighting for breath, an expression of pure agony on his face; a family maybe – a wife, two sons and a daughter – sat patiently on either side of him. They'd brought enough equipment with them for a camping trip, cooking pots and rolled-up mattresses.

They kept their eyes steadily on her as she sat down. *Please stop staring at me*, she wanted to shout. She was so het up and in no mood to be a sideshow.

The supervisor came back a few moments later. He took off his

398

glasses, looked at her and sighed heavily. He wanted the entire room to understand what a nuisance she was.

'There is no Dr Frank Steadman here, he has bifurcated elsewhere.' He flapped a hand over his shoulder.

'Look here.' Viva stood up and looked him straight in the eye. 'I'm not here because I want treatment, if that's what you think.' She broke into Hindi. 'Dr Frank is a friend of mine.'

'Oh, oh.' His face was a sudden ballet of smiles and dimples. 'A silly misunderstanding, sorry for mistake, memsahib. Please sign here, please.'

He produced a form, thudded it with stamps, shot out an order to a boy, who had appeared at her side. 'Take Madam Memsahib to Dr Steadman's room,' he said. 'Quick sticks.'

Walking down the gloomy corridor behind the boy, she caught a whiff of fried food and Jeyes Fluid and her stomach turned. On either side of her, she saw the silhouettes of patients lying in beds arranged against prison-like windows. The visitors and relatives who clustered around the beds of the sick and dying seemed completely at home here as if this place were another room in their house. Some lay on the narrow beds beside the patients; others squatted on the floor cooking meals on small Primus stoves; one woman was changing her husband's shirt.

The boy stopped to chat with a skeletal figure lying on the floor; Viva looked into the eyes of a woman, his wife, she assumed, who sat cross-legged on the floor preparing a pot of dhal for him. When the woman looked up, she surprised her with a radiant, almost intimate smile, as if to say, 'We're all in this together'.

'Careful, memsahib,' the boy said when they were halfway down the corridor. A stretcher passed them: an old man, wailing and wrapped in dirty bandages. When he leant on his elbow and vomited a trail of green slime, she felt her own mouth fill with water. How could Frank stand this?

'Here.' The boy opened a door at the end of the corridor, which opened into a dusty quadrangle. A line of grey bandages hung on a washing line. 'Mrs,' he pointed towards a small white house with peeling stucco, 'Dr Steadman is there.'

She dropped some coins into his open hand and, when he was gone, stood outside the door.

'Frank.' She knocked gently. 'Frank, it's me. Can I please come in?'

The door opened; he stood there half asleep, butterscotch-coloured hair sticking up like a child's. He blinked a few times. He was wearing blue striped pyjamas; his feet were bare.

'Viva?' He was scowling at her. 'What are you doing here?'

There was a rustling in the shadows, the crack of a branch. The boy was staring at them both, fascinated. When Frank shouted, the boy sped off into the shadows, leaving them alone.

'You'd better come in,' he said coldly. 'You can't stand there.'

When he'd closed the door behind them, he looked at her and said, 'You've hurt yourself.'

Her hand shot up. 'It's just a bruise,' she said.

'So why are you here?'

She forced herself to stand tall. 'I was hoping we could talk for a bit.'

'I'd like to get dressed first.'

He put a pair of trousers over his pyjamas; she looked away.

His room was anonymous, an exile's room. The wardrobe behind his head had two large suitcases on top of it covered in P&O labels.

She remembered him carrying them the first time she'd clapped eyes on him. How he'd walked up the gangplank towards the *Kaisar* – the cocky walk, that devastating smile, quite irritatingly sure (or so she'd thought at the time) that scores of lonely women on board would fall at his feet. No outward clues of a man in mourning and desperate for his own new start, and she, who knew so much about disguises, had taken him at face value.

The sight of his suitcases gave her a moment of bleak comfort. He was a travelling man; he'd be gone soon. This would pass.

He lit a lamp, pushed a chair towards her.

'Why are you here?' he said in the same flat voice.

She took another deep breath. Now he was sitting opposite her and she could see his face properly: his skin, his hair, his full mouth. She felt such a wave of emotion she was almost in tears before she began.

'Why are there bars on your windows?' she asked.

'There are robbers here,' he said.

She took another deep shuddering breath, shocked she'd lost control of things so early.

'Would a glass of water be out of the question?' she said at last.

'Of course,' he said in a polite voice. 'Some brandy in it?'

'Yes, please.'

He produced two glasses, swearing softly when he spilled some on his desk.

'What's wrong with your eye?' he said when he sat down.

For one brief moment she considered pretending that this had been the sole reason and purpose for her visit. By appealing to his professional pride, some bridges could be mended and he need never know why she'd come.

'I had a fall,' she said. 'In Bombay, in the market, I hit my head on the kerb. I'm much better now.'

He leaned towards her. He ran his finger along the length of her eyebrow, and looked at her.

'Daisy told me you were abducted,' he said.

'She did?' She could feel herself burning with shame.

'She was petrified,' he said. 'She thought you were dead and that's why she contacted me.' When he looked up, his face was full of a quiet, confused pain. 'You could easily have died.'

A pale dirty-yellow light was coming into the room through the barred windows. From a distance she heard the rumble of trolley wheels, the splash of water.

'I sent two letters to the home, and I didn't hear from you or from Daisy for that matter. After that, I didn't want to know. Look,' he said angrily, raising his palms like a shield against her, 'I've stopped thinking like that. I don't want to any more. I don't even know why you're here.'

She heard herself babbling. 'I didn't get the letters, I swear. They were all intercepted; everything's such a mess there now. The home is in a shambles – Daisy's been told to close the whole thing down, and it turned out, it turned out,' and suddenly to her disgust her cheeks were wet with tears, 'that half the children hated being there anyway.'

He said nothing for a while, and then, 'Did you finish the book?'

'No,' she said. 'Most of the typed pages were destroyed. Oh, I've got the notebooks, but I don't think I could do it again. So there we are. I'm sorry if I gave you a shock.'

She blew out air as if someone had punched her very hard in the stomach.

It was the first time she'd told anyone about the book; most of the manuscript pages had been either torn or defaced while she was at Azim's. They'd been waiting for her in her cupboard when she returned. She'd pretended with Toby that night; it was too painful to talk about it.

A terrible silence fell between them.

'I'm staying at Tor's house near Amritsar,' she said at last. 'I don't know how much of this you know, but Tor got married, to a man called Toby. Rose is there with her new baby. They asked me to persuade you to come for Christmas.'

'I know,' he said. 'Tor was the one who told me you were all right.' The muscle in his cheek had started to work again. 'She's already asked me; I've said no.'

'Where will you go?'

'I'm not sure.'

She felt a crushing sadness all over again. *I've lost him*, she thought, *and it's all my fault.*

'I don't blame you,' she said.

'I couldn't bear the thought of it. So!' He tried to smile, then looked at his watch as though he couldn't wait for her to leave.

There was so much pain in the room, such a weight of things that could not be said, that she stood up and wrapped her arms round herself.

'Is there anything I could say that might help you change your mind?' she said. 'There's still time.'

'No,' he said. 'I don't think there is. You see, I don't like people who pretend.'

Viva felt fear under her ribs. 'I wasn't pretending.'

'Ah, well, all better now,' he said drily.

'All right. Look,' she was almost shouting, 'I'm sorry. Does that make you feel any better?'

'No,' he said so sadly she knew he wasn't trying to be unkind. 'Funnily enough, it doesn't.'

She took his hand. 'Look, I *was* dishonest about Ooty. It frightened me.'

'What?' He shook his head.

'Can't you understand?'

'No.'

When she looked up, she noticed he'd grown thinner in the past few months. There were the beginnings of lines around his mouth. *I've done this to him*, she thought. *I've made him look older and more wary.*

Outside the hut, water was being splashed on hard ground. A dog was barking. When she looked at him she knew that if she didn't make a stand now, it would soon be too late.

'Please come for Christmas, Frank,' she said. 'I can't say everything to you all at once.'

He got up and rested his head on the bars of the windows.

'No,' he said. 'I can't change everything on a whim again. I have patients here, things to do.'

She'd passed on her hurt to him. She saw it in the way he held himself, by the look in his eyes. She'd never seen it quite so clearly before.

'Frank,' she took a deep breath and decided to jump, 'I'm not using any of this as an excuse, I couldn't, that would be disgusting of me, but do you remember on the ship when I told you my family had died in a car crash? That's not true. They all died separately.' She gripped the arms of the chair to stop herself shaking.

'My sister died of a burst appendix. If we'd been closer to a hospital she would have been all right. She was thirteen months older than me, almost like a twin.'

He looked at her sadly for a long time and then said, 'I know what that feels like. Don't you remember we did talk on the ship?'

'I know.'

She saw how his face had turned pale even thinking about it.

'Viva,' there was an edge of anger in his voice again, 'you should have told me. I would have understood.'

'I couldn't.'

'I don't think you can have any idea how closed off you can be. It's like a moat appears around you. But go on, your father.' He was listening intently. 'Tell me now.'

She took another deep breath. 'My father was killed shortly after; he was found with his throat slit on a railway track near Cawnpore with seven of the men he was working with. They think bandits killed him.'

'Oh God. What an awful thing.'

'It was. The worst thing possible. I hardly ever saw him, he was obsessed with his work, but I loved him so much. He was always in my life. He was a brilliant man and he tried so hard to be a good father to me.' She looked at him wildly. 'The awful thing is, I can't properly remember now what he sounded like, or what he looked like. If Josie hadn't died we could have reminded each other, but the memories are all fading. I hate that.'

'But what about your mother?'

'No, no, she died a year later.' She squeezed her eyes shut.

'Someone said of a broken heart – is that really a medical possibility?' She tried to smile but he didn't smile back. 'And anyway, we were never really close,' she continued. 'And I can't really remember why – perhaps it was something simple – she might have preferred my sister.

'Shortly after my father's death, she took me down to the railway station in Simla and put me on a train back to my boarding school in England. I don't know why she didn't want me with her. I never saw her again.'

'You should have said this before.'

'I couldn't.'

'Why not?'

She felt exhausted. 'I don't know – partly it's because I can't bear people feeling sorry for me.'

'Did you think I made love to you at Ooty because I felt sorry for you?'

'No.' She could hardly speak. So many things were going through her head, pain and tenderness, fury at her mother for sending her away.

When she looked up at him he had turned away again.

'Look,' she said, 'please come for Christmas. We all want you to come.'

He finished his brandy.

'No,' he said. 'I'm glad you felt you could tell me, but I can't.'

They sat in silence for a while.

'Look,' he said at last, 'when you left, I had to rethink everything. Even this.' He pointed angrily towards her eye. 'You don't trust a living soul, do you? And it's just so wearing.'

'I—' She started to speak but he put his hand over her mouth then took it away again as if she was on fire.

'Don't say anything,' he said. 'Let me finish. What happened that night at Ooty didn't surprise me. I knew it would happen and I thought you knew it, but afterwards you made me feel, you made me feel . . .' his voice broke, '. . . like a rapist when I was already so in love with you.'

'No, no, no, no,' she said. 'It wasn't like that.'

He pulled her towards him, then pushed her away.

'You've had months to get in touch with me, even if you didn't get my letters. At first I waited, and then I thought, I'm going to be slowly murdered by her if I go on like this.'

She took his face in her hands and then stopped. Outside their window, she could see Tor and Rose being led into the quadrangle.

'This is hopeless,' she said. Any minute now, Tor and Rose would burst into the room, everything would change again. 'Listen,' she said quickly, hearing the crunch of their feet on the gravel, 'I've just decided. Before Christmas, I'm going up north to Simla. It's where my parents are buried. I've got a letter from an old girl there. A trunk I was supposed to collect years ago. Once I've faced that, maybe . . .'

He was about to answer when the door flew open.

'Frank!' Tor flung her arms round him. Rose stood behind her with two parcels in her hand. 'Gosh, are you all right, Viva?' Tor said with her usual tact. 'You look as white as a sheet.'

Frank offered them a drink but seemed relieved when they said no. Rose, who'd read the atmosphere correctly, walked to the door and said that she could already see one or two stars had come out. It would be safer for them to drive home before dark.

Chapter 54

So this was it.

When Viva explained to Rose and Tor the following morning that she was going to take the train up to Simla to pick up her parents' trunk, she tried to keep her voice as calm and as even as possible, so that they didn't realise how frightened she was. When they offered to come too, she said no, she'd be back in time for Christmas and it was better they stayed put.

When really the whole trip felt like a child's dare: a breathless dash into the monster's cave and then out again. *Make it quick and painless*, she'd told herself, *don't make a meal of it.*

Now she was sitting in the window seat of the *Himalayan Queen*, the train that her father had helped to build and maintain on its circuitous route up through the Himalayan foothills, through semi-tropical vegetation and towards the towering silvery snowline of the mountains. As the funny little toy-like train worked its way through tunnel after tunnel, in and out of bright sunshine and shadowy rocks, she tried to stay calm and at one remove. Home was only a word. It needn't mean anything if you didn't want it to.

But even sitting here hurt: this train had been her father's passion, his joy. (A passion shared, she dimly remembered, by a Colonel somebody-or-other, who had shot himself through the head when two sections of the track had not joined up.)

Today it was packed. An elderly woman sat beside her whose calloused feet didn't touch the ground. She was clutching a variety of stained parcels on her lap. On the seat opposite, so close to her that their knees were almost touching, was a young couple who looked innocently happy. Newlyweds maybe. The girl sat radiant and shy in a brand-new cheap pink sari; the skinny young husband darted fervent looks at her. He could not believe his luck.

On Viva's lap was a book of poems by Tagore, randomly selected from Toby's shelves – since her abduction, her concentration had been poor.

Her feet were resting on her mother's old suitcase. She was fond of this scruffy old thing with its thinning straps and faded labels, but the stitching was worn at the seams – she'd have to replace it soon. Inside it, she'd packed the keys to the trunk, a change of clothes and Mabel Waghorn's address: 'I'm in the street behind the Chinese shoe shop,' she'd written in quavery old-lady writing. 'Close to the Lower Bazaar – you can't miss me.'

Of course, it was perfectly possible, Viva thought, resting her head on the train's window, that Mrs Waghorn had died since she wrote that letter. She'd met her once or twice as a child; her memory was of a tallish, imposing woman, someone much older than her mother.

If she was dead, she wouldn't have to go through with this. The relief she felt at this shocked her, but it felt important not to build her hopes up, although hope did not describe the mounting panic she felt at finally being on the train.

The train left another nondescript station. She put down her book and looked out of the window at houses made of cardboard, twigs, mud, old bits of wood. *I'll huff and I'll puff and I'll blow your house down.* Not much huffing or puffing needed there. They chugged past a signal box where a group of men huddled in blankets sat gazing at her. Three filthy-looking children appeared at her window. Barefoot and with running noses, they waved ecstatically at the train.

She was nothing special, she thought, waving back at them. Home was a luxury half the world did without. During the first few years of her childhood, when her father had been most in demand as a railway engineer, it had never even occurred to her to want a permanent place that you could call home. It was the happiest time of her life. All of them – Viva, Josie and her mother – moved on together like a gypsy caravan with her father every few months. Some of the places – Landi Kotal, Lucknow, Bangalore, Chittagong, Benares – she vaguely remembered; others had dissolved into a misty past that sometimes played tricks on her. On her way to Ooty, for instance, she'd made an ass of herself when she'd told Tor she recognised a little railway station – the faded blue windows, the row of red buckets – only to find exactly the same red buckets and blue windows at the next station and the next.

The train had begun its climb through dense green trees towards the foothills of the Himalayas. Several seats behind her, a booming

English voice was explaining to someone – probably his wife – that the track was only two foot six inches wide, and the whole thing a miracle of engineering and that they'd shortly be passing through one hundred and two tunnels blasted through the rocks. '*One hundred and two!* Good Lord,' a bored, affected voice exclaimed. 'What a thing.'

And suddenly she felt a proud daughter's urge to boast, to say on his behalf, 'My father helped to build this. He was one of the best railway engineers in India and it was something.'

But their voices had a bubbling distant sound now, drowned by the train's roar as it passed through a tunnel and into the light again.

How she'd loved this travelling as a child, felt sorry for children who didn't constantly have new houses to explore, new trees to climb, new animals, instant friends. She was a child of the Empire, she could see that now.

Another thought came with the force of a blow. Home was where they were, Daddy, Mummy and Josie, and she'd been running ever since.

Daddy, Mummy, Josie – such a long time since she'd dared to say all their names together. She worked it out on her fingers: she was eight, maybe nine, when she'd sat on this train with them for the last time. How strange to have got this old without them. Her mother had often packed a special picnic for trips like these: lemonade, buns, cut-and-come-again cake, sandwiches. On their last ever journey together, Josie sat next to her mother and Viva sat opposite them in a patch of sunlight next to her father. She felt again the sun on her hair, her joy at being beside him. This slender, reserved man with his gentle hands and clever face had never told her he loved her, that wasn't his way, but he did and she knew it, always; it was like moving inside an invisible magnetic field.

They'd wanted a boy but when he hadn't come, she'd stepped in without even thinking about it. She was the one who most liked to hear him talk about the things that excited him: steam engines; the point at which a horse took the strain when it was pulling a cart; the idea that the steam that came out of your kettle was an energetic dance of molecules. 'They'd be flying around like billiard balls, if you could see them,' he'd once told her.

He was there again. As her eyes wandered over the dusty villages, the towns, the parched places in between, she wanted him back with a savagery she hadn't felt for years. To talk to him again about this railway for instance. At home while he was helping to work out the complex problems of maintaining it, he would pull a large wooden box, labelled 'The Queen', out of a cupboard. He'd pour the contents on to the grass matting in his study: miniature plaster of Paris bridges, escarpments, trees, papier-mâché boulders. How cleverly he'd made what was life to him seem like a game to her. And what a hopeless task this ambitious route must have felt at times, with mountains this steep, those huge rocks to blast through.

Viva sighed so vigorously she had to apologise to the lady beside her. Why do this when it hurt so much? Apart from Frank, who still had no proper understanding of what it meant, who would give a damn if she got out at the next station, turned round and went back to Amritsar? All traces of home could be disposed of by throwing Mabel Waghorn's letter and the keys to the trunk out of the window.

The train chugged on relentlessly. At Kalka, a tiny little railway station clinging to the side of a cliff, a man with a basket of food leapt into the carriage, then ran through it as if his trousers were on fire shouting, 'Water, fruity cake, 'freshment,' but she couldn't eat, didn't want to.

She watched the young man opposite her jump from the train, dash down the platform, and buy plates of dhal from a kiosk. His young wife sat rigidly to attention, her eyes trained on him like a pistol.

In the end, it was simple, Viva thought, seeing her relief when he came back.

Home was knowing you were at the centre of someone else's world. She'd lost that security when her parents died. Nobody had been actively unkind to her after they'd gone – she wasn't beaten or sent to the workhouse, no need for sobbing violins – what had changed was that she'd begun to feel – what was that phrase? – surplus to requirements.

In relatives' homes, she'd slept in the bedrooms of grown-up children; their dusty dolls and wooden trains had stared at her from the tops of wardrobes. During the school holidays when she'd stayed at the convent, she'd been made to sleep in the sanatorium, which had made loneliness feel like a special kind of irritating illness. The relief of finally being old enough to make her own arrangements and move into that first tiny bedsit in Nevern Square had been intoxicating. She was finally and properly alone and didn't have to feel grateful to anybody.

*

In the same half-dream, she thought of Josie. It was horrible the way her memories of her were beginning to fade like a piece of music you play and play until it loses its power. Black curls, blue eyes, long legs leaping like a mountain goat from rock to rock. 'Hurry up, slow coach, jump!'

Her best memory was camping with Josie in the foothills of the Himalayas; the whole family had ridden with pack ponies and supplies and camp beds and servants following behind. They'd slept in tents under diamond-bright stars listening to the sounds of their ponies munching outside their tents, the roar of the mountain streams, their parents sitting beside a camp fire taking it in turns to tell stories. Her father's favourite made-up story was of Puffington Blowfly: the boy who was strong and brave, and never ever moaned about anything.

Later, they moved to Kashmir; the exact name of the town had gone, just as so many houses, schools, friends had. She did remember a bridge somewhere had collapsed and needed their father's attention. They'd stopped off for a holiday at a lake in Srinagar, where they hired a houseboat. She and Josie (she remembered this clearly) had been excited by their gay little craft with its chintz curtains and paper lanterns on the deck and their own miniature bedroom with its beautifully painted bunks inside. But Viva remembered crying too – something about a dog they'd had to leave behind – a dog she'd loved with a child's reckless single-mindedness and would never see again. To cheer her up, Mother said they could sleep on deck for a treat. She and Josie had sat under the same mosquito net watching the sun bloody the whole sky and finally ooze like a giant melted toffee into the lake.

Was that the night when Josie, who had a mathematical brain like her father's, had calculated the unimaginable catastrophe of one of them dying young and leaving the other on their own?

'It's one in four in India,' Josie had said. 'We may not make old bones,' she'd warned her.

Viva said, 'If you die, I'll die with you.'

She hadn't. Another shock that felt like betrayal – she could live without them.

After Josie's appendix burst, and they'd taken her to the cantonment graveyard, Viva had been obsessed for months and months with the thought of her turning into a skeleton there. She'd seen freshly dug earth around all the other little gravestones; she'd pestered her mother for details of how the other children had died. There was a small boy, she recalled, who had toddled over to a snake and tried to shake hands with it; a baby who died of typhoid the day after Josie.

Did she ask too many questions? She must have. Or maybe her mother couldn't bear her for looking like Josie but not being her, or because she'd refused stubbornly for a while to accept that Josie had gone. She had said so many prayers. She'd put Josie's pyjamas on the bed at night, put a biscuit under the sheets so when she came back she wouldn't be hungry, gone to the temple and put rice and flowers out before the gods, before she'd given up believing all together.

Shortly after, she'd been sent home to the convent. Her memory was that she'd gone alone – but surely not? She was ten years old. There must have been a companion. Why had her mother not come? Did she kiss her goodbye? These were the details that silted up your mind and made you feel like a liar to yourself and to other people. Frank was right about that, but now she still felt angry with him for butting in; yes, butting was the right word for it, into something so terrible, so final.

Twenty miles or so away from the station she found herself weeping uncontrollably. She shouldn't have come, she knew it, *she knew it*. It took her a while to get back in control, to mop up the tears, to stifle the sobs by pretending she was having a coughing fit. And then she fell asleep, and when she woke, the woman opposite was tapping her on the arm. The train had reached the end of the line. She was back in Simla.

She stood for a moment in the spot where she'd stepped down from the train. She looked at the trees dusted with snow, at the thin horses covered in burlap sacks, waiting for passengers. The one place she would never forget.

Flakes of snow fell on her hair. She watched the Englishman, still gesticulating and instructing his wife, pull away in a taxi and drive up the hill.

In front of her, in the station forecourt, was a tonga driver, feet up and sipping chai. He rang a silver bell to get her attention.

'Are you waiting for your sahib?' he asked her.

'No,' she said, 'I'm by myself. I'd like to go here,' she handed him the piece of paper, 'and then on to the Cecil Hotel.'

Frowning, he looked at Mabel Waghorn's map, his face green with cold.

'Cecil Hotel good,' he said. 'This no good.' He handed the map back to her. 'Lower Bazaar – no English pipples live there.'

'I don't care,' she said. She lifted her own case into the carriage before he changed his mind. 'That's where I'm going. It's in the street behind the Chinese shoe shop,' she added, but he had already picked up the reins and was touching the horse's rump with his whip.

When they were halfway up, he turned to look at her and went into his tourist spiel.

'Monkeys.' He pointed towards some grey langurs shivering in a tree to the right of them. 'Very big tiger and lion in the woods around here.'

She sat in the back, numb with cold. 'Yes,' she said. 'I know.'

'Tomorrow, I take you for very special ride at a nice price.' When he dropped his reins to give her a sincere look, the horse clip-clopped on, stolid and reliable. It had heard it all before.

'No, thank you.' She hardly recognised her own voice.

They were passing through a busy street, where she saw mostly English people walking in front of charming, half-timbered houses. On a billboard, there was an advertisement posted for *The Fatal Nymph* at the Gaiety that weekend. In the gaps between the houses, she saw snow, mountains, forests, rocks.

The horse was straining against his harness now, his breath like smoke as they climbed a long curving hill covered in frosted pine and spruce. They'd reached a cobbled square that looked like some sort of tourist lookout. Cold-looking European children were being led about on thin ponies by parents or nannies. On the narrowest point of the bluff was a large brass telescope.

'I speak good English.' The guide put his reins in one hand and lit a bidi with the other. 'This side very nice east to the Bay of Bengal. That side,' he pointed with his cigarette, 'Arabian Ocean. Very nice too.'

She glanced down briefly, at the two rivers, forests, the mountains sprinkled with snow.

'I didn't ask to come here,' she told him, frightened and angry. 'Why did you bring me?'

'Nice, safe holiday place for memsahib,' he sulked.

'I'm not here for that.' She showed him the address again. 'Take me where I asked to go to.'

He shrugged and took her back down the steep road into the town again. From this angle the jumble of brightly painted houses and mock-Tudor dwellings clinging to the mountains looked precarious, as though one good breath of wind could blow them away. Down in the street, she could hear the murmurs of a few strollers walking around: a tall, well-dressed white woman in brown and white tweed with a fox fur round her neck, a few army officers, but she was surprised to see how quiet it was at midday.

They stopped at the next crossroads. A black cow with a brass bell round its neck was airily depositing dung on the street corner. Viva leant out of the carriage so she could see the shop signs: Empire Stores, Tailor Ram's, Military, Army, Civilian Uniforms, Himalaya Stores.

'Stop!' She'd seen the shoe shop with 'Ta-Tung and Co. Chinese shoe makers,' written on it. The window was crammed with brogues and beautiful riding boots, chukka boots, velvet slippers with little foxes sewn on their fronts. 'Made to measure,' said a sign propped up by a pair of wooden trees. 'Lasts for ever.'

She got out her map again.

'You can put me down here,' she told the driver as she held out her money. 'My friend lives in the street behind this shop.'

He muttered and shook his head as if she would shortly see the error of her ways.

She stood for a while in the street, trying to get her bearings. To the right of her was the smart European street, well swept, and with gay little tubs of flowers; below this and down a long flight of steep and winding stairs was the native quarter, a rabbit warren of small streets and tiny lamplit shops.

She walked down the first flight of stairs.

I've made a mistake, she thought, peering into a dingy hole in the wall where an old man sat staring out. Further down, she passed a wretched-looking wool shop with sacks covering the bright skeins of wool to protect them from the snow. She looked at her map again, fumbling because her hands were cold.

Mabel Waghorn had been, she was almost sure of this, a school-teacher, perhaps even a headmistress. The map must be wrong. The street was too shabby; it stank. Flustered, she sat down on the step and then she saw a house behind a row of ramshackle tin roofs, which might just be it.

Walking closer, she stopped in front of a two-storied tenement clinging to the side of the hill and stared at it. Surely not. The house had a fabulous view of the distant mountains, but its plastered façade had peeled off in chunks and its wrought-iron balconies bulged with buckets, clothes bags, bird cages and old bits of discarded machinery.

She drew closer, still not believing, but there it was: 'Number 12,' drawn in flaked green paint on a front door with a rusty grille set in, like a Carmelite's cell. To the right of the grille was a brass bell with a rope pull, underneath it a sign written in Mabel Waghorn's quavery writing: '*I am on the first floor*'. When she rang it, there was no answer.

On the second ring of the bell, a Chinese woman stepped out of a dim doorway next to her. Behind her, in the brownish-yellow light, a man in a vest was staring out at her.

'I'm looking for this lady.' She held out her piece of paper. 'Her name is Mrs Waghorn.'

The woman ran into the house with the piece of paper. A few seconds later, she heard a broom being banged against the ceiling.

'She sleep very much,' said the woman, frowning.

'Wait,' she said, closing the door behind her.

Viva waited for about five minutes, stamping her feet, for the afternoon had turned icily cold. The mountains, half hidden in skeins of mist, an eagle flying soundlessly above her head holding a scrap of bread in its beak, and in the perfect blankness of that moment she felt herself falling through time.

'Hello.' The old girl stepping out on to the verandah had a foggy expression in her eyes as though she'd just been woken from a deep sleep. She wore slippers without stockings, and when the breeze blew her tweed coat aside, Viva saw her nightdress. They looked at each other, Viva unwilling for a few seconds to believe that this frail-looking person was Mabel Waghorn. Somehow the larky surname had made her imagine a person with a tennis racket in her hand, a vigorous pair of calves and a good memory, who could tell her things she didn't know.

'Good God!' The old woman had moved to the edge of the verandah and was looking down. When one of her slippers came off, Viva saw an ancient foot like a purple claw stuck between the iron bars of the railings.

'Good Lord!' They stared at each other for a while.

'No!' The old woman jutted her jaw forward and stared at her intently.

'No! No! No!' She had to shout to avoid the catastrophe. 'My name is Viva – I'm her daughter.'

Viva saw Mrs Waghorn's rapid change of expression. She seemed to suddenly shut down. Maybe she felt cheated out of seeing an old friend again, or maybe just too old to deal with anything out of the ordinary.

She twisted her slipper around until it was free.

'I'm frightfully sorry,' she said, 'but have I asked you to come?'

The hem of her coat blew up, revealing bird-thin legs and sensible bloomers. Viva shivered.

'I should have written,' Viva apologised. 'You asked me ages ago.' And because the old girl was cupping a hand to her ear, she shouted, 'Do you mind if I come up? It won't take long; I'm sorry if I frightened you.'

Mrs Waghorn was still staring at her, as if she'd seen a ghost.

'Come up then,' she said after a long pause. 'I'll send Hari down.'

A few seconds later, Hari, a handsome smiling boy in a Kashmiri tunic, creaked open the front door and beckoned her inside. He took her suitcase and led her down a corridor that reeked of old cats.

'Follow me, please,' he said in an echo of his mistress's posh voice. 'Mrs Waghorn is upstairs in her study.'

The staircase they were ascending was lit with candles on sconces on the wall, like a medieval dungeon, she thought. When they reached the first landing she heard the yapping of a small dog, the scrape of a stick.

'Hari?' called a voice from behind the door. 'Is that her? I'm in here.'

Hari gave Viva a mischievous, conspiratorial look as if to say, 'You're in for a treat.' 'Go inside,' he said. 'She is waiting for you.'

The room seemed so dark when she first walked in that she thought Mrs Waghorn was a pile of clothes left on a chair. When her eyes adjusted, she saw the old lady sitting in front of a paraffin heater. At the end of her knee perched a tiny bat-like dog with tragic eyes.

'Come in,' she said. 'And sit down where I can see you.'

She pointed towards a sagging sofa piled high with papers at one end. The voice, though breathless, was authoritative.

They looked at each other for a few seconds.

Viva had made up her mind not to beat about the bush. 'I'm Alexander and Felicity Holloway's daughter. Do you remember me? You were kind enough to write to me ages ago about a trunk they left with you. I'm sorry I've taken so long to pick it up.'

She saw the same look of panic in the old girl's eyes as she had earlier. Her hands plucked at the collar of her little dog as if he could save her.

'If you're from the hospital, could you go?' she said. 'I'm perfectly all right, you know. I told you that before.'

Oh dear, thought Viva, not sure whether she was relieved or sorry. Gaga, or close to it – she must proceed with caution.

'I'm not from the hospital. I promise. My name is Viva Holloway, and ages and ages ago, you were kind enough to send one of the trunks that belonged to my parents to my boarding school in Wales. The other trunk you said you'd keep until I came back to India. This is the first time I've been back since then.'

'Now look here!' The old lady was glaring and pointing her finger. 'I'm *not* leaving. I have a perfect legal right to be here.'

Her dog dropped to the floor and came to sit down beside Viva, its tail firmly clamped between its legs.

'We've upset Brandy.'

'He's sweet.' Viva got down on her knees and patted him, hoping to calm things down. 'Is he a Chihuahua?'

'Yes,' the old woman told her proudly. 'Did you know they were bred in the Ming Dynasty for catching the king's mice? I've got tons of books on them somewhere if you're interested.'

Viva felt a brief bleak moment of hilarity. Maybe that's what she'd end up doing here, reading up about Chihuahuas in Simla, for this did not look promising.

'Could you do something for me?' The old woman was staring at her intently. 'We keep treats behind the cushion you're sitting on; could you give him one? He was so good this morning and now I've made him cross.'

She pointed to a bright red cushion with an embroidered bird on it. When Viva drew it aside, she tried not to flinch. There was something disgusting there: a small paw that looked as if it might have belonged to a cat or a rabbit. It had patches of fur and a few filaments of raw flesh still attached to it.

'There's a bone here,' she said, trying not to touch it.

'Yes, could you give it to me, please? A darling man at the market gives me these for nothing.'

Shuddering with revulsion, she handed the sweet-smelling paw – a rabbit, she was almost certain of it now – to Mrs Waghorn, who dropped it between Brandy's pin-like teeth. 'They really are the kindest people in the world, you know. I do think we treat them badly.'

Viva gazed into her watery eyes. 'I'm glad they treat you well,' she said.

Under different circumstances, she felt she would have enjoyed letting the old girl talk at length about her work as a teacher here, to have told her something in return about the home in Bombay, but at the moment it seemed beyond both of them.

'Are you cold?' Mrs Waghorn's pugnacious look was softening somewhat. 'If you are, you can turn the wick up on the paraffin stove, or give it a good kick. Actually, you could do me a favour. The wick needs trimming, there's a big pair of scissors near it.'

Viva knelt down on the floor, which felt gritty under her stockings. The little stove was guttering and popping, sending out acrid black fumes.

'I had one of these in London.' She lifted the glass hood and sliced the top off a crusted black wick, and then turned the small handle. 'They can be tricky. There you are.' When she lit it again, a circle of pink and yellow flames shone brightly. 'That should do it.'

'Oh, thank you, darling.' Mrs Waghorn's eyes were watering. 'Horrid smoke. How very kind. I'm sorry if I was rude to you earlier; they keep sending women from the club to get me, you see.'

Viva turned and faced her.

'Are you sure you don't remember me?' she said. 'I'm Felicity's daughter. My father was Alexander Holloway; he was a railway engineer. I must have been about eight or nine when we first met. I remember you – I was a little bit scared of you because you were a headmistress.'

'Yes, indeed. You're absolutely right. I was head for ages there.' Mention of the school seemed to perk the old lady up. 'My husband, Arthur, and I ran the whole show: forty boarders, thirty day pupils, Indians and English. It was called Wildhern School. It was a wonderful place. That's where I met Hari—' She broke off suddenly, folded her hands under her chin and looked at her long and hard. She scrunched up her eyes and thought again. 'Do you know, I don't

417

think I do remember you. I'm so sorry. There were so many children.'

'It doesn't matter,' said Viva. 'It's my fault. It really is.'

The poor old thing looked so upset and Viva knew that if she didn't keep a tight hold of herself she might start to cry again and that would be unbearable.

'You did try, you wrote. I should have come much earlier.'

'My memory's bad,' mumbled the old woman, 'but I do remember Felicity. A lovely woman. Can I tell you more about her when I'm not so tired?'

The little dog had started to dig behind one of the other cushions. It brought out a pink whalebone corset, various dusty kirby grips and then a brassiere. Viva stuffed them back behind the cushion, glad that the old girl hadn't seemed to notice.

'I'm afraid I've tired you,' Viva said. 'I could always come back tomorrow.'

The old woman glanced at her and then at a watch that she wore pinned to her dress. 'No,' she said. 'Stay and have tea; Hari will be here in a moment. Where's Hari gone?'

She began to cough, a painful rattling sound. Viva looked around her, at the sagging heaps of old newspapers and dusty gramophone records, the crusted ashtrays. At least the paraffin fumes weren't so strong now.

'Sorry, darling.' Mrs Waghorn stopped spluttering. She wiped her mouth with a large spotted handkerchief and gave her a charming smile. 'And this is such a treat. Such a pretty girl on a dull afternoon. Tell me, are you very keen on money?' She stopped and gazed at her so intently she might have been counting the pores on her face. 'Now I look at you,' she said at last, 'you don't look as much like Felicity as I thought you did, more like your father.'

Viva almost stopped breathing, but then the door opened, Hari appeared with a laden tea tray and Mrs Waghorn lost her train of thought. 'Scrummy!' she said. 'Put it down there.' She pointed towards the camel stool.

'I've just been telling this young person,' she explained to him, 'that I taught you at Wildhern. I couldn't exist without him now,' she said to Viva. 'He's one of nature's gentlemen.'

Hari put the palms of his hands together and bowed his head towards Mrs Waghorn.

'She is my teacher,' he told Viva. 'The teacher of my life.'

'Oh, what a lovely tea you've brought us.' Mrs Waghorn was looking excitedly at the jam sandwiches, two slices of fruit cake and a large, tarnished silver pot of tea and two bone-china cups. 'And well done you,' she said, 'for remembering the cake knife.'

'Sorry about this.' She poured tea with a shaky hand and handed the rattling cup to Viva. The milk had separated into globules of fat. 'I loathe buffalo milk,' she said. 'One simply yearns for a decent cup. Now tell me something,' she said when Hari had left the room and they were alone again. 'Where do you stand on the Indian question? But can I tell you something first.' She put down her own cup and again held up her index finger for special emphasis. 'You've met Hari now. You've seen what a fine person he is, good family and so forth. He was a very good student. One of our best ever, and the only proper employment he's managed to get since he left school is as a driver or as a servant – you see, his family have no money.' Mrs Waghorn's eyes had filled with tears. 'He assures me he does not mind, but I am deeply offended by that, are you?'

'Of course I am,' Viva replied. 'It's wrong.'

'Well, good. Agreed on that one thing then. You can stay for supper if you like. I tried to speak to a woman at the club about this ages ago. Frightful woman. They think I've gone jungli, and now they've started sending people round from the hospital.'

Mrs Waghorn was starting to look agitated again.

'I'm nothing to do with them,' said Viva gently. 'I promise you, and thank you for asking me to supper, but not tonight. I'm going to go back to my hotel to have a bath and an early night.'

Through the window above Mabel Waghorn's head she could see the sky had turned into a purplish grey and sleet was turning into a flurry of snow.

On an impulse, she leant over and briefly held the old lady's hand. It was so light, like a leaf, and smelled, faintly, of cigarette smoke.

'I would like to come back tomorrow morning if I could.'

The old lady looked at her.

'Don't come too early,' she warned. 'Hari and I read books in the morning.'

'I don't want to interfere with your routines.' When Viva stood up and put on her coat, the keys jangled in her pocket. 'But I don't have long in Simla, and I'd very much like to see my parents' trunk. That's why I'm here.' She watched the old lady's eyes cloud with confusion again.

'Oh my goodness, of course, of course. Heavens! Let me think.' She put down her cup and put her finger to her temple in such an obvious thinker's pose that Viva wondered if this forgetfulness wasn't strategic after all. 'I do hope I can find the bloody thing,' she said at last. 'Have I told you about the dreadful red ants last year?'

As though red ants could eat an entire trunk, a whole decade of memories, her parents' life.

'I'm spending the night at the Cecil.' Viva tried to keep her voice calm, rational. 'Would eleven tomorrow morning suit?'

No answer. The old lady's head had sunk into her chest, her eyelids had closed. When Viva looked up, Hari was standing at the door waiting to show her out.

Chapter 55

'You can kill people but you can't kill life,' Mrs Waghorn announced at ten past eleven the following morning, shortly after Viva turned up. She and Hari had, she said, been reading the Mahabharata, which they did almost every morning.

'Do you know it?' she asked Viva. 'It's full of the most wonderful treasures. Not *the* key to life,' Mrs Waghorn added, 'but certainly one of them.'

It undoubtedly seemed to have cheered her up. On this grey winter morning, the old girl had put on a bright orange housedress and a fine set of amber beads. She'd even dabbed a little circle of rouge on her cheeks.

'I'm much more on the ball today,' she told Viva, as she stumped ahead of her into the sitting room where there was a sprig of fresh bougainvillea on the camel stool. 'I talked far too much about myself yesterday. Today, I want to hear about you.'

Viva found the touch of the old lady's hand on her arm both calming and upsetting, she was feeling fragile after an exceptionally bad night's sleep in which she'd dreamt about the houseboat in Srinagar. Talika – older and fatter – was sharing the cabin with her. The lake outside had had huge waves on it, so rough they both kept falling on the floor and Talika was furious. 'Why is there never anywhere to put my clothes?' she'd shouted, her eyes and teeth flashing with rage. She'd thrown armfuls of saris and cholis on the floor and stamped muddy footprints over the delicate silks. Viva, full of a burning shame, had watched helplessly.

She'd tried to say sorry; Talika had touched her hair.

'It's all right, Mabap,' she'd used that tender Indian word again. You are my mother and my father. She'd kissed her, something an Indian girl would never do to a European, except in dreams.

*

'I must have shocked you yesterday,' Viva told Mrs Waghorn the next day. 'This was all done on the spur of the moment.'

'*On the spur of the moment.* Isn't that a marvellous expression? Is it Shakespeare?' The old girl cocked her head to one side like an attentive bird. 'Spurs hurt, draw blood, move things along. Do you really want to do this today?' Her eyes had gone very milky and round. 'It is the most awful mess down there.'

'Do what?'

'Oh gosh, did I forget to tell you?' Mrs Waghorn's voice faltered. 'We've found it. The trunk. Or at least Hari thinks it's the one. It has your mother's name on it.'

Viva felt her heart start to pound. 'Are you sure it's the right one? Have you opened it?'

'No. Of course we haven't. It's none of our business.'

'Where was it?'

'In the box room. I was so worried yesterday, and it did take Hari hours and hours – all the people in this house throw their rubbish there. But he's such a sweet boy he didn't complain. It's filthy, I'm afraid.'

'That's all right,' Viva said. She didn't know whether to feel sorry or glad.

'The box room floods in the monsoon. I haven't been down there for years.' The old lady was breathing jerkily.

'Please,' said Viva. 'I wouldn't blame you – you've been very kind.'

The old girl sat down and shuffled her slippers; she had gone inside herself again.

'If you don't mind,' she said after a silence, 'I shan't come down with you. Hari will take you and then you can stay for lunch if you want to. Hari's mother has brought in a chicken biriyani, it's very good.'

Viva's stomach knotted at the thought of it. 'I'd better see how long it takes,' she said. She heard the scratch of matches on a box, and saw Mrs Waghorn's eyes grow milky and distant again as she lit up one of her Craven A's.

'Of course,' she said. 'Good luck.'

As they stepped outside the house, she glanced up towards the sky where a flight of rooks were passing through a pearly sky. 'I think it will be cold again today,' she said. She was shivering and she didn't want him to know why.

Hari was explaining to her in his soft voice about the box room. It was awkward to get to, he said, stepping over a bicycle. They really should have one inside the house. He led her towards a broken path that went around the house.

'Only one or two of us have use of it,' he said, ushering her down a short flight of stairs, 'to protect people's things from the miscreant. Unfortunately though, a local chap has made a bit of shambles of it by putting hay and horse food there.'

She'd pictured a proper basement, somewhere secure, but a few seconds later Hari stopped and pointed towards a ramshackle shed, with several tiles missing from its roof that seemed to be loosely attached to the verandah at the back of the house. A dog crept out of the empty spaces underneath the house, its dugs almost touching the ground. When it started to bark, Hari picked up a stone and hurled it in its direction.

'That dog is a tremendous bore,' he said, as both of them splashed through the sloppy red mud. 'It belongs to the people next door. Sorry about this.' He looked down at her shoes and ankles, now rimmed with red clay.

The shed, though flimsy in appearance, had large black iron hinges, one of which was hanging off. Hari took a key from a chain that he wore round his waist and unlocked the door. The black gloom inside smelt like the bottom of a pond.

'One moment, please,' said Hari before he closed the door behind them. He put a match to an oil lamp he carried in his other hand. 'It's very dark in here, and there are plenty of furry friends.'

'What?' she said stupidly.

'Rats,' he said, 'from the horse food I am telling you about.'

She sneezed several times. When he lifted his lamp she saw in its yellow blur several collapsed bales of straw, held together with rotten string. Weak shafts of light shone through a hole in the roof, and when her eyes had adjusted to the light she saw, on top of the hay, some broken ladders and what looked like a bundle of clothes.

'Follow me, please.' Hari's lamp was moving past the hay bales and towards the back of the shed, where the ground felt slimy and unreliable underneath her feet. Now she saw some white shapes in the dark, furniture perhaps, and on top of them a jumble of old suitcases.

'Is all this theirs?' she said. 'I was told it was one trunk.'

'Please.' He pointed behind the suitcases. 'I have put.'

He waited for her to walk past a bundle of fishing rods, and some ancient tennis rackets in their presses. It took a while for her eyes to adjust again, but when she saw it, she heard herself gasp. The large battered trunk in front of her looked for that moment like a freshly dug-up coffin. It sat on a low deal table, covered in dirt and green mould. On top of it someone – probably Hari, to be kind, to give this moment some sense of ceremony – had laid a fresh marigold flower.

When Hari put his lamp down on top of it, she saw its wooden lid sweating and mossy, almost like a live thing.

Hari stood by her, polite, impassive. She took a deep breath.

'Well, here it is then,' she told him. 'It won't take me long to go through it.'

Oh, Mummy! Oh, Josie – I left it too long.

She could hear her breath whistling in her lungs. She hadn't expected to feel like a grave robber.

She took the keys out of her pocket. Some twigs and what appeared to be bird droppings protruded from the lock and when she tried the key, it jammed immediately. She pushed again but felt it catch on the rust and grit.

'I'll need your help, Hari,' she said. 'The lock's stuck.'

There was a faint silvery rustling in the darkness as he stepped forward.

'Rats are a damned nuisance,' he said to her pleasantly. 'Please, memsahib, hold the light and I will have a go.'

He tried the key left and right and then again more forcibly.

'Step back, memsahib, please,' he said at last. He took a knife out of a leather sheaf attached to his pocket and inserted it under the lid. With one foot braced on the wall he leant into the trunk. Both of them yelled as the lid flew open.

As she looked down on the bundle of old clothes, she was trying to keep her thoughts cynical and light-hearted. So there it was, after all this time: the famous old family trunk. Her very own albatross.

'I'm quite sure there's nothing here,' she told Hari breezily. 'I'll have a quick look through and then I'll be off.'

She wanted him to leave now, but he stood quietly beside her. She heard her own jagged breath as her fingers reached out and touched something damp. A slimy sweater, then slacks, a torn pair of cricket trousers, a paisley eiderdown with a scattering of mouse droppings in the seams. She pushed her hand deeper; the smell of damp and camphor and then something worse – a dead rat? – was almost overwhelming. She touched something hard and cold. It was a saddle bag – her father's, she guessed, although she didn't recognise it – stiff with mould. Inside was a rusted hoof pick, a small ball of string and a few tarnished coins. Underneath it was a Parcheesi board, sodden with damp and gnawed at the edges. When she picked it up it snapped uselessly in her hands.

Oh dear, oh dear, still trying hard not to think or mind. Too late! Too late!

Hari was starting to look worried.

'Could you leave me on my own for a while?' she said.

'Of course,' he said. He looked relieved. He must have known, or smelt, what this would look like. 'I shall leave the light with you and lock the door, so you are safe. When should I come back?'

'Half an hour will be fine, thank you, Hari,' she said. She felt an urge to say something more: to thank him for his grace, his reticence, the gentle concern she saw in his eyes, but the door had shut behind him and she could already hear the soft slap of his shoes going upstairs again.

Alone again in the dark, she fought against a choking feeling of panic. She'd taken so long she couldn't funk it now, but the sour decaying smells, the pointless emptiness of their clothes running through her hands was horrible. Jodhpurs with the buttons missing, a stained pith helmet, what had been a pretty blue brocade jacket except for the large yellow damp stain on its collar, Josie's nightdress, a stiff satin evening dress, a tin with a powder puff in it, a bundle of letters, too damp to be legible.

'All for the jumble,' she said out loud in a bright voice that didn't sound like her own.

Her fingers closed around something soft and pliable wrapped up like a mummy in what looked like a tea towel. A softness she recognised even before she'd unwound the cloth and seen Susie, Josie's favourite doll. Josie had loved this scruffy thing with its tightly packed sausagey legs and gingham frock. Viva had been jealous of it: Josie had jabbered away at it constantly, smacking it and wheeling it around in its carriage, tucking it into bed at night under a tiny little mosquito net. It was a better younger sister than she was.

Josie had left Susie on the train once, the whole family waiting on a boiling platform while a servant went back to look for it. There had been a big row about it between her father and her mother.

Now there were rat-like bite marks on its arms; most of the kapok had been removed up to its knees. When she squeezed it, it fell apart in a foul puff of air. *Horrible.* She felt saliva come into her mouth. Susie was lying in Josie's arms on the night she died; she remembered the screams coming from her bedroom, wave upon wave of them. The sounds of vomiting, shouts of 'Do something, Mummy! Help me.' All night, feet running up and downstairs, as it dawned on everybody this wasn't just another bout of gippy tummy. Viva's own ayah had tried to stop her hearing by putting her hands over her ears, but Viva had fought free and crouched in the cupboard by Josie's door. And some time after midnight, she'd heard the screams go weak, then tiny rabbit-like squeaks and then nothing. *For Christ's sake, somebody do something!* Her mother's shriek had torn through the dark like a wild animal, a raw and bloody sound. And then the door slammed shut.

Darling, darling Josie. The doll collapsed underneath her fingers leaving a trail of grey dust down her blouse. *My sister. My only sister.*

She put the doll aside. There must be something here she wanted, could keep and make sense of. She dug down a little deeper, finding a few old letters, mostly bills, and a small household account book. Her eyes strained to read the pencil markings in her mother's neat hand: Daggett and Ramsdell cold cream 2/6, shaving cream 3/6, two pairs of wool stockings 6/. In another tin with a picture of Queen Victoria on it was a pink bridge with two false teeth set in it. Her father's. She crammed them into her pocket. The anaesthetic was wearing off; she was panting with distress. Her father's teeth. Was that it?

A clump of large red fungi had grown through a hole in the bottom of the trunk. The last layer of clothes – a great coat, a satin evening dress, wet as leaf mould and completely useless. Hari would have to burn the lot.

This was it. An insult, a joke, a great big bloody waste of time. She closed the lid again, folded her arms and leant her head on the top of the trunk while voices shouted lots of useless advice at her. Nothing had happened, that was what she was trying to tell herself. *Nothing had happened.* And even if it had, for she had just heard her own wounded cries, what on earth had she expected after all this time? Some great transfiguring moment? Parcels filled with damp but useable bank notes? Parental letters from beyond the grave full of stirring advice about how to live life from now on? So much energy squandered on a heap of rotten clothes – it was almost funny when you thought about it.

A pair of her mother's snakeskin shoes had fallen beside the trunk. She picked one up, held it against her face. One of her father's trains had lodged in its toe. A wooden train with the words '*Himalayan Queen*' painted carefully in his hand along its side. She crammed the train inside her pocket alongside his teeth.

'Viva? Miss Holloway.' She almost jumped out of her skin. 'Are you there?' Mrs Waghorn was standing at the door with a hurricane lamp in her hand, a wraith-like figure in the gloom. 'Are you all right?'

Viva heard her sneeze as she shuffled along between the bales of old hay.

'Yes, thank you,' she said coldly. She hated being seen like this. They stood looking at each other.

'Please don't cry.' She felt the old lady's papery hand. 'It's my fault and I've found something I meant to show you before.'

She held something out towards Viva.

'I can't see it,' Viva said sharply. 'It's too dark. That floor's slippery, you know; you could hurt yourself.'

'We'll have a look at it later then.' The voice that came back through the gloom had taken no offence. 'Come upstairs and have a drink with me. I think you've done enough for one morning.'

'I don't know how much to tell you,' Mrs Waghorn said when they were back in her chaotic sitting room again. Mrs W. had her back to the window; Viva was sitting on the chair opposite her. Hari had put glasses of brandy in their hands.

'How did my father die?' Viva said. 'Tell me everything you know.'

Mrs Waghorn looked surprised.

'Surely you know.'

'No. Not really. It's all got so confused.'

'He died of overwork,' said Mrs Waghorn simply. 'He had been racing around the country working on the trains, and they found him one morning at the club in Quetta. He was dead.'

'Are you sure?' It seemed to Viva that she was speaking from the grave too. 'I was told he was set on by bandits, his throat was cut.'

'Who told you these things?' Mrs Waghorn's face sagged with disbelief. 'It's absolute tosh. He died putting on his shoes. It was very quick.'

'I don't know who told me,' said Viva. 'I was at school . . . I can't remember now, somebody must have told me.'

'Not necessarily. Sometimes adults fudge even the simplest facts of life when they talk to children. They might have said he sat on a cloud with an angel or something. Or that God had moved his furniture and let him in.'

'Please,' Viva said quickly, 'tell me everything. It's all slipping away, and I can't bear it any more. I need to know what's real and what I've made up.'

'Surely your English relatives told you something.' Mrs Waghorn's expression was still guarded.

'No, or at least I don't remember. My parents were hardly ever there.'

There was a long silence.

'Now look here, I didn't know them all that well,' Mrs W. began cautiously. 'But we did like each other.' She was tapping the pads of her fingers against her palm in an agitated way. 'I'm not very good at talking about them either.'

'Please.' Viva took her jittery hand in hers and held it there. 'Don't be frightened. The worst thing for me is feeling so cut off.'

'Well.' Mrs W. fiddled with her cigarettes and then lit one. 'I've thought about this quite a lot; I'm talking about your mother now. Obviously, at first your mind goes round and round and you look for reasons.

'Here's what I've come up with. Your mother was a good-looking woman; you've seen the photographs. She was great fun to be with, an asset to your father, but I always thought of her as a Saturday's child, or she should have been. You know, the one that works hard for its living, but it was frightfully difficult with your father moving so much. And he of course,' Mrs W. swallowed hard and looked at her, 'and of course he *was* a marvellous man. We all had a crush on him.'

Mrs W.'s old grey eyes looked into Viva's. *You loved him. You loved him too.*

'His work came first of course, that's the way it usually is out here. But your mother had gifts of her own. She painted very well, and of course, as you probably know, did these wonderful things. Have you seen them?'

She leant over and put a small, hard object into the palm of Viva's hand. She took it to be a navy blue button at first: a toggle-shaped button of some elaborate design. Looking closer, she saw a woman, wrapped in a shroud or a shawl and carved out of a dark blue marble-like stone.

She looked at it suspiciously, wondering if the old girl was offering it up as some kind of consolation prize for the soggy clothes in the trunk. The tiny figure, no bigger than her thumb, seemed to radiate life. It felt important.

'I think I remember my mother doing pottery classes,' she said at last. The memory was so vague it was almost forgotten but it seemed important to keep Mrs Waghorn talking in whatever way she could, so she turned the small figure over and over in her hand. 'But never when we were around. But are you quite sure she did this? It's like something you'd see in a museum.'

'When she gave it to me . . .' Mrs W. had taken the figure back. She was stroking it affectionately as if it really meant something to her. '. . . she wouldn't let me thank her for it. She said, "It's a gift from the fire." You see, one day, I'd walked into her studio unannounced. Well, it wasn't a real studio, a hut shall we say, in the grounds of our school. She was on her knees, in tears in front of her kiln. The heat was too high, and hours and hours of work had ended in what looked like a row of burned cakes. We had a cup of tea, and I said to her – I can't remember my exact words, but the effect was, "This doesn't look much fun, why bother?"'

'And it was then she explained with more passion than I ever heard her express that sometimes when you opened the kiln there was something there that was so magical, a pot, a figure, so much more beautiful than the one you'd thought of that you tingled for hours afterwards.'

'Tingled!' Mrs Waghorn laughed delightedly. 'She told me potters call these offerings – these divine mistakes – the gift of the fire. A damn shame she stopped, wasn't it?'

'I don't know.' Viva had a hollow feeling inside her heart, a feeling that she'd been cheated of something she'd never had. 'I didn't really pay much attention to it. But why did she stop? Was it when Daddy died? When Josie died?'

'I can't remember, I really can't, but why does anyone stop? Husbands, children, moving too much. All I can tell you was that she left things of value, and that she worked very hard for them.'

Viva was still a little suspicious: Mrs Waghorn seemed so much more fluent suddenly and this all seemed a bit pat, a concocted story, the sweet before the sour course and everything a bereaved daughter might want to hear.

'I don't remember her like that at all,' she said, 'but then I was a bit of a daddy's girl. I only really remember her as well, you know, somebody who did things for you: organised meals, name tapes, journeys.'

The sketching. Out of the blue she remembered it. How the pencil and the book had often appeared with the picnic things and how cross it had made her – it was time taken away from her.

'She was consumed with her work – the pottery, the paintings, the tiny sculptures – and felt guilty about it,' Mrs W. went on, 'so she tried to hide it. It was considered not the thing to work. Still is, but it was much worse then. For women that is, the men never stopped.'

'So she was a misfit. I was too with my school, which is probably why we got on so.' She chortled suddenly like a wicked girl. 'She was tremendously good fun as well as everything else. A marvellous mimic. One of the very best things about her was that she didn't take herself too seriously. But it was also her downfall, if you see what I mean.'

No, Viva was trying not to look too astonished; five minutes into the conversation and they were talking about a complete stranger.

She remembered her mother in two ways – rustling of taffeta or silk dress, waft of scent, the twinkle of earring brushing your face on her way out to some do at the club or in the mornings, permanently rushed, often tired and always in her father's shadow.

'Am I going on too much?' Mrs W. asked. 'Tell me if you want me to stop.'

No, no, no, no.

'Please don't stop.'

'Well.' The little dog jumped up on the old lady's knee. She stroked him and, it seemed to Viva, became a dotty old lady again for a few seconds, muttering and withdrawing and watching her from her deeply pouched eyes.

'I've been meaning to ask you, dear,' Mrs Waghorn said, focusing rheumy eyes on her. 'What is it exactly that *you* do?'

Viva could have screamed with impatience. In as few words as possible, she told her about the children's home, and how she had for the past year been trying to write a book about it.

'What a *frightfully* good idea that sounds,' Mrs Waghorn pounced. She seemed fully alert again. 'I can't think of anyone who *has* let Indian children speak first. It's a very, *very* good idea. When can we read it?'

'I've stopped writing it.'

'*Stopped*.' The word was like a brisk slap. 'Whatever for?'

'Oh, lots of reasons.'

'You mustn't stop; it sounds such a good idea. I'd have gone potty if I'd stopped teaching when Arthur died.'

She didn't have the energy to explain about the troubles at the school, or about Mr Azim and Guy.

'It's a long story,' she said. 'Tell me about your school. Do you miss it?'

'Horribly,' said the old lady. 'To find work you love is a treasure, isn't it? But any chance you might start it again? The children would enjoy seeing their thoughts in print.'

'I might. Some of the notes got lost.'

'Well, you can always get them back surely?' The old lady was gazing at her steadily. 'When you smile, you look so like her,' she said. 'I expect everyone tells you that.'

'No, they don't,' said Viva. 'That's the point. Nobody I know remembers them.'

'Ooof,' said Mrs Waghorn, 'awful that.' She lit a cigarette and disappeared into smoke for a moment. 'It will get worse as you get older,' she muttered. 'You'll live in the past more and you'll mind.'

'I mind now: it's always there and I'm always trying to forget it.'

'I had an experience with my own mother once,' said Mrs Waghorn, 'which I've never forgotten. When my father was based in Calcutta, we saw them once every two years. She came home and I supposed I'd grown, or had my hair cut or something, but I was standing at St Pancras Station, by the ticket office with my suitcase waiting for her, and there she suddenly was, walking towards me. I was so excited I could hardly breathe. She walked down the platform towards me, she looked at me and then she walked straight past me. I could never quite forgive her, I'm not sure why. It was very unfair of me when you think of it, but I think something died in me that day.'

She patted her dog and then looked up. During the long silence that followed, Viva felt a moment of suspension – the old girl was still sizing her up, waiting to slip her into some garment she wasn't sure she wanted. And now it came.

'I'd like another glass of brandy,' said Mrs W. 'Help yourself too. Now, are you the sort of person who likes the truth?'

'Yes,' said Viva, 'I am.' She felt her heart skip.

'Are you sure?'

'Yes.'

'You see, I flunked it yesterday. I was so surprised to see you I didn't know what to do.'

'I know.'

'Oh dear.' She felt Mrs Waghorn's hand close around hers. 'Dear girl, please don't cry. None of this is your fault.'

'It is.' Viva could no longer stop the tears running down her face. 'I should have come earlier.'

'You are *not* to feel guilty.' Mrs W. made this announcement with some force.

'Do you hear? Guilt is a peasant's pleasure and it was nothing you did. They wanted you away because nobody wanted you to know.'

'To know what?' Viva felt her whole body freeze.

Mrs Waghorn started to mutter in some agitation to herself; she was talking herself into or out of something.

Viva poured more brandy.

'Tell me.' Viva dried her eyes, and made a huge effort to look in control. Mrs Waghorn must not stop talking.

The old lady took a sip then put her glass down.

'Your mother took her own life,' she said. 'I thought you knew.'

Viva heard herself groaning. 'No,' she said. 'No.'

'Yes.' Mrs Waghorn's eyes were bright with tears. 'But I must tell you this: she was the last person on earth who I thought would ever do such a thing. Oh, she had her ups and downs, of course she did, but she was so full of beans and she loved you so much, but such a lot went wrong. This is no consolation, but it happens to so many people out here. They get lost.'

'Oh God.' When Viva put her head in her hands she felt herself floating hazily above her own body.

'Are you sure?'

'Quite sure,' said Mrs Waghorn. 'I was the one that found her.'

'I'm going to stop talking soon,' Mrs W. said a few seconds later. Her eyelids had turned blue and she seemed slightly drunk. 'But it's my belief that a good marriage needs a flower and a gardener to keep it . . . what's the word? . . . what's that word? . . . blooming. I could never have run my school unless Arthur had been on my side – been *practical*; it's not enough to believe in other people. You've got to do the donkey work with them.'

Her purple eyelids fell. 'This is jolly tiring,' she said suddenly. 'Can you come back later? We'll talk about the ashes and other things.'

She looked worn out: an emptied paper bag, sitting there in the gloom, brandy glass in her hand.

Viva covered her with a rug; she took the glass from her hand. As she tiptoed around her, still light-headed with shock, she felt the strongest urge to kiss her on her forehead, but old habits die hard and she was almost dead with tiredness herself. She turned down the lamp and closed the door and told Hari that it was time for the memsahib to go to bed.

Chapter 56

She went back to the hotel room and lay on the bed rigid with shock, and then when the shock wore off she wept uncontrollably. She'd been so angry with her mother for so long without ever thinking about her as a separate person with her own complicated life. She felt ashamed, revolted by her own stupidity. How could she have got it so wrong – dramatising her father's death, burying her mother under a heap of carefully nursed old grudges?

When she got up, exhausted and red-eyed, the day was over and there were stars outside her bedroom window, against a dark purple sky. It was nearly ten o'clock.

She went into the bathroom and turned on the taps. Her body felt stiff as if she had been pummelled, and on her hands she could still smell the damp and camphor plus the slightly meaty smell of decay from the trunk.

She stared at the dirt that was flowing from her; she had been buried alive. She scrubbed her neck, her legs, her breasts, her arms; she washed her hair and then she lay in the water until it got cold, thinking about her mother again.

She felt already that sometime soon she might be released from the darkness. An easing – something like space or lightness.

At least she knew now. Before, she'd blamed her, even hated her for so many things: for not keeping Daddy alive, for not wanting her more, for not keeping her with her in India, when the truth was she'd been cut off from the two things that might have kept her going for a little while longer – her work and her child.

Viva got out of the water and reached for a towel. She saw her face blurry and indistinct in the steamy bathroom mirror. Maybe she'd been a ghost for years without really knowing it. That line of poetry lodged in her brain years ago at school, something about being 'half in love with easeful death'.

Half in love with easeful death, the other half floating out from herself,

434

longing to slip away into the darkness like a boat in the water, to where Josie and her parents waited for her.

She climbed into bed, putting the little blue woman her mother had made on the bedside table. Before they'd parted, Mrs Waghorn had pressed it into her hand.

'Keep it.' She'd closed Viva's fingers around it. 'It's yours. I want it to be the first thing you see when you wake up tomorrow morning.'

She was calmer now and saw it more clearly: the careful arrangement of the woman's shawl, the quizzical intelligence of her eyes as if she was in on some private joke. Its perfection hurt and thrilled her – how could something so small be so full of life?

She turned out the lamp and lay in the dark thinking about her last conversation with Mrs Waghorn.

'My mother and I had the most terrible row the last time we were together,' Viva had confessed over tea. 'I can't for the life of me remember what it was about now, or why I was so angry. I think I might have told her I hated her. *I can't wait to go back to school.* I wanted to hurt her as she had hurt me. It was the last time I ever saw her.'

'You were ten years old. All children of that age are foul sometimes,' said Mrs Waghorn. 'Particularly when they're about to be sent away. She understood.'

'You don't know that.'

'I do.'

'Look, you don't have to say things to make me feel better.'

'I'm not.'

The old girl had given her a penetrating look when she said that. Her hand had stolen over her mouth as if she was in the process of witnessing an accident.

'She was heartbroken.'

'No – don't say it, you don't have to.'

'I do. After she'd said goodbye to you she walked up to the school and had a drink with me. She was desperately upset; she knew she'd acted strangely with you, that she was losing her grip. I remember it so well because she said to me, "I couldn't even kiss her goodbye," and she'd longed to – it was so horribly sad. Too much for everyone; but why should you take the blame for that?'

Mrs Waghorn had become emotional herself at this point. She'd squeezed her hands together and swallowed several times. 'You see, he taught *me* so much too,' she'd rambled, 'and he wanted her to work, but she had to hide so much and work so hard, and then when he died— Oh, this is silly,' she'd half choked. She'd tapped her thumb on the top of her left hand for a few seconds.

Viva sat there frozen and immobile as though parts of her had jammed, watching tears flow down the deep lines in Mrs Waghorn's face and drip into the collar of her dress. She had the sense of having trespassed into some private grief, of being one part of a series of interlocking mysteries that wouldn't all be solved.

When she had composed herself again, Mrs W. had shuffled over to a locked cabinet and shown her several more pieces of her mother's pottery. A celadon green teapot, a plate, a bowl. Beautiful things.

Viva had pored over them, desperate for clues.

'Why did she leave them with you?' she'd asked.

'They were precious to her, and she'd lost so much in transit – she wanted me to take care of them.'

There was a moment of farce when Mrs W.'s wildly shaking hands had picked up a rattling cup and saucer. Some custodian. With a great effort, she held them up against the oscillating light. And then the urge to laugh had died in Viva. 'Why the pots and not me?' she'd wanted to ask but hadn't. The question sounded so nakedly self-pitying.

'I still don't understand why she sent me home?' she asked instead. 'Did I do something?'

'No, no, no, nothing like that.' Mrs Waghorn had bowed her head. After a long silence she'd looked up. 'Now, this is the point: it was my fault, I'm afraid. I said, "Send her back to England." I probably talked about the need for fresh air, the company of other children, not picking up a chi chi accent. All the things I used to say to anxious parents, and it was a ghastly mistake. And of course I did think at the time that she would eventually join you. I had no idea how desperate she was. I'm so sorry,' she said almost inaudibly.

Viva had looked across to the bowed head, the wispy white curls and the pink scalp showing through them. She'd made the usual gestures of forgiveness, squeezing Mrs Waghorn's hand, saying it wasn't her fault, she was only following the rules and so on, but another part of her cried out in agony.

She thought back to the day after the row, when she and her mother had parted: the stiff hugs, the brittle jokes they'd made, her muffled howls of pain later, doubled up in the ladies' lavatory in some railway station on her way back to school. They should never have let go. That was the truth, terrible and simple.

In the end they'd died to each other, not all at once, but bit by bit, by making themselves less vulnerable. A shocking, ridiculous, waste of love.

White muslin curtains, more stars, a silvery-green crescent moon hanging low in the sky. From downstairs she could hear puffs of music coming from a dance band, distant laughter. Her parents would have come to parties here. 'Your mother loved dancing,' Mrs Waghorn said.

Now she pictured her laughing and glamorous in her green silk dress and snakeskin shoes, her dark hair flying around her face, and felt another shift inside her. She knew something now, and must never forget it. It was money in the bank.

However sad her mother's ending had been, she had known deep pleasures: a husband she adored, work that she was good at, children who had once been a blessing. Mrs Waghorn's laughter had rung out like a girl when she'd remembered the fun they'd had together. And when she'd talked of her mother's work, she'd seemed to Viva to be years younger – ageless and invigorated still by her talent and the pots she had left behind. These things were real.

When she got up to close the curtains, a skein of cloud floated over the moon, making the whole heavens look marbled. When a light wind blew the curtains inside the room, she wrestled with them for a while, and then closed the window.

A thought had come to her, clear and strong. She must tell Frank about everything that had happened that day. If she didn't tell him quickly, she'd find other ways of hiding it and the truth would be smudged or rearranged like footprints in the sand and they'd go on not telling the secrets that were at the heart of them. That was dangerous. It could even be fatal. 'A weak specification', as her father might have said.

She dressed hurriedly, tugging on her stockings, dashing a brush through her hair. What had to be done must be done now while the pain was real – if she left it too long she could lose her nerve.

She glanced at her watch. Ten forty. The hotel's front desk might be closed, the hall porter off duty. She ran out of her bedroom into the corridor and across the hall, almost throwing herself on the lift button. Her blood was racing as the brass doors closed behind her with a thunk.

The lift took a long time to wheeze its way down to the ground floor. When it stopped between floors she felt like screaming. When the doors were open she sprinted across an expanse of highly polished cedar floor towards the turbaned man on the desk.

'I want to send a telegram,' she told him, almost grabbing the pencil out of his hand. 'To Lahore, tonight.'

He handed her a form.

'It's over,' she wrote. 'Stop. It's done. Stop.' She felt her heart jump in her chest like a large fish. 'Please come for Christmas.'

Chapter 57

Because Tor was atrociously bad at keeping secrets, she'd been forbidden by Rose and Toby to pick up Viva at the station. In the end, they'd relented – after all, the whole thing (as she had not hesitated to point out) had been her idea and it seemed mean to exclude her from the excitement.

'What happened?' she said, when she first saw Viva almost running down the platform. 'You look different.'

'I feel different.' For once, Viva didn't flinch when she put her arm through hers.

'So, tell all.' Tor ignored Rose's quelling look. 'Was the trunk stuffed with buried treasures? Did you see anyone you knew?'

Viva tried to smile, said something about being too ravenous to talk yet and, as they were walking across the car park, said casually, 'Oh, by the way, did anyone leave a message for me?'

'No,' they both said together.

'I didn't think they would,' Viva replied, and then, 'I honestly can't believe it's Christmas in two days' time,' as if that was what they'd been talking about all along.

'Sorry.' Tor didn't like to see her look suddenly so tired and upset. She'd carried on walking doggedly down the platform but looked smaller, and more vulnerable.

Her hair was covered in dust and there was a hole in her stocking.

Tor glanced at Rose. 'But we do have a small surprise for you. An early Christmas present you could say.'

'Honestly, Tor.' Rose shook her head. 'I could cheerfully throttle you sometimes.'

'Why?' said Tor. 'What did I say wrong?'

Nobody mentioned the surprise again until after Viva had had a bath and washed her hair and they were taking tea on the verandah. They were draining their cups, when Tor's eyes went suspiciously round and innocent-looking and she said she thought they should stroll down to the stables and watch the horses being fed. She said it was one of her favourite things to do at this time of the day.

Viva, who was still looking pale and rather strained, said that sounded lovely as her legs were still rocking from the train and it would be good to be out in the fresh air. She hadn't yet said a word about Simla, but they'd grown used to her being reserved about things like that by now and didn't press her.

By the time they'd organised Freddie and his ayah and told Toby they were going out, it was dusk and the whole sky had turned into a gaudy fanfare of shocking pinks and oranges and peach-coloured lights. As the girls walked arm in arm down the path together, their faces absorbed the light and they were laughing because Rose's blonde hair had gone pink.

At the end of the red dirt track, they turned to the right down an avenue of poplar trees that led to the polo ground. Beyond them were the playing fields, the school, the darkening woods where a flock of parrots had just appeared, spinning in the sunset like miniature rainbows.

When they reached the wooden benches beside the polo ground, they sat for a moment watching a couple of men playing stick and ball. Their distant yelps, the rolling thunder of hooves, made Rose sigh suddenly quite heavily.

Viva said, 'Do you miss Jack?' the kind of intimate question she usually went out of her way to avoid.

But Rose, who was looking almost absurdly young and pretty tonight in a white voile dress, didn't seem to mind. She said yes, she did miss him terribly – and then she whispered, 'Don't tell Tor because she's so longing for this to be fun for us all, but I've been having awful dreams about him. I don't know why.'

And then, because Tor was listening now, she said, in a wifely exasperated way, that Jack had only managed to telegram them yesterday to tell them that there was no chance that any of the regiment would make it home for Christmas. Something about a huge fall of snow north of Peshawar, near some mountain village, too secret for them to be allowed to know the name of. Jack would be stuck in some miserable hut in the middle of nowhere with only two of his friends from the regiment for company. Such was life, but it was a shame for him to miss Freddie's first Christmas.

'We were petrified you'd be stuck in Simla too,' Rose added. 'It must have been lonely for you there too.' She gave Viva a level look as if to say, 'Come on.'

But Viva still couldn't talk about it. She felt dazed and fragile, like someone who has broken their leg and must find a new way of walking.

She felt Rose's fingers squeeze hers. 'It's all right,' she said gently. 'You don't have to say if you don't want to.'

'I'm not trying to be mysterious,' Viva tried to smile, 'I promise.'

'I know.'

At the end of the polo ground, they stood for a while watching in silence the birds floating and turning against the crimson sky. The men cantered side by side down the long side of the pitch.

Rose was smiling.

'Isn't India the most magical place on earth sometimes?' she said as they walked into the stable yard.

'I mean, honestly, would you have missed it for anything, Viva? Even the bad bits. Do you feel that?'

'No. I mean, yes.' Viva had hardly heard a word. 'I don't know.' Her heart had started to thump uncomfortably. What was this surprise the girls had concocted?

They'd reached the stable yard. Everything was very neat here: freshly painted whitewashed walls, halters hung on brass hooks outside the stables, ropes coiled just so. Peaceful too with the horses munching their hay nets, and the gentle swish of the grooms sweeping the yard.

Two tiny Shetland ponies were stretching over their stable doors to look at them and whickering. Tor said that after winning their class at the Dublin Horse Show they'd been shipped out from Ireland for one of the maharajah's sons, but the sons were more interested in their toy cars so they were hardly ever ridden. She thought they looked lonely.

'You are so soppy,' she heard Rose tease. 'I mean, have they actually told you that?'

She heard Tor saying, 'I just sense it.' And then, 'I speak Equus, you know.'

The colours of the sunset had deepened again, and now a dozen or so pink horses looked curiously towards them over their stable doors; pink pigeons glided in dreamy circles above their heads. 'What a night!' she heard Rose say from a great distance as they drew closer to the horses. 'Let's go riding tomorrow before breakfast.'

Tor's eyes were glittering with excitement. 'I'm glad I remembered to order it,' she was saying.

Rose laughed. She and Tor started to read out the names from the brass plaques each horse had above its stable: Jezri, Treasure, Ruth, Sanya. In the last stable, a beautiful, slightly mad-looking black Arabian stallion stood behind iron bars showing the whites of his eyes. He was stamping his feet on the concrete floor. He didn't like this commotion any more than Viva did.

Tor was strolling nonchalantly up and down, murmuring at some of the horses, slipping others lumps of sugar.

Tor stopped. She turned to her.

'Now cometh the hour, Viva,' she said. 'Look and listen.'

Viva heard a slight ringing in her ears and then nothing but munching horses, the soft swish of the grooms' brooms.

'Cow-dust hour,' said Rose.

'It's enough to send you to sleep.'

'But not yet, because . . .' Tor put her hands over Viva's eyes '. . . here's your surprise.' She pushed her towards the stable door. '*Look*,' she whispered softly into her ear. 'He came after all.'

Viva's heart leapt in her chest, there was a shrill sound in her ears, but when she saw it, she had only a second to adjust her expression.

It was a foal. Nothing but a foal – still wet from its birth, lying on a heap of blood-stained straw. Above it an exhausted-looking mare stood with a damp tail and sweaty sides.

And all the way here, lit up inside, excited by the sunset, she'd imagined – oh, it didn't matter what she'd imagined – that he would be here after all, and that she'd be able to talk to him, and tell him about Simla and all the new things she'd learnt there. The longing to discharge all this new information felt overwhelming. She felt he would listen, he would understand, that she'd be forgiven and then they would all have a jolly Christmas together. *Stupid, stupid, stupid.*

There is life as it is and life as we are and she was always confusing the two.

The foal was cream-coloured with big, dark eyes and a ridiculous tail like a powder puff. She forced herself to smile at it, for the girls – how young they seemed – were grabbing her hands and jumping up and down with delight.

It got to its feet, tottered over to them to sniff their hands; they stroked its wrinkled little nose and said it felt like velvet.

'The mare lost her last foal, so she's in heaven,' Tor whispered. 'And she's very well bred too – Toby says the stallion's bloodlines go back for centuries.'

Viva made herself concentrate. If she started to cry now she might never stop and her humiliation would be complete.

The foal's pipe-cleaner legs collapsed. Its mother pushed it with her nose and made a gentle groaning sound. It hid behind her with a coquettish look and when it was suckling, the mare gave them a strange hot look, full of warning and pride. '*Mine*,' she seemed to be saying. '*Mine, mine mine.* Look, but come no closer.'

'It came last night,' Tor said, 'and the most embarrassing thing is that we took Tourmaline, that's the mare's name, out riding earlier in the day. None of us twigged at all and nor did the grooms – she hardly showed at all. Then, late last night, when I came to give her an apple, I saw this huge balloon coming out of her bottom – well, not quite bottom but you know what I mean.'

'Was it frightening?' Viva felt punched. Her own legs felt almost as wobbly as the foal's. *Stupid, stupid, stupid.* She must stop thinking like this.

'No, we weren't frightened at all.' Tor was looking at her strangely. 'We were lucky to have a professional here.' And it was then that Viva felt Rose's nails dig into the palm of her hand. When she turned round, Frank was there.

And then, she'd done something so unlike herself that the girls had teased her about it for months afterwards. 'You,' she'd almost shouted. She'd put her arms around him and hugged him fiercely; she'd burst into tears. It was just that the sight of him in that marvellous light was so overwhelming, so absolutely the most beautiful thing she'd ever seen that she couldn't stop herself. *Sometimes you know so quickly it frightens you. Your mind lumbers behind trying to make sense of it.*

He was wearing his battered linen suit; he was smiling at her and shaking his head as if he couldn't believe it either.

Thank you, God, she thought when her head was buried in his chest. *Thank you, thank you, thank you.* When he hugged her back, she cried some more.

And then everybody laughed because Tourmaline was stamping her front foot and shielding the foal with her body.

'I think we're frightening the horses,' he said. When he smiled at her she thought her heart would burst.

And then she felt shy with him, conscious of the girls staring at them and the grooms, who'd stopped sweeping. Shy and a little tongue-tied.

'I got your telegram,' he said. She noticed his shirt hanging out of his trousers. There was a slight red mark on his chin where he'd cut himself shaving. He must have dressed in a hurry.

'I was going to go to Simla, but thought you might have left already. I decided to meet you here instead.'

'He drove like the clappers.' Tor had tears in her eyes too.

'Do you promise you didn't guess?' Rose was beaming. 'I thought Miss Tor was about as subtle as a blow over the head.'

'I didn't guess. No.' Viva could hardly speak – it was all too much.

Tor checked her watch. 'I have an idea,' she said. 'There's two hours, at least, before dinner. Why don't you two go for a walk . . . ? You could actually go for quite a long walk if you wanted to,' she added innocently. 'Supper will be late as usual.'

When they were alone again, they laughed, because they'd heard Tor boom, 'See, I *can* be tactful,' to Rose as they'd walked off.

Then Frank touched her lightly on the arm.

'We're going for a walk,' he told the two grooms who were leaning on their brooms and frankly gawping at them. '*Chee apbu lamkea?*' May we please borrow a lamp?

When the groom returned with a kerosene lamp, Frank turned to her and whispered, 'There's a summer house near the river – we could talk there. Is that what you want?'

'Yes,' she said. 'That's what I want.'

She followed him back down the path towards the water. When they reached a small jetty where two row boats were moored, the sun was throwing its last rays of light over the river. They stood for a moment looking at the bulrushes, at the melting colours, now burnishing a family of mallard ducks that were floating down the river murmuring to each other. In a few moments' time, all this would be gone and night would fall.

'Are you cold?' he said, for she was shivering.

'Not cold,' she said. She closed her eyes for a moment. 'I'm just glad . . .'

She thought she might say something reasonably neutral, something that would give her a moment to catch her breath.

'Glad that we can all spend Christmas together . . .' but his arm had tightened around her and he spun her round.

'No,' he said. 'Not like that. I've had this feeling about you, for days and days now, that you've been so alone and I can't bear it any more.'

'Don't.' She put her hand over his mouth, felt the softness of his lips. 'Wait till we get to the hut,' she said, 'and I'll tell you what I can.'

Their footsteps had quickened and when they came to a small slatted bridge, he took her hand and helped her over it. On the other side, there was a shrine with candles burning inside it, set up underneath a twisted oak tree. There was a plate filled with oranges and pieces of fruit in front of it, which the squirrels had half eaten. Behind the shrine was a grass clearing, and a white wooden summer house.

'Quick.' He pulled her inside and when she shut the door behind him, she felt her blood leap.

The hut, which smelt pleasantly of cedar and incense, was simple and bare. There was a desk in the middle of the room with a pad of paper on it and some pencils, a charpoy with some faded cushions, a set of cricket stumps propped up against the wall.

'It belongs to one of the masters,' Frank explained. 'He's on holiday; Tor says we're safe here.'

When he lit the oil lamp, turning the wick down low, she saw his long brown fingers, the blondish-brown hairs on his strong forearms and shivered again. She'd never felt so out of control, so alive.

'Sit down,' he said. 'Here, with me.' He pulled her down beside him on the charpoy under the window.

'I've been so worried about you,' he whispered. 'It nearly killed me. I—'

He put his hands under her hair and kissed her – a long slow kiss that felt like a claiming. When she came up for air, her shoe had fallen off and every cell in her body felt alive and singing. It was terrifying.

He put his head quietly beside hers, a moment of submission to everything most feared, most wanted.

'Stop,' he said suddenly. 'Talk to me first. What happened in Simla?'

She took a deep breath and began by telling him about the trunk – trying to make a story of it at first.

'I mean, really, it was almost a joke – a few sodden bits of clothes, my father's false teeth. And when I think how long I'd put off seeing it.'

She told him about seeing their old family house again – Hari had taken her on their way to the railway station. How irrelevant it had looked standing in the mist, all neglected and forlorn with the woods around it, and most of the verandah gnawed away by damp. She didn't tell him about the swing, hanging uselessly by one rope and with a bird's nest inside, the swing where she and Josie had spent hours and hours together, or their upstairs bedroom with the old-fashioned wallpaper, birds and trees and fruit, torn now and dis-coloured, but still visible from the garden. Two trees had fallen down over the garden path; outside the house all the gutters were either broken or clogged with dark leaves.

And that was it. No ancient retainers had rushed out to tell her stories from her past, no neighbours who remembered them, no further clues, just the dense forest closing in on a borrowed house, as if that had been its purpose all along.

She told him how, on her last day, Mrs Waghorn had taken her to the Sanjauli cemetery where they were buried, and she'd seen all three of them for the first time, laid out in a row. It was peaceful there. The wind in the pines made a shushing sound like gentle waves, the sky a pearly white. She'd weeded the graves and put the flowers into a vase she'd brought with her and filled with water from the stream that ran nearby.

Someone had misspelled her mother's name on the gravestone and called Josie Josephine, which nobody ever had as far as she could remember.

He listened to this intently, his green eyes trained on her. When his hand tightened on hers, she felt heat rise in her and was not ashamed.

'So,' he said when she had finished, 'maybe in the end it was a good thing; maybe it helped to set your mind at rest – somewhat,' he'd added uncertainly.

He looked so anxiously protective when he said that, she knew this was a turning point. One part of her brain was telling her, *People keep things hidden from each other all the time: the soothing lie could be told, no one need ever be the wiser*, but another part of her recognised that if she fudged this, some door would be slammed inside her for ever.

She looked at him. 'My mother took her own life.'

Mrs Waghorn had added more details before they'd parted, and now, it was a great comfort to tell him as simply and fully as she could. 'When I was nine or ten years old, she got malaria. She recovered, but apparently got very homesick and low in spirits. When I think of it now, she must have been reeling from Josie's death and then my father's. I'd never really thought of it like that before.

'She rode a horse up to a hut on the ridge, half a mile north of Wildflower Hall – a beautiful place where you can see the Himalayas, and also the two rivers. She used to go up there sketching. I'd ridden up there with her myself a couple of times. In springtime you could see the most incredible flowers: celandine, and March marigold, tiny dwarf cyclamen, wild strawberries. She'd left a note saying how much she'd loved us all, but that her life was no longer bearable. "Sustainable" was the word she'd actually used. She must have stayed on the side of the mountain until she'd frozen to death. She'd left a couple of hay nets for the horse, so it would have something to eat until somebody found her.' That somebody, Viva had thought about this later, could just as easily have been a tiger or a vulture as a man. They were after all in India.

He put his arms around her. He stroked her hair.

'I had no idea,' she told him, wild-eyed. 'I'd been so angry with her for so long. I'd blamed her for everything, and almost everything I said about her was a complete lie. You were right to tell me to go back.'

'Don't you think most people make their parents up?' he said. 'When you're a child, you're not really ever interested in them, and later, if you talk to them at all, you have all the wrong conversations. Oh, my love.'

He leant over and wiped away the tears that were starting to pour down her face.

'You don't have to say it all tonight if it's going to hurt you,' he said. 'Let it come out bit by bit.'

And she had a spacious sense that this was right. There would be time to talk, and, at last, she could tell the truth. Later, in her room, stunned and wide awake, she thought of something else along these lines: that if you were lucky, very lucky indeed, there were one or two people in your life who you could tell the unvarnished truth to – shell and egg. People like Frank, and Rose and Tor. And that these people held the essence of you inside them, just as Mrs Waghorn had held the essence of her mother inside her. The rest would be conversations with people that ended when night fell, or the dinner party ended.

'Come here,' he said when she'd finished. He put his arms around her and rocked her.

'But the point is,' she told him fiercely, 'no one can ever really say why she did it. We want a simple explanation and what if there isn't one? What if all you can say is sometimes awful things happen to the best people? I think it's better to throw up your hands than try and square everything up.'

'Do you want me to tell Tor and Rose for you?' he asked. 'They were so worried about you in Simla, they had a sense something like this might happen.'

'How did they know?' She was genuinely amazed.

'I don't know,' he said. 'Friends are another mystery.'

'Not yet,' she said, all this emotion had made her feel momentarily giddy and off centre. 'I want to show you something first. Look.'

She tipped the blue woman into the palm of his hand where it lay between his lifeline and his thumb.

'Something else I didn't know about her – she was a sculptor. She made this.'

And later, she realised this was another kind of turning point between them, that if he'd flipped the little figure over and said something polite and automatic, she wouldn't have been able to stand there feeling such pride, such a strong sense that she could hold her head up high.

He turned it over, his brown-blonde hair forming for a moment a screen between her and the blue woman.

And she could tell by the way he was looking at it that he understood, and that as far as anyone is really safe in this world, she would be safe in his hands.

Chapter 58

She and Frank had walked back together through the darkness, his lamp glancing off the poplar trees, the shrine, the silver band of the river. Holding hands all the way, they'd taken the red dirt road back to Tor's house for supper. He'd stopped near the wooden bridge and pulled her behind a jasmine bush for a long, slow kiss that, even when she thought of it now, made her go weak at the knees.

She knew that for the rest of her life when she smelt jasmine, she would think of him: his arms around her, the smell of his hair, the way the kisses had changed tempo – gentle at first and then so passionate they'd had to stop, breathless and laughing and amazed.

He said he had never felt anything remotely like this before. She said she felt the same and then felt tears run down the sides of her face.

When they reached the house it was blazing with Christmas lights. What with the lights and the music wafting out, it looked like a mad little pleasure craft against the dense darkness of the trees all around them.

They ate dinner in the small dining room where Tor and Rose had lit candles and set the table with flowers. With her friends all around her, a glass of champagne in her hand and Frank beside her in the candlelight, she'd felt so full of life she could have died.

And what was strange was that she understood something, even then: that the almost electrical charge of that moment would be part of her for the rest of her life. It would be there for her, not always of course, but something you could look back on and believe in. Something she could know about herself – she'd felt the terrifying power of love.

Dinner – roast chicken, rice, champagne and afterwards a dish of lemon fluff – had gone on for hours. There was so much to celebrate, and eventually, they wound up the gramophone and danced barefooted on the verandah. They danced the varsity rag, and then sang 'Goodbye England, Hello Bombay', then Tor cracked open a bottle of crème de menthe, and tried to teach Toby to tango like Valentino in *The Four Horsemen of the Apocalypse*. Their noise woke up baby Fred. He was carried into the dining room by his ayah. They put a Christmas hat on him that the sun had half faded, and even though he was still half asleep, they'd made him chuckle, which was never hard to do. He was a jolly Bob, and when she'd looked at Frank she'd known with certainty that sooner or later they would have children.

Three weeks later, she moved in with Frank into a flat in Colaba. The small three-roomed flat cost one hundred rupees, about ten pounds, a month to rent. It had a wide half-glassed balcony on the front of it from where you could see, if you stood up and leant to the right, the sea, the boats and the misty outlines of Elephanta Island.

This was the island where the caves were full of what Tor called 'socking great' sixth-century carvings of the Hindu gods Shiva and Parvati. Colossal, magnificent, they showed the gods making love and playing dice, quarrelling and laughing. In the centre of the cave there was a gigantic and exuberant stone phallus, which confirmed, without shame, that this is it: life, and where we come from. It was given a wide berth by guides with parties known to include delicate English women.

Reaching the caves took several journeys: water had to be crossed, a mountain climbed and a cave entered. It was no easy matter, but they'd been there twice already, taking a picnic lunch, which they ate on the island. In the first flush of love, she adored making him food. She'd iron for him, kissing the collars, ridiculously in love.

During the hot days, as she sat on her own verandah, shaded by a bamboo blind, Viva often glanced across the sparkling water and towards the island. Typing and looking, typing and looking, at the island, the harbour, the boats coming and going.

Finishing the book had almost been a condition of her marriage. She'd come back from Amritsar certain most of her notes had been destroyed. He said she must try again.

A few days later, when she'd gone back to work at the home, she found a pile of torn and crumpled notes in her washstand drawer, and it turned out that Daisy had kept another chunk of the torn and defaced pages in an envelope just in case she could ever face them again.

When the children heard their stories had been revived, they got excited about the book all over again and began drawing pictures for it and writing poems. They'd helped her stick the notes together, and filled in any gaps. Once they'd started, the job had not been huge.

And it was here, on 12 April 1930, that she typed the full stop that ended her book. *Tales from the Tamarind: Ten Bombay Children Tell Their Stories.*

Frank, who was back working shifts at the Gokuldas Tejpal Hospital until his new research project began, was in their bedroom when she typed the last full stop. She stood up to ease the crick in her back. She took the pages in her arms and hugged them to herself for a moment, and then she walked into their room, put the book on the bedside table and got into bed with him.

'It's done,' she said. 'I've finished.'

'Good,' he said. He took her in his arms and held her tight. 'Good,' he said again.

There were tears in his eyes and in hers. He'd known all along how important this would be.

And lying there in the crook of his arm, she felt how much lighter she'd become in the last few months. Really, it was incredible. Like a great big stone lifted off her chest. So much had changed.

Frank was on the early shift the next morning. She got up with him at five-thirty in the morning and made him scrambled eggs on toast. After he'd eaten, they sat together on the balcony drinking coffee and watched the fishing boats coming in with their night's catch. And beyond them, just breasting the line of the horizon, they could see another P&O liner on its way to India. They came only twice a month now. Watching the scattered lights come into focus, she remembered standing with her group: Tor and Rose, Frank and Guy. Poor Nigel, the young civil servant who'd read them the 'Ithaka' poem, had gone – he'd taken his life in Chittagong during the rainy season just as he'd predicted he might. 'Oh de painin', oh de pain,' they'd sung to tease him.

She remembered their uncertain hymns, the wheezing harmonium, the childlike paleness of Rose's face, and poor old Guy – hard to imagine him square-bashing in England now.

'I've got some strong paper in my desk,' said Frank. They'd been talking about the safest way to send her book back to London. 'I'll help you wrap it and if you like, we can drop it off at Thomas Cook later.'

'Yes,' she said. She felt a fizzing elation, a drunken feeling of relief at having finished the book. He'd seen what she needed, hadn't. When you're used to looking after yourself, you don't always get it right.

Three weeks after that, they were married in the Bombay Registry Office. The churches were all booked up that weekend, which was fine with them since neither of them was formally religious anyway. They'd decided to hold the reception at the children's home at Tamarind Street which was still, by a miracle, open although the authorities were threatening to close it in June of that year.

On the morning of the wedding, half dreaming, half awake, she experienced the old familiar corkscrewing pain: it was her wedding day, Josie and her parents should have been there, but the moment came and went more calmly now. What she'd come to understand, what India had helped her see, was that mourning was no crime. It wasn't her feeling all boo-hoo sorry for herself, or being disgustingly self-engrossed, it was what you had to do to go on.

And she knew that for the whole of the rest of her life, there would be moments – today for instance, or when her children were born, or when something trivial came up that she longed to tell them about – when she would have to love them and leave them over and over again.

Three people came to the registry office: Daisy, wearing a new purple hat and sensible shoes, and Tor and Toby, who'd taken the train down from Amritsar because the old Talbot had finally died and they were too poor to replace it. Tor was the first person Viva saw as they stepped out of the tonga. Tor jumped up and down on the spot when she first saw her. When she hugged her, she whispered in her ear that she and Toby were having a baby in October.

Rose couldn't come. In her reply to Viva's wedding invitation, she said she'd be on a ship on her way home then. Her father had died before Christmas. Her beloved father dead for six weeks before she'd even heard about it. Six weeks! She was mortified to think of her mother suffering on her own.

'I'm staying for a few months to help her pack up the house,' she wrote, 'and to introduce her to Freddie.'

Jack, she added, would be staying on in India. She said he would try and come to the wedding.

'He won't come,' Viva had said to Frank. 'Bannu's miles away and he's always working.'

'You never know,' Frank had said. 'He'll be lonely without them.' Viva wasn't sure about that.

But when Viva and Frank arrived for the reception at Tamarind Street, Jack was there. Thinner and older-looking, he stood apart from the cheering children and Tor and Toby, who were madly throwing confetti. When she waved at him, he touched his hat and raised his hand shyly, and she was glad to see him.

There was no time to talk. Talika, Suday and a chattering, laughing group of children dragged her back up to her old room overlooking the tamarind tree. The girls dressed her in pale green, explaining that green was an auspicious colour for a Maharashtrian girl to be married in. They put green glass bangles round her wrists, took her Western shoes off, helped her bathe her feet and put a fine silver toe ring round her big toe. As they brushed her hair and darted and scampered around her, she felt that sense of physical lightness again. It was as though she and the children had been lifted up above the tree tops; they were flying like kites or birds, like some pure physical expression of joy.

Down in the courtyard, the drums had started again, a flute. A fire had been lit in a brazier and placed in the middle of the paving stones.

Talika ran to the window. 'They're ready for you,' she said.

And Viva, looking at Talika, remembered the pathetic little scrap she'd bathed on her second day at the home. How the child, on the day her own tragedy struck, had struggled with a broom twice her size, determined to do something useful.

Talika's eyes glowed as she held the corner of her sari. On their way downstairs she had to talk fast to tell her all her news. She told her how she'd performed the Shiva *puja* so Viva could find a good husband, how she'd drawn a picture for her and hoped it might go in the book. And Viva, looking into those eager, forward-looking eyes, saw in a jolting moment how much she owed this child, how much she'd taught her.

There was another surprise in the courtyard: Mr Jamshed, plumper than ever and wearing an embroidered tunic, stepped forward and handed her flowers and a box of Turkish delight. Behind him was Mrs Jamshed holding a dish of some elaborate-looking rice and Dolly and Kaniz, freshly shingled and looking as though they'd stepped from the pages of *Vogue* magazine in their silk dresses and smartly buttoned shoes. They were grinning their heads off.

For reasons she would probably never fully understand, they'd forgiven her. More than forgiven her. Daisy explained that Mrs Jamshed had got up early to help supervise the cooking of a special feast for them: a fish curry served on glistening banana leaves, all kinds of *pakwans*, desserts, *modak* and dumplings with coconut, all laid out on long tables in the courtyard.

The feast took two hours, and after it, much giggling and jangling behind a thin rattan curtain, and then Talika had appeared resplendent in a tangerine sari.

She cleared her throat.

'Miss Wiwa, this is our special dance for you,' she'd announced, and with a stern glance towards the troop of little girls, they'd appeared. Each girl had worn a red, an amber or an orange sari. The hundred little bells worn round their ankles had made a thrilling shivery sound you felt in your spine as they'd walked around the perimeter of the tamarind tree, the boys sweeping the path before them. Musicians appeared: fat boy Suday, playing tabla, a trumpeter from Byculla. And then the music and dance had exploded, the girls stamping and twirling, their arms graceful as saplings in the wind. When the music stopped, Talika singing in her reedy voice had prompted Viva:

> *'Aaja Sajan, Aaja.*
> *Aaja Sajan, Aaja.*
> *Come to me my lover, come to me.*
> *Come to me my lover, come to me.'*

When Frank held her hand tightly, Viva knew he wanted to kiss her, but they held back, not wanting to shock the children. Barefoot, they'd walked around the sacred fire four times, praying for long life, harmony, peace, love.

After the ceremony, Viva made a point of going over to speak to Jack, who was sitting on his own looking amused and watchful. But when she sat down beside him, she saw that what she'd taken to be English reserve was in fact an attempt to control some violent emotion. He was swallowing hard and clearing his throat. His big hands were wrestling with each other and he was sweating under the arms of his khaki shirt.

'Well done,' he said in a constricted voice. 'First class.'

'I wish Rose could have been here,' she said. 'I don't think I'd be here without her.'

'Ah, well.' He glanced at her quickly. 'Have you heard from her?' he said. His hand was crumbling a chapatti.

'Not much,' she said. 'A quick letter, last week.' Splotched, hastily written.

Dear Viva. I am so happy for you. I miss you all. Love, Rose. A duty letter, no news, making her feel that Rose was well and truly back in her shell again.

'She didn't say much.'

'No.' Jack seemed to be focusing on a spot above her head. 'Tricky time. I think her mother needs her for a bit, and of course the regiment's all over the shop, so I'm hardly ever home. So—' He made himself look at her again. 'What about you? Where are you chaps going to live?'

She told him about going back to Lahore – that when the funding came through, Frank's work on blackwater fever would resume this summer. She was, she said, determined to go too – she could work almost anywhere.

'Yes, go,' he said, with surprising ferocity. 'It doesn't work staying apart. You've got to be one thing or the other. I haven't been. I've been . . .' He said something else but she missed it. A shattering sound drew their attention away. Suday was blasting away at his tabla again; a group of children were blowing on recorders, others through combs on to Bronco paper. Frank moved towards her. He was laughing; he put his arm around her and she felt the extra glow of life beginning in her again.

Daisy, the sun bouncing off her big spectacles, stood up on top of a box that had been decorated with crêpe paper. She beamed at them. She hit a glass with her teaspoon. Tor, standing beside her, winked at Viva.

'People, people! If I might.' Daisy, head cocked, waited for silence. 'This is a good news day,' she said at last. 'Daktar Frank and Miss Viva are married, the sun is shining, we are at the feast of life. Hard times will come.' When she closed her eyes, everyone knew she was thinking about the home again. 'But we must not get ahead of ourselves.'

'Hear! Hear!' said Toby stoutly.

'We owe each other so much,' said Daisy in a faint voice. 'We owe you so much,' she told the children.

Then Talika, after a certain amount of prodding in the back from Mrs Bowman, stood up on the crêpe-covered box Daisy had suddenly vacated.

'Sanskrit poem,' she said. She took a deep breath.

'*Look well to this day*,' she read out in her piping voice.

'*For it is life.*

In its brief course lies all the realities of existence.

For yesterday is but a memory and tomorrow only a vision.'

But then a gust of wind took her poem away, it stirred the leaves in the tamarind tree and when a donkey honked thunderously in the street outside the children burst out laughing.

'Look well to this day.' Talika made a last-ditch effort to be heard and inject some solemnity into the proceedings.

Everyone cheered; she hopped down, tucked her thin arms into her sari and bobbed her head shyly.

Viva glanced at Tor, who was smiling. She thought of water rushing by, of a huge sky above them all, of being so lost she thought she'd never be found again, and then Talika tugged at her fingers. They were ready to dance again.

ACKNOWLEDGEMENTS

First I must thank Kate Smith Pearse, who inspired this book.

To the Indian friends I met during its writing: Vaibhavi Jaywant (Vicki) who showed me around Bombay with such gusto and charm. To Sudhansu Mohanty, author and friend, who looked after me in Poona and Shukla and to his wife for her help with plants and birds.

Many thanks also to Lieutenant General Stanley Menezes, Indian army soldier and historian, for the care and professionalism with which he read the book and for his many helpful suggestions. To Dr Rosie Llewellyn Jones, professional lecturer on Indian history and also the Hon. Secretary of the British Association for Cemeteries in South Asia.

My thanks to historian Dr Katherine Prior, for sharing her expertise and extensive knowledge of India with me in a series of inspiring e-mails. To Stephen Rabson, the P&O historian and to Iain Smith whose help in tracking down information on the Third Indian cavalry regiment was invaluable.

Many people were kind enough to share either their own memories or the memories of their parents with me: John Griffiths, Philip Moss, Alison Latter, Nick Rahder, Robin Haines, Toby and Imogen Eliott.

Many thanks to Peter and Rosemary Waghorn, for lending me Mrs Smith Pearse's tapes, to Corinna King for lending me her mother, Maeve Scott's tapes. To Violet Adams for her diary and to my sister-in-law, Betty, for editing it so expertly.

Special thanks to Sue Porter Davison, for her encouragement and research on my behalf and to Peter Somner for his books.

I owe Kate Shaw, my agent, a big debt of gratitude for her advice and support.

Many thanks too to Clare Alexander, for her professionalism and encouragement. To all the staff at Orion – Kate Mills, Susan Lamb – for getting excited with me and for making the book happen.

As always huge thanks to my husband Richard, who told me about the Fishing Fleet to begin with and who encouraged me to write the book. To Caroline and Delia, to my daughter Poppy for her youthful enthusiasm and to my large and loving family and extended family for early readings and helpful advice.